Praise for *The Revolution of Every Day*

"Cari Luna's beautiful, carefully rendered debut novel not only captures a specific moment in time in marvelous detail but also shows how our particular lives are moved by forces beyond us that we strive to understand and resist only at the greatest cost. A remarkable, unusual book."

—**EMILY MITCHELL**, author of *The Last Summer of the World*

"Cari Luna gets her hands dirty with her characters, digging deep and exposing vulnerable underbellies that some lesser writers might not dare explore. Masterful, precise, and utterly affecting, *The Revolution of Every Day* will change what you think about what makes a family, what makes a life, and how to love."

—**SARA SHEPARD**, author of *Everything We Ever Wanted*

"This beautifully written novel packs an emotional wallop for lifetime New Yorkers like me. I knew precious little about the Lower East Side squatters' movement while it was happening—my mistake. Luna makes a compelling case that flawed, wounded souls are often political visionaries. A major achievement."

—**SUSAN BROWNMILLER**, author of *Against Our Will: Men, Women, and Rape*

THE
REVOLUTION
OF EVERY DAY

THE

REVOLUTION

OF EVERY DAY

a novel by **CARI LUNA**

 TIN HOUSE BOOKS / Portland, Oregon & Brooklyn, New York

Published by Tin House Books, Portland, Oregon,
and Brooklyn, New York

Distributed to the trade by Publishers Group West, 1700 Fourth St., Berkeley, CA 94710, www.pgw.com

    Library of Congress Cataloging-in-Publication Data

Luna, Cari.
 The Revolution of Every Day / by Cari Luna. — First U.S. edition.
    pages cm
 ISBN 978-1-935639-64-0
 1. Squatters—Fiction. 2. New York (N.Y.)—Fiction. I. Title.
 PS3612.U527R48 2014
 813'.6—dc23

                      2013011948

First U.S. edition 2013
Printed in the USA
Interior design by Jakob Vala
www.tinhouse.com

Excerpt from *The Revolution of Everyday Life* by Raoul Vaneigem, translated by Donald Nicholson-Smith, reprinted by permission of PM Press (www.pmpress.org).

For Billy

Anyone who talks about revolution and class struggle without referring explicitly to everyday life—without grasping what is subversive about love and positive in the refusal of constraints—has a corpse in his mouth.

—**RAOUL VANEIGEM,** *The Revolution of Everyday Life*

NEW YORK CITY
NOVEMBER 1994–MAY 1995

1

Thirteen House groans and creaks, shifting her bones, old ship in a storm. Not that Amelia's ever been on a ship in a storm. Not that Amelia's ever been on anything bigger than a rowboat. Well, the Staten Island Ferry that one time, but that hardly seems to count.

"Wind's picking up out there," Steve says.

Amelia jams the chisel into the join where the stair tread and the riser meet and hits it with her hammer. The old wood gives a sigh, a puff of dust. She levers it up and Gerrit is there beside her with the crowbar to pry it out, the hundred-year-old nails giving the tread up easy.

"Wood rot," he says, which is no surprise. She smells it every time she walks up the stairs; she feels it, the telltale bounce beneath her feet—signs of wood that wants to give way.

They work from the top stair down, tossing the loosed treads to Steve. He's got the sawhorses set up in the vestibule below; he's got the orbital saw. He numbers the old treads with a grease pencil, measures them, cuts new ones from salvaged lumber.

Anne comes through the front door, bringing a cold blast of air and the smell of rain. Her rumpled work clothes make her look old, tired. A kiss to Steve's cheek and she squints up the staircase. "Those risers need to go, too." And she's right, Amelia knows. That's the thing. Push or pull at any one part of the building and there'll be six other things that want attention. And it's not just the first flight of stairs that needs replacing—it's all the stairs, from street level to the fifth floor.

"Not enough lumber," Amelia says. Because it's about compromise. It's about doing what they can, when they can.

"Ah," Anne says. "Well, there you have it."

Steve says, "We'll make it work." He seems careful with Anne these days.

Anne climbs the ladder they've raised to the second floor, throws a leg over the banister, her skirt riding up, thick thighs in pantyhose. Steve looks away, out the door, and they hear her feet on the stairs, up to the fourth floor to her and Steve's place. A door opens and closes.

"So we'll do as many flights as we can—treads and risers both—with the wood we've got. Then we'll head out tonight and get some more, finish the job tomorrow," he says.

"Just like that," Gerrit says.

"We'll find more." Steve switches the saw back on, the insistent hum of it kicking up sawdust as he goes hard against the wood. Amelia waits for him to look up at her, but he keeps his head down, his jaw set.

"*Godverdomme*," Gerrit mutters, digging into the next tread harder than necessary.

"Grumpy old bastard," she whispers, and he grins.

Soon enough she and Gerrit have the treads and risers all pulled off, the naked frame of the staircase rising up sad and open. It's like revealing the secrets of the house, uncovering some century-old shame, this undressing that they do. They are like doctors over a patient's body; not judging, just seeing with clear eyes, fixing what can be fixed. She feels bad for the old girl. It seems they'll never reach the point where everything's done that needs doing. Moving from one repair to another, even after all these years.

Steve measures and cuts the last stair and riser. He and Gerrit take up their hammers, working together in that easy wordless way of theirs, the staircase coming back together just like that.

⊞

Gerrit leans into the worn couch, watching the girls cook dinner in the community-room kitchen. The community room takes up the street-side half of the unfinished basement: cast-off chairs and a musty couch, a board-and-cinder-block bookcase, an open kitchen with a hulking old fridge and scarred counters. Amelia and Kim and Suzie are at the stove, stirring pots and chopping vegetables. Kim ladles up a spoonful of something and offers it to Amelia for a taste.

He and Steve and Amelia finished three flights of stairs today, treads and risers, just like Anne wanted. They'd been hoarding the wood for months. They brought it home piece by piece, board by board, until they had enough to replace the treads on all five flights. Today Steve wanted to please his wife, but now it falls to Gerrit to go out into the rain with him to try to find enough lumber to finish the job. For all Steve's talk, there's no guarantee they'll find so much as a single board. This is Manhattan. It's not like they can go outside and cut down trees. Not like they can drive to a hardware store and lay a credit card down, either.

They've got the Velvet Underground playing. "Oh! Sweet Nuthin'." It's Amelia's favorite song. He reaches over and turns it up and she favors him with a small smile.

Gideon hands Gerrit a beer and drops down next to him, the couch sighing with the weight. "Long day?" Gideon says.

"You wouldn't happen to have twelve two-by-fours to spare?" Gideon lives next door in Cat House. The two squats share tools and materials all the time, and Gerrit knows as well as Gideon they don't have that much lumber to spare. Twelve boards is a wealth of wood.

Gideon just laughs.

Rain beats against the metal hatch doors that lie flush with the sidewalk. Inside it's warm and smells of curry and garlic. Gerrit has a beer in his hand; there's music playing and the high sweet chatter of the girls over by the stove. Steve comes down the basement stairs and past the kitchen. Amelia pulls at his wrist, leaning toward him to whisper into his ear. She's probably trying to get him to eat before he goes out. She's always pushing food on people, always worried they aren't eating enough. Echoes, no doubt, of her own hungry days. He feels that old familiar affection for her rise up, the waif she was when she first came to Thirteen House.

Gerrit doesn't want to leave this to go on a futile search for lumber, but here comes Steve now, red-faced and blustering across the community room toward Gerrit. He supposes there is something heroic about being the ones to head out into a storm to hunt for what's needed, and Steve rarely asks for much. Of course Gerrit is going.

"Let's go," Steve says. "I borrowed Jeremy's van. Ben's coming, too. He's bringing the van around front now."

"Don't you want to eat first?"

He glances at the girls. "Anne and I ate already."

"It's early to be heading out."

"Rain like this? No one's gonna be watching to see who's climbing into any dumpsters. We're good."

Gerrit walks into the kitchen and kisses the back of Amelia's neck, goose bumps rising along her bare forearms as she ducks away with a smile. He follows Steve up the stairs, easing into his coat, and out into the rain to search for wood.

⊞

Amelia warms her hands on her bowl of curried lentils, leaning against the counter where Kim sits kicking her legs. The lentils smell good, earthy and familiar. She swirls her spoon in the bowl, watching the curry seep into the rice. She loves these Wednesday night dinners when they open up the community room and make food for anyone who's hungry. "We should cook together like this every night," she says. "I don't know why we don't."

It's been quiet so far tonight, though. A couple of crusty punks came by a little while ago, ate their food, and left. Some guys stopped in on their way to trying to get beds for the night at the Bowery Mission. Now it's just Kim and Gideon from Cat House, and Amelia and Suzie and Marlowe the only ones from Thirteen House. Well, and Gerrit was here and Steve came in for a minute, but he didn't stay to eat. He usually does.

Amelia had grabbed Steve's hand, hoping to lead him out of sight, behind the kitchen wall into the storage area, the dark corner back by the tool cabinet. She wanted a kiss, or a touch, some acknowledgment. Anything. He shook off her hand. He moved right past her.

Tonight she wants the room to be full to overflowing. She wants there to be enough noise to drown out all the shit going on in her head. She wants to hear laughter; she wants the music blasting. She wants it so crowded people have no choice but to touch each other, even the ones they don't know.

She knows people have their own lives, their own things to do. It's a squat, not a commune. But still, some Wednesdays it seems they're all down there together, everyone from Thirteen House and everyone from Cat House, squatters from Maus Haus and Utopia, kids from the park, and a steady stream of the homeless. In summer they all spill out onto the sidewalk like a party. Those nights are the best. Those nights she could believe lentils and rice are the best damn thing she ever ate.

"You think Anne'll come down?" Amelia says. "Maybe I should take a bowl up to her."

"She knows we're here," Suzie says.

There's a fear rising in Amelia, something she's been swallowing down for days. She doesn't want to speak it, saying it giving it a power, making it true. She leans against Kim's legs and Kim pets her hair while she talks to Suzie and has no idea of all the things Amelia isn't saying. *My period is late*, she would say. And Kim and Suzie would smile and say, *Well that's no big thing. It'll come.* But maybe it won't. And even so, that's only a part of it.

Denise comes down the stairs and into the kitchen, rain in her hair, rain on her glasses. She puts her arms around Suzie's waist and kisses her softly.

Suzie rubs her cheek against Denise's shoulder. "Are you hungry?" she asks, even as she's already turning to the stove to spoon out the lentils. She presses a bowl into Denise's hands and stands close and watches her eat. They speak quietly about their day, leaning in to each other, the rest of the room fallen away.

The envy rising in Amelia is ugly and tired. She walks over to the couch, sinks down next to Gideon, and takes a long pull off his beer. She nestles in under his arm and closes her eyes. The voices and the music, Gideon's warmth. She lets herself drift.

⊞

The wipers drag greasy smears across the windshield. The Con Ed clock tower could be a church spire; the Empire State Building, lit up all green and gold, could be Oz. Steve swings the van onto Fourteenth Street, heading west. He spotted a dumpster on Fourteenth and Third yesterday—a gut renovation of an old tenement. Five stories' worth of wood gotta come out of that place. There's bound to be enough.

"Look at that fucking rain," Ben says. He leans in from the backseat, his face hanging between Gerrit and Steve.

Steve loves a good hard rain at night. It's like the whole damn city gets washed clean. The people are hidden away and it's quiet, quiet. The cars glide along, their taillights stretched out behind them, staining the streets red. They are anonymous and remote, unconcerned animals. It's people you've got to watch out for and the rain flushes them away.

"Rain is good," Gerrit says. "Fewer witnesses."

Steve says, "I'm not expecting any trouble where we're headed."

He's hoping to get this done quickly so they can get back home. Anne was quiet all through dinner, quiet as he left. "I'm going to get that wood now," he said to her. "We'll replace the risers. You're right about those risers."

"Don't forget you've got first watch tonight," she said.

"That's all you've got to say?" He tried to say it with a smile. He tried to pull her in for a kiss but she moved past him, went into the bathroom, the shower hissing on. "Taking a lot of showers these days," he said. "You're the cleanest woman in town." No response, of course.

She's worried he won't make it back for a ten o'clock shift? Quarter past six now? They'll get as much wood as they need out of that dumpster—and it'll be good wood; he's got a feeling about it—and be home by seven. Six forty-five, even. "I brought you wood," he'll tell her. He'll kneel down as he says it, make it a joke that's only half a joke. *This is how I love you,* he'll be saying. *This is how I'm trying.*

He eases the van into a spot right in front of the dumpster—how's that for luck? He's never wrong when he's got a feeling like he's got tonight. Gerrit jumps out and pops the back open and Ben's up and over the side of the dumpster, poking around. Already Steve spots a decent-looking two-by-four poking up from the pile like a promise. He climbs in and grabs that board, passes it down to Gerrit to stow in the van. "What did I tell you?" he says and Gerrit smiles his tight-lipped smile.

They work quickly, tossing boards to Gerrit as they find them. Steve's thrown down four already and he thinks Ben's gotten as many or more. Steve digs through cascading plaster and lathe, snagging his skin on a jagged piece of hardware cloth. He spots what looks like another good-sized board and he kicks debris away, digging down with his feet. It comes up way too easy, though, and it's just a scrap less than a foot long. "Hey, Gerrit," he calls down. "What's the count at?"

"Five."

"What do you mean five? I passed you down four just me alone."

"Did you look at them or just grab them and throw them at me? Half of these boards are warped."

"Bad?"

"Bad enough that they won't get the job done."

He peers over the side of the dumpster at the pile of rejects at Gerrit's feet. It's true, dammit. Useless, the lot of it. "Well, shit. How's it looking over there, Ben?"

"I've hit bottom over here."

"Five boards," Steve says.

"Five boards," says Gerrit.

"It's a start," says Steve. "It's a good start."

Steve climbs out of the dumpster, his hand slipping on the rain-wet metal, and his shoulder comes down hard against the edge. The gutted building sits dark, plastic rustling where its windows used to be. Shirley Riley lived in this building when he was a kid. Her dad caught them kissing right there on the stoop one summer day when they were twelve and he made like he was going to chase Steve away with a hunting knife. Though maybe he was only half kidding. Either way, Steve never kissed Shirley again. He'd had his eye on Cat by then.

"Shirley Riley," he says, pulling the van away from the curb.

"What's that?" Gerrit says.

"City full of ghosts," Steve says. But he doesn't mind. It's how he knows he's home.

"Now what?" Ben says.

"I've got another idea." He heads south on Third Avenue and then east on Sixth Street to Avenue D, pulling up in front of a burned-out building.

"It still smells like a bonfire over here," Ben says.

"X Squat," Gerrit says. "There's nothing in there but cinders."

"Yes, but what's *outside*?" Steve points to a staggered semicircle of blue sawhorses with white stenciled lettering: POLICE LINE DO NOT CROSS.

"Oh, man. I don't know," Ben says.

"We need the wood," Gerrit says, climbing out of the van. He goes around to the back and opens the double doors. "Get moving. This has to happen fast." He tosses a barricade into the back.

Steve grabs one up in either hand and passes them off to Ben, who fits them into the van. They get twelve of them that way, Steve and Gerrit hauling them to the van and Ben nestling them in together. "That'll do it," Steve says. That'll more than do it. That'll do the risers and then a few boards to set aside for something else.

They jump in the van. "Go!" Gerrit says, and Steve pulls away fast from the curb, the tires squealing.

"Subtle."

"We've got to be sure to paint these or we're screwed if we ever get raided," Ben says.

"Sure thing," Steve says, but Gerrit turns around in his seat to look at Ben and says, "We will have much graver concerns if we ever get raided."

Ben snorts. "An accent doesn't make you smart, man. Just makes you born someplace else."

Steve feels Gerrit go tense a second, but then he laughs and it's all okay. They've got the wood, no one's behind them in the rearview, and they're headed home. *Wood*, he'll say to Anne. *I brought you wood.*

2

"Gerrit, I'm pregnant."

Amelia practices saying it. She says it to the tenement bricks all sharp-edged in the cold, clear winter light; says it to the leaf-bare trees, their sidewalk planting pits studded with cigarette butts and shards of glass; says it to the old bodega cat on Tenth and B, who dismisses her with a blink of his rheumy eyes. One of his ears is freshly torn and the bodega is lousy with mice. He's got his own problems.

The guys playing basketball in Tompkins, so caught up in the game they don't even bother to catcall at her? They've got their own problems. A kid in a gray hoodie dribbles the ball up the court, and what's that steady thump of ball meeting ground drumming out? What's he trying to forget each time the ball meets his palm? A shot and a miss and then his eyes catch Amelia's and he smirks and nods at her, a quick jerk of his chin as if to say, *Yeah, I missed. No big thing.* But then his eyes drop away, shoulders rounded as he runs after the others, and she doesn't buy it.

The Chinese delivery guy on the bike, four or five orders hanging heavy in plastic bags from his handlebars? He's got his own problems. He's got to be at least fifty. Puerto Rican kids hoot in fake Chinese as he rides past, fast as he can.

Fourteenth Street and Second Avenue. She's been wandering for blocks, trying to build up the courage to tell Gerrit but only growing colder and more nervous. She turns onto Thirteenth Street, heading east, toward home. She sinks her hands deep into the pockets of her worn peacoat and her fingers graze the fresh pack of Marlboros in the right pocket, her excuse for leaving the bike shop early.

She bought the smokes and a pregnancy test at McKays, took the test right then and there in the drugstore bathroom. A pink cross appeared, bright and clear, seconds after the pee hit the stick.

Pregnant. She's imagined it before. She'd always assumed she'd just go and get an abortion and that would be it. She hadn't anticipated this fear, like her body's been hijacked.

Her mother was only seventeen when Amelia was born. Twenty-three might seem a long way from seventeen, but it isn't. Not really. Her mom used to say, "Amelia, you're like a gun to my head." Amelia doesn't want that for herself. Doesn't want a life like cold metal up against her temple.

Ahead of her on First Avenue, a cab cuts across two lanes to the curb to pick up a fare. A chorus of horns swells up, fading into a distant whine as the cars race away. All these people speeding by in their cars and cabs, running to catch buses, racing toward the subway. All these people moving so fast, shouldering past her on the sidewalk, dodging around her, and all she can do is stand up to that stream, stand still and not let it take her.

The light changes and she crosses First Avenue. Two red cars in a row along the crosswalk. Maybe that's good luck. It's about damn time she had some.

⊞

The boom box sits on the kitchen table, its back panel taken off and its innards spilling out across the white enamel surface. When Gerrit found it in a trash can over on University, he was nearly certain it could be salvaged. Now, after two days of tinkering, he's not so sure. These newer stereos have computer chips in them, wires and connections he can't recognize. He's beginning to think they're manufacturing them in a way that you can't fix just so you'll have to buy a new one as soon as the first little thing goes wrong.

Older electronics—TVs and stereos and radios and the like from the seventies and eighties—are easy to fix. He finds them, repairs them, and sells them. Appliances, too, he can fix, and either they get used in Thirteen House or they get sold. A chunk of the money goes to the communal fund for building supplies and utilities, then a chunk to his and Amelia's coffee-can savings plan for food and toilet paper and that sort of thing; the rest goes in his pocket for cigarettes and subway fare, sometimes a book or a movie.

He and Amelia get by. They run a bike repair shop downstairs, in the ground-floor storefront. He's taught her to fix bikes and she isn't bad at it. She's got nimble fingers, good for some of the finer work he has trouble with. He describes what needs doing and her fingers just do it. If only she were a bit more patient. She was sixteen when she moved in with him, and he thought she would settle down and get more focused with age, but seven years on she's still with that mind going everywhere at once, still high-strung and distractible.

High-strung and distractible, but his. Seven years ago he wouldn't have predicted anything like this little life they've built together. He wouldn't have dared even to hope for it.

She'll be home soon. He'll hear her feet on the stairs, then her hand at the door. Thin as she is, all angles, and her hair cut short like his, sometimes he'll look at her fast and swear she was a skinny Dutch boy, some leggy little punk from back in Amsterdam, back in the day. Then she'll turn to face him full on, those red lips of hers and the long lashes and she's all girl—short hair and bony shoulders, but all girl. She'll step inside, step right into that sunbeam that's cutting through the room. The sun will fall across her face, golden, and then that flush in her cheeks. Amelia.

⊞

Amelia is sunk down into the turned-up collar of her coat, the late afternoon sun sending her shadow long and crazy out ahead of her on the sidewalk. There are cells dividing, a body unfolding inside her.

Apartment windows are cracked open to the cold to balance overzealous radiators, and there's a comfort to the sounds drifting out. Each window Amelia passes hints at the warmth inside: people talking, people laughing, kitchen sounds, the steady pulse of music. Now salsa, now reggae. Now opera, now rock. Voices in English, in Spanish, in Korean, in junkie gibberish. And she's a part of it, at least as long as the sounds of all those lives wash over her.

A cabbie tunes in to 1010 WINS, his cab parked at the curb, door hanging open and his left foot propped on the sidewalk, a makeshift ottoman. He's got bodega coffee, a sandwich wrapped in cling wrap. He nods to Amelia as she passes. Can he tell? Is it in her face now? How can such a huge secret not show around the edges?

Crossing Avenue A and halfway down the block toward B. The bike shop security gate is down, the lights out, the compressor in the basement quiet. Gerrit must be upstairs already. She'll have to gauge his mood before she tells him, read the room for signs. Gerrit speaks a subtle language of doors and windows and furniture, and she's become fluent in it over these past seven years. A slammed door means come pay attention to me—come win me over so I won't have to be mad anymore. A quietly closed door means it's better to steer clear until he cools off. A wide-open window in winter means he's confused or stressed and needs the cold air to help him think. A window shut tight in full summer means trouble brewing. Combine that closed window with an overturned table or the couch shoved to an angry angle and it's best to take a very long walk, maybe find someplace else to crash for the night.

When it's really bad he'll pace, his heavy black boots scuffing along the floor. "Shhh," she'll say. She'll stand behind him, her arms wrapped around him, and breathe into the nape of his neck. He's only an inch shorter than she is, but he always seems so small when she holds him like that, his body temporary, ready to slip away. She pulls him tight to her and his heart flutters against her forearm where it crosses his chest, a frightened wild thing, like the field mice she'd catch as a kid and hold in her cupped hands, unaware of the terror of her enormous human face.

No matter what his reaction is, she thinks, he'll mean well.

And now here is the gray metal door of Thirteen House and she fits her key into the lock. Inside, the air is warm. She smells coffee, hears the voices of friends downstairs in the community room laughing, and someone singing along with the rumbling old stereo. The Pogues. Sounds like Ben and Suzie taking the parts on "Fairytale of New York."

Home. She feels it settle down around her, the warmth, the safety. Her palm finds the banister, the good solid oak worn smooth from a century of hands. Her feet find the stairs, the new treads solid and sure beneath her feet. She climbs to the third floor.

Gerrit is at the kitchen table, the carcass of a boom box before him and tools spilled across the tabletop. She kicks off her boots and pads into the main living space, the big room with its spring-shot couch and old stereo and book-shelf, the kitchen area, where Gerrit sits looking at her, his face soft and open. She loves it when he looks at her like that. Like seeing her come through the door is the very best thing that could have happened in that moment; like he wasn't really sure she was coming back. No one but Gerrit has ever been this happy to see her.

God, he's going to be so angry.

"Gerrit?"

"Toss me a cigarette, yeah?"

She hands him the fresh pack of Marlboros from her coat pocket.

He jerks his head toward her. "You going back out?"

She forgot to take off her coat. Or maybe her subconscious is anticipating the need for a quick getaway. In which case, her subconscious fucked up when it let her take off her boots. "Gerrit . . ." She slips the coat off, hangs it on the back of the chair across from his. She feels the coat's rough weave, the metal bones of the chair frame through it. He's unwrapping the cigarettes, cellophane curling around his fingers.

"Gerrit, look. I think . . . I mean . . . I know. I definitely am . . ."

He packs the cigarettes, *smack smack smack* against his thigh, draws one out to light. "What? Are you okay?"

"No. I'm pregnant."

His face draws tight, all the features and lines collapsing into a tiny crunched-in center so that his eyes nearly disappear and his thin lips are just white strips of the tautest flesh. The unlit cigarette in his hand trembles. "You're pregnant."

"Gerrit."

He's quiet. Far too quiet. His body's gone shrunken and tensed, a coiled spring. "Who's the father, Amelia?"

"I'll take care of it, okay? I'll get rid of it, if that's what you want."

"Get rid of it? This isn't some stray dog that followed you home. Do what you want. I won't be the one to tell you."

He tries to light the cigarette, but his hands are shaking and he can't get the lighter to strike. Two, three, four tries. Finally it catches on the fifth and he inhales deep, like the cigarette's a respirator, like he's drowning.

Steve taught her to salsa up on the roof late one night, Anne and Gerrit asleep and the boom box turned low. He held her against him, sang quietly into her ear. She couldn't understand the words, but he sang them like they were for her. If she had the baby, it might grow up to be someone like that, a man who would dance with a girl late at night on a rooftop. A man who would hold a girl and sing to her.

"I don't know what to do," she says.

"*Stomme sloerie,*" Gerrit says, spitting the Dutch out like it's something gone rotten in his mouth. *Stupid slut.* "I should have known what I was getting when I brought you home."

And what is there to say to that? She goes to her room, lies down on the bed. She wishes she'd taken one of her grandmother's quilts when she left home, though it probably would have been ruined in that year of going from building to building, sleeping in the park, in doorways. By the time she ended up at Thirteen House, all she had left fit in her small backpack: a notebook, her grandmother's knitting needles, a few photos and postcards. Her clothes were gone. Her money was long gone. And Gerrit took her in.

The way Gerrit looked at her just now—his face closed, lips twisted in disgust—all it took was him looking at her like that, calling her a stupid slut, and she's that dirty wasted wreck again, sixteen years old and junk sick on St. Marks and not worth a damn to anyone unless she lifts her skirt.

⊞

Steve's at the stove, got some burgers frying. Anne's standing by the table, her broad midwestern ass swaying unconsciously to the Héctor Lavoe song on the stereo. He loves that ass, but it ain't built for salsa. Still and all, he flips the burgers, dances the three paces over to her, grabs her hand *pa' sacarla a bailar.* She half smiles, pulls away. *Ay, Annie,* he thinks. *You didn't used to pull away so quick, girl.*

"Periódico de ayer" plays on, Lavoe's voice hanging like fog between them. Fourteen years together and Anne still doesn't speak much Spanish. You'd think she'd be a little curious, at least. Want to know what the inside of her husband's head sounds like. If she lived half her life, dreamed more than half her dreams in some other language, he'd want to know. He'd want *in.*

Gerrit's voice rises up through the floor, angry. Amelia's voice lower, placating. Can't make out the words, just the feel of them. And best not to try to overhear, anyhow.

Living like they do in the squat, you learn early on to give what space you can. He goes to the stereo and turns the music up a notch, gives them just a little more room.

Amelia's not a girl to pull away. You can always get her to dance. Stiff and shy at first, but she'll try. And before you know it she softens, melts right into you.

"I got a letter from my mom today," Anne says.

"And what does Mama Barrett have to say?" The bi-weekly missive from his nervous mother-in-law, who hid her purse behind her behemoth *culo* the few times he and Anne went to Akron to visit. Who pretended first not to notice and then later not to care that her older daughter had married a Puerto Rican. A homeless Nuyorican who brought his young wife to live in a former crack den. Steve is all kinds of welcome in Akron.

Anne tugs the sleeves of her thermal shirt down over her hands, clutching the ends in her fists. "She wants me to come for Christmas."

"We could do that. It's been a while since we went back."

Her thumbs worry against the sleeve fabric, threatening holes. *Why so wound up, Annie?* His Annie. He loves her. *Remember that, cabrón. You love this woman. This wide-hipped, flat-assed, prairie-voiced woman with the heart big enough to take in all your bullshit and give it back to you as something bigger and cleaner. This is your wife. Love her.*

"Shit!" The burgers. He gets them off the heat. "Gonna be a little well done tonight, babe."

"She wants just me to come. I'd go along with Cindy and Ron and the kids. They're driving."

"And you want to go. Without me." Cindy, her little sister in Brooklyn Heights with the banker husband and the two fat blond babies. Before she met Steve, Anne had been the good daughter. Cindy oughta thank him. She's been on the rise ever since.

"Yeah," she says. "I think I do."

Cindy's kids. A boy and a girl. Not babies anymore. Michael's in first grade now; Lara just turned three.

"That what you and Cindy were up to in their kitchen on Thanksgiving? Planning your solo trip back home?"

"No, it's like I said. Mom just mentioned it in the letter. And then I called Cindy and we talked about me driving out with them. It doesn't have to be a big deal."

"No big deal. You tell me what to think of a mother who welcomes you home but not your husband; a mother who wants you to leave your husband alone on Christmas."

"I just want to be with my family," she says. "A normal Christmas. It's been a long time. I know it's kind of screwed up, and of course I'd rather have you there, but ..." But she wants to please her fat bitch of a mother. She wants to be the good girl again.

Or maybe she's had enough of him. Maybe she wants out.

Monogamy isn't Steve's strong suit, but nothing ever got so out of hand as the affair with Amelia did. He never let anything else, any other woman, go on that long. What if after all these years of straying and never—not even once—getting caught, what if now that he's finally put that behind him, *now* Anne leaves him?

"What do you mean 'a normal Christmas'?"

"Let's just think about it, okay?" she says. "Let's just say maybe I'm going. Just a few days, no big deal. You don't even like Christmas."

It's like she's halfway out the door and wanting him to pull her back in. "Hey," he says, "I would miss you, is all." He goes to her. Her shoulders are tense. She doesn't want to give over, but he holds her against him and she leans into his chest, wraps her arms around his waist. "Let's eat, okay?" A kiss on her forehead, a hand to smooth back her hair. His wife.

He lays the burgers on the toasted buns, puts the plates on the table. A little plate of tomato and onion slices, a salad, a can of beer for each of them. He cracks his open, takes a swig, cold and metallic. He pulls out her chair for her and she sits. The music plays on as they eat, the dead *cantante* the only voice in the room.

⊞

Gerrit shuffles through faces and names in his mind, wondering who it might have been. Amelia's history of betrayals, large and small. His history of looking the other way. These habits of theirs now taking weight.

She is carrying another man's child and expects Gerrit to fix it. He will, of course. It's what he does.

The first time he saw her, she was draped across some crusty punk on St. Marks in the middle of the *godvergeten* tourist carnival between Second and Third Avenues— cheap sunglasses, novelty T-shirts, dirty runaway kids asking for spare change. She was sitting with a bunch of punk kids panhandling in their aggressive, counterproductive way. She was skinny and dirty, but obviously fairly new, because she looked scared. He met her eyes and she looked right back at him and he knew she was scared. He knew she didn't want to be hanging on that kid with the ridiculous tattooed face. Gerrit thought maybe she was asking for something with that look, but then she leaned back into the kid's chest and looked away, so Gerrit kept walking.

But after that he made a point of going down St. Marks every day, and sometimes he would see her there with that same group. Her glossy blond hair grew dull and matted. She'd been skinny when he first saw her; before long she was all bones and torn clothes. Ragged plaid skirt and her kneecaps jutting out from fishnet tights. Wasted. It hurt him in ways he couldn't explain. She was just another runaway kid, no different from the rest of them in Tompkins Square Park and all through the neighborhood, huddled like rats wherever you looked. If they all fell into the river, he wouldn't waste a second's regret on them. But this girl, the way she looked at him . . .

Probably eight, nine months after he first saw her, dead of winter and dead of night, he was riding his bike home along St. Marks, and there she was, alone. She was trying to light a cigarette but the wind kept blowing her matches out. He slowed as he rode past her. "Hey," she called out to him. "Got a light?" She made this pathetic wave with her cigarette.

"You shouldn't be out here alone this late," he said. "And it's cold. You should be inside."

"Yeah. I kind of . . . I mean, I have a place where I . . . I just can't . . . " and she started to cry. "I don't want to go back there. I can't stay there anymore."

He had her perch on his rear rack, the milk crate usually strapped there balanced in her lap, and brought her back to Thirteen House. The squat was much rougher then than it is now, but they'd already tapped into the electric and gas lines, so it was warm and dry, and it was safe. There was hot running water and his tub was good and deep. He made her toast and a can of soup; he drew her a bath. She came out of the bathroom with that matted hair gone; she'd found the scissors in his first-aid kit and cut it herself by feel in his mirrorless bathroom. She looked even younger then, shorn and exposed, all eyes and mouth.

She came to him. Whoever the father is, if she even knows, she came to Gerrit for help. It was one of her little indiscretions, one of her cruel girlish flirtations, with unlooked-for consequences. She did not do this to hurt him. He needs to remember that.

He goes to her bedroom door. She's left it open just a crack. She's lying curled on the bed, her back to the door. He thinks of the baby, thinks of the three of them together: a family. They could do it. He and Amelia have been together for seven years. No one would think anything amiss.

"Amelia." She's all shoulders and elbows and knees, her jeans riding up long skinny calves—all angles and then that silent, stubborn back. "We can have the baby. Together. If you want to keep it."

She shifts over on the bed to make room for him, and he sits beside her and strokes her hair. Up close, he can hear the hitch in her breathing; he can see the quilt darker and wet beneath her cheek.

"You don't care who the father is?" she asks, her voice muffled by the bed.

"I'm the father, if that's what you want." He drags the pads of his fingers along the back of her neck, the crude tattoo there, hand-done in one of the punk squats before she came to stay with him. She said it was supposed to be the Chinese character for strength, but that some Chinese guy had told her after it was done that it didn't say anything at all. "It'll be good. You'll see. We'll be a little family, the three of us."

She rolls over to face him, her eyes red-rimmed. "A little family." It isn't gratitude on her face, or even relief. Just fear.

"Yes," he says. "A little family."

"And just like that you're the father."

"Yes."

She kisses his fingers, a gesture so intimate it nearly undoes him. From no one else in the world could he stomach it; when she does it, it's this small, perfect gift and she knows it. He leans in to steal a kiss on the lips, and she indulges him. And a second kiss, indulged. Only when he goes in for a third does she roll away from him, face buried in her pillow. "I'm going to go lie down," he says. "Are you cooking tonight?"

She nods.

"Wake me up when you want to eat." He goes to his room, closes the door, and lies down on his cot in the near-perfect windowless dark. A baby. Well.

⊞

Through the thin drywall, Amelia hears Gerrit's cot groan as he settles into it. She remembers the way it would cry out every time he shifted and turned that first night she stayed. She was lying in the alcove, which they would later wall off to make into a bedroom for him when she moved in for good and he insisted she take the large front room with the windows. But that first night it was still an alcove and the front room still Gerrit's, and she was thinking about how it was warm and dry in his apartment, and how organized the squat was, and how nice everyone had been to her, if maybe a bit wary and looking at Gerrit with smiles and raised eyebrows when he'd introduced her around.

She reached up to touch her hair, cut short and clean and new, and there was the feeling of freshly washed cotton against her skin, the T-shirt he'd given her to sleep in and said she could keep. She'd eaten; she'd bathed. And she felt safe. He'd said she could stay as long as she wanted, and to make herself at home. There had been only two cans of soup on the shelf, but he'd still insisted she eat every drop of the can he opened for her. She hadn't had an appetite, the detox already creeping in, but she ate what he offered because she saw that it pleased him. She'd eaten the soup, choked down the toast. Smiled sweetly and thanked him.

She pictured what her life could be like at Thirteen House. Without the hunger, without the cold, without the fear. Without the rush of the dope and the awful crash when the dope was gone. So she decided to go cold turkey.

Stupid teenage bravado. She actually thought Gerrit might not notice.

And she thought she should make herself useful to him. There was only one thing she could think of that she was maybe good at, one thing he could want enough that he would still want her around in the morning, and in a week, and in a month. So she was the one to open that door. *Stomme sloerie.*

She crawled out of the cocoon of the quilt and took off the T-shirt. She slipped through his bedroom door, left cracked open like an invitation, and eased herself beneath the scratchy wool blanket that covered him. It was dark; he was just a lean shape, a man-shaped shadow among angular furniture shadows, and she found him by feel and pressed herself against him. He startled awake.

"What are you doing?" he asked, and she tried to think of how she would do it in a movie—a really good movie with a powerful, quirky girl who has a happy ending— and she said "*Shhh*" and pressed her finger to his lips and then her lips to his lips. His arms went around her and she thought he would roll on top of her, but he didn't, so she wriggled down beneath the blanket and tugged his sweatpants off and crawled back up his body.

He smelled good and clean, not like the boys from St. Marks, and she took him into her mouth. He made appreciative murmurs, muttering things in what she knows now was Dutch. He was hard for a while, but then he started to go soft and she couldn't get him hard again. She tried with her hands and with her mouth and nothing worked and

finally he stopped her. He said, "It's okay. Roll over." She
turned over onto her stomach and he moved behind her.

"Spread your legs, just a little," he whispered, and his accent and the feel of his breath against her neck made her
want him, really want him and not just trying to be nice
and useful anymore. Something hard slipped inside her. It
wasn't his cock, because he was rubbing that against her ass;
it seemed half hard again and she was relieved at that. And so
she thought it must be fingers from his right hand, because
his left hand was on her shoulder, pulling down each time
his hips thrust up against her ass. It felt different than fingers, longer than fingers, but it was warm like flesh and it felt
good, really good, pushing pushing pushing toward the front
instead of just in and no one had ever done that before. And
just like that, she came. Her first time unless she counted
the times she'd done it to herself, alone at night in her room
back home. Feeling this now, she didn't think that counted
so much. She pushed back against him, but he'd gone soft
and he rolled over onto his back and took his hands away.

"I wanted you to come, too," she said. That wasn't how
she'd thought it would go. She'd gone in to thank him and
instead he'd gotten her off, and there he was looking tense
and ashamed and maybe annoyed. She realized maybe
she'd forced herself on him, since he'd been asleep and all.
She thought about what had happened and she whispered,
"Do you wish I was a boy?"

"No," he said. "That's not it at all." He pulled her close
with his left arm, her back to his chest. He kissed her and
said that she should get some sleep.

By morning the detox was full-blown. Gerrit told her later he'd woken up to find both of them soaked in her sweat, and her skin hot with fever. He said she was shaking and crying, clawing at her belly. He'd run to get Suzie, who'd been there herself only a couple of years earlier.

Gerrit had known Amelia only a few hours. Suzie had met her for five minutes the night before. Same with Ben, with Steve and Anne. And there she was, sick as hell in Gerrit's apartment, and they not only let her stay, they insisted. Suzie cleaned her up when she puked on herself, helped her to the bathroom and steadied her shoulders when she nearly passed out from the cramps and diarrhea. When she tried to sneak out, Steve stopped her. She screamed and scratched and kicked and he pinned her down until she gave up and slept. When she woke up, Gerrit was there. He sat up with her three nights straight when the insomnia hit. He held her; he told her she was safe.

A week later she came out the other side, and they held a house meeting and voted her in. They said she could stay, as long as she stayed clean. So she stayed clean. She leaned into the work of the squat. And the people of Thirteen House became her family.

The nights were rough for a long time, nightmares riding her hard, and so she stayed on with Gerrit instead of making her own space in the building. And then it was a month in Gerrit's apartment, then two months, then three. And so of course people assumed that Gerrit and Amelia were a couple. She wanted to love Gerrit that way. She tried so hard, in the beginning, to love him that way. But it just didn't take. So she let everyone believe it simply because it made life easier. When she saw the way people in the neighborhood treated Gerrit, with such respect, it made her feel good that everyone thought he was her boyfriend and that he valued her above all the others. As Gerrit's girlfriend, she didn't get messed with. The punk boys stopped whistling and saying the shit they said, and they stopped cornering her in alleys and expecting her to put out, and everything just got so much better so quickly. And then a year went by, then two, and by then the building was full but she'd long since stopped considering the possibility of her own apartment, anyway. The lie had grown into a life around her.

There have been other guys over the years, and people shake their heads and think she's cheating on Gerrit, think that Gerrit—the open-minded Dutchman—is letting his younger lover have her fun. She thought she would meet a guy one day and fall in love and move in with him, leaving Gerrit's home to make her own. But that day always seemed just off in the distance, and so she didn't worry about the practicalities and particulars of how things are now. And then she fell in love with Steve. Maybe she should have seen it coming. Maybe things had been quietly going in that direction for a while, but she'd like to think not. She'd like to think they were overtaken by passion, the both of them.

It had been a late night in the community room, just the two of them, that first time, eight months ago. Amelia and Steve staying up, everyone else already gone to bed. There was nothing inappropriate about it, the two of them—night owls both—staying up together. It seemed innocent enough.

But she had felt him watching her closely all that night, long before they were alone, laughing at all her jokes. Suzie and Denise had gone to bed first, then Ben. Then finally Gerrit had called it a night. Anne hadn't come down at all—Steve said she wasn't feeling well.

So everyone else went to bed and Steve moved over to sit next to Amelia on the couch. They were quiet, listening to the music Steve had put on—Tito Nieves, she thinks it was. "Te amo"? "Sonambulo"? Memories of that first time blend and blur with the nights that came after. They listened to the music; they listened to the sounds of the house, feet on floorboards and water through pipes. And then there was silence above them, and even the street outside falling quiet. And then his hand on her leg, his breath on her cheek, fingers turning her head toward him. And then his lips on her lips.

She'd thought about Anne, for a moment. Just a moment. And then she hadn't. Then she'd thought only about Steve's mouth on her throat, about his hands sliding her jeans down her hips. How rough his calluses felt against her skin. How soft and small she felt beneath him. How good that was, how safe. To be that small, to be that sheltered.

When it was done Steve cradled her to his chest. "Sweet girl," he whispered. "Sweet, sweet thing."

She would have run away with him, if that's what he had wanted. But that wasn't what he'd wanted. He chose his wife.

And now, there's this baby. If she has the baby, Gerrit will become the father, and they will be a family. Forever. No big love to sweep her off her feet. Not Steve, not anyone else. She'll have to let that go.

⊞

Anne moves through the apartment, sliding the chairs back under the kitchen table, wiping the counter down, lining their shoes up on the rack by the door. Steve's stretched out on the couch, the book he's reading raised over his face to block the glare from the bare bulb overhead. He broke its frosted glass dome when he was changing the bulb. He said he'd get a new one right away, but it's been at least a month, maybe longer, with the hard white light blasting down on them. She'll go get a new dome tomorrow; she'll do it herself.

"Why don't you come on over here," Steve says. He sets his book down on the floor, the spine cracking; he reaches out to her.

She lies down on top of him, his arms around her. Her cheek on his chest, she rises with each breath he takes. She wills her body to go heavy, to be still, to be present. *He's trying*, she thinks. This should warm her more than it does. "What are you thinking?" she says.

"*Sancocho*," he says. "I want some *sancocho*. Like my mom makes. Not that watery Colombian crap they sell over on Delancey."

"You should make some."

"You'd like that?"

"Sure. Why not?"

"Yeah. Okay. Maybe I will. Maybe tomorrow." He slides a hand under the back of her shirt, fingers plucking at her bra band. "Wanna fool around?"

She laughs but it sounds empty. "I can't. I've got first watch tonight."

"It's only nine thirty. A half hour with your old man isn't enough?"

If he really wanted to, he would have just started kissing her. "Maybe later," she says, but she knows they won't. There's a relief in that and beneath it a queasy nervousness, the understanding that she should not feel relieved not to have to make love to her husband.

She rolls off him and he picks up his book, holding it up to block the light.

"I'll get a new dome for that light tomorrow," she says.

"I'll take care of it."

"No, that's okay," she says. "I can do it." She pours herself a cup of coffee, picks up the book she's been reading, and slips into her shoes. "I'm heading down for my shift," she says, but when she turns to the couch he isn't there. She can see him through the open bedroom door, standing by the window in the dark. She walks out, pulling the door quietly closed behind her.

She sets up the folding chair in the vestibule and settles in for the four-hour shift. Coffee in her favorite mug, a good book—a mystery Steve wouldn't approve of as serious enough but dammit, it's okay to read things just because they're fun, she thinks, just because they take you out of your own head for a while.

Ben comes through the front door and smiles to see Anne sitting in the watch chair.

"You're early," he says.

"A little extra precaution can't be a bad thing."

"Wanted to get out of the apartment, hunh?"

"Is it that obvious?" She dog-ears the page she's reading and lays the book on her lap.

"Only to an old friend." Ben sits down on the pocked tile floor, his back against the wall.

It should be comforting to know that her problems with Steve aren't passing invisibly by the people who care about her. She should want to be seen, to be understood. She should be open to comfort and sympathy. She knows this. Instead she wants to pull her sweater tighter around her and sink down behind the battle-scarred fortress wall of her marriage. Put on the brave public face and fall apart in private.

They're all so mixed up in each other's lives. Some people need that; some people found their first true family in Thirteen House. She gets that. But for Anne, the degree of intimacy can sometimes be unnerving. Suffocating. But this is Ben—one of her oldest friends. Where does the urge to push him away come from? Why the desire to hide?

"Where are you coming from?" she says.

He pulls a face. "The Bronx."

"How's your mom?"

"The same. She won't listen. Dad's getting worse all the time and she won't ask for help. You've seen her—she's a tiny thing. Now she's hauling him up out of his chair, in and out of bed, to the john. 'Get some help,' I say to her. Medicare'll spring for a home health aide a few hours every day. Won't cost them a penny, but no."

"She wants to take care of him herself."

"Dad's no help, the bastard. He won't tell her different. 'I don't want some little nurse coming through here, ripping us off,' he says. Like someone takes a shit job like that just for the chance to steal my mom's porcelain Jesuses."

Anne smiles. She and Steve went to Ben's parents' apartment for Thanksgiving one year. The place was lousy with Jesuses. Steve accidentally knocked one off a side table with his elbow, the big oaf, and Jesus suffered a slightly chipped toe. Ben's mother spent the rest of the day pushing statuettes away from table edges, eyeing Steve nervously anytime he moved. Steve's joke about watching the chipped toe to see if it would magically regenerate probably didn't help.

"I gave the old man a bath today. That's not something they tell you about when you're a kid—that when you grow up you'll maybe have to wash your dad's hairy old ass."

"It's good you can get there, though, that they're just a train ride away." When Anne left Ohio at twenty-one, following her little sister, who'd moved to New York for college the year before, she hadn't thought about what that would mean for their widowed mother as she got older. She hadn't thought about her mother at all. She thinks about her now, though; she thinks about her a lot.

"True. But it's hard to be there, you know?"

"I'm going home for Christmas, I think," Anne says. It's been four years since she went back, four years without seeing her mother.

"That'll be good."

"It's been too long."

"Good for you, then," he says. "Your mom will be happy to see you."

"She will," Anne says. "She'll be happy." They'll have a Christmas tree, of course. They'll take the Christmas boxes down from the attic and she and Cindy can show the kids all the old ornaments, all their favorites. They'll take over, make the big dinner, the ham and the sides, the pies. Mom will want to do it all, but it's too much. They'll have her sit at the kitchen table and roll out the pie crusts while they do the heavier work. Mom and her girls, together in the kitchen. After all this time.

Cindy and Ron have gone back every year since the kids were born, because that's what you do with kids. You seek out home, you seek out the old traditions, for the kids' sake. Anne should have been doing the same, for her mother's sake, and for her own. A person needs roots, she's realized. A person needs her family, those old comfortable connections. A person needs to be loved, simply and honestly. How childish, to have shrugged that off for so long. As if her mother were a heavy anchor instead of a touchstone.

Ben pulls his sketchbook out of his bag, flipping it open to a half-filled page, one of the intricate drawings he does, cogs and gears hemmed in by mazelike pipeworks. "Want some company for a little while?"

"Sure. That'd be nice." She sips her coffee and finds her place in her book again. She's going home. Just a few more weeks, and she'll be home.

Home. She hasn't thought of Akron as home in years. For fourteen years, New York has been home. And she met Steve just a few days after arriving, so he and New York are inextricably tied. There is no home for her without Steve.

He would bring her things when they were first married: a dwarf orange tree in a red enamel pot; a coin flattened on a subway rail; a stranger's lost notebook, the words "Angel, O Angel, O . . ." scrawled across the only marked-up page.

"I see you everywhere," he would say.

He wrote her poems on scraps of paper. He sang her songs. He held her and his chest was as broad and as deep as the city's skyline. He held her and his body was the world.

It isn't like that anymore. Either he's gone small or Anne has grown too large to be contained; when he holds her now, she sees only what's beyond him, waiting over his shoulder. He holds her and she feels the wind and the encroaching dark. He is neither the city nor the home that shelters her from it.

If only he would bring her a poem, a twisted piece of metal, a single ripe orange. Anything. If only he would come through the door and say, "Look at what I have," and place it in her hands, proof that he thinks of her, that he carries her with him still.

⊞

Light stings Gerrit's eyes awake. Amelia leans through his bedroom door, the hallway light blazing over her head. She says, "Look. Let's not tell anyone yet. About the baby. Let's keep it to ourselves for now." He nods, because what is there to say, and she says, "Dinner's just about ready."

The clock reads nine thirty. "You let me sleep a long time."

"You seemed tired, I guess. And I kind of lost track of time. Thinking." She shrugs and trails away down the hall.

The main room is warm from her cooking, the air thick with garlic and olive oil. There's brown rice; there's kale with garlic, stir-fried tofu. She's a skilled dumpster diver, that girl. She goes out on a weekly run with Suzie, hitting the dumpsters behind the markets and restaurants around town, and they almost always come back with enough food to feed the whole building all week. Usually they find enough to share with other buildings, too. Gerrit knows he could walk into any squat in the neighborhood some weeks and find everyone eating the same food, thanks to those weekly runs.

Plus she's got a kid who works produce at the Met supermarket on Second Avenue totally charmed. Anything wilted or bruised or just a touch overripe that he's supposed to throw out, if it's still edible he sets it aside in a bag for Amelia to pick up at the end of his shift. He always tucks something fresh and perfectly salable into the bag, too. The poor kid is half in love with her. She knitted him a cap to thank him, and Gerrit's never seen him without it since.

Gerrit lived on canned soup and ramen noodles heated on a hot plate before her. He would have gone on that way forever but then she moved in and pressed for a stove. Once she started talking about it others wanted them, too. When they started looking, it seemed there were ovens everywhere. The yuppies, already starting to move into the neighborhood back then, like their appliances shiny new. Landlords ripped out perfectly good kitchens, littering the streets with stoves, sinks, and minifridges. It was a salvager's bonanza out there. Steve's handyman work in rental buildings all over the neighborhood sometimes had him replacing two functioning stoves in one day. He loaded the old ones into the back of a borrowed van to bring home rather than setting them out for garbage pickup like he'd been instructed. In a few weeks they'd easily collected enough for all ten apartments.

The city was full of gas ranges—they didn't find a single cast-off electric range. There'd likely been gas lines connected to each apartment when it was a functioning rental, but by the time they'd taken the building over most of the plumbing—valuable or not—had long ago been torn out. Like any other project they'd done in the squat there was a learning curve, and Gerrit was sure they'd blow themselves and the building to bits, but once they got the hang of it, it was just a matter of following the steps from beginning to end. He had to admit it did them all good to be able to cook real food, to have working kitchens.

He sits down at his place at the table and Amelia serves him, standing behind him and letting her arm brush his shoulder as she spoons out the rice. *We'll be okay*, that touch tells him. *We're going to be fine.*

"We should go out tonight, get a drink at the International," he says. "Celebrate."

"Celebrate what?"

"The baby."

She forks some kale, plays with a stray grain of rice on the table as she chews. "I can't drink with the baby."

"You'll have a ginger ale."

"But we can't tell anyone."

"We need an excuse to go get a drink? Come on."

"I'm on second watch tonight."

"We'll be home by eleven so you can grab a nap before shift. I promise."

She drops her fork and pushes back from the table. "Gimme a few minutes," she says. Her boom box hums on and he hears Ani DiFranco through the open door of her room. What is it with these young girls and Ani DiFranco? All that righteous anger; men as tormentors, as things to be gotten past, overcome. He leans back to peer down the long hallway. She's standing by the bed, naked to the waist, changing her shirt. She does it on purpose, he's sure. When she wants to get to him she leaves her door open like that. She undresses right in front of him, walks naked from the shower to her room.

He's watched her body go from skinny teenage angles to lithe womanly angles. He's watched her small breasts grow, hardly perceptible, but noticeable to him. He's watched the smooth skin of her belly and her ass go from childish pink to this perfect adult glowing white. He's watched it all. God, how he wants to touch her. Lights on, eyes open.

She turns to him, her little nipples impertinent as a smirk. *Kleine kuttekop.* "Going to a fashion show?" he asks. "Get your clothes on and let's go."

⊞

Anne hears footsteps on the stairs behind her, then Gerrit's voice followed by Amelia's girlish laugh.

Gerrit's hand is light on Amelia's back, ushering the girl toward the door. "We're going out for a drink," he says. "Can we bring anything back for you? Coffee?"

Anne shakes her head. "Have fun." She watches as they walk through the door and are gone.

Amelia had smiled shyly at Anne, her laughter falling away as she and Gerrit walked by her. If Anne were Amelia's age, what would she think of Anne: sunk into the folding chair, gone soft around the middle, bags under her eyes? Anne, the downer voice of reason, always demanding accountability and logic. She's thirty-six. Just thirty-six! But she feels old. Stuck.

When Anne moved to New York, she must have come across women who were then as she is now. But when she thinks back to the various radical groups she'd been part of—the meetings, the planning, the small fruitless actions they launched—she first remembers the men. She remembers the old Communist survivors of McCarthyism with their beards, their intellectual reserve, their insistence on grounding everything in theory. She remembers the young hotheaded anarchists, talking loud and looking for trouble. She remembers the earnest, deliberate men. She remembers the men she thought of as middle-aged and maybe a little creepy, who were probably around the ages she and Steve are now. Some called themselves Communists; some called themselves anarchists. It was generally the ones who didn't call themselves anything at all who spoke the most sense.

She remembers that the young women listened intently and read voraciously but only nodded their heads in meetings, offering at most small words of agreement. She remembers that the older women mostly cooked food for the meetings and made the coffee.

Anne had graduated from Oberlin the previous spring with a degree in poli sci, her head full of Marx and Debord, but also Simone de Beauvoir and Susan Brownmiller. She and her sisters in the women's studies department had taken their male classmates—those radical schoolboys—by the scruffs of their necks and shaken feminism into them. There was no need for splinter women-only meetings at Oberlin; men and women were on nearly equal footing, it had seemed. And so she blustered into the New York scene from the safety of that world, running her mouth.

Young girls today don't understand how bold an act that was, a girl of twenty-one speaking her mind in a meeting—Anne hadn't fully understood it herself at the time. They take all this shit for granted. They're happy to be the ones cooking the food and pouring the coffee because they don't realize that not so long ago that would have been the extent of their participation.

Anne had been in New York for just three days, sleeping on the floor of her sister's NYU dorm room, when she found a flyer posted outside the dorm about some radical meeting on the Lower East Side, a group organizing around housing rights. She'd grabbed it, eager to have something to do that felt familiar.

The meeting was held in the back room of a comics shop on Fifth and A after closing. Folding chairs, a card table with pamphlets and flyers, an urn of weak coffee. It was a small group, maybe ten people. She slipped into a chair in the last row. An old man with a Marxist beard was at the front, running the meeting, but Steve, sitting in the second row, seemed to be the center of things. Two young women sat on either side of him, leaning in close and smiling as he spoke. The men mostly nodded in agreement while Steve talked. He talked and talked. And as he talked, his eyes looked out over the room and skimmed right past Anne.

She knew she was plain; she'd learned to pride herself on it. Her plainness, she reasoned, allowed her to pass through the world less subject to the male gaze—if not totally free of its burden, then at least not completely shackled by beauty. *Look at those girls fawning over the tall guy with the big mouth*, she'd thought at that first meeting as she watched Steve holding court. *Look how they seek out his eyes, his attention. Look how they push their hair back from their faces.* She pitied them.

"You can call it a theory," Steve said, "but spatial deconcentration sure as hell looks like real government policy to me. I've lived in the neighborhood all my life, and I've watched the city cut our services, making it harder and harder to live here, trying to force us out. I've watched them look the other way while whole blocks burned. If we take those burned-out buildings, it's a counterattack. It's a legitimate assault on their system. We take those buildings and we hold them, and they're out of play in the gentrification game."

"That sounds pretty, but how do you intend to hold the buildings?" Anne said, and all heads in the room turned to her. She sat up straight in her chair and squared her shoulders. Steve, that big blustering loudmouth, looked at her and smiled.

"You're new," he said.

"You talk a lot," she said, but she said it with a smile. And before she could stop herself, her hand went to her hair and swept it back from her face.

When the meeting ended he went up to her. He folded his big hand around hers. "I'm Steve."

"Anne."

He held on to her hand a beat too long, and she let him.

That night she stayed with him on a mattress on the living-room floor of his friend's apartment in the Jacob Riis projects. They made love quietly, to not wake the children asleep in the next room. He held her and whispered his plans: He was part of a small group that was going to take an abandoned building on Seventh and C. They would squat it and make a home. He talked of bringing the homeless in to live with them, turning the basement into a soup kitchen, founding a school for radical thought. They would plant a vegetable garden on the roof and fruit trees in the backyard. Did Anne want to join them? Did Anne want to be a part of it?

It was the two of them together from that night on: Steve with his big mouth and big heart; Anne, practical, reining him in, demanding that he at least consider logic and simple common sense. Plans coalesced. She found herself at the center of things; she demanded her voice be heard and it was. They were doing something real. It wasn't theory, or a vague idea argued in a coffee shop.

Their first squat would be a disaster from start to finish, but they hadn't known that yet. And if they had known it, that wouldn't have stopped them. They were fierce. They were united. In 1979, even their love was a revolutionary act, his golden-brown hand across her pale white flesh. She was giving the finger to everything she'd fled in fatly safe suburban Ohio each time she took Steve's brown, uncut cock into her mouth.

All that fire in them, all that radical energy has gotten tamped down by the long years, the hard daily work of this path they chose together. Hell, the hard daily work of life—any life.

If she were to run upstairs right now, if she were to grab him and shake him and say, "I'm right here! I'm still here!" what would he say? He would blink those big brown eyes and say, "I know, baby. I know."

But he'd be wrong. And she'd be lying.

⊞

Steve stares out the bedroom window. It's cold—no way to totally draft-proof hundred-some-year-old frames—but he doesn't mind. He had the same kind of tired tenement window in his room as a kid, across the street and up the block a ways. The cold never stopped him from standing by it all hours of the night, staring out, hoping to see something. Shooting star, spaceship.

All he ever saw was Crazy Louie dragging his decrepit Chihuahua for a late-night walk; old man Hoffman coming home from his shoe repair shop on Avenue A; gangs of teenage boys, all slick and sharp-edged, cutting jagged lines as they walked right down the middle of Thirteenth Street. Juan Carlos Ramirez. Manny Miranda. Miguel Angel del Prado. He mouthed their names like incantations, breathed them, didn't dare give them voice. The kings of Thirteenth Street. The princes of Loisaida. All dead years ago. Princes die young around here.

Thirty years gone since then. New Juan Carloses, new Mannys, dozens of Miguel Angels since then. Same old story in an endless loop. It was probably the same story when the neighborhood belonged to the Jews. The black kids over on Avenue D are probably living out the same shit, too. People aren't so different. Times haven't changed so much. Young is young. Poor is poor.

And here Steve is, forty-two years old, still standing at a bedroom window looking out on Thirteenth Street. But he's done some good here in the old hood. Carved out a place in the world for himself and his wife. He and Anne and the other homesteaders, they're taking Loisaida back from the crackheads and dealers one abandoned building at a time. Call them squatters, fine, but homesteading's what this is really about. Staking a claim. Taking back the land. Loisaida—as much his ancestral home as Puerto Rico. More so.

A gang of teenagers slides down the street. Boys like lion cubs, testing their teeth.

Steve grabs his coat, heads down the stairs.

"Going for a walk," he says to Anne, who's planted on the folding chair in the vestibule, empty mug by her feet and a book in her hand. A quick kiss to her cheek and he's out the door.

It's a beautiful night, cold and clear. Nights like this, Steve feels like he could follow the streets and they'd take him anywhere. Walk east into the river and across to Brooklyn; walk north into the low mountains of Rockland County. Walk south and jump off the island's end, swim through the harbor and right on out to sea.

Maybe he'll head over to the Brooklyn Bridge. Walk halfway across, just to look back, see the city lights in the water. The lights in the water like some second city, a city of the drowned. He always thought that when he and Anne had a kid, he would spin it into a bedtime story. "Hey, kiddo, guess what? There's a whole 'nother city in the East River. Folks who drowned and came back to life, only now they live in the river. They breathe water. They eat tin cans and tennis shoes."

Instead he takes a right on Avenue B and up to Fourteenth. The all-night Chinese on the corner is lit up, the cold white fluorescent lights a beacon against the rolled-down security gates of the stores around it. Chicken wings and rice $2.99. Spare ribs $1.95. A black guy in a banker suit waits for his food. He leans his shoulder against the bullet-proof glass walling off the register and kitchen. A thick scar cuts across his cheek like words escaping his mouth.

On past the Chinese and around the corner. Madame Rosa Palm Reader gone dark for the night. The plastic and grime of Fourteenth Street shut tight. Only the dime-bag bodega is open along this stretch. Across the way, light gleams still from some of the windows of Stuyvesant Town, the redbrick towers with their backs turned to the tenements to hide the secret playgrounds and quiet treed streets at the center. When he was a kid he'd sit in the Oval in Stuytown—that park at the heart of it with the fountain and the benches and the smooth, looping walkways. The trees and the playgrounds. He'd watch the shiny kids in their shiny shoes, and pretend he lived there, too. Or he'd imagine he was a fish in that fountain, a magic fish that ate all the coins thrown in there. A wish-eating fish.

Up the block, he spies Ivan, that old queen all done up in his dress and wig and the whole bit, just turned the corner from A onto Fourteenth and walking west. Five kids come around the corner—same kids Steve saw out his window. They're silent and quick, sleek like sharks, but Ivan feels them following him; you can see it in his walk, all nervous and clipped in those high heels, not his usual strut.

Steve knows Ivan from way back, like grade school way back. They'd sit on their stoop sometimes, swapping comic books while their dads played dominos at a card table on the sidewalk. Steve breaks into a jog. Easy, like he wants to catch up to a friend. Casual. "Hey, Ivan! Wait up!" Usually Ivan won't respond to that name when he's all dressed up, but Steve's fucked if he can remember what he *is* supposed to call him. And now he knows for sure that Ivan knows the kids are after him because he responds to his guy name, that big platinum wig swinging around a beat behind the rest of him when he turns.

Steve meets the kids' eyes as he passes them. *I see you, motherfuckers.* That's enough. They melt around and past him and Ivan, a muttered "fuckin' faggots" and on ahead to First Avenue, where they disappear around the corner, headed downtown.

Ivan spits on the ground, adjusts his wig. "Like goddamn baby piranhas, I swear to God."

Steve offers his arm. "Let me walk you a ways."

Ivan laughs and it's the same high, ringing sound from when they were kids. "You're a good man, Estefan. Go home to your wife." He kisses Steve's cheek and walks on, swinging his skinny Rican ass more than strictly necessary.

"And how am I supposed to explain the lipstick on my face?" Steve calls after him. He watches until Ivan crosses First Avenue and sinks into the safety of the crowded sidewalks there.

He buys a beer and a paper at the bodega, a cup of coffee for Anne. He goes home to his wife.

3

There's a knock at the door. A heavy fist, like it's used to banging on doors with a certain authority. A nervous-making knock, especially coming this early, the sun not even half risen over the East River. Amelia's riding out the last twenty minutes of her four-hour night-watch shift. She squints through the peephole.

Marlowe emerges from his first-floor apartment, drawn out by the sound. Amelia is grateful for the dense wall of his body beside her.

"A big guy," she says. "No uniform."

Marlowe leans into the door, hunching down to take a look. "Yeah?"

"Steve," the guy says, his voice coming tinny and muffled through the heavy metal door. "I need to talk to Steve. Tell him it's Rick DeBlasio."

Steve's already coming down the stairs. He's pulling on his coat. "Saw through my window."

"Careful," Marlowe says. "Guy looks like a cop."

"That's 'cause he is one." Steve passes between them, a squeeze to Amelia's arm and out the door, falling into step beside this Rick. They walk east, the two men easy with each other, shoulders nearly brushing.

Amelia and Marlowe stand in the doorway, cold air swirling through the vestibule. "I didn't know Steve knew any cops," she says.

"Steve's been around a long time. He knows everybody."

The sun is rising, the tenements that line Thirteenth Street going golden as the light hits them. Steve and this guy Rick walk into that light. The squatter and the cop. Amelia waits, watching them until they turn right onto Avenue B and disappear.

Marlowe scratches his hip, peers out the door to where Steve and Rick have dropped from sight. "Gonna get dressed. Start some coffee."

She nods, only half hearing him.

When Steve comes back around the corner, he's alone. Amelia's in the doorway still, shivering in the cold. She sees him stop at a pay phone. Sees him run a nervous hand through his hair as he talks into the receiver. He hangs up and walks toward her. The sun blooms behind him, those black curls of his all ablaze in the light. She almost forgets herself and calls out to him. She almost runs to him, coatless and no shoes and all. It's hard not to want to be the dog nipping at his heels, brushing against his hand to be petted.

Last night at the International she swallowed his name with each sip of the sticky-sweet ginger ale she hadn't wanted.

He comes through the door, a sunbeam cutting across the vestibule like it got caught up in his hair. "The city's filing papers against us and Cat House. Go let them know next door. Tell them we're calling a meeting. Our community room in a half hour." His eyes are hard and bright. A tiny muscle twitches in his jaw.

"Jesus." She drops her forehead against his chest and he cups her head with one palm. She takes in the familiar smell of him. Just a moment like that, and then he lets her go.

"They've got to get a judge to sign off first," he says. "Rick's bought us some time, warning us like he did. Now go on. We've got to get everyone together, get things moving."

She finds her boots and slips them on. Steve's stopped on the stairs, watching her. "Gerrit awake already, you think?"

"I doubt it," she says. "He's never up this early." But Steve knows this nearly as well as she does.

He nods, turns to go up the stairs.

She steps out coatless into the cold. Cat House is quiet. She lifts a hand, gives a hesitant knock on the red metal door. Readying herself to give the news.

⊞

This is how history happens in America—desperate people crowded into a musty basement, ready to give themselves over to a lawyer who's supposed to be their savior. In Amsterdam, when they heard the police were coming they barred the doors and took to the rooftops. They stockpiled bricks and stones. They prepared to fight. Here they talk and wring their hands, hoping pieces of paper will save them. Gerrit can smell the fear coming off them all, the smell of fear and paper.

Steve called Irving Fischer—the great class warrior—straight away after the tip-off from Rick. He called the lawyer before he'd even told anyone in the buildings what was going on, as if it were his decision alone. Gerrit hasn't heard any objections, though. They're all bowing and scraping, calling the lawyer "sir." He's stooped and round-shouldered, this Irving Fischer. He's gray and slack-jowled and haphazardly shaved, shuffling papers with thick clumsy fingers, digging in his shirt pocket for the pen that's tucked behind his ear. This man is supposed to be their best hope. *Godverdomme.*

In come José and Nena, their daughter, Carla, trailing behind them in leggings under a ruffled purple nightgown and a sweatshirt pulled over it. It's comforting to see that going on fourteen she still sleeps in a little-girl nightgown, comforting to see the softness in her early-morning face.

Cat's holding court at the back of the room, the squatters from Cat House gathered around her chair. Gerrit doesn't understand why everyone's so fixated on the legend of Cat. They say she got into a drunken brawl with Allen Ginsberg in Tompkins Square one hot summer night back in the seventies, and she won. They say she broke Iggy Pop's heart. But so what?

"You should have known Cat back in the beginning," he wants to say to them. "She's just another junkie hanging on to clean by her fingernails. She's nothing you want to be; she has nothing to offer you." There's no shame in having been an addict once you've fought your way clean, but Cat wears her ex-junkie badge like it makes her holy. She walks around like she's been through hell and come out the other side with some special knowledge that she isn't ready to share just yet. Heroin doesn't make you a martyr and getting clean surely doesn't make you a saint.

Cat catches Gerrit looking at her and he looks away. *Teringwijf.*

Gideon is tipping his chair back like a school kid, the front legs bobbing in the air. He's talking to Fletcher and Chrissie, laughing. It's a forced laugh, fake bravado. Chrissie's in sweatpants and a ragged T-shirt, looking like she crawled out of bed and headed straight over for the meeting, as most of them did, no doubt.

Steve's crouched next to Irving, who's seated at the front of the room. Gerrit looks to Amelia, sunk down into the couch between Suzie and Anne. He catches her eye and she gives him a wobbly, nervous smile. "I think we've got everyone," he says to Steve, who rings a sledgehammer against the concrete floor to bring the meeting to order.

"Okay, folks," Steve says. "This is a fucked-up way to start the day, I know. Let's get this thing going so we can get on to whatever comes next. Irving Fischer is here to help us figure out the best course of action."

Irving stands to address the group. His hands are steady, his stance firm. There's no sign of the bumbling old man who was slumped in the chair a few moments ago. "I made some phone calls before I headed over here." He glances at notes scrawled on a yellow legal pad. "Here's what we're looking at. The city is claiming that the squatted buildings at 537 and 539 East Thirteenth Street—your buildings—are in danger of imminent collapse. The city is pulling together the paperwork to post emergency evacuation orders so that repairs can be made."

"Repairs?" Chrissie says. "Since when does the city repair squats?"

"Giuliani's gonna come fix the leak in Suzie's sink that's eating through my bathroom ceiling?" Ben calls out.

"We *fixed* that," Suzie says. "Jesus Christ, we fixed that weeks ago."

Irving holds up a hand for silence, but he's smiling. "It's a workaround. There will be no getting you back into these buildings if you're evacuated. What we need to do is make sure they don't get you out. I'm going to file for a temporary restraining order this morning. If we get that, it buys us some breathing room and a chance to plead our case. And it means the city will have to work harder to back up their safety claims."

"Those safety claims are bullshit," Steve says.

"And they never sent any damn inspectors," Gideon says. "Anyone had inspectors come by?"

There've been no inspections, but Gerrit knows this isn't really about safety anyway.

"So the safety claims are false," Irving says, "and you've been squatting these buildings for over ten years now. That's good. Possession is established by use. We show

how long you've been here; we show the work you've put into these buildings, how much you've improved them, and we have a good case for adverse possession. After ten years of continuous, open use without complaint by the owner, you're supposed to have right of title."

Right of title. Gerrit has no interest in "owning" the building. It was good space wasted in a place where housing is sorely needed, and so they, the people, claimed it for that purpose. They claimed their right to housing. But going legal is a pyrrhic victory, at best. The system grants them what they've already taken, and by doing so makes them a part of the very machine they're fighting against. The squatters take title to the building and they become landowners themselves. Neutralized. Neutered.

Anne says, "It seems too simple."

"Simple, yes," Irving says. "Easy, no. The city holds title to both buildings. Of all the absentee landlords we could be up against, in many ways the city is the toughest. They're not trying to get you kicked out on trespassing charges. They'll use other government agencies against you: Housing Preservation and Development, the police, the fire department. First we need to stop the evacuation orders. We go to court this morning and hopefully get the restraining order. Then we take it from there, and the real work starts."

"And if we don't get the restraining order?" Ben asks.

"We bar the doors," Gerrit says. "We put up barricades. Hold the buildings."

Irving smiles. "One step at a time."

"They say he's great in court," Steve whispers to Gerrit. "Does a regular Clark Kent to Superman thing. He's the one who stopped the Utopia Squat eviction last year."

"Yeah, but what about Glass House?" Gerrit says. "Papers and lawyers didn't save them, did they?"

Steve twists his mouth and shrugs. He's already made up his mind, casting his lot with the lawyer, the courts.

There's a calm to the whole group that wasn't there before the meeting and it nettles Gerrit. They're making hopeful noises, talking about taking the city to court, talking about getting legal title to their squats. It's all in Irving's hands now. Irving is going to take care of it. Irving is going to make everything all right. It's dangerously blind naiveté.

This is Giuliani's New York. The city isn't simply going to roll over and hand them the buildings. It will come down to force in the end. Battering rams versus bricks. It always does.

⊞

Cat hauls ass up Fourteenth Street. It's nearly eight in the morning and she's not the only one running late, hers just one more pair of feet in the Wednesday-morning crush of work-bound bodies. She moves, small and quick, picking her way through the crowd, weaving around the slow-movers, the shufflers, the newsstand gawkers. She gets hung up at the light at Third Avenue. There's a guy next to her shifting from foot to foot in expensive shoes, like that's gonna make the light change faster. Or like if he stops moving he'll get stuck there, have to spend the rest of his life rooted to the corner. At night, the club kids on their way to the Palladium would wonder at him, some mysterious holdover from the morning world. The light changes and she matches his pace, then blows on past him. Middle-aged Jewish chick in secondhand combat boots: one; impatient Prada-footed yuppie: zero.

A delivery truck rattles past, Chinese characters and a line drawing of a lobster in red on the driver's door. Someone's spray-painted RICE DICK across the side in a loose black scrawl.

She'd kill for a breakfast-cart tea, but no way can she show up with a cup in her hand like she had time to wait on line for tea but not to get to work when she said she would. That damn meeting.

Cat never wanted to be a leader, didn't ask for it. She played no part in the building coming to be called Cat House. In the beginning they just called the house Five-Three-Nine, but her reputation being what it is, everyone in the neighborhood got into the habit of referring to it as Cat's house and it stuck. She hates the name. It's like the weight of the place hung on her.

And now everyone is looking to her to have the answers and say what's what. Cat has no fucking clue what's what. When it came time to choose two reps from each building to go down to the courthouse with the lawyer, and they all looked to her, she said, Nuh uh. No. Send someone else. So Gideon and Chrissie went instead, and good for them.

She's had enough of the noise and the drama. She just wants to come and go without anyone bothering her.

Hang out with her cats. Sleep late. Make tea and toast. A person's entitled to take a break. Say, "I've been part of this human race for forty-one years and I'd like to step off the ride for a while." Not die or anything. Just step off to the side and watch everyone else run the circles for a change. Or not watch. That would be even better.

Like now, for example. Except she has to work. She couldn't have gone to the courthouse even if she'd wanted to. She promised Dan she'd be there at seven to help set up and here it is 8:05. The farmers' market opened five minutes ago. Fuck this. Forty-one years old and worried about being late to a job selling onions. This isn't what she'd expected from her life. Though, truth be told, her expectations ran out at thirty and she's been winging it since then. Who would have thought she'd live this long, anyway? You don't set about making plans for a cushy middle age when you expect to die young. But she didn't die, did she? Joke's on her.

8:07. The white-peaked market tents rise up ahead of her on the west side of Union Square. That first glimpse of the tents gets to her every time, even after five years of working for Dan. A quiet feeling, almost like hope. That she should belong there, be a part of it. There's a pleasure to it, moving crates, stacking vegetables, making change for customers. After a lifetime of tying things up as convoluted as she could manage, she's come to find that what she wants more than anything are the small, simple things. She likes to smile at regular customers, show them she remembers. She'll say something like, "How'd you like that miner's lettuce last week? We've got a good price on it to-day." It's funny, the things that keep you going.

She crosses Fourth Avenue with the light and jaywalks a quick line across Fourteenth, then cuts through a crowd of homeless guys ranged out on the steps up to the park. She catches sight of Benny, a sweet little drunk she knew back in the day. He's got a pile of sugar packets between his feet. He rips one open with stained fingers, then pours the sugar into his mouth. He's got the shakes bad and there's sugar caught in his beard. She picks up her pace to get past him.

The steps are low and deep, like waves of concrete. She half runs across the park and down the steps on the far side to the Windmar Farm tent, one of about ten farms at the market today. The market's smaller this time of year, a lot of producers closing shop for the winter. But not Dan. He's there year-round, even though by December it gets to be just storage apples and root vegetables and the hardiest of winter greens. Windmar's tent sits, as always, between the egg farmer and the pork and beef farmer. "Breakfast, lunch, and dinner," Ron, the egg farmer, likes to say of their little row.

Dan's tables are already set up and heavy with produce. Radishes and turnips, beets purple as a bruise. The wind blows through the market, carrying the bitter-green winter smell of the brassicas: kale, cabbage, collards. It's got to be the cleanest smell in the world. And then the hint of fresh blood coming off the meat stand. That's got to be the truest smell in the world.

She shouldn't have snuck by Benny like that. She'll bring him some food later, first break she gets.

"Sorry! Sorry!" Cat winces as she approaches the tent. Dan's weighing turnips for a pinched old lady in a down coat that smells of cat piss. *Easy*, she thinks. *That cat-piss coat is gonna be yours before you know it.*

"No matter," Dan says. "It's slow to get started when it's cold like this."

His daughter is stacking carrots. Her fingers thick as the carrots, her squared-off swimmer's shoulders hunched to the work. Milk-fed farm girl with neither the patience for nor the understanding of Cat's kind. She'd been hoping the girl would stay back on the farm today. No such luck. No luck at all today, it seems.

"Hey, Riva," Cat says.

The girl doesn't so much as glance up. "We finished loading up the truck at ten last night. We woke up at four this morning, and drove two hours in the dark to be here on time."

"Look, I'm sorry, okay? There was this meeting—"

"We don't need you here now. We needed help with setup. We don't need three people working the stand at the end of November."

"I said it's alright, Riva," Dan says.

The girl's got her mouth bunched up tight like an asshole. She graduated from college in the spring and came home to join the family business. She's been riding Cat hard ever since. Big bad boss lady.

Cat knows they don't need three of them working the stand today, but Dan's too kind to lay her off for the winter. She stuck with him the last five years while Riva was away at school and it was just Cat and Dan on their own. She worked in the snow, the cold, the rain. So maybe Cat's earned a bit of loyalty in return. Maybe Miss Riva can screw herself.

"The city's trying to evict us," Cat tells Dan. "We had to meet with a lawyer this morning." She might be homeless by the end of this shift. She'll be weighing turnips while the police padlock her front door. She's too old to start over, too tired. She doesn't have any kind of savings, not enough job to pay any kind of real rent. No real skills to get a better job.

"That's a hell of a thing," Dan says. "You let me know if there's anything I can do, okay?" Good old Dan. That kind face of his. He has no idea, and why should he? He turns away to help a customer and Cat puts out a few more acorn squash.

It turns out that knowing famous people does not amount to being famous. It turns out that a youth spent hanging around with people who did big things is not the same as having done a damn thing herself. She lived her twenties and thirties full throttle, with fuck all to show for it. She's a legend on the Lower East Side. A legend who's bound to freeze to death sleeping in a doorway before too long. Wouldn't her mother be proud, if she'd lived to see it?

No, this is not the life Cat thought she'd signed on for. Not nearly.

⊞

Sunlight blows Centre Street out like an overexposed photo-graph and pigeons swoop in graceful arcs across the frame, as if they've suddenly remembered they're doves. Steve, pushing through the heavy courthouse door, could open up wide and eat the world. Shoulders like mountains. He feels that powerful. "Request for a temporary restraining order is granted" and the gavel coming down just like in the movies.

Gerrit's sucking hard off his cigarette, loping along beside him. Still got that frown of his on. Still got those shoulders all hunched.

"Gerrit, man. You're the kid who made a face and it got frozen that way. Smile. We won." Steve nudges the smaller man with his elbow and boosts the smokes from Gerrit's coat pocket. He shakes one loose, then hands the pack back.

"We haven't won anything."

Those beady little eyes, that pinched little mouth. How is it Steve's never noticed before how much the man looks like a possum? That's Amelia rubbing off on Steve. He feels a stab of guilt, bitter as bile. "No," he says, "but it's a start. Today, right now, the news is good. Today we are the mighty, the winners, the all-fucking-powerful *ganadores de la puta Loisaida*. Don't you want to hold on to that for a while? They'll try to beat it out of us soon enough anyway. I won't do the job for them."

Footsteps come up fast from behind, heavy booted feet. Steve and Gerrit whirl around but it's just Gideon come out of the courthouse and wanting to catch up to them. Steve can see Chrissie trailing behind a ways down the block. Maybe he and Gerrit should have waited for them. Weird, maybe, the way the two of them just barreled out of there on their own. But that's their way—Steve and Gerrit against the world. And again the guilt rises up like something bad he ate. But that's in the past, Steve and Amelia. That's a done thing.

"Hey," Gideon says, falling into step next to Steve. "Where you guys running off to?"

"Home," Gerrit says.

"Gonna catch the train?" Gideon asks.

"Walking." Gerrit picks up the pace, but Gideon sticks with them, his big face open and eager.

"That lawyer for the city's something, hunh?" Gideon says. "Elaine DeMarkis, *Esssquire.* She's like one of those Upper East Side girls you sit a little too close to on the six train just 'cause they smell so good."

"She's trying to get you evicted and you're wondering how she smells?" Steve says.

"Yeah, I'm not so worried about her, I guess. She's wound up real tight, like it wouldn't take much to make her crack. Did you see the way she was tapping her pencil on the table? Tapping it like crazy. *Tap tap tap.* Like Morse code or something. Hell, I don't know. Do you think they'll do it? Get us out?"

"The city doesn't look away when it thinks you're sitting on a pile of its money," Gerrit says.

They turn right onto Canal, merging into the midday Chinatown bustle. An old man working the battered red newsstand on the corner shouts in Chinese to no one in particular. Speakers outside a pawnshop blare syrupy Cantopop. Three teenage girls who should probably be in school come giggling out of a bakery, trailing the scent of eggs and sugar in their wake. A blonde in a short-skirted business suit high-heels it across Canal, and Steve's fickle heart beats two or three beats just for her.

"New York's always run on money," Gideon says. "That's nothing new. Money and power."

"Neither of which we have," Gerrit says.

"So then you need to know what you've got that the people who do have the money and power want, and there's *your* power." Gideon falls into step with Steve. "You know what I'm saying, right?"

Steve eyes Gideon, his earnest farm-boy face. All these years in the city and he's still running those old New York movies in his head. "I know what you mean, the money and power trip, but I'm not playing that game. That game's exactly what's killing this city. You ever have a hamster?"

"What?"

"A pet hamster. When you were a kid. You have one?"

"Nah. Had a dog."

"Well, you know what happens if you get a boy and a girl hamster and they have babies? If you leave the babies in the cage with them, the parents eat them. They eat their own babies. *That's* New York for you right there. The bitch mother who eats her own babies. I'm not gonna play their money games. Irving's gonna help us get title to those buildings. We're coming out on top this time. I can feel it."

Ahead of them, Canal Street rushes headlong across Bowery and into the open mouth of the Manhattan Bridge.

"Kronos ate his babies," Gerrit says.

"Zeus's father," Steve says. "And Zeus got away. And?"

"Do you remember how Zeus got away? His mother fed Kronos a rock. Trading power we don't have for money we don't have won't save us. And we'll see what happens but I do not believe the lawyer and the courts will save us. This is the world. The best we can do is watch our backs and carry a big rock."

Gideon snorts and pats Gerrit on the shoulder. "You're one angry dude, man, but you're alright."

Gerrit glowers and hunches deeper into his coat collar. "Steve, I'll see you back at the house." He turns south onto Bowery, moving deeper into the heart of Chinatown.

"You think he's right?" Gideon says.

Steve watches his friend's retreating back, the way he makes himself smaller as he walks, arms pulled in, head down like he's walking against the wind. It's like he wants to pass through the city without being seen at all. "No," he says. "Not this time." They cross Canal and head north on Bowery, toward home, bearing the hopeful news.

⊞

Anne reaches under the wobbly bar table and takes Steve's hand. This morning she'd been resigned to losing the house, but Steve had been so sure, so strong in his belief. "It'll be fine," he'd said. "You'll see." And he was right. At least for now, he's right.

He's glowing tonight, that special shine of his that first took her in. Even in the dim bar light, he's glowing. He looks at her with his eyes lit up and warm. He squeezes her hand.

Amelia sits slumped in her chair, sullen. Gerrit's no better, hunched over his beer, spinning the usual stories of how things went bad in Amsterdam, even his accent thick with resignation. He won't allow for any optimism here. He won't allow for even one night to enjoy their victory, however small. Anne's father, an armchair philosopher given to sweeping pronouncements at the dinner table, liked to say, "The European man is a conquered man. Their empires are gone, their lives turned over to history." Maybe he was quoting someone else. She's half tempted to tell Gerrit about it, if only to get him a little riled up. He would almost have to show some optimism in self-defense.

Steve is drinking whiskey tonight, like they've had some kind of windfall. Like they're made of money. *But it's okay*, she tells herself. *It's okay to celebrate once in a while.* He says she needs to loosen up. So here she is, loosening up.

"Cheers," she says, raising her beer. Gerrit clinks his bottle against hers, Amelia raising her drink a beat behind him.

Steve's already drained his glass. "This round's on me," he says, pushing back to stand, but no one else is ready for another. He comes back with more whiskey. "I knew it," he says. "I fucking knew it. Didn't I tell you?" He turns to her. "Annie, honey. Didn't I tell you? I said everything would be okay."

"It's not okay yet," Gerrit says.

"It's a fine beginning. An excellent beginning," Anne says, smiling at Steve, patting his leg. He's looking at Amelia, watching her fiddle with the straw in her glass.

"The whole thing makes me nervous," Amelia says.

"That's Gerrit's voice in your head, telling you not to trust it," Steve says. "Relax. At least for tonight. What's with that soda you're drinking? Let me get you a real drink. Gerrit, you can't spring for a real drink for your girl?"

"No," Amelia says. "I'm good."

"A beer?" Steve says. "Gin and tonic?"

"She's on antibiotics," Gerrit says.

"Antibiotics." Steve rubs his palms on his jeans. "Nothing serious, I hope," he says, glancing at Anne.

Amelia coughs out a little laugh.

"It's nothing to worry about," Gerrit says.

The way Steve worries over Amelia, his gruff fatherly way with her, was sweet when the girl was sixteen. Anne was proud that he saw that need in Amelia when she first moved in. But she's not sixteen anymore. It's time Amelia stood up a little, found her own strength; well past time. Steve and Gerrit both still treat her like a favored child.

Steve would have been a good father.

No. Push that down. They're celebrating.

Steve's got a big hot hand on her thigh, he's nuzzling into her hair with his boozy breath. They're celebrating.

⊞

Amelia walks home from the International between Steve and Gerrit, silent. Gerrit and Steve and Anne have been rambling on all night about what's going down with the city, and they must not care about her opinion—or maybe it doesn't occur to them that she might have one—because she hasn't said much at all and no one's even seemed to notice.

"All I'm saying is that a piece of paper from the court doesn't give us enough protection that we can let our guard down," Gerrit says.

Anne's got her hand looped through Steve's arm, hugging close to him on his other side. Steve's lit, of course, shambling along, his free arm brushing against Amelia as they walk. His hand finds its way under her coat hem to grab at her ass, and Anne walks along completely oblivious. It's sad, yeah, but it's also kind of funny. It got to be a game with her and Steve when they were together, to see how far they could push it without getting caught. Seems like the game's back on.

His reaction to Gerrit's antibiotics excuse was priceless. She should tell him she's got the clap, just to see the look on his face. She should tell him she got it from him.

They stop at a red light and Amelia tucks Gerrit's scarf tighter against his neck, tugs his cap down over his ears. She makes a show of kissing him, knowing Steve's watching.

Anne says, "No one's saying we should let our guard down. But I don't think it does us any good to be going into this from a position of violence—with some kind of siege mentality."

"*Lammeren ter slachtbank*," Gerrit mutters. *Lambs to the . . . something.*

Steve shakes a fresh cigarette from his pack, lighting it off the stub of the old one. Amelia watches the way his lips meet the cigarette, the way his eyes go half-closed on the first draw. "Gerrit's right," he says. "We need to be prepared."

"Who's on the door tonight?" Gerrit asks.

"Ben has first watch, Suzie second," Anne says.

"We'd better do a bike watch, too," Gerrit says. "Have someone keeping an eye on the block from the outside. I'm not sure how much we can trust the city to hold to that restraining order. I'll take first watch."

Gerrit's all charged up now, energized by the idea of the threat to the squat. Amelia hasn't seen his eyes this bright in ages. Maybe years. Not since a bunch of kids tried to mug them one night, a few doors down from their building, and he'd pulled out his knife. He'd told them he wouldn't be mugged on his own block, and they could try but someone was going to get cut, and the kids had backed down and run away. Amelia had waited until they'd gotten home safe, then had lit into him, saying he could risk his own life but not to drag her into it, that the kids might not have backed down, that they'd been outnumbered, what if they'd had a gun?

"But they didn't have a gun," he'd said.

He has that same look now. He's going to get on his bike tonight, and he's going to circle the block for hours, watching for trouble. Half hoping, no doubt, for trouble. Amelia wonders how much this has to do with the house and how much it has to do with boredom, with things having been too quiet for too long. Sometimes Gerrit just likes to fight. He's got something to prove, and he'll likely have to go on fighting forever, because she doubts he's ever going to feel like it's been proven.

A week after Amelia first arrived at Thirteen House, the worst of the detox just beginning to ease, she and Gerrit were sitting quietly at the kitchen table. It was snowing again. She was doodling clusters of circles on a pad and wishing she had something to knit, and he was fixing a small transistor radio. He held it on his lap, below the table, so all she could see was his left hand turning the screwdriver handle.

Out of nowhere, casual, like he was talking about the weather, he said, "Kids teased me when I was younger."

"Oh, me too," she said. "Really bad. I hated school."

"Kids teased me. Just because I'm missing some fingers from my hand." He pushed up the sleeve of his flannel shirt and set his right forearm on the table. The forearm was short and thin and pale white, tapering sharply down to two impossibly long fingers. No wrist, no palm. Just a forearm and then the two hooking fingers pressed together and quivering against the white enamel of the table.

Was it a hallucination? A trick? She couldn't make sense of what she was seeing.

"What did you do to your hand?" she sputtered. Before she could think and realize what she was seeing and just shut the fuck up, that was what came tumbling out. And she recoiled. She knew she was recoiling after it was too late to stop. His face sagged and crumpled. He tugged his sleeve down and rushed to his room, closing the door behind him.

A week she'd been living with him already. How could she not have noticed? She had spent most of that time sweating out the dope on the thin mattress Gerrit had found for her, her bones aching, her skin sharp and buzzing with a sick electricity, but even so . . . She'd never seen his right hand, and never having seen it, her mind filled in the absence, giving him an unremarkable right hand to match the left. Then that normal right hand of her mind was abruptly changed for his real hand. She wouldn't have predicted her reaction to his hand any more than she would have predicted the hand itself. She would have thought she was better than that, more generous than that. She was not. How awful, to find out she could be so small.

She went to the closed door, leaning against it. "Gerrit," she'd said, dragging her knuckles against the scarred wood. She'd opened the door and gone and sat beside him on his cot.

"I'm sorry," she said. "God, I'm sorry. I'm an ass . . . I'm so sorry."

He rolled his sleeve up and rested that right half-hand on her leg. It lay there warm and trembling, like something not ready to be exposed to air or light. She didn't dare to move; she held her leg as still as she could beneath that hand.

"There was this drug called Softenon," he began, quietly. His voice was tight, as if he was struggling to be calm, to be patient with her. "Thalidomide—it's called thalidomide here in the States. Did you ever hear about it?" He told her the story, then. About how his mother had been given some pills for morning sickness when she was pregnant with him. About how he'd gotten off lucky—much luckier than many—and how very badly other victims had been deformed. He told her about how his two fingers had been joined by a web of skin, and how he'd had them separated when he was fifteen so they would be more functional. Except the result was nerves running along the inside of each finger that had never wanted to be so close to the surface, and how painful the simplest pressure was. How a tool slipping between those fingers was enough to blind him momentarily.

It hurt her to think of how skilled he was at hiding that hand, and the reasons he'd had to become so good at it. Her own reaction, just one more reason. "I didn't notice," she said.

"You'll only ever see it when I want you to. It's okay. I surprised you." He said it was okay, but he wouldn't meet her eyes. Other than his hand on her leg, which he seemed to have laid there to challenge her rather than to touch her, he held his body apart from hers. Rigid, distant. "See, it's not just my hand. It wasn't you, wasn't that I didn't want you. I did. I do. It's my cock, it doesn't work like it should. Sometimes it does, but usually . . . It wasn't you. I want you to know that."

He should have done it differently, made it less of a surprise, less of an ambush. She has always wished she could go back in time and react differently, erase that first horrified look from her face, wipe it from his memory along with every other horrified look he's seen his whole life. Or at least erase hers, so that she wouldn't have turned out to be like all the others, exactly like everyone else.

⊞

It's just past 2:00 AM. One more time around the block and he'll call it a night. Gerrit pedals slowly, eyes on the shadows, scanning stoops and doorways. There's a guy in gray security-guard pants coming off the late shift; a drunk girl stumbling ahead of a drunker boy; a homeless guy sifting through the trash. No signs of trouble.

At Thirteen House Amelia's windows are dark; Steve and Anne's windows are dark; Suzie and Denise's windows are dark. Streetside, only Ben's lights are on, his shadow crossing the window shade as Gerrit rides past.

He thinks of the Vogelstruys, a lifetime ago in Amsterdam, spring 1980, Gerrit as young then as Amelia is now. They woke in the squat one morning to find they were under siege. The long-anticipated war with the police had finally arrived. They'd waited and waited. They'd stocked their arsenal, built their barricades and fortifications. And even so, when the attack arrived, it came as a shock. All these years later, his stomach still roils at the memory of the tear gas, at the echo of booted feet on the stairs, the police in their riot gear.

Everything changes depending on vantage point. Above the police, throwing rocks from the windows and the rooftop, the fight is about defending the house. Meet them at eye level, on the stairs, in the rooms, and it's about saving your own ass.

Gerrit, Claar, Max, and Frits had rushed to the roof, hurling down the stockpile of rocks and bricks they'd collected in the weeks leading up to the siege. Then the door gave way, the police streaming inside the building. They'd heard their comrades as the wave of police had moved through them—sounds of bodies hitting the floor, sounds of boots meeting flesh. Gerrit and Claar had jumped across to the neighboring rooftop and gone inside, running down the stairs, aiming for the street. Cops followed. Gerrit was caught by the arm, dragged by his hair. Claar was pushed down the narrow staircase. He remembers the sick crack of her head as she hit bottom, the look of simple surprise on her face in the moment before she lost consciousness. How she lived through that, how any of them did, he still isn't sure.

He's told Amelia the stories. He's told all of them how bad things can get. But they hear his stories like fairy tales. He's from the Old World, no different than their long-dead Italian/Polish/Puerto Rican great-grandmothers who darkened their childhood bedsides with tales of wolves that steal children and magical old men with dark secrets in burlap bags. Amelia and the rest of the squatters are American. They are shiny and new. They are entitled and untouchable. Inevitable. He hopes they never have occasion to learn otherwise.

Back at the house, he hefts his bike up onto his shoulder, thumbs his key in the lock, and slips inside. He's greeted by that good honest smell of fresh lumber and plaster, and also the more worrisome smell of must and wood rot. Over the years they've rebuilt most of the joists, replaced crumbling plaster ceilings with drywall, fixed the roof. But there's still so much they haven't had time or money to do, like the rear facade. It's not watertight; it needs repointing. Until they can get that done, water will keep finding its way in, softening the wood around the windows, compromising the building's structure. Already the weather is too cold to work with mortar. If they can hold on until spring, they'll do it then.

Suzie is on the folding chair by the front door, dog-eared paperback in hand. "Nothing?" she says.

"Quiet. Here, too?"

She nods.

Footsteps on the stairs, Ben headed down to relieve Suzie. He has a deck of cards in hand, and a thermos tucked under his arm. "Hey, man. Want to play?"

"No, I'm headed up to bed."

Marlowe emerges from his first-floor apartment, coat on, ready for his shift. He's wearing the green scarf Amelia made for him a while back. Amelia said he cried when she gave it to him.

Her knitting is like magic. She'll take a huge old sweater bought for a dollar at the Salvation Army, unravel it, wash the wool, and knit two smaller sweaters, a hat, and maybe some mittens from it. Gerrit's got a drawer full of warm socks she's knitted for him from recycled yarn, a scarf, two watch caps, three sweaters. She has no idea that when you slip on that hat or scarf or sweater she's made for you, you feel the work of her hands in it. You feel her love for you. That was why Marlowe cried. Gerrit gets it. He feels the same way every time he pulls one of those hand-knit sweaters over his head. The girl thinks she's invisible. She has no idea, the impact she has on people. Seven years he's been trying to get her to see it. Maybe she never will.

"Sure you don't want to take a bike?" Gerrit says to Marlowe. "I've got something in the shop not exactly big enough for you, but close."

"Nah, man. My feet will do just fine." He claps Gerrit on the shoulder as he passes, slaps hands with Ben, a nod to Suzie, and he's out the door. His shoulders fill the doorframe, and then he turns right and is gone, just the sound of his footsteps on the sidewalk and then the door falling closed.

Gerrit takes the stairs to the third floor, to the apartment he and Amelia share. He imagines her asleep in bed, the covers pulled up to her chin. She looks like a child when she sleeps, her lips softly open. He'll climb in beside her and she'll nestle into him and he'll hold her like that and drift off to sleep. Or she'll wake up just enough to move against him in that way she does, her way of asking him to touch her. He'll slide a hand between her legs, feel her skin heat up, feel her breathing go shallow and quick. He'll hold her and touch her, and through the windows by her bed, down on the street, there will be the sound of cars passing, the sound of the wind off the river, the sound of Marlowe's heavy footsteps circling the block, watching over Thirteen House and all its people.

4

Amelia stares at the bike tools laid out on her workstation. She's used them nearly every day for years now, since Gerrit first started to teach her how to fix bikes, but somehow today she can't make sense of them. They may as well be dental tools, instruments of torture, tuning forks.

"You're quiet," Suzie says. She swings her bike up onto a repair stand, the lean corded muscles of her forearms flexing beneath the red scales of twin tattooed koi fish. "You've got to help me with the gears. There's this grinding sound and then it slips when I shift down." Suzie moves easily around the small workspace, gathering up tools.

"Gerrit could get this done a lot faster," Amelia says.

"And we can get it done, too. Roll up those sleeves, woman. What's wrong with you? Where's that man of yours today anyway?"

"Meeting at Irving's."

Suzie nods, her sleek cap of black hair iridescent under the shop lights, like a crow's wing. "Some ugly shit. But we'll be okay." And if they're not okay, what's it to Suzie? She's got a family to fall back on—a family in Connecticut, with money, no less. So her mom's got a pill problem and her dad's got a girlfriend. It's still a family. When Suzie told Amelia her story, she said, "There are all kinds of ways to have it hard," but if she called them and said she was homeless, wouldn't they say, "Come home. You and Denise come stay with us until you get your feet back under you"?

If her mom were still alive, Amelia wouldn't have run away. Even if her mom was still drinking.

"I'm not feeling so good," she says. "I need to get some air or something." She rushes out the back door, stumbling into the yard with its building materials under tarps, its discarded bicycle parts, its broken cinder blocks and cigarette butts. She leans against the wall and pukes, a thin white spattering on the gray-brown dirt.

"Whoa." Suzie is in the doorway. "You okay?"

Amelia wipes her mouth with the back of her hand.

"Holy shit. You're pregnant!" Suzie practically squeals it, and loud enough for anyone near the back windows to hear.

"It's just a stomach bug or something. Don't be stupid."

"Are you sure? Because you've got that look. It's a special kind of queasy. I've seen it before."

"That's not it." *Yes, that's it*, she wants to say, but everything feels too close right now, too immediate: the broken cinder blocks and the dirt; the sun in her eyes; Suzie and her knowing smile. To say it out loud would be to give life to the new lie. Suzie will assume Gerrit is the father, and Amelia won't tell her otherwise, and just like that there'd be a new layer packed on to the old lie, and this time the baby caught up in it, too.

"Well, it'd be cool, you know, if it was. You and Gerrit. First baby born in the house and all. It'd just be . . . it'd be a good thing. We could use a good thing right about now, don't you think?"

"I should get knocked up for the good of the community?"

"I was just talking. So you're not pregnant. You feel okay enough to help me fix this bike?"

Amelia follows Suzie back inside. Suzie knows. She didn't believe the stomach bug excuse or she'd be worried about catching whatever it is that Amelia's got.

Whatever it is that Amelia's got. Jesus.

Last night Amelia lay awake in bed, poking and rubbing at her belly and trying to find evidence of what was going on inside but feeling only her own usual self. She listened to the familiar night sounds of the building, heat through the pipes, floorboards creaking under feet. And she got to thinking about her choices, and how maybe there was a third way. Something between having the baby with Gerrit and getting rid of it. How maybe she could go off somewhere where no one knows her and have the baby there. Maybe someplace in the Midwest, or north, way north close to Canada. She could go there, find a hotel, and get a job as a room maid. She knew a girl who'd done that once and who said it was easy work to get.

If she gave a different name at the hospital and just slipped out real quiet one night, they'd have to take care of the baby, wouldn't they? Or she could find an adoption agency and plan it all out in advance. She could go through their books and choose the right couple. And the couple would pay for her hospital stay and bring her flowers after the baby was born, and then they'd take the baby home and Amelia would be free to move on.

Except then there would always be a kid out there, her and Steve's kid, not knowing either of them. She doesn't think she could bear that, the not-knowing of it. Choosing to walk around the rest of your life with someone missing.

And Gerrit is planning for the three of them, a snug little family. She owes him so much already.

Stupid little tadpole. She's starting to feel something like love for it, and that scares her. That means she's already taking too long to make her decision. She has another few weeks to decide, maybe a month, tops. And then she would be having it and it would be a question only of stay or go, keep it or give it away. Stupid tadpole. It never asked for this. Both of them, stupid creatures who didn't ask for it, in it together.

She thinks of her own mother, pregnant with her at seventeen, her older boyfriend leaving town as soon as he got the news, never to be heard from again. She thinks, for the first time, of how scared her mother must have been. And, no, abortion wasn't legal back then, wasn't as easy to get as it is now. But it was still an option, as her mother reminded Amelia more than once. "I could have gotten rid of you," she would say. "I could have, and I didn't, did I? You remember that." At the time, Amelia heard it as a threat. Only now, her mother years dead, does Amelia hear it as a plea, as evidence of love.

⊞

Cat's got a little bit of happiness in a brown paper bag. Falafel with hot sauce, Sun Chips, a Dr Pepper. When she gets home she's gonna sit at the window to watch the world go by while she has a picnic lunch all by herself. She's celebrating today, though she's not sure precisely why. The restraining order, maybe. She was relieved as hell to get that news yesterday, even though she knows their asses are still hanging out there.

Whatever it is, she slept in till ten this morning and when she woke up the cats were purring and the sun was shining and all her usual aches and pains were quiet enough that she didn't have to mind them at all and she caught herself thinking, "Damn, what a beautiful day," and determined to do something nice for herself. Falafel, chips, and a Dr Pepper. Doesn't take much these days, does it?

Thirteenth Street is quiet at midday, the kids gone to school or hiding from it; adults at work or sleeping one off. The occasional car rumbles past her as she walks. Used to be all you'd see was old beaters creaking on by, but the cars are getting nicer little by little. Gentrification rolls in all caught up in the bumper of a Camry. And why not? Who says a shitty neighborhood has to stay shitty? Who says New York is New York only if there's a knife at your throat? Change is the city's only true constant. Someone has always been getting rolled over to make room for someone else, and money pretty much always at the root of it. All the way back to the Dutch and the Indians, yeah? She should point that out to Gerrit one of these days.

Not that she's in any rush to lose the roof over her head. She hopes they can hang on. It's just that she won't be all that surprised if they can't. It's the nature of things. The rich eat the poor, then shit them out into the crappy run-down tenement corners of the city. Then more rich folks, and folks who want to *be* rich folks, move to the city and they need more room. But it's a fucking *island* and there isn't all that much room left, right? So the crappy corners start to look better, especially to the ones who aren't rich yet (and probably never will be, sweetie, sorry to break it to ya), and they move on in and eat the poor all over again, but where is there left to crap them out now? Across the river, in Brooklyn. And when the rich have gobbled Manhattan all down, then what? Roll on over to Brooklyn and take over the poor neighborhoods there.

She walks past Thirteen House and sees Amelia and Suzie doing battle with a bike in Gerrit's shop. Suzie, the poor little rich girl; Amelia, the white trash runaway. She's okay though, Amelia, a sweet kid. And if what Cat's heard about her is true, that she had no one at all left alive and that's why she ran away to the city, well then that girl is in as much trouble as Cat if the shit really does come down. Though Gerrit'll take care of Amelia, of course. Tell her exactly what to do and what to think while he's at it. He's got a funny way of looking after that girl. Not that it's any of Cat's concern.

The real reason men like 'em young? It's the girl's willingness to submit to Daddy's authority. Get enough of an age gap and a certain kind of girl will defer to a man on nearly everything. Amelia's that kind of girl.

Cat? Cat's a grown-ass woman.

Through the red metal door of Cat House and up the stairs. Falafel with hot sauce, Sun Chips, Dr Pepper.

"Yo, Cat!" Gideon sticks his head out of his tagged-up apartment door.

The paper bag's starting to go soft from the falafel grease and the condensation coming off the Dr Pepper. "Make it fast, man. I've got a hot date with a pita." She shifts her grip to hold the bag from the bottom.

"Me and Chrissie just got back from the meeting with the lawyer. You want me to bring you up to speed?"

She waves him off. "Yeah, but later, okay?" She half turns away, then . . . *shit*. "It can wait, right? I mean, we're not expecting the villagers to show up with torches and pitchforks just yet, are we?"

"Nah. It'll keep. Not much different from yesterday, actually. I think we're already talking in circles."

"Cool. Well then I'll come back down later, okay?"

"Cool."

She's halfway up the next flight of stairs when he calls after her. "Hey, but Cat? I thought *we* were the villagers?"

"Sometimes you're the villager, sometimes you're the monster. The tricky part's knowing whose turn it is."

"So we're the monster?"

Gideon takes her way too seriously. Everyone does. She's not sure how she managed that.

Alone in her apartment, she settles down onto the wide windowsill and takes the falafel from the bag, the pita gone soft from the oil. She takes a big bite, feels sauce drip warm between her fingers. That's half the pleasure of it—eating alone and not caring about the mess you make of yourself.

Yeah, so maybe they're the monster this time. And maybe the monster needs to find a way to wake those villagers up, point their flames and pitchforks uphill to the castle, where the real trouble is. Ah, but Cat doesn't have it in her to wake anybody up. Leave the revolution to Gerrit, to Steve, to the young kids they gather around them who've still got enough energy to muster the kind of outrage that sends you tilting at the castle walls.

Probably the falafel and chips shouldn't taste as good today, the Dr Pepper shouldn't taste as sweet, with all that they're up against. But they taste damn good, and Cat's gonna eat every last bite. Then, and only then, will she go downstairs and find out what the lawyer had to say.

⊞

"Do you think we'll get away with them as they are?" Gerrit says. "It's too cold to work with the mortar." He and Steve are on the roof, surveying the parapet walls, which will need to be reinforced. The same restraining order that's keeping the city from evacuating them right now is also supposed to put a stop to all repairs on the buildings in question, but the closer to code the buildings are when the inspectors come, the stronger their case in court. The work continues, quietly, slowly, the way it did in the beginning, so no one would know it was going on.

"It'll have to do for now. I'm more worried about the rotten lintels in the back. They're gonna say those are structural damage." Steve squints into the fading light of dusk, out over the tenement rooftops to where the projects on Avenue D shoulder up double, triple the height of the rest of the neighborhood, and beyond them the river. The tip of his cigarette glows an angry orange as he takes a hard pull. Gerrit motions toward Steve's jacket pocket and Steve tosses him the pack of Marlboros.

"The first time we stood on this roof a wrong step would have landed us in the basement," Gerrit says. Eleven years ago, they opened the building: 537 East Thirteenth Street. It had been abandoned since the early seventies, a crack den most recently. Steve had had his eye on the building for a while. He'd grown up just a block away and was partial to Thirteenth Street the way a person is about wherever he passed his childhood, if it was mostly a good one. Then one night the police busted the crackheads and Steve put the word out and their group moved in as soon as the cops' backs were turned.

There was no way of knowing how long they'd be able to stay, but they settled in and went to work. The building needed all new joists, a new roof, new walls, new floors. It needed a sewer line and gas lines. The broken-down shamble became Thirteen House, the first working squat on the block. There have been countless repairs and restorations over the years, and they've done them together, scavenging the supplies where they could. Gerrit learned carpentry in the Amsterdam squats. Steve's friend Ricardo knew some plumbing. The rest they figured out as they went.

A few years in, Ricardo moved on. His cousin José took over his space, bringing his family with him. Having little Carla, six years old then, running through the halls, leaving hopscotch squares and flowers and hearts chalked onto the sidewalk out front, solidified something, a reminder of what they were doing, the community they had set out to build; here was a child, deserving of a safe place to live and play and be loved. Gerrit's never said as much to José and Nena, but now he thinks he should thank them for what they did when they brought Carla to live in Thirteen House. He digs at the parapet with his toe and the mortar crumbles, cascading over the tip of his boot.

"I'm not ready to leave," Steve says, his voice thick.

Gerrit thinks of Amelia, the way her hand rests on her belly when she thinks he isn't watching. That baby will need a secure home. If that means going legal, if that's how things have to be done, so be it. Never let it be said that Gerrit cannot adapt. "We're not leaving."

Gerrit met Steve on the morning of his second day in New York. 1983. Straight off the plane, he'd headed to the Lower East Side, the address of Maarten, a friend's cousin, in his pocket. Maarten had left Amsterdam the year before and had fallen in with the homesteader movement in

New York. He introduced Gerrit to Steve, who was getting ready to open the abandoned building on Thirteenth between A and B that would become Thirteen House.

Maarten left New York only a few weeks after Gerrit's arrival, and so Gerrit found himself shoehorned into the role previously assigned the older Nederlander. Gerrit was seen as someone of consequence, battle-hardened, a leader. The degree to which the New York squatters idealized the Dutch movement sat uneasily with Gerrit.

In Amsterdam, many *krakers* wore keffiyeh around their necks; they were supposed to mark the squatters' isolation and outsider status, but it was also a simple fact that the scarves were handy for quickly covering one's face during a riot, to hide one's identity or protect (well) against plaster dust and smoke and (poorly) against tear gas. Soon, though, the scarf became part of the *kraker* uniform, and they'd all started to look alike. When Gerrit left Amsterdam, he'd left behind a movement that was stumbling to its inevitable end, consumed by itself. The initial impulses and spontaneity had given way to self-consciousness, active engagement with the media, pointless actions, costumes and poses.

Now in New York, squatters wear the Palestinian scarves to copy the Amsterdam *kraker* fashion. It's supposed to make them look authentic, he imagines, but it's just more costume, more outsider's pose. It runs counter to so much else he knows about these people—the sincerity that moves so many of them, the belief in the choices they've made—in the larger political implications of what they're doing in the squats.

Gerrit's early days in New York were hard, learning to live and work as a Nederlander in a crowd of Americans. He'd never been abroad before, never before been surrounded by so many very different sorts. It was the Wild West as he'd always imagined it, though with rubble and trash instead of tumbleweeds—but with cowboys, for sure, and lawless lawmen. The sound of gunfire at night. Wild dogs and crazy men ruling the streets after dark. All of it.

It was magical and terrifying and it took time, more than he let on, to get used to. These Americans, the way they argue; the way they won't back down from a fight no matter how wrong they are; the way they then shrug off the fight and move on to the next thing so easily; their distractibility, like children; their pride—their ridiculous, beautiful pride. He can't say he understands them, even now, but he knows he'll never go back to Europe. He knows he'll die in New York.

5

One day Gerrit will figure out how it is that Steve can get him to do such clearly ill-advised things as hitting up a construction site in the middle of a Friday afternoon. He and Ben are following Steve on a scavenger mission, lured by the promise of perfectly good PVC pipes that some obscure change in building codes rendered unusable for a building NYU is putting up. Another dorm? Classrooms? Who knows. The university is swallowing up downtown building by building, block by block.

"Remind me again why we're doing this in broad daylight?" Ben says.

Steve says, "The security guard's a friend of a friend. He'll let us in."

"And then he turns around and says we stole the stuff."

"Not gonna happen. He's a good guy. He just doesn't want to see good stuff go to waste."

"Let's hope we can get it all in this granny cart," Ben says. He jerks his chin toward the beat old folding shopping cart he's dragging behind him.

"I couldn't get ahold of Jeremy to borrow the van. If there's something really good we can't haul ourselves, I'll try to hook up with him later," Steve says.

Steve's jacket is missing a button; his shirt is stained. These would be meaningless details on anyone else, but Anne has always been so careful to keep him squared away. She would joke about it—her ongoing battle to make him at least *appear* respectable.

"How's Anne?" Gerrit says. His mother used to say that an unkempt husband is a sign of trouble at home. It's an old-fashioned sentiment, perhaps, but the more years go by, the more Gerrit's come to favor the old-fashioned sentiments.

Steve looks at him sharply, almost startled, tugging his fingers through his hair as if the mere sound of his wife's name draws his own attention to his disorder. "Good," he says. "You know. Worried like everyone else. But yeah. She's good."

They fall into silence, marking the blocks in bootfall. The shopping-cart wheels give a faint metallic whine, the smallest complaint beneath the hum of traffic. They pass in and out of conversations, lives rising and falling around them. An old man weeps into a pay phone. A mother slaps her son. This is what it is to live here. A postcard glance, maybe a word or two, maybe a whole sentence overheard, and that's all you'll likely ever know of that person; and then the next one; and the next. There you all are, crammed in together and still somehow terribly, awfully alone.

Gerrit wishes he'd gone with Amelia to her doctor's appointment. She said she didn't need him there, that he shouldn't trouble himself. What she meant was that she didn't want him to go.

Of course she needs him. She needs him so much more than she wants him. He wishes he didn't know this. He wishes, too, that he didn't know that he *will* trouble himself. He will do whatever it takes to care for her. *Someone* needs to look after that girl.

Amelia's time before she came to stay with him couldn't have been good, but she won't talk about it much. When he brought her home she had bruises on her arms and thighs, and on her neck. She'd been with the St. Marks kids for ten months, and doing heroin most of that time. He doesn't like to think about what she must have had to do to get it.

There was the detox at first, and he was afraid of what he'd done in bringing her home, what he'd brought into his life and into the house. She was such a wreck—a thin sheen of sweat on her skin, and the bags under her eyes gone blue like bruises. There was such fear in her. He held her and told her she would be alright, but he wasn't sure at all that she would be.

In those early months when she was afraid to be alone at night, he would lie beside her and watch her sleep. She would mutter and cry out. She would twitch and shiver beneath whatever nightmare had grip of her and more often than not wake up screaming. There Gerrit would be, holding her, petting her, telling her that she was safe, that she was home. "*Ik ben hier,*" he would say. "Here I am." To this day, he doesn't know what the nightmares were about, or where the bruises came from, though he can guess.

She was much more interested in his stories. She wanted details about Amsterdam, about the squats; about punk in Europe in the early eighties and what did he think of punk now, all these years later; about the clearings and how he came to be in New York. That's how he started teaching her Dutch. As he talked he would use a word in Dutch here, a phrase there, and she would repeat it, her mouth working around the unfamiliar sounds. She would ask for bedtime stories about *de buurt*, and he would lie in her bed beside her and stroke her hair and tell her tall tales and true tales about his days back in the Amsterdam squats. She would curl up ready to drift off and she'd listen, lips half-parted.

Some nights his hand drifted beneath the hem of her shirt and brushed across her nipples or spidered along her rib cage and she didn't stop him. Some nights he would lie behind her and she would wriggle her ass against his crotch, and he'd slip his hand into her pajama bottoms. On those nights, when she'd shift her shoulders a certain way, or adjust her back against his chest just so, her body became a country separate from her head and utterly open to the attentions of his hands.

They never discussed it directly, but she seemed to especially like the long fingers of his right hand inside her. He'd use them, the sensitive skin between the two formerly joined digits soothed in the wet and warm, slipping deep inside her and scissoring and twisting against the contracting walls.

They never kissed; they never tried to make love, even within his limitations. There were just these half-stolen caresses in her bed some nights where their eyes would never meet and neither was allowed to fully acknowledge that it was happening, even as it happened. In the morning, it would be as if nothing had.

Gerrit wonders, sometimes, what it is in him that allows him to accept this relationship of half measures. Amelia, his lover only at night, only in the dark. Amelia, his lover only as long as their eyes don't meet. Amelia, by day no more than his roommate. But he loves her. She loves him. She doesn't say so often, but in the long spaces between those times that she does say it, he trusts that love is still there. He is a strange man, the demands of loving him strange, and so he has come to understand that this is how it is between them; this is how it will be. Seven years of hushed touch in the dark; seven years of her sneaking around with other guys, but always coming home to him. There's such tenderness in her when she comes back; such a beseeching softness in her when she's done with whatever boy and back home where she belongs. He has come to understand, to accept, that this is their version of normal. He loves her. He gives her the space she needs, the space that ensures she will always return to him.

Their life together has grown into a C-shaped thing, Gerrit forming the strong closed left and Amelia the right,

cracked open to the world, always wanting to peer out to
see what's next, who's next. A baby will close that up. A
baby will make them whole. Is that ridiculous? It feels ridiculous to be thinking of them that way, to be thinking of
the shapes they make and the way the baby will change and
define them. It's true, though. A baby will contain Amelia
at last. It's what has been needed all along to make the girl
cleave to him. Cleave—a good, biblical word. Strong, like
too few words in English. Strong like Dutch. Yes, she will
cleave to him.

⊞

It feels good to get away from the building for a while.
It feels good to be out walking with just Gerrit and Ben,
heading out for supplies like it's any other day. Like there's
no Acme anvil dangling over their heads, the rope fraying.
Jesus, all the expectations now. Steve's drowning in expectations. He was the one to get tipped off by Rick; he was
the one to call Irving; now he's the one they're all coming
to, wanting to be reassured, trusting him to tell them what
to do, how to fix this.

He's supposed to lead Thirteen House into some bright
new future where the rules have all changed, where they
not only fight off eviction but also somehow come out
owning the buildings, and he can't even get his wife to
spend Christmas with him.

What kind of wife doesn't want to spend Christmas with
her husband? Yeah, but what kind of husband leaves his

wife's bed to ball his best friend's girl on the roof? Anne's right to leave him home for the holiday, he thinks. He's lucky she doesn't just leave his sorry ass altogether—if she really knew what kind of man she married, she would. Though maybe she's on to him. Maybe that's what this Christmas thing is building up to. She'll get into Cindy's Volvo wagon, sit in the backseat between the two kids, and drive off to Ohio without him. Leave Steve to play the third wheel at someone else's table or sit home alone, eat some cheap take-out, and watch out the window as Christmas lights blink on and off on the fire escapes across the street. And then maybe she just doesn't come back. Maybe she moves in with Cindy and her family, sheds Steve like a bad habit.

Cindy's kids—Michael and Lara. Anne's got their names tattooed in a puffy red valentine on her chest. She had it done last summer, when they decided enough was enough with the trying and the miscarriages and all. "Only babies I'll ever have, right?" she said when she showed it to him. That wasn't like her, going off and getting tattooed like that. And the worst of it, how ordinary it is. A heart over her heart. The kids' names in script. Now they've both got to look at it for the rest of their lives every time she gets naked or her shirt collar shifts.

He wanted to say, "Why not get four black teardrops tattooed somewhere, one for each baby we lost? Or four broken eggs? Four dead sparrows? Four awful, silent plane crashes?"

He wanted to say, "Why not get *my* name tattooed over your heart?"

Went and had some other man's children's names tat-tooed on her body. Did it like a brand. Like a mark of shame. Right there on her chest, the symbol of everything she wanted and couldn't have. Everything Steve promised and hadn't made good on. So she borrows her sister's luck, her sister's blessings. It's not right.

Who could blame him for wanting to slip away some-times, for wanting someone young and uncomplicated, someone lean and hungry, who'd fuck in the basement stairwell; who'd fuck on the roof or across the counter in the dark, shuttered bike shop; against the wall in the late-night hallway right outside her own apartment door, with Gerrit asleep inside?

Who could blame him for wanting that when there's a dark shape in his bed that looks like his wife but is re-ally just a twisted mass of loss and pain and longing? And blame. She blames Steve. She blames herself. She blames God, like he's gone and stolen her babies and tied them up into his long white beard just to spite her, to punish her for something, only she doesn't know what, so how can she make it right? Her babies, her babies. They were Steve's babies, too. His babies died, too. He didn't go tattooing someone else's babies' names on his chest.

That tattoo, it's like a target, like she's daring him to stab right through it. Another man might. Steve, he's just gon-na work harder, gonna love her harder. When he broke it off with Amelia two months back, he chose Anne all over again. That's how he said it to Amelia, he said, "I've got to choose Anne." He's got to make it work.

He lights two cigarettes, hands one to Gerrit, who takes it with a nod. Steve says, "Hey, remember that time we busted into the old SRO?"

Gerrit winces. "Let's hope today goes a bit more smoothly."

"Good story?" Ben says.

Not really, but Steve tells it like it is. How they'd snuck into the abandoned flophouse to salvage some light fixtures, doorknobs, that kind of thing, only it wasn't as abandoned as they'd thought. How there'd been this old junkie looked like he was eighty if he was a day, pruned up and skeleton skinny, come up out of the basement moaning with his awful toothless mouth agape and Steve thought he was a ghost and nearly shat his pants. He's told the story so many times he can tell it without thinking. He can tell the story and the whole time his mouth is going he can really be thinking, *Gerrit, hermano, lo siento. Perdóname. Ay dios, lo siento.*

⊞

Anne presses down on the coffee grinder, feeling the metallic whir of its motor vibrate against her palm. Her sister's kitchen commands the entire back half of the first floor of their three-story brownstone. Late-morning light floods through the sliding glass doors that lead to the small backyard, the landscaping cut back for winter and the flagstone patio swept clear of leaves. Anne makes coffee while Cindy squints at a cookbook propped up in a wooden stand on the wide island that separates the table from the food-prep area. She adds chopped carrots, onion, and celery to a slow cooker, plops in a pork roast raw and red.

"I think you're supposed to brown the meat first," Anne says.

"Eh." Cindy waves her off, moving to the sink to wash her hands. She puts the lid on the slow cooker, turns the dial, and drops into a chair at the table.

Anne brings her a mug of coffee, gets the half-and-half out of the refrigerator.

In runs Lara, chubby bare legs, pink bottom peeking out beneath the hem of her shirt, her big brother's baseball mitt on her head. "I'm a clam!" she shouts, flapping the mitt up and down on her head. She runs around the table and through the wide arched doorway of the family room, where the floor is strewn with toys and cast-off dress-up clothes. She drops the mitt and flops onto the couch, grinning at Anne, her fat little feet bicycling in the air. "I want Barney!" she sings out, and Cindy rushes over to pop a tape into the VCR. That awful music, that inane theme song.

"That'll keep her for a while," Cindy says.

It's Anne's first day off in weeks—cold and flu season, a substitute teacher's bread and butter. It's been good to have the work, and it's a comfort to know there's a nice check coming at the end of the week. It's good, too, though, to have a day off, to call in and be told she won't be needed today, to catch the four train and cross the river to Brooklyn Heights and sit in her sister's kitchen, drinking coffee, watching that delicious girlchild run around.

"I read that article in the *Times*," Cindy says. "Steve came across a little . . . militant."

"He . . . yeah. He gets . . ."

"Strident?"

Grandiose. "He shouldn't have talked to the press at all. There's nothing to be gained by it."

"It can't be a bad thing to make your voices heard. To get your points across in your own words?"

Anne shakes her head. "It never works out that way. The press wants a spectacle, something that sells. They don't want us calmly explaining our position. So Steve gets the idea that he's going to give them what they want, but he's going to turn it around on them, make it work in our favor. He's going to enter the spectacle and use it to stir up some sympathy for us, some understanding. Only that's not how it came across, is it?"

Cindy twists her mouth and raises her eyebrows, giving an apologetic lift of the shoulders.

"You can't shrink what we're doing into a news-ready sound bite and let that stand for some kind of truth about us. It's limiting. He shouldn't have talked to them at all." Anne had told him it was a bad idea. Gerrit had told him it was a terrible idea. Everyone else was all for it, mostly because Steve can make anything sound like a good idea when he's looking you right in the eyes. Though apparently *Times* reporters are immune to his charms.

"Yes, well, overall the article was favorable, I think," Cindy says. "It showed your people in a good light. There were those sympathetic quotes from some of your neighbors.

The laundromat owner likes your friends quite a bit." She flicks a crumb of toast off the table. "Is Steve joining us for Christmas?"

"No. I told him Mom wanted just me to come."

"You blamed it on Mom?"

"It was your idea to leave him home," Anne says.

"Because you need some space. You need some time apart to figure out what you want. I meant for you to tell him that."

"If I could tell him that and have it go well, there wouldn't be so much to figure out in the first place." She should have just invited Steve for Christmas. It's not like her mom's house is some magical retreat that's going to grant her peace and clarity. "Anyway, it's done. He isn't coming."

Cindy shakes her head and sighs. Anne wishes, for just a moment, that they were twelve and nine again and she could slap that know-it-all look right off her little sister's face. Or she could say, "Marriage must be a lot easier when your husband is never home." That would knock that look off her face just as quickly. But she won't say that. She would never say that.

Lara is standing in front of the TV, doing a frantic approximation of whatever dancing is going on onscreen.

"Barney," Anne says. "I don't know how you stomach it."

"The thing about Barney is he's pure love. There's no subtext or side jokes for the adults. Pure love. Once you see that it's not so bad."

"It's a guy in a purple dinosaur suit singing nursery rhymes."

"Pure love. I'm telling you." Cindy sips her coffee. "And it buys me some peace in twenty-three-minute chunks. It's hard to beat that."

Peace. Cindy wants peace. This sun-filled kitchen, that pink-bottomed cherub. The big house with a weekly cleaning woman. Michael is at school now, but Cindy and Lara will go pick him up at three. They'll bring him a snack; they'll talk about his day. All of Anne's wanting and not having rises like a bitter fog. *So push it down. Beat it back.*

"I could babysit more often," Anne says. "On the days I don't get called in to work. It would give you a chance to get out and do things on your own."

"You wouldn't mind?" Cindy frowns, a deep groove appearing between her eyes.

"Of course not."

"Right. Well, okay. Yes. Thank you."

Through the sliding glass doors the light moves on, less insistent now, and Anne imagines the sun drifting overhead to gild the corniced rooftops of Brooklyn Heights, the limestone stoops and front gardens, the backyards, the promenade along the river. A blue heron lands on Cindy's back fence, an improbable, impossible thing. Anne stares at it and it stares back. It *sees* her. All angles and wings. "Cin!" Anne hisses and points. Just that sound, that motion is enough to ruin it. As Cindy turns to look it takes off. Its wings beat the air, heavy, languorous, and then it's gone.

⌗

Amelia walks down Thirteenth Street, a bottle of prenatal vitamins rattling in her pocket. Pregnancy confirmed, the baby due July 16, which seems so far off. So much can happen in eight months. They could be evicted long before then. They could be homeless.

Gerrit insisted she go get checked out, get the proper care. He's already decided they're having the baby. He looks so happy when he talks about it. So hopeful. She can't tell him that she's still not sure she can keep it. She can't tell him how scared she is. She'd be taking all that hope away.

And she isn't sure she won't have it. The thought of not having the baby is becoming scarier than the thought of having it. And best to take good care of it, in case she does keep it. So she went for the exam. She'll take the vitamins.

As she approaches the building she sees Ben pushing a shopping cart loaded down with supplies, bits of wire and tubing popping out every which way and a load of lumber stacked on top. Gerrit is guiding it from the front and Steve walks along beside them, waving his arms around, talking loud. She pushes the bottle of vitamins deeper into her coat pocket. Closer now, she hears Steve telling Ben the story about a nighttime salvage mission that went way wrong. She's heard the story, involving Steve, Gerrit, a torn pair of pants, and a stray cat, too many times before, and it's not that good. She's pretty sure Ben's heard it before, too.

Gerrit looks at her, raises an eyebrow, and she nods. Yes, everything's fine.

"Hey guys," she says. "Nice haul." The cart is loaded down with good, fresh lumber. What looks like enough plumbing to outfit four or five sinks with all new parts. White, unmarred PVC pipes. Even some copper tubing.

"You know how NYU is. Always so sloppy with their materials. This stuff was in a dumpster," Steve says.

"Waste not, want not," Amelia says.

"And idle hands are the devil's something or other." He tousles her hair, letting his hand slide down to rest, just a moment, at the bare nape of her neck. His touch, and then the next moment the loss of it. "So grab an armload and get to work. You want to do the plaster in the vestibule or the new floorboard in the fourth-floor hallway? I didn't see you signed up for any work crews this week."

"No, man, let her rest today," Gerrit says. "She hasn't been feeling well."

Ben says, "What? My back is killing me and I think I need a root canal. Can I go inside and put my feet up, too?"

Amelia says, "I'm fine. I'll do the wall." She likes plastering. There's a certain art to it, building layer on layer, each one finer than the one that came before, that's more satisfying than simply driving nails into pieces of wood. She likes the way the best work becomes invisible, how she knows she got it right if no one can tell anything has been done at all.

"You're going to push yourself too hard," Gerrit says.

He's going to give it away. Steve will know she's knocked up before she's even gotten used to the idea herself. Before she's even begun to figure out how to tell him. "Gerrit," she says. "I'm *fine*. I'll go mix up some plaster and get to it."

Gerrit's lips purse into that tight white line again.

"Hey, look. It's fine. I swear I'm fine. Okay?"

He nods reluctantly.

Steve says, "Good. Gerrit, you want to help her? Ben and I can get the hallway."

Used to be, Steve would have made sure he was the one paired up with Amelia. Now he isn't even looking at her as they maneuver the cartload of materials through the front door. She and Gerrit will stay down here, Steve and Ben will go up to the fourth floor, and that will be that. How quickly things can change.

⊞

Gerrit crouches beside Amelia, his back against the vestibule wall.

"Hand me that mesh?" she says. She's on her knees, squinting at a six-inch hole he made in the wall last week trying to figure out why the vestibule light kept shorting out.

"So it went well with the doctor?" He gives her the plastering mesh she's already cut to size.

"Fine. It went fine. They drew some blood, gave me an exam, sent me home with prenatal vitamins. I have to go back in three weeks for the first ultrasound." She threads a bent paper clip through the center of the mesh and fits the panel into the hole, poking in the corners with a slim fingertip. "The baby's due July sixteenth."

"Let me see the vitamins. You have them with you?"

"My coat pocket."

He finds the bottle and runs a finger down the list of ingredients. "Did you ask what's in here? Are you sure it's all safe? What's magnesium stearate? What's silicon dioxide? Did you ask?"

"It's fine. The doctor gave them to me. It's just vitamins."

"You can't trust so blindly. Why do you need to take these? Just eat good food. Just take care of yourself."

"You're a fucking nut," she says. "You're paranoid."

"Am I?" He waves his right hand at her. "A doctor gave my mother some pills. So they must have been fine, yeah?"

"And if she'd asked if it was safe, the doctor would have said yes. So what do you want me to do? Everyone takes prenatal vitamins. It's nothing new. Really. It's fine." Her nimble, well-formed fingers gently pull on the paper clip until the mesh sits flush with the wall, then ease the paper clip free. She doesn't understand. How could she? She loads up the trowel with plaster, considering the hole in the wall. She bends to the work, her shoulders rounded, Gerrit a mere distraction.

"I just want you to think. What you put in your body matters now. More than ever, it matters. You have to ask questions. You have to look out for yourself, and for the baby."

Chemie Grünenthal told doctors thalidomide was nontoxic, a miracle drug with no side effects, safe for pregnant women. They had no reason to believe that was true. What little testing they'd done hinted that it was *not* true, that there were, in fact, severe side effects, but there was more money to be made by making claims first and apologizing later. Ten thousand babies were born deformed, maybe more. Nearly half didn't live to see their first birthdays, many more dead before their tenth. The survivors, like Gerrit, were paid off.

Gerrit's right hand was determined to be worth 100,000 guilders.

"Imagine it, Amelia. You're having terrible morning sickness, or you can't sleep at night, and your doctor says he has these pills that will help you. Perfectly safe little pills, gentle little pills. And you trust your doctor and you take them. And then your child is born with flippers for hands, sprouting directly from her shoulders. Or no hands at all. No arms. No legs. Why? Profit. Your well-being is measured directly against the drug company's bottom line. Don't you get that?"

Ten thousand babies. The courts settled with Chemie Grünenthal, saying money was recompense enough. No criminal action. The night after the settlement was announced, twelve-year-old Gerrit stood in the hallway outside his parents' closed bedroom door, listening to them argue. "You can't say the money won't help," his father said. "Who's to know what will happen to the boy after we're gone, how he'll get by? What if he can't find work? He's limited, and people limit him more still. The money will be a help."

He heard his mother crying, a full weeping she'd never allowed herself in Gerrit's presence. "But how dare they? They pay us off with money they can well afford to part with and just like that they're washed clean. Just like that. How dare they?"

She never said so to him, but Gerrit knows his mother carried always the guilt of what happened to him, because it was she who opened the bottle, she who brought capsule to mouth. He knows his hand was the reason she didn't have more children, that she was afraid it would happen again or that something worse still might happen. He knows this because his stupid aunt Griet let it slip one night, half drunk at a family Sinterklaas party when Gerrit was eight. "Your mother always wanted a houseful of kids, the poor duck. Wanted a boatload of kids. But after you, she didn't dare try for more, did she?" Aunt Griet had patted his head and lurched away, leaving him stunned in the dining room, the *pepernoten* he'd so looked forward to eating gone to cardboard in his mouth. He understood then that he was a disappointment to his mother, that he had ruined her life. Another little gift the thalidomide gave him.

In the end his mother must have given in to his father's logic, because they accepted the monthly payments. Gerrit didn't begrudge them that. The money helped the family. But when he left Rotterdam for Amsterdam, he turned his back on that money, letting it accumulate untouched in a savings account. He dipped into it just once, to buy his plane ticket to New York. He has not touched it since— will not touch it. It's blood money.

"The doctors won't protect you," he says to Amelia. "The government won't protect you."

"Just vitamins," she says. "I hear you. I do. But you're working yourself up over nothing here."

"How much is your hand worth to you, Amelia?"

"Gerrit," she says. "Let it go. Please. Just let it go."

Softenon-kindje. Thalidomide baby. Thalidomide victim. Thalidomider. Deformed. Disabled. Walrus boy. Lobster boy. Flipper. Flid. Freak.

Gerrit still hears the taunts, still feels the kids chasing him. All these years later, full-grown man and still he's always hunched as he walks; always waiting for a hurled rock to hit the back of his head. He couldn't get out of Rotterdam fast enough. He fled for Amsterdam when he was sixteen and never looked back. He visited, from time to time, to see his mother. His father had died when Gerrit was fourteen. His mother followed his father when Gerrit was twenty—cancer, too young—and then there was no reason to ever go back to Rotterdam, long may it fester.

Rotterdam, witness to his daily shame, his daily torture. *Rotjeknor*, where he buried his parents, where he tried to bury the boy with the half hand. But that boy followed him to Amsterdam; he followed him to New York.

For a time he thought about cutting it off, getting a prosthesis, and then making up some fabulous story about an industrial accident or a fall while rock climbing. But the boy won't let him. He wanted to cut the hand off, but contemplating it felt like contemplating suicide—something to brood over while drunk, but not something to be done. The threat, always the threat . . . but the reality, the thing that is known, no matter how awful, is the thing to cling to in the end. He hates the hand, but he knows it. That hand is him, in ways he can't begin to untie.

"Kids teased me," he always begins when showing it to someone for the first time. "Kids teased me when I was younger. Just because I'm missing some fingers from my hand." Simple like that, he says it. "Just because of this small thing." Which is a lie. It is no small thing, no matter what he tells them. No matter what he tells himself.

Thalidomide made him what he is, despite all his life-long protestations to the opposite. His life has been a series of reactions. He is a spring, pushed down and punching back out at unpredictable angles. Reacting, reacting. He is who he is in reaction to how he was born—not what he began as, but what he was made, the transformation the chemicals worked on him in the womb. Ruining his hand, ruining his cock. Making him small, wiry, weird. Making him fearful, angry, hunted, haunted.

But for some tiny pills down his mother's throat, because she felt a bit of morning sickness, it could have all been different. He is not supposed to admit this. He is supposed to be proud. Strong. Able. "I wouldn't choose to be born any different," he tells people. "This hand has shown me how strong I am."

But sometimes he'll catch sight of his right hand, his goddamn stunted hook of a hand, and he'll be overcome with such revulsion, with such fear, such anger. That this small thing, this slight percentage of his entire man's body, should be allowed to define him; that it should have shaped his life the way it has.

As a teenager he learned that there was something crueler than the girls who recoiled from his hand, laughing at his nervous advances; something crueler than the ones who blushed and stammered and couldn't escape fast enough because their inbred Dutch properness was battling with their animal instinct to flee from the monster. Cruelest were the girls who would choose him because of the hand. To choose him made them feel holy. Their goddamn pity for him, their saintly desires to fuck him, because of all the good things they could then think about themselves. Those girls were the worst.

Even so, he'd tried to accept the charitable fucks and noble blow jobs when they first became available, when the local girls started to bud and bloom and kids started pairing off, sinking into the dark parts of the city at night. He had expected to be excluded from that, was taken by surprise by the way these budding, blooming girls would offer themselves to him; the church girls who might be frightened by the advances of the other boys whose chests were broadening, whose hands were growing big and strong and insistent. He'd tried, and time and again he'd failed.

This was not entirely a surprise. When he was twelve, he'd started overhearing the other boys talking about jerking off. It had become a near-constant part of the conversation in the schoolyard and in the streets. He'd gone home and tried and sometimes succeeded and sometimes failed, but had known from the way the other boys talked that he was different—that it was more difficult for him and that he wanted it much less.

He'd stammeringly, tortuously asked his doctor— red-faced and mortified but needing to know—if he was different in this way, too; if it wasn't just his hand that the thalidomide had taken. The doctor, the understanding if stern doctor who had taken Gerrit on as a sort of favored pet, had explained it to him then. That yes, there was another difference to Gerrit. Perhaps it was his testosterone levels, perhaps it was simply a matter of stunted development, the way he was shorter and slighter than he might have been. The doctor had said they could do tests if Gerrit liked, but there was nothing to be done most likely. He told him that other boys' penises were somewhat bigger on average, which Gerrit already knew. He told him his testicles were somewhat abnormal. That there was no knowing without further tests if Gerrit could one day be a father, but that it was fairly certain, from what Gerrit had described to the doctor, that his sexual function was not normal because of the thalidomide. That his sex drive was lower than normal. That he could not consistently maintain an erection the way a normal boy could. That this would impact his life, and that the doctor did not want to pretend it wouldn't. He said Gerrit should try to come to terms with his limitations now, should try to find happiness in his life differently from other boys. He should accept this difference, should not expect to have girlfriends, a wife, children. These things were most likely out of reach. The doctor did not want to mislead Gerrit, did not want to give him false hope. Further tests could be done, but the doctor saw no point. Gerrit was stunted. He was abnormal.

Gerrit never told his parents about this conversation with the good doctor. He never told anyone. Later on, in the Amsterdam squats, when he met a girl—Marrije—who saw him as he was and loved him, who wanted him without pitying him, he tried to forget what the doctor had said. She was patient, he tried to be patient, and maybe one try out of five would work. Those times were more than he'd ever hoped to have and he was—in spite of himself, in spite of his hatred for this very emotion—grateful to her. He was not impotent. He and Marrije made love. And when the traditional methods failed, there were others, which she'd taught him.

But even good things end, and there came an end to Gerrit and Marrije, and when he left for New York he never spoke about her again. Amelia knows nothing about Marrije. Amelia thinks Gerrit is impotent. Amelia has no idea.

His desire is less than it might be, that's true. It's good, in a way. He doesn't have that distraction as other men seem to. His desire flares up from time to time, and over the years he's satisfied it either on his own or with a girl, if there was one, but it hasn't been the constant presence, the constant need for sex that he sees in other men. So it hasn't seemed so terrible to move through these seven years with Amelia, to sometimes touch her silently in her bed at night, to never acknowledge it in the daylight. To never have her—not since that first night—turn to him, touch him. To know that she assumes it is pointless, that she assumes he can't, not ever, and so to never try, because he has never corrected her mistaken beliefs about what he is capable of.

She isn't patient like Marrije was. She won't make the leap past her schoolgirl's idea of what sex can be, and he's been too cowardly to push her, afraid of losing her entirely. It has been enough to get her off, simply, and then go back to his own room and touch himself, to smell her muskiness mixing with his own, even if she's asleep in the next room.

Now she's pregnant by some other man, and she's treating Gerrit with increasing distance, like a tolerated uncle, like a friendly cousin. Maybe he should have pushed her more. Maybe he should have insisted on what is possible. But so much has always been unsaid between them, and who knows where the truth lies with so much not-saying. How deeply they've misunderstood each other.

6

Amelia and Suzie cut west across First Avenue. On the corner of St. Marks and First, the two perpetual drunks are propped up like ghoulish dolls against the outside wall of the shoe store no one ever goes into. The fat one is passed out, a lit cigarette stuck into the drool-slick corner of his open mouth. It's a filterless. Amelia wonders if he'll wake up when the ember reaches his lips. More likely it'll just get snuffed out by the slug trail of spit. The short skinny one salutes her. "Spare some change for an American Indian?" Amelia smiles and shakes her head.

"Those guys, man," Suzie says. "I can't remember them ever not being there."

Amelia thinks of the deep creases in the short one's face, his eyes small and shrouded in folds of loose skin, and the weakness of the hand that saluted her, and she thinks, not without sadness, *He'll die soon.*

"The tall one was gone for a while this spring," Amelia says. "Rehab."

"Yeah, that's right. I thought he'd died, but then he turned up again in the summer."

"I saw him come back. It was something—all cleaned up. I kind of thought he'd make it." He came back one July day, striding right down the center of St. Marks against the traffic, the king of some invisible parade. His black hair was gleaming, and it streamed out behind him as he walked his long-limbed walk. He wore clean white jeans, a new-looking black T-shirt, a black leather vest. Bright white sneakers. A huge smile, and his glasses new, too. Many of the people on the street knew him and recognized the transformation, Amelia among them. They all smiled at him and he smiled back.

That very night, Amelia saw him passed out on the sidewalk in front of that same damn wall. Dirt and cigarette burns on the white jeans; leaves in his hair; his limp dick, fat and purple, in his hand; lying in a puddle of his own piss.

"In here," Suzie says, passing through a black metal gate and up some stairs.

There's a guy sitting at the top of the stoop, knees bouncing, fingers bopping along the step at either side of his skinny ass. "Hey," he says. "Hey, girls."

"Amelia, this is Craig," Suzie says and he stands, wiping his palms down on his thighs, then jabs a hand out to shake.

He leads them into the building, up five flights to the top floor, where he swings his apartment door open.

"Jesus, it's like the Bronx Zoo in here," Suzie says.

The small studio is dark and warm, tree branches criss-crossing overhead. There's a boa constrictor curled around one branch, and Amelia spies three really big lizards stretched out on others. "I don't want to ask how many animals are in here that I'm *not* seeing," she says.

Craig laughs, a raspy huff of a laugh. "No worries, no worries." He carefully meets Amelia's eyes and then Suzie's, and leaves the apartment door hanging open to show that they're safe with him. Thoughtful guy. So he's a little jumpy. So he's turned his apartment into a jungle. So what. He reaches up and brings down a big green iguana. It lies across the full length of his forearm, its long clawed toes digging into the scarred leather of his jacket. The tail hangs down nearly to the floor.

"Are you sure this is what Denise wants?" Amelia says.

"She's always wanted an iguana. A really big one."

"Her name's Esmerelda now, but it's cool if you change it," Craig says. "She won't mind."

"Can I hold her?" Amelia says. She puts out her arm and he nudges Esmerelda onto her. The lizard is heavier than she looks, all muscle. Amelia strokes her side, the beaded skin iridescent green and blue. Esmerelda blinks a heavy-lidded eye, darts her tongue out. "She's something, isn't she?" Amelia murmurs. She looks up at Craig, beaming. "She's really something. Maybe I'll get an iguana one of these days. Look at her eyes. Look how she looks at you. Like she's got all the answers and she's just waiting for us to be ready to hear them."

Craig smiles back. "Exactly, man. Exactly." He eases the lizard into a cat carrier. "I tell you what. Next iguana gets dropped off here looking for a home, it's yours."

"Really?"

"Absolutely."

Suzie laughs. "Oh, Gerrit will love that."

They go back down the stairs. Suzie's got the cat carrier in her hand, Esmerelda with her tail curled around herself peering out the grated metal front. They hit the stoop, sunlight, and Amelia bursts out laughing. It spills out of her, she doesn't even know why, really. She digs in her bag, finds the apple she tucked in there, and hands it to the short Indian as she and Suzie walk past.

"I can't eat this," he calls after her, pointing to his near-toothless mouth, but she's already halfway across First Avenue. Maybe he can trade it for something else.

They head back to the squat to set up the cage before Denise gets home from work. Suzie's been planning this for weeks, building the six-by-eight-foot enclosure in Ben's apartment so Denise wouldn't see it. She saved up, used really good materials. All new two-by-fours, hardware cloth. She built it in panels, because it won't fit through the apartment door once it's put together.

That's the kind of thing Suzie and Denise do for each other. Amelia loves their love. It gives her hope to see love like that, and it's enough some days just to be around it. Today is one of those days. She feels grateful. Craig's crazy jungle apartment and Esmerelda's wise eyes and helping to put the cage together so Denise can come home from her shitty job to find that the woman she loves has given her something she has always wanted. Amelia gets to help make that happen. She lets the laughter rise up again.

"Are you crying?" Suzie says. "What's wrong?"

How does she say it? *Thank you for letting me be a part of this. Thank you for letting me warm myself by your fire awhile.* "Nothing. Life is good sometimes, you know?"

She stoops low to peek in at Esmerelda, who blinks one slow brown eye.

⊞

Steve hauls everything he needs for the job up to the second floor in the old granny cart. A box of tiles, a duffel bag full of trowels and the like, a tub of mortar, a tub of grout. He knocks, hears quiet footsteps padding toward the door and the peephole cover sliding open. "Handyman," he says. "I'm here about the bathroom floor."

A woman opens the door slowly, peering around it. She's young, early twenties. A sort of sweet, plain face and soft-looking shoulders in a brown T-shirt and the rest of her hidden behind the door. She eyes him nervously, like she doesn't want to let him in. Like, who left this big Puerto Rican dude with the crazy mop of hair on her doorstep and what's she supposed to do with him?

"Your super, Mike. He called me. You've got loose tiles on your bathroom floor, right?" He should have hustled to get here and get the job done earlier, when she would have been at work.

She slips farther behind the door, her body totally hidden. Maybe he caught her off guard and she's not wearing any pants. But a normal person says, "Just a minute!" when they hear the knock and they real quick throw some pants on before opening the door. "Do you have, um, ID?"

Hijo de . . . "That says I'm here to fix your tiles? No. Look, how am I gonna know your bathroom floor needs fixing if your super didn't call me? Didn't Mike let you know I was coming?"

"Well, no. Okay, so, I just think if I could see—shit!" A fat gray cat darts out the door and makes for the stairs and she runs out after it. Jeans with that T-shirt. Kind of doughy around the middle but cute enough; she's got those heavy tits he likes and you don't get those without a little belly to match.

The cat doubles back to sniff Steve's boot and he scoops it up. Its fur smells like incense.

She takes the cat from him. "Okay, so come on in," she says. Apparently only legit handymen help you catch your runaway cat.

Through the door and the smell of incense is strong. It's a studio—can't be more than three hundred square feet—and she's completely filled it with stuff. Shelves loaded down with books. A sun-faded armchair in the corner next to a bookcase with more books. The mantel of the bricked-up fireplace cluttered with candlestick holders and photos and a haphazardly placed collection of ceramic birds. A small TV with *Star Trek* action figures ranged across the top. The cat nests into a pile of black fabric on the floor that looks to be a suit—work clothes she's just changed out of, most likely. The little main room has two windows looking out through security bars onto Ninth Street, then there's a five-foot-long kitchen/closet combo on the way to the bathroom. Sink, stove, and minifridge on one wall, closet on the other. She's got two squares of counter in the kitchenette; one holds a microwave and the other is piled with books.

Steve parks the granny cart in front of the minifridge and starts to unpack his tools. She's sitting on the futon, reading. Her back and neck are stiff, the book held up at an awkward angle in front of her. She knows he's looking at her and there's nowhere to hide in the tiny apartment.

"What's that you're reading?" He says it casual, gives her a slow smile, hoping to put her at ease.

She holds up a battered paperback copy of *Anna Karenina.*

"Nice," he says. "I really dug parts of that, but I couldn't get into all the farming chapters, you know?"

She gives him a feeble smile and shrugs, then puts the book down and picks up a remote control. The six o'clock news hums on.

What? She doesn't believe he reads? Maybe he never got a degree, but he went to college. Spent nearly three years at CUNY, studying literature, thinking he'd go all the way through to PhD, become a professor. And all the while his father wondering what the hell Steve was doing with his time and money reading books, thinking about books, talking about books. What use was that going to be for the son of a factory worker?

Turned out Steve didn't have it in him to even finish his bachelor's. Got caught up in girls, in booze, traveled for a while. He always meant to go back, and he just didn't.

He'll go on great reading binges sometimes, reading anything he can get his hands on. Skip sleep to finish a book, finish one book and immediately pick up the next one, like he's chain-smoking them. But then there are times when he can't read at all, when the thought of it hurts him, an almost physical hurt. Those times it's like the books are mocking him, who he thought he was, thought he might become. Those times the scraps of poems in his pockets burn him with a shame that sinks so deep it gives over to rage when it hits bone.

Okay, *papi*, he thinks, here's your boy on his knees on a white girl's scuffed linoleum floor, tools spread out before him. This is more like it, *verdad*? Here's what you knew your boy was worth all along.

That girl out there, she doesn't even see him. He could be any *pendejo* on the corner, a middle-aged Latino who doesn't merit a second look. Maybe he's Puerto Rican; maybe he's Dominican. She doesn't care. Maybe she pictures him playing dominos at a card table on the sidewalk all summer. Maybe she pictures him with eight snot-nosed brown kids and a wife with a huge ass in tight pants. Most likely she isn't picturing him at all. He should have looked around for a book he could really talk about. Something he could dig into, flash her a little piece of knowledge. Like that one right there—she's got the big collected works of Ginsberg on the toilet tank, a piece of toilet paper stuck in for a bookmark. He could talk her ear off about Ginsberg. He *knows* Ginsberg. Sort of. They've met, anyway. They have people in common.

There was a time not so very long ago he could have had a girl like that on her back in minutes. He doesn't want her, plain as she is, but he might have gone for it anyway, just to do it. That time is past. She's staring at the TV, clutching the remote, waiting for him to be done and gone. Afraid that if she reads her book he'll try to talk to her about it again. *Déjala, hombre. Se acabó . . . se acabó . . . Estás viejo ya.*

The bathroom stinks of fresh cat shit. He pushes the litter box out into the kitchen and sets to work.

7

Saturday afternoon in the laundromat. Steve measures the time in washer cycles. They've made it through a soak and a rinse, but he's not sure Anne's gonna get through to the final spin without losing her shit.

She's got two washers going and she's worried there won't be any open dryers when the washers are done. "Did you see that guy? He keeps feeding quarters into the machine but his clothes have to be bone dry by now. He saw me looking at his machine and that's when he put in another quarter."

"Laundromat anxiety," Steve says. "You've got to let go. Breathe deep. Zen laundry, baby. Zen laundry."

"Look—our washers are done now and there aren't any dryers."

"Feel your ass sink into the seat. Become one with the molded plastic chair, Anne. There is no laundry. There are no dryers. Say it with me."

"You aren't funny. And there *are* no dryers."

"I'm a little bit funny."

"No. You're not."

"So maybe not. But we've got coffee, we've got books. Is it so bad if we have to wait a few minutes for a dryer?"

"We should put a washer and dryer in the basement."

"And then you'll be stressed out that Suzie's hogging the dryer or that Gerrit left his wet clothes in the washer overnight. And you know what that water bill would look like?"

"Those two dryers are done. Whose stuff is that? Did you see?"

Here we go. "Didn't notice, no."

"I'm moving those clothes into a cart."

"If it gets you into another catfight with a tranny, you're on your own."

"Such a gentleman." She empties the clothes from one of the stopped dryers into a cart, then grabs another cart and starts in on the second machine. "Bring one of those wet loads over to this one," she says, tapping the dryer she just emptied. "Quick, before someone else takes it."

A harried-looking woman with thinning brown hair and two kids at her heels rushes in just as Anne pulls a threadbare pink towel from the dryer. She's probably a single mom, probably younger than she looks; they almost always are. She snatches the towel from Anne. "Get your hands off my shit!"

"If you aren't around to take your things out when the dryer stops, I'm perfectly within my rights to take them out myself."

Ay, Annie.

"My clothes better all be here." The woman moves off to an empty folding counter. The older kid, a boy, pushes the little girl around in a cart while their mom stuffs their laundry into a sack. He takes a corner too fast, spilling the girl out onto the floor. Steve waits for the wailing to start, but the girl just stands up and brushes lint from her knees, both kids eyeing the mom to see if she noticed. She either didn't see or is pretending she didn't. She waves them out the door, the heavy laundry bag on her back.

"Why do you talk to people like that?" Steve says.

"Like what? I was within my rights."

"Like *that.*" It's that suburban thing, that midwestern thing—*say it*—it's that *white* thing. "We should start dropping our laundry off. Something about the laundromat gets you going."

"We can't afford it." She tosses the last of their wet clothes into the second dryer and slams the door shut.

"It's not that much more expensive than what we're paying in quarters and detergent to sit here all afternoon and bitch at each other."

"Maybe we should take some of that money you send to your mother every month and put it toward the laundry."

He wired cash to his ma in Puerto Rico this morning, same as he does every month. How long has Anne been pissed about it and keeping quiet? "You don't like it that I help my mother out? A widow, seventy-two years old, her only son how far away in New York, and I shouldn't help her out?"

"Your mom's the one who moved away, not you," Anne says. "And she lives with your sister, for God's sake. Who's the money really for? Your mom or Lettie?"

"So my sister should look after our mother all on her own? Lettie is there in PR so she helps with the day to day. I can't help with the day to day, so isn't it the least I can do to send some money to be sure they're taken care of? My mother doesn't have a teacher's pension to fall back on like your mom. Forty years pushing little tubes into bottles at the perfume factory till her hands twisted like oak knots."

"But do you have to send so much? It's like I'm working to support us while you work to support them."

Anne's glaring at the dryer like it's Steve's mother tossing around in there, clutching their money in her gnarled fists.

"This isn't about my mother. What's this about?"

"Everyone warned me about marrying a Latin guy, that I would always be taking second place to your mother."

"You want a husband who doesn't care about his mother? How can a man who doesn't love his mother love a wife?"

She snorts and force-feeds another quarter into the second dryer.

"And who is everyone?" He grabs her arm, harder than he meant to. Her flesh is soft under his grip, like he could sink his fingers straight down to bone.

"Nobody. Forget I said anything." She pulls away, sits down, disappears behind her book.

He drops into the chair next to her, picks up his own book.

"You know what my mom told me?" she says from behind her paperback. "She had a friend who was engaged
to an Argentinian guy here in the States. Her friend went
back to Argentina with the guy to meet his family. The first
night she and the guy walk in, and the mom doesn't like
the way the guy has his shirt tucked in or something, and
she opens up his pants and retucks his shirt like he was
four years old."

"And your mother sends you dish towels like they don't
sell them in New York, or like we wouldn't have the sense
to buy them for ourselves. What's your point?"

The door swings open and Cat rides in on a gust of cold
air, laundry stuffed into a pillowcase.

Anne sees her and drops down farther behind her book.
"Fantastic."

Doesn't like his mama. Doesn't like his ex. *Lord, please
forgive me for having had any kind of life before I met my
darling wife, who was a flawless virgin bathed in angel spit
until I got my filthy claws into her.* "Hey, Cat," Steve calls
out. Forget what they tell you about honesty, intimacy.
Marriage only works if you hold some corners of yourself
back. Look how Anne hates Cat just for having been his
first all those years ago. What would she do if she knew
everything? If she knew him through and through, she'd
be gone. Her goddamn head would explode.

Cat stuffs her clothes into a washer. Always plenty of
washers open, never any dryers. Anne's right about that.
She's weird as hell about it, but she's right. "How's it going?" Cat says. Something black falls to the floor. Leggings,

small enough for a child. She shakes them out, tosses them into the washer. A pang shoots through him sharp and quick. Not all memories live in the head. Cat, she lives in his body. Somewhere between his lungs and his heart, she's eternally sixteen years old: snake-hipped like a boy, wild red curls. Fiery little Carolyn Weider from up the block whom he promised to love forever if she gave it up to him under her yellow gingham quilt while her parents were at work. He thinks now that maybe he's made good on that promise after all. He didn't say he'd stay; only that he'd love her.

"Do you even like me anymore?" Anne whispers.

Cat's jaw twitches.

"Of course I do." He takes her hand and squeezes it. Hollow, hollow gesture. She deserves better.

Cat sees it. She knows.

"Sometimes you act like you don't."

"I do. I do."

She pulls her hand away and goes back to her book. Her lips tremble. This is the part where he's supposed to take her into his arms and let her cry against his chest and they'll finally break through all of their bullshit. Except he doesn't reach for her. And she doesn't reach for him. And then the moment is past. Again.

Your problem, viejo, is you never had any business getting married. Your problem, cabrón, is you think you can skate by on love alone.

He watches their clothes tumble together in the dryer, hoping for some kind of sign—he doesn't know what, their shirtsleeves linked or something—that everything will be okay. But it's just a dryer, their clothes just dumb pieces of cotton. The machines rumble and drone and an old man in a coffee-stained shirt snores under the sports pages and Anne is turning her book's pages faster than she could possibly be reading them and he looks down at his empty, useless hands and when he looks up again, Cat is gone.

8

"The bracing on the rear wall is good," Gerrit says. "It's solid. Let's leave that for now." They're sitting at Steve and Anne's kitchen table, running through the repair list—an executive meeting of sorts. As usual at Anne and Steve's, there's freshly baked bread and good strong coffee. Gerrit runs a hand along the oak table's familiar surface, the grooves and pits. It's an old table, deeply scarred in places but strong. Anne found it on the street outside an Italian restaurant years ago, and Steve and Gerrit hauled it home for her. There had been one broken leg, but Gerrit had fixed that easily enough.

"Where do we stand on getting an independent engineer in here?" Anne says. "We don't want any surprises when the city inspectors come through."

"Ben was on that," Steve says. He grabs a broom from the corner, knocks the wooden handle—three sharp raps—against the ceiling. "Ben!" he shouts. "Yo, Ben!"

Footsteps overhead become footsteps on the stairs and Ben comes through the door, shirtless in well-worn jeans. Ben has aged. They all have. Gerrit looks around the room and sees tired adults. Ben is all of thirty now; Gerrit is thirty-six, Anne thirty-six, too; and Steve is the grand old man at forty-two. They're young yet, but nothing as young as they were at the beginning.

Gerrit expected his old friend Ben, all lean muscle and elbows, to come through that door and instead here comes this man whose belly is starting to hint at softening, whose face has gone craggy and set, like something carved from rock. Even the tattoos across his arms and chest have started to blur, the once-clean lines spreading, muddling into each other. Gerrit suspects that if he were to look in a mirror he'd see the same changes on his own face that he sees now on Anne's, and on Steve's. They've been so busy surviving they haven't noticed their lives hardening around them, fixing them into place. They are now all they're ever going to be. This is their life. Here it is.

Gerrit's life before Thirteen House ended in smoke and all-consuming fire. That's not something he's told anyone here in the States, though certainly by now some of them have earned that much trust from him—Steve and Anne and Amelia. Especially Amelia. Some memories are too big and deep, some memories go right down to the bone, and to drag them out of the past and make them part of his story now is more than he wants to do.

They know there was a fire at his last squat in Amsterdam, started by an especially thuggish landlord who wanted things to move faster than the usual legal channels would allow. He's told them that much—about the fire, about the landlord—but he hasn't told them about Marrije. He hasn't told them about Jurrie.

The landlord had sent threats, then he sent muscle, and when those didn't work, he sent fire in the form of a Molotov cocktail through a window in the middle of the night. Gerrit and Marrije had been asleep on the ground floor, and awakened to the sound of breaking glass. They'd rushed from room to room, waking everyone up, getting everyone out, but they hadn't thought about checking the attic.

Gerrit should have noticed that Jurrie's sleeping bag wasn't in its usual spot. He should have thought about Jurrie going up to the attic to sleep sometimes when the sound of everyone else's breathing and snoring and farting got to be too much. He wasn't cut out for group living, for so much proximity to other bodies. Everyone knew Jurrie went upstairs, but no one thought about that in the rush to get out, the heat and smoke rising. They stumbled coughing out of the building and onto the late-night streets and by the time someone thought to say, "Jurrie! Anyone seen him?!" the staircase had collapsed and the whole building had gone up and the fire department and police were on the scene. They'd had to slip into the dark, to make themselves scarce.

Gerrit would like to be able to remember how he'd tried to run back into the building to get Jurrie, how the others held him back, crying that it wasn't safe, but that wasn't what had happened. None of them, Gerrit included, made a move to go back in, and they would have been fools to do so.

Jurrie died and the flames never even reached him. He died from the smoke, as the papers reported the next day: a single squatter, identity unknown, found dead in the attic. It was Marrije who placed the anonymous call to the police, giving Jurrie's full name so his family could be notified.

The group split up, finding spaces in this squat or that. Gerrit and Marrije talked for a while about opening a new building, but it was mostly Gerrit talking and Marrije listening. Or not listening, but sitting silent. She did a lot of sitting, a lot of looking out of windows after the fire. A month after the fire, she told Gerrit she had decided to go back to Utrecht to live with her parents and finish her course at the university. She would be leaving the next morning. There was no talk of Gerrit going with her, and he understood she was not offering that as an option.

They were sitting in a squatter coffeehouse, the Koffiebar Roodmerk, that good old place that he had loved. After that day it was just one more thing lost to him, the chairs, the tables, the very walls thick with her leaving. She was tracing the circular stain her coffee mug had left on her napkin, tracing it around and around as if it were only a matter of following the circle long enough and it would break open and become something else, reveal something she'd been missing. "And so that's that," she'd said. *Afgelopen, klaar, uit.* Under her breath, as if she were alone, as if she'd already left him behind.

Afgelopen, klaar, uit.

In the morning he walked her to Centraal station; he kissed her good-bye. She had just one small bag with her—they'd lost everything in the fire. She'd pressed a sweaty little square of paper into his hand, her parents' address on it. "Write to me," she'd said. He said he would. He carried that square of paper around Amsterdam for weeks. When he walked the streets and found there was nothing for him there, no reason left to stay, he bought a one-way plane ticket. He carried that square of paper all the way across the ocean to New York.

He carries it still in his pocket. He'd copied the address in indelible marker on the inside of his left boot, but he was afraid of losing it and tattooed it across his right calf—on his own one night, hunkered down on the floor with a single lamp beside him, sewing needle and thread and a pot of India ink. He tattooed the address, but no name. He lost his nerve at the thought of seeing her name every time he took off his pants.

Amelia, first seeing the tattoo, said, "So this is where I should send your body when you die?" She'd been joking, but he said, without thinking, "Yes." She assumed it was a relative's address and he didn't bother correcting her.

Marrije's address—or rather the address of her parents, the address where she spent her golden-haired childhood—tattooed on his leg, but he's never used it. He's never written, never visited. He never speaks her name out loud unless he's alone, absolutely alone, and then only when it is wrenched out of him, at the smallest hours, and when things are at their very worst. He isn't even sure what she means to him anymore—their time together was so short. The pain of her loss is mostly a well-worn groove in his brain, mostly a habitual ache. Marrije loved him. And he lost her. And he hasn't been loved that way since.

9

Jimmy D: dead. Susan J: dead. Leroy, Marnie, Monica: dead. Tim and Andrea gone upstate to be farmers and JoAnn gone upstate to jail and whatever happened to Sailor and Slim, those goddamn cokehead twins from Milwaukee with the violet eyes? Gone, gone. Jesus, they're all gone. Cat walks through Tompkins and the faces turn away from her or look through her and she doesn't know them anyway. All these new faces. All these young kids. They just keep coming.

That one over there by the dog run could have been Cat herself twenty years ago. She's a translation of Cat for this decade, holding court on a bench, surrounded by other kids—one poor boy is actually sitting at her feet. Razor thin, this nineties girl, and wrapped in black, hair an iridescent oil spill piled just so atop her head. An Italian greyhound shivers in her lap. Cat had favored reds and oranges, silver and gold; her own hair always a wild auburn tangle and eventually these coiled dreads. The dreadlocks sit so heavily now and she wishes she could be rid of them, their weight, their history, but they are an armor of sorts and she doesn't think she would have the courage to face the world without them.

In her own day, when it was her turn (midseventies, mostly, though she rode the aftershocks of her local sort of fame well into the eighties), Cat would float through the halls of the Chelsea Hotel in a silver dress that barely covered her ass; she'd stalk through CBGB, the sound of her name in a hundred different voices falling like leaves at her feet; she'd walk through this very park and every eye would be on her. She fronted a punk band called Tonsillectomy and she thought maybe she'd be a rock star, but she just ended up another name on the very long list of people Lou Reed was rude to.

Yeah, but Lou's alright. He knew her name for a while, back then. That's what Cat was best at—getting famous people to know her name. Whatever the hell that was worth.

Anyway, downtown's got a short memory. Five, ten years from now that girl over there will be a housewife in Nyack; she'll be a secretary in midtown; she'll be an ex-junkie stacking squash for a piss-poor living. There's another girl just like her, right behind her; she's on her way. She's driving up from North Carolina. She's dropping down from Wisconsin. She's that girl over there, but younger, quicker, dumber. That girl before the shine wore off. You don't get to keep that shine forever. Cat looks at the girl and can see it's already half gone but she doesn't know it yet. Cat didn't know it either, not until she'd spent it down to nothing.

Goddammit.

"Cat!" someone calls out. "Yo, Cat!" And she sees Steve, all long-limbed and wild-haired, walking toward her. God bless that motherfucker.

"Steve-o," she says. "You look like hell." They lace fingers like old times. His hands are cool and rough, nothing like they used to be. When she thinks of Steve's hands, she thinks *smooth*, she thinks *heated*. These are working hands now. And that's okay. They're the hands of a grown man. Useful hands.

"Headed home?" he says, and she wasn't but she nods yes. She wonders how close they'll get to Thirteenth Street before he lets go of her hand.

"I was walking through the park," she says, "looking at all those goddamn kids."

He drops her hand as they come around the basketball courts toward Avenue B. "Oh yeah?" His eyes follow the bouncing ass of a barely legal Dominican chick.

"I'm thinking maybe I'll get the band back together."

Asshole actually has the nerve to snort. "None of you could even play your instruments."

"Yeah, but nobody couldn't play their instruments better than us." Never mind that there's no one to call to get the band back together. Jane OD'd. Karen got cancer. Nicole got famous. The last time Cat saw Nicole she was stepping out of a limo, had to be nearly ten years ago now, all dressed up and headed into a party in some Gramercy Park townhouse. Cat was lit—this was back when she was still using—and Nicole pretended not to hear Cat calling out to her. Fancy actress, but not such a good one that she didn't give it away that she'd heard. Her jaw went tight and twitchy but she kept on walking, eyes fixed straight ahead. Bitch. Cat used to hold Nicole's hair for her while she puked. Used to lie to her parents for her when she was too high to come to the phone. Still, Cat might have done the same, positions reversed. No—fuck that. She wouldn't have.

"How about I let you take me out for a coffee?" she says.

Steve shakes his head. "Got to get home to Anne."

"Ah. The wife. Hey, remember that time we rode all the way out to Flatbush to go roller-skating and we almost got our asses kicked by those Brooklyn kids?" *But we got away and then we made out the whole way home and when the train barreled out of the tunnel into daylight across the bridge our faces were so close I thought the sunlight was a halo sprung up over your head.*

They're at Thirteen House, Steve glancing around him before reaching out to rub her shoulder. "Yeah. Yeah, I do." His touch is distant, brotherly.

"Yeah." She swats him on the ass. "Go on. Get on up there to your wife."

"So long, Carolyn," he says, almost a whisper. It's been so long since Cat felt what it was like to be Carolyn that it might as well be a stranger's name—some girl dead and buried, someone she caught a glimpse of once or twice in the mirror before she lost her for good.

⊞

Anne came through the door cursing, kicking off her work loafers so hard they skidded across the room and under the kitchen table. When she reached for a mixing bowl and the bread flour without so much as lifting her eyes to acknowledge his presence in the room, Steve began to consider his escape routes. He'd have to walk past her to leave through the door. Bad idea when she's in a cursing, shoe-kicking, bread-baking mood. The bedroom window, maybe? Down the fire escape and out to a bar for a while?

But he was feeling brave, and maybe a little guilty, and so he marched straight up to her, rubbed her shoulders. "Bad day, hon?"

Which is how he now finds himself parked on the couch, pretending to read. She told him to leave her be, but you don't live with a woman for fourteen years without learning a thing or two about her, and one thing Steve knows for sure is that he damn well better not actually leave the apartment when she says to leave her be.

She took a shower while the dough was rising and he hoped it would calm her, but she came out wet and pink, her face twisted as angry as a just-born baby. Now she's kneading the dough, pushing it harder than strictly necessary, picking it up and slamming it back down onto the counter, little gusts of flour rising up to cloud her wrists. Fold and push and *slam*, fold and push and *slam*. He wonders if the bread will taste like rage or submission.

"You want to talk about it?" A risky tactic, but how long can he sit there on the couch like an asshole, watching her work over that lump of dough?

She sighs, a burdened kind of sigh. Fold and push and *slam*. Fold and push and *slam*. "I got called into the principal's office today." She stops kneading, her fingertips tensing, dimpling the fleshy surface of the dough. "I was covering a middle-school social studies class the other day and we got to talking about homelessness. So I told the class about us, about what we're doing here. Some parents complained. They don't want a squatter teaching their kids." She snorts. "Like they let subs teach, anyway. Zookeeper, that's about it."

"That's bullshit. You're in the union."

"He said he doesn't like it that they can't reach me by phone, that they have to wait for me to call in every morning. Said he doesn't want my 'lifestyle choices' to distract the students." She waves her hand in front of her face. "Anyway." She plunks the dough back into the bowl and covers it with a dish towel, sets it aside for the second rise.

There's a slash of flour cut across her collarbone, dough crusted around her wedding ring. His love for her is worn, heavy with habit, but it wells up sharp and clear now. "Oh, Annie. Baby." Her face goes crumpled and red again, but this time when he reaches out she lets him hold her, the earthy scent of the flour mixing with that milky smell of her skin. No woman has ever smelled as good to him as Anne. That's why he married her; that's how he knew she was his.

"We got the other utilities hooked up legally, no problem. I don't see why we can't get a phone line," he says. "But you know what? Fuck them. They should be thanking you for the example you're setting for the kids. They should be begging you to talk to them about why we squat. This is

New York City, for fuck's sake. They think these kids don't know about homelessness? They think that none of those kids have ever been homeless themselves? And here you are, actually doing something, taking action for yourself, and they want what? Want to hide you away?"

"I am to be sure to keep my 'politics' from interfering with the education of the students. But they want me gone. He didn't come out and say it, but . . ."

"Bullshit. We'll fight this. They can't get rid of you because of where you live."

"I'm just a sub, Steve. They'll call me in less, or they'll find some other reason to let me go." She fists tears from her cheeks. "The phone thing, maybe, or something else."

"We'll get a phone. We can do that."

"What are we doing here anyway? Why are we still here? Because it's not so clear to me anymore. Is this really such a noble thing? I can see the other side of it." She shakes her head and pulls away from him. "I just want to get out of the city for a while. I can't think straight here. There's too much going on, too much waiting to go wrong. I'm going home for Christmas."

"This is home."

"You know what I mean."

"Okay. I'll miss you. But okay. Go."

He thought that was what she wanted to hear, but she looks at him now like he's slapped her. She uncovers the dough and starts to punch it down. She hasn't let it rise long enough yet, but she's punching it down anyway. Punching so hard the bowl it's in rattles against the tabletop.

"Okay then," she says. "So I'll go."

"What?" he says. "What did you want me to say? You want to go, you say you need to go. So go! Fucking go!"

And so now she's crying again. She goes into the bedroom and closes the door behind her.

Steve covers the dough bowl and sets it aside to rise again.

She says she can see the other side of it. *What other side?* Should they both work two jobs to afford the rent on some shitty little place? For the privilege of handing over all their money to some landlord every month? Or more likely these days to some management company hired by a massive real estate conglomerate. Should they work their lives away to feed into the great corporate machine?

No. A person has a right to life, liberty, and the pursuit of happiness. Isn't that the bill of goods they're selling the kids in the schools?

The way things are now, the way money rules—a person doesn't have to just bow down and swallow that. It only is the way things are until people say no. Until they decide that there's a better way to live, and rise up. That's what they're doing here in the squat. They're standing up. They're saying no. No, we will not be drones in the great corporate hive. No, we will not sacrifice our time and happiness to the all-consuming goddamn maw of consumption. No. We're going to take this unused land, and we're going to build a home on it, and we're going to live here, together. A community of resistance. Sharing this land, pooling our resources, helping each other. We will spend our time thinking, making art, sleeping, making love, raising children.

Outside, streetlights blink on. Windows in the building across the street are dark, the wage slaves still at work. Steve's done odd jobs in that building. The apartments are two hundred, maybe two hundred fifty square feet, and they rent for almost as much as he and Anne make in a good month. Why are people willing to work so hard for the privilege of living in a dark little shoe box in a shitty tenement building? Do they ever think about what they could be doing if they didn't have to work all the time? What they could be doing for themselves, their families, their community? What would this country be like if its people were freed from the yoke of the forty-, fifty-, sixty-hour workweek? What could they accomplish if housing weren't bought, sold, rented, but was a right?

His sister, Lettie, she teases him. Calls him Fidelito, little Fidel. So be it. They're on the right path here at Thirteen House. It's the rest of the country that's out of step.

Anne's being tested now. Her courage, her convictions are being questioned. That's what he'll tell her when she comes out of the bedroom. *Stand with me*, he'll say. *I'm here with you. Stand with me.*

⊞

Amelia's skin smells so strongly of curry she thinks it must be coming out of her pores. She stood at that stove cooking for hours tonight. They got a big crowd for the community dinner, people coming in off the street in a steady stream from the moment they opened the doors at six until just a little while ago. It's going on nine, past curfew for the shelters, and it's just family left now—nearly everyone from Thirteen House and at least half of Cat House. Marlowe pulls the doors closed and they settle in. Dregs of the lentils forming a crust in the big pot and Kim and Fletcher and Gideon getting a poker game started and Suzie and Denise trying to get Marlowe to dance to some Prince song.

Amelia sets the pot to soak and sits down on the couch. Gerrit follows her across the room and drops down next to her, too close. She picks up her knitting, working the stitches fast, her left elbow jutting out toward Gerrit. He doesn't move away, just lets her elbow graze his arm with each stitch. Anne and Steve are sitting in the pair of threadbare armchairs to the right of the couch, Steve in the near chair. Amelia slides away from Gerrit's arm, her knees tilting down toward Steve. "Hey," she says.

Steve clears his throat. "Hey." Nodding to her and Gerrit both. Anne's eyes are cast low, fingers picking at a small hole in the leg of her jeans.

Three quick stomps sound out on the metal cellar doors and a voice calls, "Ahoy the house!" Laughter through the community room and Suzie says, "What are we, fucking pirates?" and someone else says, "Hell yeah, we are." Marlowe goes through the interior door and climbs the short flight of stairs. There's the dull clang of metal on cement as he throws the cellar doors open, then feet on the stairs.

In rolls the rest of Cat House: Linda and Chrissie, Big

Ron and Rolando, with Cat bringing up the rear. Cat, the pirate queen, her red dreads wound up like a crown, the yellow tips of the flame tattoos that cover her back and shoulders just barely visible at the collar of her bulky army jacket.

Steve hauls himself up from the armchair, offering it to Cat, who takes it silently. He lowers his big body to perch on the arm of the couch next to Amelia; she lets her knees brush his thigh.

"Steve," Gerrit says, and at the sound of his name Steve jumps. "There's room if Amelia and I squeeze together." Gerrit moves in close to Amelia, who shifts her body until it's hard up against the couch's arm. He slides in closer to her.

"Wouldn't want to crowd you," Steve says, but takes the offered spot on Gerrit's other side, folding his body tight.

The heat coming off Gerrit's body is insufferable. He keeps moving closer. If Amelia moves any farther away, she'll have to climb onto the couch arm. She'll fall right off into Cat's lap. Which would be awkward, to say the least.

Cat keeps sending warm little glances Amelia's way. It's thrilling, but somehow terrifying, too. Like the time she passed David Byrne on the street and he looked at her and smiled. Like, here we are, two people walking down the same street, and isn't it nice? But her legs felt shaky for two full blocks after that smile. Here was this remote person from some fabulous celebrity planet, smiling at her. Not on some separate planet after all. Just another person walking down Second Avenue.

With Cat's history—with everyone she's known, everyone who's known her: the rock stars, the poets, the activists; with everything she's done, everything she's seen—why should she take the time to show this kindness to Amelia? What could Amelia possibly offer Cat?

And there's Steve on Gerrit's other side. He can hardly look at Amelia and he doesn't even know about the baby yet. Anne all solid and still in that armchair. Steve loves Anne. He chose Anne. That's not going to change.

This must be the loneliest feeling in the world. She's had that thought over and over since she found out for sure about the baby. She'll think it and then an even lonelier moment will come along to knock that earlier loneliness off its post. It's got to be radiating off Amelia in waves. There's no way everything seems fine. Maybe Cat can see that. Maybe Cat keeps looking at Amelia because she can see Amelia is drowning. Maybe Cat could reach a hand down, haul her clear.

But it's Suzie reaching a hand out to Amelia. "Dance," Suzie says. "You will dance now. That's an order."

"I just cooked fifty tons of lentils and now you expect me to dance?"

"I do."

She looks up at Suzie and realizes she wants to say yes. Tired as she is, she still wants to dance. So what else is there to do but slip her hand into Suzie's and follow her out into the middle of the room where Denise and Ben are already dancing to an old ska tape Ben dug up.

"Wait!" Suzie says, flipping through the stacks of cassettes and CDs piled up next to the boom box. "This one's for Amelia."

Bright, whining keyboards. It's ABBA. "Dancing Queen." *Glissando*, Amelia thinks, the word swimming up from the depths, a remnant of her middle-school music class. *Glissando*.

"Oh, hell no," Ben says. "Who brought that crap into my house?" But he's smiling. Everyone's smiling. Even Amelia. She closes her eyes, she throws her head back, she dances.

10

Daybreak, the sky to the east gone thick like jam. It's easy to love this city in the small hours of morning, before the sun cuts the buildings to hard angles, before the sidewalks fill with raised voices and swinging elbows.

Cat's dad used to work a newsstand right here in Union Square, on the southeast corner. Starting the year she turned ten and going on until she was sixteen, he'd wake her up at four thirty so they could be there when the trucks dropped off the morning news. Hot coffee and toast standing up by the kitchen sink and then out into the predawn streets, her hand in his long after she was too old for it, because who was there but them to see it and because even then she sensed there was something sweet and fleeting in their mornings together. At the stand, he'd slice the strings on the heavy bundles with a box cutter and together they would stack the papers as the sun came up. She'd think about her mom still asleep and warm in their apartment, the sun finding her bedroom window before it moved west to Cat—*no, to Carolyn*—and her dad, the piles of newspapers, the rows of candy and gum, the packs of cigarettes. When it was time to leave for school, she'd palm a pack of Lucky Strikes to hand out in the school-yard. The old stand's been gone at least twenty years now.

Dan passes a vegetable crate down from the truck, the sudden weight of it rocking her back on her heels, the dirt-and-cheese stink of winter squash. Cat is sick as hell of winter squash. She lowers the crate to the ground and turns to accept another, but Riva's stepped between Cat and the truck.

"Get started on the displays," Riva says. "I'll finish un-loading with Dad." Because she's younger than Cat, be-cause she's stronger, because she's a full head taller with shoulders like a goddamn football player. Dan nods to Cat and passes a crate of storage onions to Riva. They slip easily into a rhythm, moving faster than Cat and Dan ever have. Cat keeps her head down, works on stacking the onions.

There's a bitter wind blowing, bone-cutting cold com-ing off the East River. Cat remembers lying in bed the first morning she refused to go to work with her dad. It was cold like it is today, the wind rattling through the gaps around her bedroom window. She and her folks had had a fight the night before—a big one. About Steve, of course. She'd totally blown her curfew, and her dad got in her face about how she was running around with Steve, getting a reputa-tion. How they had raised her better than that. Her mom just sat quietly at the kitchen table, turning her teacup around in her hands. "This is bullshit!" Cat had screamed, and watched her mother wince at the profanity. "If he was Jewish you'd be falling all over yourselves to invite him to dinner. You'd have me married off by next week."

But Steve was trouble. Of course he was. Cat was the only one who couldn't see it at the time. That morning she buried herself deep under her blankets until she heard the apartment door fall shut behind her dad. When he died of a heart attack six months later, they still weren't really talking. She's tried to blame Steve for that, but she can't. That one's squarely on her shoulders.

She thinks back to Steve and Amelia at dinner the other night. There's something going on there. That prick Gerrit gnawing on the girl like a bone and all the while she's watching Steve like she doesn't know when to breathe without his say-so and Steve's sitting there jumpy as a thief. He fucked Amelia, no doubt. Isn't that just like a man, to cut the most vulnerable one from the herd and devour her. Oh, that stupid girl; that poor, stupid girl.

No wonder Cat's dad hated Steve. It's all so clear, watching from the outside. But Steve was every bit as young as Cat back then. Whatever the hell he's gotten up to now, he should know better.

"Wake up, Cat." Riva thunks a crate of carrots onto the table and an onion falls from Cat's careful stack to the ground.

"What the fuck?"

"You're daydreaming."

"I'm stacking fucking onions."

"Excuse me?" Riva pulls herself to full height, hands on her hips.

"I said I'm stacking the goddamn onions." Cat gets up close, sticks her face right under Riva's, smells the coffee-and-cornflakes stink of her mouth; she's not afraid of some farmer's daughter barely out of her teens.

The girl's chin quivers and she blushes hard. "Riva," Dan says, "why don't you go get the cashbox out of the truck? Make sure we've got enough singles to make change." He stoops to pick up the fallen onion and Cat sees that the skin on the nape of his neck has gone thin and crepy; the seat of his jeans hangs loose. Dan's getting older; only a matter of time before Riva starts running the show. He sets the onion down on top of the stack and smiles. "Now the fucking onions are stacked; come help me unpack the rest of it."

Dan can't be more than ten, fifteen years older than Cat, and look how he's aged since they met. Farming's hard on a body. "You're a lucky man, Dan," she says. "Got your daughter to help you run the business."

"Don't pay too much attention to Riva. She's got to learn how to talk to people."

"Nah. She just doesn't like me. That's okay." Cat lifts a bunch of rosemary to her nose, the sharp green scent scouring her lungs clean. No, it's not okay. When Dan retires he'll have his daughter to keep the family business going and the money coming in. He'll have his wife, Sandy, whom Cat's never met but whom she feels she has come to know through the big lunches she packs for Dan, the way she folds his paper napkins just so and always tucks in a few homemade cookies; his sandwiches on fresh thick-sliced bread, heavy with meat and the vegetables from the farm. Cat's always kind of hoped that one day Sandy would send along a sandwich for her, too. Five years and no sandwich.

When Dan retires, Riva's first order of business will be to can Cat. And so then Cat's gonna find herself retired, too, because what the hell else is she qualified to do anymore? Who's gonna hire her skinny old ass? How strange to have reached this point, to find herself wishing she'd had a plan, only now when it's too late. How strange and how awful to feel herself this alone in the world, and to know that it's her own damn fault.

"She'll like you fine, Cat. Give her time." But he's just talking from some reflexive urge to reassure her. He's eyeing the parsnips and beets; he's mentally tallying the sales from Monday and Wednesday, wondering how much they'll clear today—Friday being the slow day in winter, and how much tomorrow, Saturday, the biggest day in every season. He's thinking about what he'll plant in the spring, and about how many parsnips he'll sow for next winter, how many beets. He's thinking about cabbage moths, about aphids. He's thinking about powdery mildew and the rising cost of gas. He's not thinking about how it's going to be for Cat when Riva takes over, and why should he? His retirement, even if it comes next week, is a remote thing to him. For now, there are crates to unpack: bunches of winter greens cold and damp; leeks lined up like squat white soldiers; the sweet milky smell of the carrots. They work steadily, their bodies bending to the task.

The sun rolls along up Fourteenth Street and the ghost of a habit turns Cat's face into the light. She shields her eyes and looks east, half expecting to see her father, a sun-blown shadow in the diorama box of his newsstand.

⊞

Amelia crosses Second Avenue toward Kiev, the diner's windows leaking greasy yellow light into the gray afternoon. Inside, at the takeout counter, a fat little troll of a man, ratty green cape on his shoulders, gnarled wooden walking stick in his hand, squawks for "matzoh brei with three eggs, and a Diet Coke." Stringy hair tangling into his beard, faded Superman T-shirt, braying Lower East Side accent. "That's three eggs for the matzoh brei!" He's got thick silver rings on his fingers, chunks of amber worked into the wood of his walking stick.

"Amelia, Amelia, Amelia Bedelia." Gideon does that singsong of his and waves her over to the table he and Kim have claimed by the window. That big smile and stubbled chin, the ever-present flat cap. She slides into the chair next to his and kisses his cheek. She smells black cherry soda on his breath.

Across the table, Kim's looking woozy with red lipstick smudged to one side and eyeliner pooling like thumbprints under her eyes. "Rough day?" Amelia asks.

Kim grabs her hand, turns it over, traces the lines of Amelia's palm with a jagged nail. "Your luck's right here," she says, jabbing a nail dead center of Amelia's palm.

"Deep-grooved, fat luck right here. Missed you, bitch. You never come out to play anymore."

Amelia's palm itches where Kim's nail dug in. "It's the cold. Makes me tired."

Gideon snorts. "The cold makes you huddle up with Gerrit for warmth. He's been looking especially smug lately, the Dutch fuck."

"Gerrit doesn't know how to look smug," Kim says. "He can only scowl and look very, very serious." She draws her brows down over her eyes.

Amelia throws a sugar packet at her. "You look like an angry Muppet." The waitress comes by and grunts toward the laminated menus. "A bowl of mushroom barley soup, Dr. Brown's Black Cherry," Amelia says.

She isn't feeling sick like she thought she would. Not since that one time she puked, and maybe that was stress and not the baby. She's tired all the time, but otherwise she could almost forget she's pregnant. When she first thought she was pregnant, she felt it. There was a difference, a fullness below her navel, something going on. Either that feeling has gone away, or she's grown so used to it that she can't feel it anymore, even if she concentrates really hard. She wonders if the baby has just stopped growing and died. She wonders if not wanting a baby hard enough can kill it.

Almost a full week to go before the ultrasound and there's no way to know until then if there's still that little lump of life in her or not. She doesn't know which she hopes for more, or which scares her more. She doesn't want the baby, but she can't bring herself to wish it away. She doesn't want the baby, but when she presses her hand to her belly she finds a new softness to it, and that softness pleases her.

"So you've got the flyers?" Gideon asks.

Kim draws a white paper bag from her backpack and divvies the stack of paper inside it into three piles, handing Amelia and Gideon each a pile. The paper is still warm from the copy machine. *Defend the Squats!* it says along the top. Which squats? And why? Amelia's not so sure about the way they're going about trying to get support.

"We should be pushing the homesteader angle more, don't you think?" she says. Shouldn't people know they aren't just a bunch of punks crashed out in crumbling buildings? That they aren't freeloaders out to get something for nothing or whatever it is people are thinking about them? Shouldn't people know how hard they work?

Kim shrugs. "This is what Chrissie gave me to copy. The outreach committee came up with it."

"I think it's fine," Gideon says. "You don't want to get too complicated. Like, 'Here's the problem. Here's who's having it. Here's how we need your help.' Simple, yeah? Let's not get too caught up in the squatter/homesteader thing."

"Yeah, it's simpler," Amelia says, "but then let's say you go to hand out these flyers and someone feeds you the usual shit, says, 'Why should you get to live rent-free?' Says we're stealing, sponging off someone else's property. So then what do you say? How do you get them to understand it's not like that?"

"I don't engage with that noise," Gideon says. "There's no point to it."

"But that's just it. We're asking people to help us protect something and they don't even understand what it is we're trying to save. I mean, not all squats are the same. You've got the hardworking ones really trying to do something, helping the community, you know? And then you've got those other buildings . . . one step up from a crack den, right? And we're not the same, so—"

"Aren't we? What makes you so special?"

Amelia pulls back to see his face. There's no smile there. What the hell? "I'm not," she says. "I never said I was." How can he lump their buildings in with the broken-windows, rotting-floors, piss-bucket wrecks she crashed in when she first got to the city?

He shakes his head like she's gotten it way, way wrong. "You fucked your way into a stable building full of worker bees so you've got a snug little place carved out now. You mean you aren't the same girl who was crashed out on the floor of that dump of a place on Avenue D back in the day with a bundle of plastic bags for a pillow, no heat, no Con Ed, one wrong step and you're falling straight down to the basement? I saw some punk girl blowing a crack dealer in an empty lot on my way over here. That couldn't have been you, huh? That wasn't a road you could have gone down?"

"I didn't fuck my way in. It's not like that."

"Yeah, you work hard. And you and Gerrit have stuck together a long time now. But why'd he bring you home in the first place? And how'd you get him to let you stay?

You think everyone's forgotten that skinny little chick in the fishnet tights? Look, I'm not saying you did anything wrong, then or now. I'm just saying there's not all that much difference between any of us. People are just people, Amelia Bedelia. Even Biff on Fifth Avenue. Just people."

"You know what? Fuck you." Anger rises up in her, a fierceness she didn't see coming. "I only did what I had to do. Same as that girl in the vacant lot. I did what I had to do *to not die*. Ever think of that? Ever fucking think of that?"

"Easy there, kiddo." He lifts his palms up, warding her off, a dismissive smile on his big dumb face. "That was kind of my point, right?"

They were all just clueless kids trying not to die. Gideon was no different before he moved into Cat House. So where does he get off attacking Amelia now? "What did you have to do to survive, hunh?" she says. "All alone in the big city? You weren't much older than me, right? Sixteen, seventeen? I remember you from back then, too. Getting into big old cars with greasy old men. I remember."

And he goes quiet; he loses the stupid grin. So there's that, at least.

The door swings open, a burst of cold air with it. There goes the troll man, a plastic bag in one hand, walking stick in the other. He shuffles past their window and Amelia stuffs down the urge to knock as he goes by, to wave to him, make him see her. *I see you, Matzoh Brei Troll. Here we are together in this crazy fucking city.* She doesn't do it. She never has the nerve to act on the connections she feels. People hold themselves apart here. Why are they all so afraid of each other?

"Damn. Why did we sit so close to the door?" Kim rubs at her eyes, the smudged liner streaking out toward her temples. "You and Suzie doing a dumpster run tonight?"

"I don't think so. Maybe tomorrow." Amelia's too tired to even think about climbing in and out of those dumpsters, digging through trash bags.

"We've got someone making a run tonight," Gideon says. "I'll pass word on that Thirteen could use the extras."

"So you're being nice to me again now?" Amelia says.

Gideon takes off his cap and scratches his head, his scalp showing through pale and shiny where his dark hair has thinned. "Yeah. Ignore me, Amelia Bedelia. You know I love you."

"Sure you do, asshole." Jesus.

He smiles his toothy grin and squeezes her thigh. He kisses her ear, a soft pop of a kiss. "I'm off to the john." He ambles to the back of the restaurant, that easy rolling walk of his.

"Gideon was a cowboy in a past life," Kim says. "I just know it."

"Gideon's a cowboy in this life."

The food comes and the smell of mushrooms from Amelia's soup bowl is like a fist to the gut. Her mouth goes wet and metallic. She pushes the soup toward Kim. "Want it? I'm not hungry, I guess."

Kim takes up the spoon. "It's not like you to not eat."

"Yeah." So much for no symptoms. She presses a hand to her belly again, trying to feel something past the nausea, trying to sense the little body growing in there. She finds she's relieved to be nauseous, to have evidence. *Oh hey*, she thinks. *There you are.* Such a huge, lonely thing to keep to herself. "So, Kim? I want to tell you something."

"Mmm?"

"A secret, okay? You can't tell anyone yet." Kim nods, dunking her grilled cheese into Amelia's soup. "Okay, so the thing is, I'm pregnant."

Kim pauses, sandwich stalled in midair, soup droplets puddling on the table. "Does Gerrit know?"

"Yeah."

"Wow. What are you gonna do?"

"I don't know. Keep it? Maybe? I don't know yet."

Kim points her sandwich at Amelia, then takes a bite. She wipes at her lips with the back of her hand. "I got pregnant once. Before I moved here."

"What happened? Did you have it?"

"Have you seen me with a kid?"

"No, I'm just asking. I mean, maybe you gave it up for adoption or it's with your parents or . . . I don't know."

"I didn't have it."

"Oh. Was that . . . ?" Was that what? Amelia isn't sure what to say. Does she say she's sorry? Does she say *good for you*? "That must have been hard."

"You just . . . you get used to it." She pushes the soup aside. "It was the right thing. Can you imagine me with a nine-year-old? She would have been nine by now. Going on ten."

"She?"

"Yeah, I don't know. You get used to it."

Gideon settles down next to Amelia again, and Kim's face goes closed. The air is thick with frying onions and boiled potatoes. Sounds of Russian from the kitchen, and Spanish from the table behind them. Gideon talks about some graffiti in the bathroom and Kim stares out the window, not hearing him.

Amelia wants to run out the door, leave the chatter, the smells, the nauseating soup, the thick stack of bullshit flyers behind, and run after the troll man. She wants to follow him to whatever hole he lives in, whichever bridge he lives under. She wants to watch him eat his matzoh brei, his thick lips slick with the grease, bits of matzoh and egg in his beard. She wants to tell him her secrets, and she wants him to reach out one of those fat hands and pat her head and tell her that he understands, that it's all going to be okay.

Coming on dusk, the gray sky going over to a dirty mottled purple. The nausea is passing, leaving behind a dull halo of unease and a gnawing hunger. She takes back her soup—Kim's not eating it anyway—and tucks in.

11

Thursday dawn never came, night just fading into progressively paler shades of gray as Cat watched sleepless at her window, a kitten curled in her lap. A little girl, a calico, left yesterday in a cardboard box on the Cat House doorstep, which seems to be the neighborhood's default response to its unwanted felines. Cat's already got fifteen of them, though, and this new little one wasn't exactly greeted with a warm welcome by the other cats. Cat had been hoping Griselda would take to her, as she sometimes does with kittens, but that bony old bitch just turned her head and pretended to sleep while the other cats blocked the kitten's path to the food, the litter boxes, the prime napping spots.

She snugs the kitten into a satchel and heads outside, the soft pink nose shunting the flap open at the corner, tiny nails needling into Cat's hip through the canvas. She rests a hand inside the bag, gently restraining that muscular little body until the kitten dozes, lulled by the motion of her

walking. She'll bring the cat to Jack Pohl. He could likely do
with some company; it'd do him good, having something
to look after. Old Jack Pohl, Aspirin Jack. She's neglected
him lately, caught up in her own shit. She'll take him for a
walk to buy some kibble and kitty litter, help him get all set
up. She's got her pay from yesterday's market in her pocket,
and more coming from tomorrow's market. She'll buy him
breakfast; wouldn't that be a turnaround? He'll like that.
He's all about the gestures, Jack. A gentleman of the old
kind, no matter how come down in the world.

A true gentleman, never mind he never has gotten off
the dope. He has an old-money inheritance and a discipline about his habit that's allowed him to find a magical balance. The heroin as much keeps him alive as it kills
him, so you'd be inclined to think he's replaced his blood
with junk, that he's preserved in it. Maybe because he
never got greedy with it, maybe because he's careful not
to shoot more than he needs, just take that edge off and
keep going. And because, with his money, he's never had
to go without unless he wanted to. Once a year, beginning
on his birthday, June fifth, he'll take two months off clean.
A junk fast, he calls it. Junkie Lent. He'll pass most of that
time looking like hell, snarly and sour and not wanting to
see her. And then on the morning of August fifth he'll start
up again with a freshly lowered tolerance, the sweet sleepy
junk shuffle returned.

In the old days, when she was still using, Cat would stay
away all June and July, turning up at his door on August
fifth with a little plastic packet for him, a welcome-back

gift. They'd shoot up, then float east to an automat there used to be on Twenty-Third and Sixth, where he'd buy her cheese sandwiches and watery coffee. Over squares of stale coffee cake he'd tell her she had to clean up her act: get off the dope; get some decent friends; get some decent sleep.

"It's okay for you to use, but I should get clean?" she'd say.

"Heroin and I have reached a certain understanding after all these years," he'd say. "And I'm old and wrinkled and unlovely. You, my dear, are still young and lovely and it would be a shame to waste that."

"You're not as unlovely as all that," she'd say, patting his dry hand, its shot veins.

"Marry me," he'd say every once in a while. Cat, she'd always smile and say, "Ah, Jack. You're too good for me," and she'd mean it.

He was prouder than anyone when she picked up that one-year NA coin. And he was on her ass more than anyone when she stopped going to meetings a few years later. But she's still clean—ten years clean—and at least partly with Aspirin Jack to thank for it. Hanging on by a thread, but clean. *So go to a meeting, asshole*, she thinks. But no, too many people up in her shit, telling her what to do. Too many kids with three minutes' sobriety thinking they've got it all figured out. She's not one for *groups*.

Twenty-Third and Twelfth Avenue. His tumbledown SRO nudges up from the ground like a mushroom on the Hudson's dank shore. She slips in through the unlocked door, past two gangly freaks on the nod in the vestibule, and up the spindly stairs to the third floor. The air is thick with the stench of mold and piss and booze, and that acrid burning smell—telltale of countless small fires, drunks and junkies nodding off with their hot plates left on. No crackheads in the SROs, usually. They flame out too fast to pay the meager rent. That was one thing she learned in those NA meetings—when you hear someone say, "And then I started smoking crack," you know they're almost at the end of their story.

The kitten stretches and mewls as Cat reaches Jack's door. It's locked fast and there's no answer when she knocks, so she waits and knocks again. The door next to Jack's opens and some wasted ghost wanders out, bare distended belly and stick-thin arms, bulging frog eyes and a tequila stink. Frog-man croaks, "The old man's gone."

She ignores him, knocks again.

"He's not gonna answer, lady. He's dead. Get it?"

"What? When?"

He scratches his belly, tugs up his sagging pants. "Yesterday, I think, or maybe the day before it was, they hauled him out of there. Gone a while before that, though. He was starting to stink. I complained to the manager about it, the stink. I don't pay my rent to smell dead guys through the wall."

No. No no no no no no no. Jack died alone. She promised him that he wouldn't die alone, that she simply wouldn't allow it. "You feel like dying, you wait for me. I'm gonna hold your hand. I'm gonna brush your eyes closed. Don't you go dying without me, old man." And what did he do?

"Hey, is that a cat?" The kitten's climbed out of the bag and is clawing her way up Cat's jacket to perch on her shoulder.

"No, it's a fucking monkey," she says as she turns back toward the stairs, one hand on the kitten to steady her. Last thing she needs right now is to chase a scared kitten through these greasy halls.

Goddammit.

Downstairs to the manager's apartment on the ground floor and she pounds on the door, which swings open, a fat woman in a housedress, angry and looking like she might hand Cat's teeth to her. "Why you gotta bang so hard on the door?" she says, her accent faintly Russian.

"Jack Pohl," Cat says. "Room 308."

"Yeah?"

"He was my uncle."

The woman's face softens. "That kitten," she says, "is yours?"

"She's nobody's cat now. You want her?"

Cat leaves with a paper grocery bag of Jack's worldly possessions, the kitten given in lieu of his back rent. The rain soaks the bag and it rips before she can get halfway up the block. Sour-smelling clothes, a few paperback Westerns, a manila envelope of old photos. No cash, no dope. His works in their soft leather case—the pair of antique silver-and-glass syringes (*They weren't antique when I bought them, dear*)—and his silver watch were missing, too. No surprises there. She found his bankbook: fifty-three bucks left from a balance that started in the hundred thousands many pages and years before. She stuffs the photos into her bag, hauls the rest to the river, and dumps it in.

Ask me again, Jack. Ask me to marry you. On the scummy surface of the Hudson, his threadbare black topcoat fans out like a floater.

⊞

Gerrit insisted on going along to the prenatal exam, but now that he's there beside Amelia in the Planned Parenthood waiting room, he isn't so sure he belongs. An armed guard checked through his backpack on the way in and made him leave his pocketknife at the front desk. Gerrit and the security guard are the only men to be seen. Around them, mothers chase after toddlers; middle-aged women page through cheap paperbacks; teenage girls look out nervously from behind their hair. There's a young one crying quietly in the corner; she keeps looking from the door to the clock.

"I don't think her boyfriend's going to show, poor thing," he says to Amelia, who's sucking noisily on a ginger candy—she says they help settle her stomach—and knitting a sock.

"Who?"

He gestures toward the crying girl.

Amelia shrugs and goes back to her knitting. "Better she learn that lesson now."

"Nice," he says. "What lesson would that be? I'm here with you."

"Yeah, but I'm not here for an abortion. And I'm not sixteen anymore."

"I noticed." He picks a piece of lint from the shoulder of her sweater and smoothes her hair back from her ear. She hasn't changed that much. He can still look at her and see the scared sixteen-year-old. "I still would have been here if you were sixteen."

"If I were sixteen and you'd knocked me up, you'd be headed to jail if you turned up here admitting to it."

"You're being difficult on purpose."

"Fine. You're a prince among men. We know this already."

A nurse comes into the waiting area. "Amelia?" Gerrit follows Amelia, who follows the nurse, through a pair of heavy swinging doors, down a glaring white hallway that smells of antiseptic and bodies, through another door. Exam Room 3. Dull green walls. A burgundy table with those strange stirrup things. A complicated-looking machine with a computer monitor attached. Metal instruments lined up on a sterile sheet on a counter. Harsh light. Gerrit begins to sweat. He wants to run from the room, but he asked to be there. He insisted on being there. *Kom op*, he tells himself. *You aren't the one going on that table.*

Amelia is undressing as if he weren't there, as if he didn't have eyes—the way you undress for your bedroom walls. He gathers the clothes she's tossed on the exam table and folds them. He sits on a plastic chair in the corner and holds her clothes in his lap. They're warm from her body, her body now wrapped in a blue paper gown. Her head and collarbones emerge from the squared-off blue. She looks so thin in that paper gown—too thin. He worries that she isn't eating enough. He worries that she still comes home sometimes smelling like cigarettes, though she insists she's quit. "We'll go out for dinner tonight," he says. "Indian, if you'd like. Or pierogis. Whatever you want."

She shrugs and the gown makes a shifting, whispering sound against her skin. He thinks of her ribs beneath the paper, the pale taut skin that stretches over them. He thinks of the baby, somewhere deep inside her.

A doctor comes in, businesslike. Amelia's feet settle in the stirrups and Gerrit finds he has taken a chair just behind the doctor's right shoulder. He finds he is staring between Amelia's spread legs, the skin of her slim thighs mottled white and red in the cold room. A light beats down directly over the doctor's head and Amelia is opened up by a clear plastic device that looks like a cross between a duck and an instrument of torture.

There's a blur of swabs and test tubes, the snap of latex gloves, and then the plastic duck is out, tossed in a biohazard bin, and now the computerlike machine is humming to life, the doctor easing some plastic wand thing inside of Amelia.

"Come here where you can see," Amelia says. The ultrasound, the reason he'd wanted to come along. He shoves his right hand deep into his pocket, safe from the doctor's clinician eyes, and goes to stand by Amelia's side.

On the screen is a pulsing grayscale ocean. The doctor points out the parts: the head, the butt, the heart. They can see it. They can hear it. The heartbeat is so fast and Gerrit feels his own pulse race to try to match it.

"Amelia," Gerrit says. "Amelia, you've made a heart."

It is small, it is alien and strange, but there is a heart. The doctor pronounces the baby perfect. Gerrit is gratified to see tears on Amelia's cheeks as she watches the beating heart on the screen.

⊞

It's raining when Amelia leaves the clinic, Gerrit bumbling along beside her. Dead gray skies over the looming old buildings on Bleecker. Gerrit's got the printouts from the ultrasound tucked carefully into his inside coat pocket, and he keeps patting his coat to make sure they're still there.

"Take it easy the rest of the day," he says. "I'll look after the shop on my own." Like he's doing her a big favor; like he's the generous boss giving her an afternoon off.

They walk up Bowery. Puddles swell to erase the street corners; the frayed hems of her jeans drag wet at her boot heels. Behind the smudged windows of restaurant-supply stores, stoves and sinks sit dull and silent. Stainless steel and sharp edges. Cavernous refrigerator cases. Land of lost alien robots. Ageless men with square heads and big shoulders wrestle a greasy old grill from the back of a truck. Their eyes skim right over Amelia.

There is something inside of her that's better than her, and she feels her body closing in around it like a fist. How can anything good be growing inside her? Amelia, who sometimes forgets her last name. Who sometimes forgets her mother's face. What's leaching into the baby from her bones?

"That was something, wasn't it? I've never seen any-thing like it," Gerrit says.

"The baby?"

"Yes, the baby. Of course, the baby."

Of course, the baby.

"We should start thinking about what it will need," he says. "I can build a crib. We'll turn my room into a nursery."

"And where will you sleep?" she says.

He grimaces and feels for the ultrasound printouts again, and she knows he's thinking he'll be sleeping with her. Mommy and Daddy snug in the mommydaddy bed, and if they're going to go through with this charade she guesses that is how it will be. One day after another, play-acting until it starts to feel real. Tell a lie long enough and it starts to sound true even in your own head.

She imagines what a miscarriage would be like. Doubled over with cramps, huddled on the toilet. The blood and the tissue in the water. Tears. Less blood than she would have expected. Or maybe more. More, she thinks. And she'd struggle to stand, blood sticky on the insides of her thighs, and she'd try to clean herself with a washcloth and it would come away iron red, the blood still coming. She'd find a pad in the box under the sink, press it into her underpants, then stumble out to the living room. She'd be crying. Half afraid, half relieved. Full of the loss and the pain and the blood.

Maybe Gerrit is there to bundle her up, hail a cab, get her to the hospital. Or maybe Gerrit is gone, off some-where who knows where and she bangs on Steve's door, collapses against the doorframe and weeps, and it's Steve who bundles Amelia up and hails a cab and gets her to the hospital. She'd come home that evening, pale and drawn and weak, and Gerrit would be waiting at the kitchen table, and she'd have to tell him what happened. Except he would already know. She wouldn't have been able to bring herself to flush the toilet. Water full of baby.

But here, now, Gerrit walks beside her, his hand reaching again and again for those ultrasound printouts, oblivious to her tears. Amelia is sick with fear and something like longing. It's almost romantic the way it could end like that. The blood and the pain. The penance built right in. And not her fault.

She wipes her tears away and maybe it isn't so much that Gerrit didn't see them as that he was giving her some space, because now he draws her hand into his warm coat pocket. "It will be good. You'll see. *Ik zweer het.*"

And didn't she choose Gerrit? Didn't she make that choice when she decided to stay? The failure to move is a decision to stay. She can have the baby, and she can stay with Gerrit. She won't meet another guy and fall in love, get married, have his children, build a life with him. But who's to say that ever would have come to pass? Who's to say that anyone would have wanted to keep her forever? Steve didn't.

In all her twenty-three years, only her grandmother and Gerrit have ever found her to be worth keeping.

Something quick and fierce wells up in her chest.

"I'm keeping the baby," she says. Out loud for the first time, and it sounds true. Terrifying and true. "I'm going to have it."

12

Amelia trips up the stairs. Dust motes in the sunbeam from the skylight overhead and the air close and musty and she's too warm in her peacoat and sweater. She's lugging a heavy grocery bag, free produce from the kid at the Met. Tomatoes, cabbages, apples. She feels dizzy. She walked without noticing past her own door and up the stairs and here she is at Steve and Anne's door. There's the smell of bread baking and she can hear kitchen sounds, someone moving around in there. Amelia leans against the door, just leans her shoulder, just a rest, but then everything tilts and she's on the floor somehow, the thunk of her head against the door and Amelia sliding away . . .

"Amelia!" Anne's kind hands on her arm. Anne's kind face floating over hers. She lets Anne lead her into the apartment, lets Anne lead her to the couch, and she closes her eyes, sinks into the couch, grateful for the smell of baking bread, for the sound of Anne calling her name from far off.

Hands around a warm mug, mint tea, steam rising, mixing with the scent of the baking bread. Warm kitchen, Anne's warm gaze on her.

"Now," Anne says. "Better?"

"Still woozy," Amelia says. "I guess I overheated; this heavy jacket, this sweater. How long was I out?"

"A few seconds. Not even a minute. Do you want a doctor? Want to go to the hospital?"

"No . . . no . . . I'm okay." She takes a small sip from the heavy pottery mug.

"Want to tell me what's going on, then?"

"What? Nothing."

"You don't seem too surprised at having passed out on my doorstep, is all." Anne looks at her, kind eyes, set mouth. She must know.

Anne is the last person she should tell. But she already knows. Amelia can see it in her face. She knows.

Anne says, "You aren't using again, are you? After all this time—"

"No! No. Look. Okay. The thing is, Anne. The thing is . . . I'm pregnant."

A nod, lips drawn. Another small nod. "Yes, well, that would explain it. Healthy young girls don't just go falling into a faint for no reason."

"I suppose not, no."

"So, a baby. Well, that's"—something Anne can't do; something Anne wants, has wanted for years—". . . that's wonderful, honey. Wonderful. And Gerrit must be so happy, too. Proud."

"Proud, yes. Gerrit is proud, happy. He's happy."

Quick sharp movements as Anne sets her tea mug into the sink, wipes down the counter, brushes her hair from her eyes. Quick darting glances, to her hands, the clock, the window. To Amelia's belly, back to her own hands.

"A baby. Well, Amelia, that's wonderful. I'm happy for you. I am. Happy. And if you need anything . . ."

"Yes, thank you."

"Okay, well if you're feeling better . . ."

"Right. Okay, so thanks."

The air is cooler in the hallway, the smell of baking bread fainter as Anne closes the door behind her. Amelia walks down one floor to her and Gerrit's apartment. So Anne knows. And then Steve will know.

She shoves through the apartment door, finds Gerrit at the table, piles of legal-sized paper before him, his perpetual scowl. He grunts his greeting, turns back to the papers.

She drops the bag of food on the table. "I passed out in front of Anne, so I had to tell her about the baby. She knows now." She goes to the bathroom, pulls the door closed behind her, draws a bath. Let him chew over that. Let him figure out what's next.

⊞

Gerrit opens the bathroom door and hovers in the doorway, nervous. She said it was too soon to tell anyone—that they had to wait until thirteen weeks to tell anyone—and it's still just nine weeks and yet she's gone and told Anne.

Anne, of all people—the one person it would hurt and that's where she starts.

Her body is long in the water, pink tips of nipples a blush of color in a field of white. Only the smallest of changes to be seen yet, and only then if you really know her body like he does. Her breasts have gotten fuller. Her angles and edges are starting to soften.

"You're starting to soften, Amelia. Your body. You're changing."

"Close the door. There's a draft."

"There's no belly yet, but your breasts, you can see it in your breasts. Softer, yes. You look soft."

She closes her eyes, ears beneath the surface, shutting him out. Her body is open and floating, as if he weren't there. After all these years he has become like the furniture to her, like the walls. She can strip down in front of him, bathe, shit. It means nothing. It's not intimacy. It's something duller than intimacy. It's habit. It's comfort borne on the steady buildup of days, sharing the same space, but in body only.

"You don't love me, Amelia," he says, and her eyes pop open, her lips twist. A sigh and she sits up, water streaming from her head and shoulders.

"I do," she says. "You know I do."

"You love me like a brother, like an uncle."

"Yes. I love you."

You love me like your ankles, he thinks. *Like your collarbones, your ears. You love me as you love the things you need and never think of.* "So you told Anne. I thought we were waiting a few more weeks."

"I passed out on her doorstep. I kind of had to say something."

"How did she take it?"

"Yes, I'm fine, thanks. Did you miss the part where I passed out?"

He closes the door and sinks down against it to the floor. "Are you okay?"

"Anne took it okay. As well as she could have, you know?"

"That must have been terrible for her," Gerrit says. "The miscarriages."

Amelia shifts in the deep old claw-foot tub, moving toward him, tipping those slim shoulders out, hanging one arm over the edge, water dripping to pool on the tiles beneath her hand. "Yeah," she says quietly. "But it's Anne. She took it okay, you know?" She shrugs, slides back into the tub, all the way under the water, eyes closed. He watches her, watches the water rock her gently back and forth, waits for her to surface.

She breaks through and comes suddenly to stand, swaying in the old porcelain tub. The water pours off her body, the fading light of day from the window behind her. She looks like she might take off, float up and out the window, the light behind her like it is, her eyes wild.

"Amelia," he says, standing to reach for her. Her wet skin slips from his grasp as she steps from the tub and goes to the window, naked and dripping.

"I think it's a boy," she says. Her eyes in the soft light coming on dusk are huge and luminous things. "A boy,

I think." She turns her back to him, looks out the window. Her shoulder blades are sharp as knives, jutting out at him, fending him off.

⊞

Amelia settles into the small couch and takes up her knitting. Mittens, pale green merino unraveled from a thrifted ski cap. She was making them for herself, but she's thinking now maybe she should give them to Anne. Anne loves green, and Amelia already has two pairs of mittens. And the way she's feeling lately—always too warm where it used to be she was perpetually cold—she's wondering if she'll ever need mittens again. Hands like hot water bottles. Side effect, she supposes, of all those chemical reactions going off in her belly all day and night. Heat given off by the body at work, by the building of another body. So the mittens will be for Anne, if that's not too perverse.

Amelia knits on the couch and Gerrit's gone back to scowling at legal papers, night now fallen outside. She hears Anne and Steve's voices, muffled by the ceiling and the distance, but there and recognizable. The sound of their door opening and closing, feet on the stairs, and here it comes: she can picture Steve lifting his hand to the door, then a pause, and here it is now, the knocking, a soft rapping on their door, and Gerrit says, "Come in."

The door pushes slowly open. Steve is in the doorway, looking at Amelia, his eyes full, his face full with what he now knows. Steve a quivering arrow in the doorway, poised to shoot; Steve vibrating with everything he's not saying.

Gerrit says, "So Anne told you?"

Steve sighs but the tension doesn't ease in his arms, in his legs, in the trembling of his hands, and he turns to Gerrit, says, "Yes. Congratulations." He smiles a tense smile at Gerrit and Gerrit smiles back, a big smile, a triumphant grin of a smile. Steve is nodding and trembling still and "Yes, a baby. That's just great, you guys" and Amelia rooted to the couch and wanting to sink into it, wanting to be gone, to be anywhere but there; or wanting Steve to grab her up into his arms. Wanting Steve to grab her and run out the door and down the stairs, the two of them running together, far away from the squat, from Anne and Gerrit. Wanting Steve to take her away, to tell her he's so happy, to tell her he loves her, loves Amelia, loves the baby, their baby.

He moves, heavy feet, heavy limbs, Frankenstein walk across the kitchen. Slaps Gerrit on the back, a forced chuckle. Can't Gerrit see it? Can't he see how Steve is acting? Steve turns to face Amelia, and the tension falls away, the forced grin dissolving into grief, real grief on his face, and he goes to Amelia, drops to his knees at her feet. "A baby," he says. "How wonderful, Amelia." He speaks these words, his back to Gerrit, but his face is saying it is anything but wonderful. Or that it is wonderful and terrible, all at once, which is exactly what it is. Wonderful and terrible. An awesome awful thing, this baby. He rests those big warm hands on her belly and he looks at her with his face open and grieving, and his mouth forms a silent shape: "Mine?"

Amelia nods, her hands over his hands, pressing his warmth into her belly, into their baby, and then Steve is standing, leaving, weeping fat silent tears, and he's gone, out the door, down the stairs, the heavy door to the street swinging open and slamming shut and Steve is gone.

"Taking it hard," Gerrit says. "What with him and Anne not being able to. I was afraid of that."

"Yes," Amelia says. "Me, too. I was afraid of that, too." She follows Steve in her mind, outside, down the street. Going who knows where, alone. Upstairs, Anne is shifting chairs around. Slamming pots into the sink. Moving furniture around her losses.

⊞

Amelia hadn't wanted to hurt anyone. After that first time with Steve in the community room she told him they couldn't do it again, that it was wrong, that people they cared about could get hurt. She tried to do the right thing. Kind of. But then Steve's hand would brush against hers as they passed on the stairs, or they would be working together in a tight space and she would feel the heat coming off his body. He would look at her with those dark eyes. Soon they were meeting in the basement, meeting on the roof, rutting like rats in the darkest corners they could find. Hiding, stifling cries, smothering moans. They got bolder as time went on, groping in the hallways, daring to bite, to scratch, to leave a mark. Hungry, always hungry and craving.

The guilt each time Anne smiled at her or said something kind: that wasn't strong enough to stop it. The guilt each time Gerrit spoke Steve's name, the awkwardness each time she saw them together: that was nothing compared to the hunger she felt. It was love. True love! How could she stop such a thing? Why would she want to?

Amelia wanted to run away with Steve, to be out in the open in the light of day; to lie in a bed with him, to stay there all night and wake up together, naked in the daylight; and that's when he said enough is enough. That's when he said it had to end, that it was over. One last time, but then it's over. And then it was over. And then her period not coming and now—now the baby.

Maybe she should have told Steve sooner, told him before she told Gerrit. But she knew, didn't she? She knew all along what his answer would have been, if Gerrit hadn't already been lined up to slide into the daddy role. He chose Anne when he ended things, and that was that. Steve won't be moved. When he wanted her, he had her. When he ended it, it was ended. Steve won't be moved.

"Do you love me?" Amelia asked when he was ending it.

"I love Anne," he said.

"Yes, but do you love me?"

"I love Anne."

"But me?"

"No, Amelia," he said. "Not like you need me to."

⊞

Beer and tequila, then just tequila, and tequila makes him mean and stupid, but fuck it. Steve's wallet's gone empty so he digs in his pockets for change and he's only got sixty-three cents and two subway tokens and he doesn't know anyone in here tonight. When you want to drink alone the place is like a goddamn high school reunion, but need someone to buy you a round and you don't know a soul.

He slides off the barstool, just a stumble, he's fine, and the little bartender in her little black tank top, pale arms with their too-new tattoos, she gives him a look and says, "You alright there, hon?" Hon, she calls him, like she didn't just refuse him a buyback that he really had coming. Hon, like she thinks she's some wised-up old-timer local broad and not some kid barely out of college *que todavia huele a avion y maleta.* He leans over the bar, close to her face as she'll let him get, which isn't all that close, and says, real slow so even her white ass can get the gist, "*Me cago en la puta leche de tu goddamn puta madre,* little girl," and he stumbles shambles shuffles out onto the street, and the moon is fat over the Con Ed clock tower and it's laughing at old Steve, a father at last.

There's a guy walking a dog and the dog looks at Steve with these big soulful eyes like he understands his pain, one dog to another, and Steve drops down to embrace the shaggy mutt and the guy—a short dude in a too-big parka—says, "Get your hands off my dog!" Steve hugs the dog tighter and it starts to whine and the guy says, "Get off!" and shoves Steve's shoulder and Steve tries to kick out at the guy while still holding on to the dog and the guy hauls off and kicks Steve full in the face. Direct hit, a good one, goddammit. Flash of white, flash of black, then hot hot heat and all that booze burning up and out onto the sidewalk and Steve goes down in a puddle of his own puke and blood. *Hijo de . . .*

The guy and the dog run away and Steve's lying on the sidewalk with a bloodied mouth and the stink of puke and tequila on him, staring up at the sky. *Oh it's a hell of a world you're coming into, baby, and you've got one hell of a daddy. I'm sorry for it.* He fishes in his pocket for his smokes and his Zippo and he must not have tightened it enough when he was messing with it in the bar because the lighter fluid's seeped out into his jeans pocket. He takes the lighter out and shakes it over himself, what little fluid didn't already soak into his jeans raining down on him. He's flammable now. He should light this shit up, have done with it like an old Buddhist monk. Go to flames right here on Seventh Street. But he can't because his fucking lighter is empty. And he laughs and cries because he can't set himself on fire so he might as well go home.

⊞

Anne feels the pressure build up behind her eyes so strong she thinks she might be sick. Steve is drunk again. And even so, doesn't she go downstairs when he stands on the sidewalk bellowing her name? Doesn't she wince an apology to José on night watch as he helps her haul Steve— all six feet two inches of him, bloody-nosed, stinking of beer and tequila and, inexplicably, kerosene—up the four flights of stairs? And then she says, "I've got it from here. Thank you. Really," to José and she smiles and closes the door, Steve leaning all his weight against her, and she lets go. She steps away and lets him fall to the floor. All six feet two inches of him, all two hundred however many pounds of him, down to the floor. He's crawling toward the bedroom but she says, "No. The couch. You get your sorry drunk ass to the couch." And he crawls to the couch.

Maybe that's cruel. He's broken. The news about Amelia's baby, Gerrit and Amelia's baby, has broken him. Of course it has. Gerrit getting what Steve wants, what Anne wasn't able to give him. So he went out. He got drunk.

But he should have stayed home with her. This is something they're supposed to be walking through together. It was the same with the miscarriages, the way he pulled away from her, the way he wallowed in his own pain, like it was greater than hers—like it was even close to equal to hers! He can't begin to comprehend those losses. He can't begin to grasp what it is to bleed a baby out of your body. Four times! Four babies loved, and then gone. He knows only the fact of the losses. Anne, she knows the way the blood felt, the way it smelled. She knows the rubbery strength of the egg sac from the third baby. She held it in her hands after she passed it. It was warm and slick with blood. And empty.

She can't stomach the thought of him lying in bed next to her, stinking and sweating like that, moaning and crying. Laughing. It's the laughing mixed in with the crying that gets her. It's pathetic. Pathetic and weak. She closes herself in the bedroom. She leans against the door, listening. He's restless out there. He's going to break the couch with all that tossing around. Then a big thump, a groan. "Annie! Shit!" and silence. She peeks out the bedroom door and sure enough he's passed out on the floor. She goes to him; she stands over him. She resists the urge to kick.

13

It's coming on six o'clock and the sun long set, snow beginning to fall, easing all the hard edges as Amelia walks home. And then she's inside and there is Steve coming down the stairs. She hasn't seen him in two days—since he found out about the baby—and she finds she's surprised that he looks the same, that the news hasn't somehow transformed him. He sits down on the stairs, hanging his head, and that thick black hair falls across his face. The loose curls cast shadows like waves along the scarred plaster wall, waves that rise and fall with his breath, tremble as he trembles.

"Why didn't you tell me?" he says. "Why did I have to find out from Anne? Do you know what that was like? Finding out from Anne?"

"I wasn't even sure I was going to keep him. And then I knew I had to keep him—that I want to keep him—and then . . ."

"You should have told me."

"Yes."

"Him?"

"Just a feeling. That it's a boy. I have boy feelings." She sits down next to him on the step, squeezing herself into the small space between his body and the banister. His big, warm body. "Let's go to the roof," she says. "To the basement. Somewhere we can talk in private."

"No." He stands and she feels the loss of him, of his warmth, in a panicked animal way. She grabs for him, catching the hem of his coat.

"Don't go," she says.

"I don't know what to say to you. We can't talk yet."

"When?"

"Soon. We'll talk soon." He's moving again, headed down the stairs to wherever it is he's going.

"Steve!" It comes out choked and desperate. He turns and looks at her, and she is aware of the shape she's making, of the small huddled thing she is becoming, crouching on the stairs, clinging to the banister. Desperate animal. Little mouse, little panicked thing.

He sees her like that, and she can't tell if it is pity moving across his face, or love. He climbs back to her; he lifts her up. "Gerrit's at the legal committee meeting?" he asks, and she nods her head yes. He says, "Anne, too," and carries her to her apartment, opens the door. He carries her to her bedroom and lays her down. "In a bed, for once," he murmurs. His kisses are hard and urgent, his hands rough over her body. Amelia wraps her arms around him, trying to pull him down to her. She feels his broad back, feels the heat of his skin through his shirt.

He pushes away and crosses the room to the window, his forehead pressed to the glass. "I can't do this." And then he's out of her room, rushing through the apartment. She races behind him, but he's faster, and as the apartment door falls closed between them she hears him sob, and it's the lowest, saddest sound in the world.

⊞

Amelia is chopping onions. The white chunks tumble away from their rings; one slice, another, another. Her tears fall to the cutting board. She'll cook them into the soup, along with the chopped onions.

She hears Gerrit open the door behind her, stomping his boots at the threshold. "Freezing out there," he says. He brings a cold draft with him, and the scent of snow on wool. She hears the sound of the couch accepting his weight; the sound of his boots clunking off; the sound of him groaning and stretching. Outside their apartment, she hears footsteps going up the stairs; the sound of a door opening; Anne's voice, then Steve's in greeting. She reaches for another onion.

Steve carried her to her bed, he laid her down, and then he ran from her. She is carrying his baby and he ran from her and now she can hear him right above her head, making dinner for his wife. Amelia is making soup, which she will feed to Gerrit, whom she does not love, while upstairs Steve cooks for Anne, whom he loves. Steve, who does not love Amelia.

Maybe Amelia and Gerrit do belong together, she thinks, if only because they are both unloved.

Gerrit comes up behind her, hands on her shoulders. He kisses her cheek, the rasp of his stubble on her skin intolerable. He swipes at her tears with his fingers. "I've never seen an onion get to you like that before."

She shrugs his hands away. "Every onion is different."

Gerrit is getting bolder, more demanding. Ever since the baby. Ever since he swooped in to save the day again. He's claimed Amelia and the baby both, and he reinforces that claim every chance he gets. These touches, these kisses, like they're a homey little couple in some fifties TV show. He comes to her bed every night now. Hot breath at the back of her neck, insistent hands.

She should have put a stop to it years ago, but it hadn't seemed like too much to ask. He had given her so much, and all he took in return was to touch her sometimes. Shyly, sweetly. And he was gentle. She would lie still and close her eyes, and it wasn't bad; sometimes it felt pretty good, really. It wasn't too much to ask. But it's every night now, and his touch is getting stronger, bolder. He wants her to turn toward him. He wants her to touch him, too. She can feel it. He's changing the rules on her.

"The engineer came through this morning, the one Irving hired," Gerrit says. "Steve and I showed him around."

"Yeah," she says. "You told me."

"Right, well, nice guy. He said the building looks good. Says we're mostly up to code."

Onions finished. She starts on the carrots, fat orange

coins falling from the knife. One piece goes skittering across the counter and Gerrit snatches it up, pops it into his mouth.

"He gave us a list, things to take care of that the city inspectors might make noise about." There's a fleck of carrot at the corner of his mouth. His pointy little tongue darts out at it, pink as a worm.

Carrots slide from the cutting board to the bowl already half filled by the onions. The celery now. Overhead there's the sound of water running, the sound of the oven door opening and closing, the sound of glasses. Anne's voice high, Steve's voice low in response.

"Steve didn't turn up at the meeting today," Gerrit says, head cocked toward the voices upstairs.

"Weird," she says. "Not like him."

"No. We were all a little worried, but it sounds like he's okay."

"I didn't see him around here."

"Hunh. Yeah, well . . ."

"Dinner in about an hour," she says.

"We're eating late tonight."

"Yeah. I got distracted. There's apples if you're hungry." The onions, the carrots, the celery into the soup pot, where the oil's already hot and ready. She stirs the vegetables in the heavy pot, watching them go glossy with the oil and the heat.

Upstairs the stereo hums on. Salsa. "They need to turn that shit down," she says. "Too damn loud." She cries harder, though she swore she would not.

Gerrit turns her away from the stove and into his arms, pulling her tight against him, swaying to the music.

"This is how I know everything will be okay," he says. "This, right here." He closes his arms tighter around her, humming softly in her ear.

Upstairs, the song seems to go on forever.

⊞

Anne's skin glows pearly white in the streetlight filtering through the window. Asleep on her side, covers thrown off and her bare hip rises like a nearer moon and it's all Steve can do not to throw himself across it, to weep for forgiveness, to weep for mercy.

He is an ape. He knows he is an ape, because the simple fact of Amelia carrying his child has every cell south of his brain wanting to ditch sweet barren Anne for the good breeder. Survival of the species. Which hardly makes him less culpable.

But it's too easy with Amelia. When she started to talk about love and running away together and he ended it, she cried but she took it. She nodded and swallowed it, like she'd never expected more from him. From anyone. And now today he picks her up and carries her off to bed like a caveman and she goes along with it, just like she always went along with it when he'd fuck her against the basement wall or bend her over the stair rail or push her head down to suck him off on the roof like some back-alley whore.

She looked so lost, huddled on the stairs. When she called out his name, her voice breaking, her vulnerability inflamed him. Caveman. Ape. And not one word from her about him helping with the baby in any way or even acknowledging it's his. It's almost criminal, the way she lets him treat her. The kindest thing would be to stay away from her.

But it's his baby. His *baby*, and Gerrit's letting everyone believe he's the father. *So what's it gonna be, Estefan?* A baby and a lifetime staring at the sweet face of a girl you don't love, a girl who expects nothing from you or anyone else? And all your friends hating you for what you did to Anne and Gerrit and you hating yourself, too, until you drink yourself into an early grave after being a shitty-ass dad to the poor kid who didn't ask to be born into the mess you've made for it. Or no baby, ever, and the woman you love, the wife you chose and then cheated on, growing fat and bitter, choking on her childlessness and hating you for it. And watching your best friend raise your child, watching that child—a boy, she thinks, a son!—watching your son call Gerrit Daddy. Watching that little Dutch bastard walk *your* kid to school, teach *your* kid to ride a bike.

Anne stirs in her sleep, her forehead pressing against his chest like she wants to burrow inside him. She sighs and her fingers scrabble against his skin.

It's Anne or the baby. If he chooses the baby, he might as well put a gun to Anne's head right now and pull the trigger. At least she'd die without pain that way, and he wouldn't have to see the betrayal on her face.

Perdóname. Perdóname, amor. Make it all okay. Oh, Annie, say it's all okay.

He didn't mean to speak out loud, but maybe he did. Or maybe they've just been together so long she heard it from where it got stuck in his throat, because she half wakes and threads her fingers through his. "You're crying," she says and that breaks him wide open. He pulls her close against him, whispers, "Bad dream," and pretends to drift back to sleep. Soon her breathing slows and deepens and he rolls away from her, looks to the window, where a single star's gotten lodged in the upper right corner.

Perdóname, mi niño. Forgive me, baby, for failing you before you're even born.

14

The last time Amelia's mother went away it was the middle of winter. Ten-year-old Amelia woke up and got herself dressed for school, like always. Made her own breakfast, like always, because her grandmother—a nurse—worked the early shift at the hospital. She poked her head into her mother's room on her way out to the bus stop to wake her up, let her know her breakfast was on the table, and instead of finding her mom asleep, hunched up into a ball beneath the quilt, blond hair a tangle over her face and that smell of booze and smoke and rot Amelia had come to associate with morning, there was just the bed stripped bare, empty dresser drawers, the closet door hanging open like a broken jaw, and she'd taken all her clothes and she was gone again.

There was some relief in it, because things were quieter, easier when her mother wasn't there. But quiet and easy doesn't mean better. Doesn't mean things were the way Amelia wanted them. Because she wanted her mom, of course. She wanted her to be there when she left for school, to be there when she came home. And sometimes she wasn't drunk, sometimes she wasn't passed out or taking Amelia's odd-jobs money. Sometimes Amelia came home from school and her mom was at the kitchen table with Grandma, drinking coffee, and she would smile and smooth Amelia's hair back from her forehead. Sometimes it was like that, exactly the way she wanted it to be. And those times almost made up for all the rest of it.

Her mom was gone only five months that last time. Not a long time at all, by her standards, but when she came home she was sick as hell, and not two months later she was dead. Ruined liver, ruined brain. Died in her own mother's arms as Grandma was helping her to the toilet. Just sat down and died. Like Elvis.

No matter how bad things got with her mother, Amelia loved her. Loved her desperately. And no matter how much Amelia fucks things up, her baby will love her. Amazing that a girl like Amelia, a girl who had nothing, who owes everything to Gerrit, could suddenly have something so huge, and all her own. Sweet babe. She's all he's got. She's going to be his whole damn world. She's determined to deserve his love, determined to do right by him, to be the person he'll need her to be.

⊞

Anne watches the white tiled walls streak past the car window as the Volvo barrels through the Holland Tunnel,

Ron's fingers twitching on the wheel, the talk radio he'd been blasting gone to static.

"We're underwater," Michael says, poking Anne's arm. She's sitting between the kids in the backseat, her feet perched on the center hump. Lara's already asleep in her car seat, damp little fingers resting on her belly. Michael's got his slight seven-year-old frame pressed up against Anne's side. She puts her arm around him and he nestles in close.

"I know it. They tunneled right under the river." The tunnel walls rush by. "Do you know which river?"

"The Hudson!"

"That's right. Okay, we'll cross over into New Jersey soon. Watch for the border sign." Any moment now they'll leave New York behind, heading toward the swamps of industrial Jersey and then pushing west, her trials in the city traded in for the softer complications of the Midwest. In her mind she sees Steve standing coatless in the middle of Thirteenth Street, watching the car drive away like he was some bad romance-movie hero. She shouldn't have looked back.

Michael presses his hands to the window, looking out intently. "Where is it? Now?"

"Soon, soon . . ."

His back is alive under her palm, his shoulder blades tensed, poised for flight.

"Now!" A thick blue stripe against the otherwise white wall. NEW YORK on one side, NEW JERSEY on the other. Almost as soon as they're upon it it's behind them.

"Mom!" Michael says. "Mom! You and Dad were in New Jersey and me and Aunt Anne and Lara were in New York! Just for a second, but we really were."

Cindy turns around and smiles. She wasn't paying attention. She has no idea what he's talking about. "Okay, sweetie."

"Aunt Anne, are you sad?" Lara says, half awake and looking at Anne through heavy-lidded eyes.

"Maybe a little, honey."

"You miss Uncle Steve," Michael says.

She smiles and snugs him closer. "I'm fine."

She brought Steve home for Christmas the first year they were together. They caught a Greyhound bus out of Port Authority, her, Steve, and Cindy. No Ron in the picture yet and Cindy as ragtag as any of them. They'd eaten peanut butter sandwiches out of Anne's backpack. They'd split a single can of Coke at a rest stop outside Stroudsburg. Anne and Steve had just opened their doomed first squat on Seventh and C, and they were full of hope, the boundless dumb optimism of youth. They'd leaned in close to each other as Cindy slept across the aisle. They'd whispered their plans. It was all possibility then. Real life, real action. Life without constraints.

There are no half measures at twenty-one, when time stretches out full and limitless, the momentum of the teen years still pushing like an insistent hand at your back. She threw her lot in with Steve, and with the squat. She never stopped to ask herself what she really wanted, what kind of life she hoped to have.

A life without constraints—that had been the goal. Her life does not feel free of constraints. Anne is not free. She doesn't know anyone who is. Maybe that's the kind of thing that can seem attainable only at twenty-one. Even the fiercest of anarchists lose their teeth to age.

That first wreck of a squat hadn't been bad enough to discourage them. It had been just enough of a taste to get them fired up to try again, to get it right the next time. The right building, the right people. And they did that. Dammit, they did it. So now what? Now that their great experiment, this small daily revolution of theirs, has just become her life, now that she knows it's no better to be defined by your home than to be defined by your marriage, your job, your sex.

She rests her head against Lara's car seat and closes her eyes. That must be the moment when they emerge from the tunnel. That must be the precise moment when they shuttle out the New Jersey side and onto that great rushing highway, because the world outside her closed eyes goes flooded with light. She squeezes them tight against it.

田

So Anne's left to spend Christmas without him. So, okay. Steve picked up some takeout *sancocho* and a bottle of Maker's Mark, with the idea of getting quietly drunk alone. It was a good idea, he supposes. He should have kept it to that. Instead, after he got drunk he went and collected Amelia and brought her upstairs. And now she's sprawled out next to him, her skin and the sheets smeared with grease and bits of meat because as he was fucking her in his sloppy bourbon-brained way he spotted the half-eaten *sancocho* and it had seemed like a good idea to pour it on her. And she'd let him. Which, well . . . there you have it.

She's got a gentle little swell to her belly already, the baby eager to announce himself. She runs a hand over her hip and smiles, holding up a palm slick with stew. "Let's go take a bath," she says. A bath together. What a cozy honeymoon. He grunts, rolls over, pretends to sleep, but she's pawing at him, clambering over him like a puppy. "Come on!"

"I like showers," he says.

"A shower, then," and she hops out of Anne's bed, pads naked through Anne's living room to the bathroom. And here goes Anne's husband following the twitching white globes of that little ass into the shower, half hard again already never mind the bourbon.

Amelia looks back over her shoulder, eyes quick and hungry. The hunger of youth. That's what first drew him in, what kept him coming back—Amelia's hunger. If Anne would just once look at him the way she used to, look at him with any kind of heat and need . . .

⊞

There wasn't much of a fuss between Anne and her mom when they arrived. It's about the kids now, of course. Lara wiggling like a puppy to get at her grandma, Michael excited but hanging back, shy, having not seen her in almost six months. Then Anne and Mom hugged, and there was instant relief, the familiarity of her mother's body against her own.

Now the kids are asleep and Ron feigned exhaustion and closed himself off in Cindy's old room, and it's Anne and Cindy and Mom in the kitchen just the way Anne wanted it to be. Mom warms up slices of blueberry pie and Cindy finds a tub of vanilla ice cream in the freezer.

"This is why it's so hard to get kids to go to sleep," Cindy says. "They're convinced grown-ups stay up late eating secret desserts."

"They'll get their fair share of pie and then some after Christmas dinner, I suppose," Mom says. She takes the three big wedges from the oven, and Cindy tops them with the ice cream. They do it without speaking, like it's something they do all the time. Their wordless ease with each other is new, or new to Anne. There's Mom and Cindy together and then there's Anne, the visitor. It's her own fault; she stayed away too long.

Oh, but Mom looks old. The crepy skin of an old woman, the trembling thin lips of an old woman.

Anne looks older, too. She could see it in the way her mother scanned her face when she walked through the door, in the way she placed a cool hand on Anne's cheek.

Mom sets a warm plate down in front of Anne, ice cream already starting to melt, the white running into the blue of the berries. It's a gorgeous mess. "Steve couldn't come with you, Annie?" she says.

Cindy sits silent, lips pressed shut. She was right when she suggested Anne come by herself to get some space; that's what Anne needs. Or it seemed like it, back in New York. Now Anne thinks about how Steve's absence here is also her own absence there, and she wonders how he'll fill it, what might creep into her life when she's left it unguarded.

"He had to work," Anne says. "And there's a lot going on with the building right now. It was going to be really hard for him to get away."

Mom takes a bite of pie, a flake of crust sticking to her upper lip. "Your sister's told me some of that. She sends the articles." She glances at Cindy. "They worry me."

"It's going to be okay, Mom."

"You could be homeless."

"She'll never be homeless, Mom," Cindy says. "She's always got a place with me. She knows that." She nudges Anne's leg with her own. "You know that, right?"

"I do." She does. It would be insufferable living under Ron and Cindy's roof, beholden to them, but it would be a roof. "And then Steve and I would find another place on our own. We'd be fine. Really." That's not entirely true. Where would they go? Where could they afford to go?

"You could come back home," Mom says, quietly, decidedly. "You can always come back here."

Anne tries to picture living in her childhood bedroom again, the faded lilac walls, the pilled purple bedspread. She could get a teaching job. She could have pie and ice cream with Mom every night.

"Steve, too," Mom says. "Of course Steve is welcome, too."

Is that not a given, that Anne would return home with her husband? But he isn't here now. She could slip back into her old life and it would be as if she'd never left home, as if she'd never met Steve at all. A middle-aged spinster schoolteacher, living with her mother in Akron, Ohio.

"Steve's a good man, Annie. He makes mistakes, maybe, but he's got a good heart." Mom swipes the last bit of blueberry from her plate and sucks it off her finger. "I've never said that to you before. I should have."

"Everyone makes mistakes," Anne says.

"Everyone does. That's right." Mom pats Anne's hand and stands to put her plate in the sink.

What did you tell her?! Anne mouths at Cindy, but Cindy shakes her head. Nothing. She didn't say a thing.

Everyone makes mistakes.

When they lost the first baby, Steve was sad but optimistic. Miscarriages happen, he said. It would be okay. Then they lost the second baby, and he got quieter. When they lost the third baby, then the fourth, Anne looked to him and he was gone. He turned his back on her, like she'd failed him. She thought she would leave him. She took her bag out of the hall closet early one morning and unzipped it. That was as far as she got. The bag was back in the closet, empty, when he woke up.

He's trying to make it right; she feels that. But the loneliness of the past year ghosts around her still. It pushes at the spaces between them and the spaces grow deeper, colder. She doesn't know how to find a way through it. She isn't sure what she'll find if she does.

15

New Year's Eve. Ninety-four giving way to ninety-five. Halfway through the decade now, the downward slope of the century. Gerrit stands alone, watching the party. Everyone from Thirteen House and Cat House is up on their rooftops, crossing back and forth from one roof to the other, drinking, singing, shouting down into the street. There is a new intensity to their togetherness. The two squats are a blended family now, brought closer by their shared fight.

All around them the rooftops are alive with the shadows of bodies, the echoes of voices. Amelia stands by the parapet, looking out over the city. Steve is a large, dark shape beside her. Gerrit hears Amelia's voice, cast low. He hears Steve rumble in return. They're standing close to each other, standing there together a long time now. She's been so shut down lately, so quiet. It's good to see her talking to someone, even if he'd rather it be him.

Anne stands in front of the fire they've built in a metal trash can. The firelight washes over her and she looks softer, younger than Gerrit has seen her look in a long time. Competent and quiet from the beginning, Anne has always worked with her head bent to it, slow and steady, dependable as rain. But lately her face has taken on the careworn, weathered look you see in old photos of pioneer women—a face incapable of surprise. She's passed from the plain-faced, fresh-scrubbed girl he first met on Steve's arm all those years ago to become something rougher and stronger.

But there she is now beside the fire—the Anne he remembers. Denise grabs her elbow and whispers something into her ear and Anne laughs, her head tipped back, mouth open, showing her strong white teeth. It's good to see her laughing. He hasn't seen much of Anne, apart from the endless committee meetings, since she found out about the baby. He hasn't seen much of Steve, either. Gerrit would have thought it would take more than a baby to separate them.

Steve lurches away from the parapet and into the firelight, his shadow blowing up huge and crazy—all wild hair and shoulders—across Anne and Denise. Gerrit catches Steve's eye and smiles. He's half-drunk, so likely there's a speech coming.

True to form, Steve clears his throat and squares his weight. "My friends," he booms. "My neighbors. We find ourselves here, gathered together at the end of another year."

And the friends, the neighbors, the squatters of Thirteen House and Cat House, draw in closer to him and to the fire, smiling at one another, knowing how Steve gets.

"Nineteen hundred and eighty-two, it all started," Steve intones, carnival-barker-like, warming into it. "The Wild West eighties, when crack was king. I never thought I'd be so nostalgic for the crackheads. Never thought I'd miss the crunch of those little vials under my boots. Crunchy like thin ice on the sidewalk each morning. Crunchy like cutting a fresh path through old snow. Never thought I'd miss that, but we didn't know at the time the way those crackheads were shielding us. The way they were insulating us against the rising yuppie tide. The hungry real estate ghost."

He throws his arms wide, throws his head back and howls. It's a thin sound, from the lungs, not the gut—not so much a howl as the memory of a howl. "I wrote something. A little something to mark where we find ourselves tonight." He produces a crumpled piece of loose-leaf paper from his pocket.

All this sentimentality makes Gerrit queasy—the way Steve will pull out a piece of paper and read these things, so unashamed. He never knows where to look while Steve is reading, never knows what to say to him when he's done.

"This is New York!" Steve shouts. "What's left of it. Bitch Manhattan gone over to money, gone over like a whore. Rolled over, pimpled ass up and bruises on her mottled old thighs. Freaks and artists into the river! Smooth these streets over, clean up the dirt. Crack was king but there's a new king in town."

Gerrit looks over at Amelia, hanging back at the parapet, eyes fixed on Steve.

"End of the century, baby, and our time is up. This ain't
the Lower East Side anymore. It's the East Village, home to
trust-fund punks and the edgier stockbrokers, all so proud
of their geographical daring. Living their new downtown
lives like they think downtown lives should be lived, but
cleaner, faster, sleeker. The tenement charm without the
tenement life.

"No more slow-smile leatherboys with unironic tattoos.
No more bearded communist daddies with soft bellies and
hard eyes. Good-bye to the forgotten guitar genius with
his thin-armed jangling walk and his rock 'n' roll banter in
his claustrophobic top-floor studio. Good-bye to the ag-
ing actor with his whispered Buddhist chants, perched on
a stool day after day in the caged basement vestibule of his
subterranean St. Marks castle. Good-bye to the miracu-
lously middle-aged junkie with her sweet nodding head
and her needled arms. Money's pushing into the Lower
East Side. All-consuming consumer class. Into the river,
freaks and artists. Rents are rising, prices rising. We're all
going condo and to hell with the cost."

He sways unsteadily on his feet. The paper trembles in
the firelight, and for a moment Gerrit thinks Steve is about
to let it fall into the flames. No one speaks; no one moves.
Steve takes a pull off a whiskey bottle and continues.

"Wait!" he reads. "But not yet, not just yet. There's still
a foothold here, a crack to work your fingers into there.
Hang on, hang on. It's not over yet. Pigeon shit and

garbage and soot, sure, but where else does the light look like this, the water towers rounding out into the sky coming on dusk?

"This is our city. Go ahead and love her, because we've still got a chance. Our city; our beloved, hated city. From up here on the rooftop, look down and the streets are a pulsing, living thing. From up here, can you tell anyone apart? The street-smart braided hippie; the practiced young punk; the Wall Streeter, slumming on Avenue B? It's just people, all just people flowing along down the street. Street music. Music of feet and cars and the underscore of the subway rumbling beneath those feet and aren't we all here, now, all of us in it together?"

He pauses, arm raised high as if to punctuate the point, but then the point goes lost and he stands there, big and wavering, flickering like the flames of the fire. His hand drops, the paper limp in his fist.

"The beginning of a new year and who's to say if we'll all be here together come next New Year's . . . We might not win this one. I'm . . . it's getting so I'm just not sure how the cards will fall."

He goes quiet, his face closed and dark, and he takes a hard swig off his bottle and stares down into the fire. Steve in typical form might have spat that mouthful of whiskey into the flames, but he swallows and rocks back on his heels. Everyone waits a moment or two, but he doesn't say more. There's a collective embarrassment. Gerrit feels it all around him. Urgent sips off bottles and hungry drags off cigarettes. They're pretending to hope, pretending everything will be okay, but the pretending is starting to wear thin, the hope starting to wear out.

It's coming on midnight. Voices from a party across the street float over the rooftops. The blinds are up, windows open to the cold—the room's all lit up and they've packed the place with bodies. They've started the countdown, they're chanting down the seconds. The good people of Thirteen House and Cat House, Gerrit's people, gather at the parapet, gazing down into that party, hushed and listening to the countdown. *Six . . . five . . . four . . . three . . .* Gerrit draws close behind Amelia and reaches for her hand *. . . two . . . one . . .*

Fireworks. Gunshots. Shouts from the apartments, and from the streets below. On the rooftop of Thirteen House they crane their heads, hungry for glimpses of the party across the street, bright bodies of hope moving past the windows, kissing, shouting, singing their way into a new year.

"Aren't we all here, now, all of us in it together?" Amelia whispers.

16

It's five gray days into the new year, and the hopes of New Year's Eve are already in tatters. Gerrit can see it in the faces around him—the dull realization that change has not come. They have not been transformed. They will not be transformed.

Steve walks beside him, the habitual cigarette in the corner of his mouth like he's some movie gangster hero. He shakes another loose from the pack and offers it to Gerrit, then lights it for him. His Zippo clinks open and the nauseating sweet stink of the lighter fluid hits Gerrit's nose, turns his stomach a half turn, only to be forgotten with that first drag.

They pass the Mexican place on Eleventh and A; it's shuttered and dark. "I heard the rent went up first of the year," Gerrit says.

"Getting so a body can't eat around here," Steve says. "Getting so there's nothing to be had but sushi and top-shelf booze. It's like we engineered our own extinction."

Gerrit draws on his cigarette. "It's been a long time coming. It was already happening when I got here in eighty-two."

"Nah, man. The Tompkins riot. That was the tipping point. That was when everything started to change," Steve says.

"Things were already changing or the riot wouldn't have happened at all."

Gerrit remembers that hot August night, 1988, police with their badges covered, marauding gangs of cops, stampeding police horses. The police rushing through the streets in mobs, grabbing random people, clubbing them, handcuffing them. Passersby, gawkers, people just trying to get home knocked down, bloodied.

It wasn't that Gerrit couldn't have imagined such a thing possible—he'd survived as much in Amsterdam: he'd been shot by water cannons, been beaten and choked by billy clubs, been pushed off barricade piles and dragged by his feet. He'd been tear-gassed, he'd been jumped, he'd been bombed. But that was then, and that was there. That was limited to the squatters and the police; an action and a response, no civilian casualties. In Amsterdam, the attacks were precise. Brutal, but precise. There was a certain fairness to it. As a *kraker*, you knew going in what you were risking.

The night of the Tompkins riot, there was no such fairness. Instead, random brutality. Mob mentality. And not by the people, but by the police. These things weren't supposed to happen in America—least of all in the People's Republic of Tompkins Square Park.

We don't live in a police state, as long as you do what you're told.

Gerrit remembers a man in a bathrobe and slippers, pulled from his bed by the noise, maybe, standing in the middle of Avenue A, blood pouring from a gash in his forehead. He remembers a girl, about twenty years old, walking dazed through the crowd, wringing her hands, crying, her shirt torn to rags. He remembers a cop grabbing him by the shoulder, raising his nightstick over his head, and as Gerrit braced himself for the impact someone threw a bottle. It smashed just past Gerrit's feet and, the cop distracted, Gerrit slipped away. He ran straight for Thirteen House and found Steve running back home, too.

Police helicopters buzzed and whirred overhead, searchlights staining the rooftops all around them. Gerrit and Steve hugged close to the buildings as they ran, not wanting to be spotted running from the scene, not daring to take the time to walk. When they reached the building, they were the last ones home. Barricades slammed into place and they hunkered down, waiting for the police to come clear the neighborhood, waiting for the battering ram. They didn't come for them that night, but they're coming for them now. It was only a matter of time.

Rick is waiting for them at a basement bar, the Blue and Gold. He's deep in a booth, beer in front of him. He's got his back to the wall, front and back doors both in his line of sight. It's a cop's habit, but a fugitive's, too: Always keep your back to a wall. Always keep entrances and exits in sight. That way they can't surprise you. That way, you can't ever say you didn't see it coming.

"Beer?" Steve asks and Gerrit nods.

Gerrit sits across from Rick, pressing his own back to the wall. "And here we are with a cop," Gerrit says as Steve sits next to him, setting two beers down.

"We were talking just now about the Tompkins riot," Steve says.

"Yeah. I wasn't there that night. And that's all I have to say about that." Rick takes a deep gulp from his glass. Big hands, scarred knuckles. He shifts in his seat, revealing a revolver strapped to his hip: worn black leather holster, police issue; heavy gun, dumb black metal. Gerrit wonders how many times it's been pointed at someone out on the street, how many times it's been fired outside of a practice range. Rick is Steve's friend. Gerrit accepts him because of that, but he doesn't know the man.

"Now, I found something out," Rick's saying, "and maybe you're not going to be so happy to hear it, but you should know." He digs in his pants pocket and comes out with a folded newspaper clipping. He opens it and tosses it onto the table. "This guy"—he taps a thick fingertip on the grainy black-and-white photo at the top of the article: DEVELOPER BIANO'S 20K TO GIULIANI CAMPAIGN OVER LEGAL LIMIT—"Donald Biano. Major Giuliani contributor. Got his hand right in the big guy's pocket. They've got your buildings marked for him. They're talking privatization. The plan on the table is to turn your buildings into low-income housing, which Biano's group would manage. There's all kinds of tax credits wrapped up in that. And then in a few years the ownership reverts to Biano and he gets to jack the rents up to market rate."

"Shit," Steve says, rubbing his eyes. "Shit, shit, shit."

"This isn't a surprise," Gerrit says. "We could have guessed this."

"But guessing and knowing are two different things," Steve says. "They won't back down. It's more than the idea of what the buildings are worth. It's real money. Real right-now money."

"Biano's no joke," Rick says. "Some shit you've found yourselves in. I'm sorry for it. I am. I wish I could do more."

"You're doing plenty," Steve says. "At least we know what we're up against."

"For what it's worth," Rick says.

"For what it's worth."

Outside the bar, it's pushing toward evening. Through the basement window, Gerrit sees the feet and legs of the passersby. So many people coming and going, moving through their own lives, their own problems and fears. All of them living together in these few square blocks, and what do any of them know about the lives around them? They're alone, all of them, and there's nothing to be done. No help for it.

There will be no last-minute reprieve, barring a miracle in court. With the big money come the big guns. He'll go down screaming; he'll go down throwing bricks. But he'll go down. He knows it.

⊞

"You don't really need me here," Anne says. "You've got this covered." She and Ben are hunting for the clog that's got the toilets backed up on the south side of the building again. They started at the top in Ben's bathroom and worked their way down the line to Marlowe's on the ground floor with no luck, no simple snaking the clog out. So here they are in the basement, where the stack vent meets the sewer line.

"What if I just like the company?" Ben says. He grimaces as he pries open the junction cover on the soil stack. One of the original members of Thirteen House was in charge of the early plumbing projects because his father was a plumber. When they tied in to the sewer line and ran the pipes through to the apartments back in eighty-four, he headed up the show, acting like he knew exactly what he was doing. He didn't. When he moved out in eighty-seven, he left the botched plumbing behind as his legacy. They've had to cut through the walls behind the toilets so many times to find the clogs in the soil stack that no one even bothers to fix the drywall anymore.

"What we really need to do is rip this all out and do it right," Anne says.

Ben grunts. They don't have the money for that kind of project, or the time. The city inspectors could come through any day. This is not the time to start tearing out all the plumbing.

"Here's your clog," Ben says, and fishes out a big, gooey, stinking thing bound together by hair. "Jesus. It looks like someone flushed a cat."

"Wow," she says. "That's the worst one yet." In the early days that sight would have pushed her right over the edge.

But pipes get clogged. Toilets get backed up. This is the world. Things break and you fix them. She holds a bucket out to Ben so he can drop the clog in.

"Ben, man, there was shit water coming up out of my bathtub drain." Marlowe walks in with three mugs of coffee.

"One of those cups better be for me," Ben says.

"Yeah, one's for you." Marlowe hands a mug to Anne and sits down against the wall. "You two need a hand?"

"Nah. Just about done here." Ben nudges the bucket with the clog toward Marlowe. "Check that beast out."

"Oh fuck, man! Get that thing away from me!" Marlowe jumps up, sloshing coffee on his pants. "That's not cool." He edges toward the bucket and peers in. "Is that a cat?"

"I've got it from here," Anne says. "Go get your coffee." Ben soaps up at the utility sink while Anne eases the pipe back into place and tightens the fitting. It grips nicely, and there's a satisfaction to that. Her hands have become capable hands. She turns the knob on the main shutoff and listens as water bangs through the pipes, the faucets they had everyone leave open hissing and sputtering to life. Someone upstairs cheers.

"Let's hope they don't all try to flush at once," Ben says.

Anne sits down on the couch and puts her feet up on the rickety coffee table. Steve will be home soon from that meeting with Rick. Or maybe he won't. He's been hard to pin down since she got back from Ohio. Hyperattentive one minute, completely gone the next. Marlowe sits down next to her, and Ben takes the armchair to the left of the couch. They sit like that, quiet, companionable.

"The trip back home was good?" Marlowe says.

"It was. Yeah." She smiles, takes a sip of coffee. She almost asks if he went anywhere for the holiday, out of some long-ingrained reflex, but where would he have gone? Marlowe doesn't have anywhere else to go. Before Thirteen House, he was a marine and then a drunk and then a crackhead. He moved into Thirteen House five years ago, got clean, got sober. He took to the squat like he was joining a rebel army. "It was good to get out of the city for a little while," she says, "to get some space." Some space. The space had been good, so good it got her thinking that maybe she wanted more of it. But then she would think of Steve and she wanted him, too.

"Space," Ben says. "I've got plenty of that."

"Mmm-hmmm," Marlowe says.

Ben and Marlowe both alone, both wishing it were different. Everyone wants to be loved. Isn't that the most basic, the most obvious thing she could possibly say? But it's true. It's true. Everyone wants to be loved. *I love you guys*, she thinks. *I love you both so damn much.* But she doesn't say it. They sit there in silence, the three of them, drinking coffee.

She came back from Ohio to a house buzzing with Amelia's growing pregnancy. They're all hungry for hope, and they've latched on to this baby as their good omen. Anne sees Amelia, sees that rounding belly, and she's surprisingly okay with it. Not completely okay, but it's a dull ache she feels, not the knife to the gut it was at first. A dull ache is manageable. It seeps into the fabric of her days. It occurs to her that there have been other dull aches in the background all along. She has borne them, scarcely registering them. She can bear one more. The dull aches are the symptom, not the disease. It's the disease that needs to be addressed, but first she needs to name it.

Its name is not baby. Its name is not Steve—this, too, surprises her.

If the city takes Thirteen House, they will be setting Anne free. She loves this house; she loves its people, her people. And she wants to leave them. She wants to break out of this "life without constraints." There is no step up within this life; there is no moving forward. There is nothing but the clinging and scrabbling to maintain their impoverished status quo.

Endless revolution with no development is meaningless. They're trapped in a cycle here. No—Anne feels trapped. She will not speak for the others.

The air in the basement still smells faintly of shit, and she realizes none of them have bothered to get rid of the clump in the bucket. The cumulative hair and nail clippings and crap from all the bodies on the south side of the house, bonded together to form a stinking hulk, a shit monster.

Set me free, she barely dares think. *Take this house and set me free.*

17

Amelia rides uptown in the creaky old van driven by Jeremy, that creaky old hippie. Suzie is up front in the passenger seat and Amelia bounces along on the bench seat, the city slipping by them in red and white and neon, the city such a different animal when you cut through it by car. Moving fast, away from the sound and smell of it, and it's swift and layered and beautiful. Especially on a winter night like this, late enough and cold enough for most of the people to be tucked away, and it's just you and the cabs and the late-night streets and the lights, and you remember why you love this city. Easy to love her again. To look out the window and find the Empire State Building all lit up and the Chrysler Building up ahead and gleaming, and it's enough to make Amelia go all heart-full and giddy. Enough to make her want to reach out and embrace it all.

The van rolls along First Avenue to the Upper East Side. Jeremy's not a squatter, but he's sympathetic. He's been around forever, and he's happy to pitch in for a small cut of the haul. He drives them on these weekly excursions into the foreign territory uptown, where the dumpster diving's the best, the pickings the freshest, the most abundant, the most outrageously, ostentatiously wasteful.

First stop, a bagel place on Eighty-Third and First. Amelia and Suzie get out of the van and go around the back down the alley, Jeremy circling the block so as not to draw attention. A wad of black trash bags tucked into each of their jacket pockets. Pop open the dumpster and rip open a trash bag and there are the bagels, dozens of them. Six or seven dozen, easy, all on their own in the trash bag, no garbage mixed in. Nice and clean.

Next stop, Gristedes. Yogurt, cheese, milk expiring day after tomorrow, still good for a few days. Slightly dented cans of soup. Boxes of cereal with the cardboard bent in. People don't want to buy dinged cans. Don't want to buy boxes that show they've been touched by hands before theirs. It won't sell and out it goes and all the better for them, who need the food, who can pull this stuff from the garbage and clean it up and feed themselves and their friends. Save it from the landfill.

But there's something sad about it, Amelia thinks. The mountains of food. An entire building could grow fat on what they find in the trash. They did the Upper West Side run last week and found five wheels of perfectly good brie behind Fairway. Entire wheels of brie. Who knows why they were tossed. Along with a bucket of olives, bags of slightly bruised apples, bananas showing just a touch too much brown.

It feeds them, yeah, but you have to wonder what's going to become of a place with so little tolerance for dings and dents, for bruises, for small scars.

The bags are full of food, the floor of the van loaded down with groceries. It's a good haul, really good. They'll drop some off at Cat House, at Utopia Squat, at Maus Haus. Plenty of food to share. As the van ambles back downtown, Suzie and Amelia divvy the goods up, getting a bag ready for each building.

First stop is the farthest south and east, dropping food off at Utopia on Fifth and D. Rolling up Avenue D, they head north, over to Maus on Seventh. Then toward home. They drive west on Thirteenth Street. There are four guys in front of the building to the left of Cat House. The light over the door is out, the men blending in with the shadows.

Suzie says, "That doesn't look like hanging out."

"Can you see who it is?" Amelia says.

"No one I know. No one who lives in that building, pretty sure."

"Big shoulders, short hair," Amelia says. "Undercovers?"

"I'll pass the word along to Cat House when I run the bag in," Suzie says. "Amelia, you want to go home and let our guys know? And Jeremy, you mind swinging back over to Utopia and Maus to give them the heads-up? Just so the night watches know to be on alert. Maybe nothing, but better to let everyone know, yeah?"

"Hey, Jeremy? Just watch until Suzie and I both get safe inside before you drive off, okay?" Amelia says.

"Come on. It's not like they're waiting to jump us," Suzie says as she climbs out of the van with the bag for Cat House.

Jeremy catches Amelia's eye in the rearview mirror. "I'll wait."

Amelia goes into Thirteen House with their bag of food. Marlowe is on the door tonight. It seems Marlowe's always got night watch lately. He's an insomniac and he says if he's going to be awake he might as well make himself useful. She tells him what's up, then goes upstairs to find Gerrit and tells him. He runs upstairs to tell Steve and Ben and then you can feel the whole house buzzing with it, waiting and wondering what's going to come, if anything.

⊞

It's well past 1:00 AM, and the food is all divided up. Everyone heads toward bed, except Marlowe on the door and Ben on the roof, Suzie circling the streets on bike watch. Amelia feels kind of sheepish, like they overreacted to a bunch of guys standing around outside in the dark.

"We're all so jumpy," she tells Gerrit. He's climbed into bed with her again. He presses against her. The heat coming off his body, the new boldness of his hands. She talks, trying to distract him, trying to calm herself, trying not to mind his being there, and she says, "Maybe we got it wrong. Maybe they weren't up to anything."

"It doesn't matter," he says. "You were right to let everyone know. We have to be on guard. Even if they aren't up to something tonight, it's good to keep your eyes open like that."

He's kissing her neck now, easing his hand beneath the waistband of her sweatpants. She rolls away, but he pulls her back against him. He's half hard and she feels a little jolt of fear, wondering just how far the rules have shifted. "Shhh," he's hissing in her ear. "Shhh." Those hands. She wants to elbow him hard and run from the room, but she doesn't. They've struck this deal over the years, this unspoken deal, and she can't go back on it now. Certainly not now, with the baby. She closes her eyes. She tries to like it.

Banging on the door downstairs reverberates through the hallways, right up into their apartment. Shouting from the roof, shouting now on the stairs, in the hallway, and they're both up, grabbing for boots, grabbing for coats, out into the hallway.

Ben is in the hall, eyes wide, nostrils flaring, shouting, "Eviction Watch! Let's go! Let's go! Over to Cat House, people, let's GOOOOO! Lock your doors behind you, barricades down!"

Boards are wedged into place to bar doors and windows, apartment doors are locked, then everyone rushes downstairs and out the front door. Nena closes it behind them, little Carla standing behind her wrapped in a blanket, and they hear her slide down the heavy steel bar that braces that door. They're twenty strong, together, angry, adrenaline pumping, and Amelia thrilling to it, even though she's scared. Thrilled and thinking, finally, finally something is happening. Something, whatever it is. They've been waiting and here it is, it's happening now.

Next door, their friends at Cat House are outside, arms linked and blocking the door, and here comes a group from the other direction, coming from other Eviction Watch squats, and everyone joining in, linking arms. The cops are there, three cars with the lights going, and a battering ram—scarred blue metal beast—leaning against one of the cop cars. But only six cops for all these squatters.

Amelia finds Kim. "What happened?"

"Anonymous report about a gun. Someone seen going inside with a gun."

"Seriously?"

"Yeah, some bullshit, right?"

"And there you have it," Gerrit says, his arm linked through Amelia's and now she's glad to have him beside her, glad for his touch. It's cold out, near freezing, but she thinks the shaking in her legs has nothing to do with the cold. It's an awesome sight, all these people—fifty easy, maybe more—come together to defend their neighbors.

"*Godverdomme*," he says. "We should have left you to guard the house with Nena. If there's any pushing or shoving at all, promise me you'll get off to the side?"

She nods. "Yeah. I promise."

Steve's in front, talking to the officer in charge. Cat's beside him, angry, obviously working hard not to spit, not to take a swing at the cops. "There are no weapons in this building, officer," Steve says. "I can vouch for that. We can't let you search, though. Not without a warrant. There are residents who aren't home. We can't allow you to come through. There are no guns here. Could it have been a drill? Or a nail gun?" Steve turns to the group gathered behind him. "Anyone working with a nail gun tonight?"

Ben says, "Yeah. I was."

The cops don't know who lives where. The officer in charge says, "Nail gun?" and turns to the other cops and says, "I'm not looking to haul fifty people in tonight. All that paperwork. I'm satisfied I see a nail gun." The other cops nod and shrug. Who wants to do all that paperwork? "Okay," he says to Ben. "You bring out that nail gun. And when you bring it out, you do it nice and slow and pointed to the ground and we'll be okay. Okay?"

Good thing Ben knows Cat House as well as he does, and good thing they all pitch in with the work and know where everyone's tools are kept, because Ben goes into the building and three minutes later (a very long three minutes and no sound but shifting feet and clearing throats and the cops looking as nervous as the squatters) he comes back out—nice and slow—and he's got a nail gun and turns it toward himself and hands the butt end to the cop, who fires a round into the sidewalk. He nods and hands it back.

"Okay, folks. Have a good night."

Just like that, they're gone. And everyone is cheering and patting each other on the back and excited. They sent out the call, they set Eviction Watch in motion, and it worked. It totally worked.

"Fuckers," Gideon says. "Good thinking on the nail gun, guys. That was quick thinking."

"If that's the best they can do, we've got no worries," Suzie says.

Cat snorts and says, "Baby, that was nothing. You just hang on because this thing is just getting started."

But still, tonight, success. Tonight, they've done something. No one wants to go back to sleep. They all crowd into the Cat House basement community room—because they can, because the building is still open—and someone hauls out some booze and someone else puts on some tunes, and they break out the food that Amelia and Suzie brought back. Ben stands on a table, waving that nail gun around and hooting, and everything is good and hopeful. Everything is right with the world, for now.

18

Amelia didn't tell Gerrit about the appointment; she didn't tell Steve. She's been waiting for this ultrasound, hungry for another look at the little creature she talks to in her mind. She wants to share it with no one.

Steve gave a small corner of hope to hold on to, up on the rooftop on New Year's Eve. He said he was thinking about her and the baby and his responsibility to them. It sounded good that night, standing with him in the dark, his voice soft and low, his hand sometimes brushing against her, but three weeks later it's gone stale and worthless like all New Year's promises. All that talk about responsibility, but not a word about love, not a word about her or the baby being anything but a burden for him to shoulder.

The shortest wait yet at Planned Parenthood. They whisk her in almost right away—the privilege of the happily pregnant. No tears, no hand-wringing thoughts of abortion. No wondering if the boyfriend will show. Just pregnant, babyful, and she walks through those swinging double doors, close on the heels of the nurse, who's chatting to her happily, all the nurses and aides smiling at her and breezy. They must like seeing this. Too much seeing things the other way around, too much watching the hard choices made.

Pants tugged down, shirt tugged up. Cold gel on her belly and the screen flickers on, the wand running across, and there it is. So changed now at sixteen weeks from the little fist clutched around a thumbprint of a heart at nine weeks. So changed. Arms, legs, face. A full perfect profile. The sonographer names all the parts. Together they count the lobes of the brain, the chambers of the heart, the fingers and toes, the testicles.

A boy. Her son.

⊞

It's beginning to get to Gerrit, the way Amelia keeps to herself. She's silent as they work together in the bike shop, silent as they sit at the dinner table at night, silent through the planning meetings. She goes to bed without a word, wakes without a word—hardly a glance at Gerrit. She's gone inside, with the baby. They're in there together, deep inside her where he can't reach. He can't break through.

"I don't know what to do for her," he tells Steve when they run into each other on the street and sit down on a stoop to talk. "I don't know what she needs from me. She's changed. The baby is changing her, and not the way I would have thought."

"What did you expect?" Steve spits out of the corner of his mouth and fixes his gaze toward the river, thousand-yard stare.

"I thought she'd get more serious," Gerrit says. "I thought she'd settle down, grow up."

"And she has."

"But she barely talks to me at all. It's like having a spoiled teenager around. And she sleeps all the time. Goes to bed early, wakes up late."

"Hard work, making a baby. Let her sleep."

"She won't let me in. It's my baby, too. Shouldn't I have some part in this?"

"Is it?"

"What?"

"Your baby?"

"Jesus, man." Steve, of all people. Amelia's running around was never much of a secret, but no one has dared to ask that question, to say it to Gerrit's face. He looks at his friend and sees how tired the man looks. Beaten. Gerrit wouldn't have ever thought it. Steve, their firebrand, their warrior. In the last two months he's aged ten years or more, bags carved deep under his eyes. Gerrit realizes that the change in Steve came when he found out about the baby. He feeds off the fight with the city. That isn't what's dragging him down. It's this baby, the baby he and Anne will never have, that's killing him.

"Steve, man. I know you and Anne must be hurting, what with the baby. I want you to know that. Amelia and I, we both know that it can't be easy for you."

Steve tosses away his spent cigarette, grunts, and heaves his big body up off the stoop. "You and Amelia talk about that? How hard it must be for me and Anne?" He spits again, the fat wet glob hitting the pavement just beyond Gerrit's boots. "Amelia's the only one making that baby," he says. "You let her do it however she needs."

What does Steve know about what Amelia needs? Gerrit knows, as much as anyone can. Steve walks away, all big-shouldered and sure, noble in his loss. He wears his barren marriage like a shield, his mantle of suffering. Telling Gerrit what to do, how to be with Amelia.

"She had an ultrasound yesterday," Gerrit calls to Steve as he's moving down the block. "A boy. A boy for sure."

Steve stops for a second, two seconds, three. Head down, shoulders down. And then a nod, his back still to Gerrit and a small nod to himself. Then he lifts his hand to wave good-bye, to wave Gerrit off, still his back to Gerrit and he walks off to wherever he's going.

"I'm going to have a son!" Gerrit shouts to the retreating back. "A son!"

19

Gerrit is late opening the shop. Amelia used to be the first up. She would get the coffee going, get the breakfast going, then she'd shake him awake, droplets of water from her just-washed hair raining down on his face and the good clean soapy smell of her the first thing he'd know each day. There would be coffee and toast or oatmeal, some puttering around, and by ten or so they would head down the stairs together, quiet, still tucked into themselves.

They would walk downstairs and outside to the shop, Amelia turning the key in the lock and Gerrit opening the security gate; turning on the lights; going down to the basement to turn on the air compressor, that hunched metal beast shuddering and coughing awake; snaking a hose through the cellar doors to the sidewalk so people can fill their tires. Amelia would put out the tools they leave in the waiting area: free to tune up your own bike, free to come inside and learn how to do it. Gerrit would turn on the radio, swinging the day into motion: maybe NPR or maybe music, one well-worn cassette or another thumbed into the player. It would be the Clash, usually, to get them going, or the Velvet Underground if it was raining or if they were tired or feeling especially easy and tender with each other. By noon they'd be talking and laughing and Amelia cracking jokes and Gerrit rolling his eyes, sometimes rewarding her with a small smile, indulgent as with a child.

But not today. No more, hardly ever. She sleeps late now, later than him. She rolls into the shop at noon on the days she turns up at all, and her work is sloppy and distracted. It's hard work she's doing with the baby. He reminds himself of this. She's tired. He tries to understand that it's not about him. It's not a rejection. But he feels the loss of it. He misses the banter that made the work lighter. He misses having her to turn to, to say, "Hey, let's knock off early and get burritos" or some such thing he almost never said, but now in retrospect feels like the kind of thing they used to do all the time. It's the things he wishes they'd always done that he misses, now that they aren't likely to be done at all.

So he is alone this morning, the new usual, opening the bike shop. Gerrit can't help but feel hunted, to be on the verge of losing both the apartment and the shop, spaces he's worked so hard to build. He's broken too many of his old rules. He's stayed too long here, gotten attached to this place. No more "one small bag and be ready to move, sleep with your boots on." He's dug in; he's gotten comfortable. There is something to be lost now, in fact and not just in principle. If they lose the fight, it won't be like before. It won't be just a matter of shrugging and turning to find a new building to open. His whole world, from the last eleven years—his true adulthood in its entirety—is tied up in this little community, in this group of buildings. For all his talk, he is terrified. He does not want to start over.

The security gate rolls up with a screech. Inside, the shop smells of metal and oil—good smells, the smell of honest mechanical work. It's another cold day, but Gerrit throws the back door open anyway, lets the frigid air fill the room. He wants that burn of skin on cold metal as he works. He wants to see his breath in the air. Let Amelia close the door if she comes in.

Gerrit has always loved navigating a city by bike. It's a very particular way of traveling. You see the streets differently, experience them differently. Pedestrians going by in a blur, the rush of horns, riding the crest of the traffic's waves. Sudden stops, almost getting doored all the time. If you're fast, if you're good, weaving through the traffic, getting there faster than the cars. Going ways the cars can't go, going ways you aren't supposed to go, but if you're swift enough, if you're daring enough, you can go anywhere at all in the city on a bike, fastest way around by far.

But the danger, the anger of the drivers at having to share the road with you. The idiots who throw open cab doors without looking, stepping out on the street side. The constant risk of getting a wheel stolen, a seat stolen, the whole bike stolen. No one owns the same bike for more than two years here.

Gerrit used to ride through Rotterdam perched on the rack over his mother's rear wheel, a fistful of her coat to hang on to for balance and the soft spray of water drawn up by the tires misting his bare calves where his too-short jeans hiked up. Moving through the gray rain-wet streets, faster than bullies, faster than hate, safe within his mother's motion. When he got too big to ride on the rack and was given a bike of his own, it wasn't the same. He would ride along beside her as they went about their errands and eye the rack, a basket now tied to it where he once sat. He wanted to make himself small, to crowd into the basket with the groceries and ride there, hunkered safe behind his swift-riding mother, forever.

Now his own bike has a milk crate strapped to the rack, and most days he doesn't think of anything in particular when he loads it with food or tools, or something found on the street that might be useful. But some days, when the cold is especially wet, when the rain is soft and light like a mist, if he's out riding just after dawn and the whole city is hushed and damply gray, he'll remember those rides with his mother. Lately he's been thinking about child seats, about strapping his own son into one and letting him feel the city fall past him, the mist on his face, the motion of his father moving him through his city. He wishes it were safer to ride here, as safe as it was back in Rotterdam. Gerrit wonders if, when the time comes, when the boy is old enough, he'll have the courage to put him on the bike. So many cars, so many doors. How do you keep a child safe in this city?

The shop door opens. Ben walks in and pulls three cups of bodega coffee from a paper bag. He hands one to Gerrit.

Steam rises up as Gerrit thumbs the lid's plastic tab back. He raises the cup to Ben. "Cheers."

"Amelia's not here?"

"Sleeping in again," Gerrit says, feeling his face redden. "She's tired a lot these days."

"Sure, sure." Ben settles his weight against the counter, his fingers toying with a socket wrench. "Let her sleep while she can, right?"

The shop door whooshes open again and in comes Amelia, clutching an orange, holding it out in front of her like a talisman to ward off evil. "Inspectors," she says. "A runner just came by. City inspectors are coming tomorrow morning. Ten o'clock." They don't have phones, so Irving sends a kid from his office over on foot when he needs to reach them. "Irving heard I'm pregnant. He sent the kid with a box of oranges. Nice, right?"

Gerrit herds Ben and Amelia out the door and tugs the security gate back down.

"And thus no work shall be done in ye olde bike shoppe today, my friends," Ben says, and runs upstairs to gather whomever can be found for a meeting.

"It'll be okay, right?" Amelia asks. She stops at the top of the basement stairs and leans against Gerrit, her head on his shoulder. He welcomes the contact, whatever her reason.

"We've got to be sure we're ready," he says, putting his arm around her. Her back is newly plush under his hand, her body softening around the baby. "Let's start with that."

⊞

Ten o'clock comes and goes. Closing in on eleven. Steve and Gerrit wait outside the building for the city inspectors to show. Gerrit paces the sidewalk, muttering in Dutch, driving Steve crazy with it. People come in and out of the building, trying to pretend it's a morning like any other. Trying not to ask the obvious question when they see them out there, still waiting.

They worked all night—all of them—checking and double-checking the repair list the independent engineer had given them, making sure everything was done. They'd finished a few minutes before 9:00 AM. Then word came over that they were done at Cat House, too. Both squats finished enough and cleaned up enough to pass an inspection easily if they'd been rentals. In fact, finished way better than a rental building would need to be. There's still work to do—a hundred years old, the buildings, and there will always be more work to do—but there's no way the inspectors could come in today and say the buildings are unsound. No way they could evict them based on safety. Not legally.

Amelia's been sitting in the vestibule this whole time. Every time the door opens Steve looks in and there she is, looking at him, her sweater riding up on her rounding belly. It's disturbing how fast she's getting big, like she's swelling with all his dirty little secrets and she's bound to blow. A time bomb, that girl. No way his kid's gonna come out looking anything like Gerrit.

Finally, half past eleven and here come the inspectors. Two of them, cheap sport coats under puffy winter parkas, khakis, hard hats. They look like regular guys. Just normal guys with jobs to do. Maybe this won't be so bad. Maybe it'll go okay.

They nod to Steve and Gerrit, each shaking Steve's right hand and each hesitating when they go to shake with Gerrit and he grudgingly offers the left hand, the right tucked deep into his coat pocket. Steve's seen it a hundred times before, this reaction to Gerrit's left-handed shake. Some folks pick up quick enough and respond with their left hand, making for a fairly normal shake. Others leave that right hand out there, and the result is a dainty little meeting of hands, Gerrit's left fingertips resting in the other guy's confused right palm. The inspectors both opt for the right-handed shake, then step away, awkward and quiet.

They survey the facade. One of them—the shorter of the two—scratches some notes on his clipboard. "We'll start in the basement and work our way up," the tall one says. "We'll do the storefront last." They move inside, Amelia stepping onto the stairs to let them pass along the ground-floor hallway, down to the basement. The tall one walks right past her, but Steve notices the short one give a nod. Not an unfriendly nod. Just regular guys, doing their job.

Down to the basement and Steve does his level best to hold his tongue as the inspectors hardly look at the things he and Gerrit point out to them. The little one holds the clipboard close to his chest, making note after note but rarely giving anything more than a glance.

They move quickly from water heater to furnace to circuit box. They look at the ductwork, checking the wiring, the exposed plumbing woven through the ceiling beams. The joists, the windows. Gerrit shows them the electricity meter. "Our Con Ed's totally legal," he says. "We installed the meter last year. They inspected it and approved it. We pay our bill every month."

"And before last year?" the tall one asks. He moves on, walking the perimeter of the room.

"You can see we put in a French drain," Steve says. "These old basements can get real wet. We haven't had any flooding at all since we put it in."

"Smart," the short one says, shooting a glance toward the tall one.

They're done with the basement and all the mechanicals in less than ten minutes. Done with Marlowe's first-floor apartment, moving up to the second floor. "We rebuilt the stairs completely," Steve says, giving one of the steps a good thunk with his boot heel. "Every level rebuilt and reinforced."

The tall inspector aims a finger overhead to a riser on the flight above them. POLICE LINE DO NOT CROSS in white letters, hung upside down.

Shit. They'd meant to paint that.

"City property," the short one says, making a note on his clipboard.

Up the stairs and on into the second-floor apartments, and up and up like that, no more than a glance at anything and always with the scribbled notes. Floor after floor, apartment after apartment, then up to the roof. They pop their heads out the roof door but don't step outside. "We wouldn't want to risk falling through," the tall one says, and Steve all but spits as he says, "The roof is sound."

Gerrit pushes past them to do an angry tap dance on the tar, but they've already turned around to go back downstairs. As Steve and Gerrit follow the inspectors down so they can pretend to look at the storefront and the backyard, Steve mutters, "A complete sham."

"We expected as much," Gerrit says.

Amelia smiles sweetly from behind the work counter as they go through the bike shop and out to the backyard, but the inspectors don't acknowledge her. Gerrit shakes his head, kisses her cheek. She rolls her eyes at Steve after Gerrit's gone past her. *Ah, Gerrit,* Steve thinks, *you poor sad fuck.*

Outside, in the yard, the inspectors gingerly lift the corner of a blue tarp to peek at the building materials stored there. And then it's over, the inspectors headed next door to go through the motions at Cat House. All that buildup, all that preparation, but they'd known what was coming anyway. They'd hoped it would be fair, but they'd known, hadn't they?

20

The squatters fill the seats on the left side of the courtroom. Amelia feels the collective anxiety like a thick veil
of smoke over them. She tries to catch the city lawyer's
eye, but the woman hasn't cast so much as a glance their
way. *Here we are,* Amelia wants to say to her. *These are the
people you want to put out on the street.*

A bailiff steps to the front of the courtroom. "All rise
for the honorable Judge William Sykes!" A small old man
glides, surprisingly quick, from a door behind the bench.
Dark eyes beneath outrageous gray brows.

Irving snaps to attention and there's that transformation everyone's talked about. The judge walks in and Irving's stooped shoulders settle and square themselves.
His face goes sharp and focused. His fumbling hands go
quiet and still. Look at that. It seems to be true, the legend
passed from squat to squat, the stories told about Irving
Fischer the tiger, the class warrior, the defender of the just

and downtrodden. Go figure. Amelia allows herself just the smallest corner of optimism.

Irving comes on strong right out of the gate. "Your honor, the fact that our report, filed by an unbiased independent engineer, directly contradicts the findings of the city's inspectors is reason enough to uphold the restraining order.

"Counselor DeMarkis is showing no respect for this court, for the legal process, for the rights of my clients. The city claims the buildings are in danger of collapse, and yet you have before you a report from an independent engineer that plainly states that not only are the buildings sound, they are up to code. I move to have this entire case thrown out. With such obvious falsehood, Ms. DeMarkis is demonstrating exactly how concerned the city is with the safety and well-being of its citizens."

"Could the judge really just throw the case out and that's that?" Amelia whispers to Kim. It seems impossible that the whole problem could go away so easily. The judge just claps his hands together and they're saved?

"Dunno," Kim says. "Maybe so."

Cat, sitting in front of Amelia and Kim, whispers, "Don't get your hopes up."

The lawyer for the city, Elaine DeMarkis, she's young, maybe thirty. There's something too deliberate in her, the way her hair's pulled back severely from her forehead, the way her glasses perch just so. She opens her briefcase and Amelia spies an asthma inhaler, a pack of Camel Lights, a worn paperback book. DeMarkis slumps a little in her chair and Amelia thinks she can see the woman's real face leaking through around the edges. But she catches herself, sits up straight, the muscles of her jaw tightening. She stands, her black heels tapping along the floor as she makes her way around the table to the front of the room.

"Counselor," she says, "let's keep things in perspective. Your clients have been living rent-free in these buildings for years, while thousands of others in genuine need wait for low-income housing."

Irving smiles. A patient smile. An indulgent, grandfatherly smile. "I thought this was about public safety and imminent collapse? These are hardworking people. Have you even looked at them? Look at these people seated behind me, Ms. DeMarkis. The city has failed to protect their basic human right to housing, and they have taken that matter into their own hands."

Irving approaches Judge Sykes and DeMarkis sinks back down into her chair. This probably isn't how she pictured her career going when she was paying out all that cash for law school. Why would you take a government job instead of working in a fancy law firm, unless you want to help people? She must have meant well, Amelia thinks. And now here it is her job to do Giuliani's dirty work. Amelia almost feels sorry for her.

"Your honor," Irving says, "these buildings are rightfully the property of their residents, by way of adverse possession. They have lived there, openly and continuously, for over ten years. And never an objection by the so-called legal owner of the property, the city. Not a peep, your honor.

By these facts alone, they fulfill the criteria of adverse possession. But it goes beyond that. It goes to the heart of why the city, after decades of neglect, now suddenly wants these buildings."

He paces the front of the room, waving his hands. It's like a movie, Amelia thinks; it's almost too much. But the judge leans forward in his seat. He's listening. "In the seventies, when our beloved city was choked by crime and drugs and poverty, families fleeing for the suburbs, corruption rampant at the highest levels; when the president of the United States *told us to drop dead*, the landlords fled as well. They abandoned their buildings in the poorer neighborhoods. They left them to rot.

"And rot they did. What do abandoned buildings do to a neighborhood? They drag it down. The drug trade moves in; the buildings become havens for crack dens and prostitution. The streets around those buildings grow more and more dangerous. More families move away, more buildings go vacant, and the problem grows until entire blocks, entire neighborhoods, once vibrant and bustling, are lost."

Irving casts his arm out toward the gathered squatters. "These people, whom the city now seeks to evict, took what was left for dead and brought it back to life. And with their buildings, and others like theirs, they have brought the Lower East Side back to life. The streets are safer; crime is down. Professionals want to move in. Families want to move in. This revitalization has, ironically, been the downfall of my clients. These buildings have become desirable real estate and the city wants to hand them over to developers in the interest of money, in the interest of Big Business. Your honor, we cannot allow that to happen.

"My clients are working artists, PhD candidates, carpenters, schoolteachers. Two of them run a bicycle repair shop that provides free bicycles for the neighborhood kids, and teaches them how to repair them. Counselor DeMarkis, are you saying you want to evict these people, who are themselves in need of low-income housing, to replace them with other people who need low-income housing? Because I was under the impression that we were talking about the soundness and safety of the buildings. If we're going to have a different kind of discussion, Ms. DeMarkis, we are entitled to a different type of hearing. We are entitled to argue for adverse possession."

Judge Sykes sits drumming his slender fingers. He's frowning, but in a thoughtful way. Amelia can't read his expression.

DeMarkis says, "This is a matter of public safety, as demonstrated by the inspectors' report. Those buildings are dangerous. But since you brought up the bike shop, let's talk about that. I'm assuming this bike shop charges sales tax? I'm assuming they're up to date on their taxes?"

Beside Amelia, Gerrit growls. "Taxes. *Klotefascisten!* Take my home and charge me for the privilege."

Yeah. So maybe DeMarkis doesn't mean well.

Judge Sykes says, "Enough. I find these contradictory engineer reports highly suspect. Counselor DeMarkis, if the city is indeed claiming this is a matter of safety, which I do believe is the issue at hand, and the city is claiming this inspection report is accurate, then as the titled owner of this property, the city is responsible for the repairs. I do not, however, find cause for evacuation. The city is hereby ordered to complete the necessary repairs without displacing the residents. Request for emergency evacuation denied." He bangs his gavel and leaves the bench, disappearing through the heavy wooden door.

"Did we win?" Marlowe says. "For real?"

"Holy shit," Kim says. "Did the judge just do what I think he just did?"

Amelia looks to Gerrit, and even he's sitting there slack-jawed, but then he shakes his head and says, "This just raises the stakes. With Biano involved, they'll just come at us another way."

"And you'll be waiting, good soldier that you are," Cat says, standing and slipping into her coat.

Gerrit stiffens at Amelia's side. "That's right. I will. Where will you be?"

Cat laughs, throwing her head back, and her complicated earrings make a small plinking sound. She pats Gerrit's shoulder as she goes past, sweeping down the aisle and out of the courtroom, the scent of amber oil lingering in her wake.

⊞

Cat stops outside the courthouse to light a cigarette and let the crowd of squatters stream past her all bright and triumphant. She falls in a few paces behind the crowd, wanting to be with them, but quietly. Wanting to be part of the celebration without having to perform the role of "Cat."

Everyone's got broad grins, everyone's chattering happily, except Gerrit. Gerrit's face is pinched, his eyes darting around like he's scanning for police snipers. Amelia is grinning along with the rest of them, her arm linked through Kim's, but then she looks to Gerrit and he scowls at her and the smile fades from her face. She drops Kim's arm and falls back to walk beside him, her shoulders rounding to match his, her footsteps getting heavier and more clipped. The lightness she carried just moments before, gone.

Damn him that he's got the power to drag the girl down like that. And damn her for letting him, Cat thinks. Someone ought to step in and wake that girl up.

21

Coming on sunset. The end of February, and finally it feels like the days are getting longer. Gerrit and Amelia are winding things down in the shop, putting away the communal tools, shooing the boys—it's always boys, almost never any girls—toward home. Amelia yells, "Go do your homework!" and the kids laugh and wheel away on their bikes.

The boys ride in tight circles, popping wheelies, calling to each other with that certain kind of laughter that's caught between boy and man. Ringing high still, but something coarser beneath it, something knowing. Amelia's watched a lot of these kids grow up, and the older they get, the more distant, the more inscrutable. Some of them have started making her nervous in ways she doesn't care to name. Black and Latino boys hardening into the kinds of teenagers she'd hesitate to walk past at night. She feels ugly, thinking this. But there it is.

She tugs up the elastic band on the maternity jeans she found at the Salvation Army. They're a size or so too big, but at the rate she's going they'll fit before long. Absent-minded hand on her belly, the little frog kicking and flipping away. She leans against the frame of the open door, looking out onto the darkening street. Behind her, Gerrit mutters to himself and sweeps the floor.

"Amelia." Her name, quiet and low, and there's Cat standing in front of her, out of nowhere, big eyes lined thick and kohl-dark. Creases in the pale leathery skin around her eyes and mouth, and that heavy crown of red dreads piled up on top of her head.

Amelia glances at Gerrit, sweeping, his back to her. Cat tips her head, raises an eyebrow.

"Gerrit," Amelia says, pulling her coat around her. "Heading out now. Cool?"

"Yeah, yeah." He waves her off.

Amelia walks along a step or two behind Cat, resolving to go wherever Cat intends. But she goes only as far as Cat House. She opens the door and Amelia follows her up—silent all five flights to Cat's top-floor apartment.

The hallways and doors in Cat House are pretty heavily tagged up, but Cat's door is clean, painted a glossy black. Heavy iron doorknob, a scrolled old knocker. The door swings open onto a cavernous space. She has the whole floor to herself—herself and her cats. The smell of cat mixes with a thick layer of incense and dust.

Cat flicks on a lamp beside the door and sleek bodies spill out from the dark. Black cats, white cats, tabbies. Ten of them, or more. They mill and weave around Cat's and Amelia's feet. The apartment has no interior walls. A door on the far wall, flanked by litter boxes, is most likely the bathroom, but other than that the space is completely open. A broken-down couch. A mattress on the floor, piled high with quilts and pillows. Torn hippie tapestries on the walls. Ruined plaster molding. A double-burner hot plate, some dishes stacked in a milk crate. Along the wall across from the front door are four windows shrouded in faded red velvet drapes. Cat still hasn't spoken.

And then she says, "I used to be with Steve, when we were in high school. You've probably heard about that."

Amelia nods. Steve's first love. He's got her initials scratched into his arm, a crude, hand-poked tattoo, done by Cat herself. CW. Amelia knows the *W* stands for Weider. Carolyn Weider. That's who Cat used to be. Amelia would run her fingers along that tattoo, hoping to find in it some connection to Steve's younger self, who he was all those years ago, when he was even younger than she is now. She would trace that tattoo, trying to find a way in.

"And then some years back, we started fucking again."

Steve undressed in this dim room; Steve sprawled out on that mattress, waiting for someone who is not Amelia and is not Anne.

"Just for a few months. Right before you showed up, in fact. A momentary lapse of reason on my part, because I knew better by then. He's something, isn't he? Makes it real easy to have those lapses. Makes it real easy to forget yourself. Who you are, what you want. Men like Steve, they can get a girl into all kinds of trouble. You know what I mean?"

Amelia sinks down onto the beaten old couch, which sends up a puff of dust and mildew. Adrenaline hits her like a sharp, cold needle. Cat doesn't invite anyone up to her apartment. Amelia has walked into something. A trap, a snare. How does Cat know? She's going to use it against her somehow.

"You've seen me with Steve?" Amelia says.

"I've seen you with Gerrit, too." Cat perches on the closest windowsill, lights a cigarette with a strike-anywhere struck on her boot. She takes a deep drag, all the lines around her mouth and eyes flaring awake.

She's shed her bulky army coat and sweater, stripped down to a thin tank top and black leggings. She's surprisingly small with all those layers gone. A skinny little thing folded into herself, the masses of her hair the very biggest thing about her. She moves closer, sits on the edge of the couch beside Amelia, and when she leans over to turn on another lamp, Amelia sees the flame tattoos that cover her shoulders and back.

It occurs to Amelia that everyone talks about Cat's flame tattoos, but as far as she knows, no one's seen more than the little bit on her neck. No one but maybe Steve. She can't recall ever seeing Cat without a long-sleeved shirt, even in full summer. How is it that everyone can know about tattoos that most of them have never seen? That anyone would care enough about hidden tattoos to tell others? The flame tattoos are legendary, another story about Cat that gets passed around, handed down to the new kids. One of those Bermuda Triangles of logic that sprout up around the woman.

But now Amelia can see them. The flames blanket her shoulders and back like a prayer shawl, creeping up her neck toward the hairline. What Amelia didn't expect, what isn't a part of the story they tell each other about Cat's tattoos, is that the flames grow over and around an intricate map of scars. There are countless deep scores in the skin of Cat's upper back and shoulders. Rivulets dug into her flesh, disappearing into her tank top. And now Amelia sees that the habitual long sleeves cover scarred arms. Old track marks; shot veins; papery, ruined skin.

Cat turns to Amelia, so close Amelia can see the fine red veins in her eyes. She eases the hem of Amelia's shirt up, slides a cool dry hand across her belly. The baby rises beneath her touch, an elbow or a heel poking toward the surface. "If you just roll with whatever's happening to you, just go along without complaining, letting people do what they want with you, take what they want from you, you end up empty. Know what I mean?"

Cat's touch is steady and sure. It doesn't feel like the hand of someone laying a trap. Cat's face is not the face of someone positioning herself to reveal a secret, or to conceal it for a price. Her hand on Amelia's belly is kind. Her face is kind.

"Steve's a hard man to say no to. And poor thing, you never stood a chance, did you? Little orphan girl and here comes big daddy gonna scoop you up and love you.

Something tells me if I'd been the one to bring you home instead of Gerrit, you would have fucked me. If I wanted to, I bet you'd fuck me right now, and you don't even like girls, do you? Why is it that anyone can do anything they want to you? Do you ever wonder about that?"

"It's not like that," Amelia says.

"Oh."

"Steve didn't get me to do anything I didn't want to do."

"And Gerrit?"

"It's not like that with me and Gerrit. It's not just his hand, the thalidomide thing. We're more like roommates." She watches Cat's face for a reaction, but she doesn't look surprised. Not at all.

"You don't owe Gerrit anything."

"I do, though. I owe him everything." Amelia stands, her sudden movement sending cats scattering. "I should go."

Cat tilts her head and narrows her eyes, considering Amelia's face. She stays like that several long, slow moments, and Amelia fidgets under her gaze. "You come visit me anytime," she says, finally. "My door's always open to you."

Amelia nods, backing toward the door. She makes her way down the stairs and out to the street, cat hair and incense clinging to her coat. She feels Cat's eyes on her long after the door closes. She's not sure what to tell Gerrit when she gets home. Not sure if she'll tell him where she's been. And if not, not sure why it should feel like such a secret.

⊞

Cat hears the front door slam shut and looks out the window to see Amelia standing on the sidewalk, staring out onto the street. Not turning to go into her own building, not turning to walk away, just kind of stuck there. That's a girl who needs to get shook loose, Cat thinks. For all her time on the street that should have wised her up, she's somehow young for her age, an innocent. And caught between those two grown men. Those greedy men.

Cat's sick of herself. She pulls her sweater back on, heads out her door and down the stairs. She walks into the basement community room to find Chrissie, Linda, and Fletcher glaring at each other, Linda's new mutt sniffing around their feet.

"Cat!" Chrissie pulls herself up straight. "Help us settle something?"

She should have stayed upstairs, made a cup of tea. Maybe had a nap. "Yeah?"

"We've got a problem with little Clash here." She motions to the dog, who's now gnawing on the toe of Linda's sneaker. Dogs—Cat's not a fan.

"Actually," Linda says, "the problem is with Fletcher." She wipes her palms on the belly of her purple sweatshirt, like just saying his name got her palms greasy.

"Clash went after our cat and got a piece of him," Fletcher says. "Me and Chrissie spent all last night at the emergency vet."

"Yeah and then Fletcher busted into my place this morning waving a pellet gun around and saying he was going to shoot the dog," Linda says.

Jesus, Cat thinks. She should have stayed upstairs. "Did he shoot?"

"No," Linda says, "but—"

"He broke into your space?" Cat says.

"He knocked, then kind of pushed in when I opened the door. I got in his face and he left. I want to call a house meeting. I shouldn't have to worry about some jackass waving a gun around in my apartment."

"It was just a pellet gun," Chrissie says.

"Still." Linda hauls herself up to sit on the scarred for-mica counter of their little communal kitchen. Her heel slips and kicks the cabinet, spooking the puppy, who pees on the floor.

"Nice," Chrissie hisses.

"You could totally kill a dog with a pellet gun," Linda says, her voice shaky. "When I was growing up, a kid in our neighborhood took out someone's Chihuahua that way."

"Okay," Cat says. "Fletcher, the pellet gun and the threat, totally not cool and you should fucking know better. But what's this about Clash getting a piece of the cat?"

"That's what I was saying," Chrissie says. "It's not the first time he's gone after a cat. Linda needs to get control of that dog or he shouldn't be able to stay. I mean, not to say that Fletcher should be waving pellet guns around either. But maybe we need to revisit the pet rule. It's a free-for-all with so many animals running around the place now. Maybe pets should get voted in same as people."

God, yes, thinks Cat. *Let's please have a meeting to talk about voting on which animals get to come live in the squat.*

Let's be sure it's no less than three hours long and that at least one person cries and runs out of the room before it's over. That's exactly what we need. More meetings. More voting. Jesus.

"I get a gun in my face and the problem is me and my dog?"

"A *pellet* gun, Linda," Chrissie says. "It was a pellet gun. Are you going to clean up that pee before someone steps in it?"

Cat sinks down into a chair and closes her eyes, letting their voices blur. She used to have an apartment over on St. Marks, all hardwood floors and the old-style moldings around the windows, a tin ceiling. When she came back to town in seventy-three, beat down and needing a place to get her feet back under her and her own mother turned her away, a friend took her in. And when that friend left town a couple years later, she left the apartment to Cat. It was a great old place, run-down but sweet, and the sun would come in in the morning and pour across the floor. You could lean out the window and look at the little backyard where the super grew fig trees in barrels. Money was tight, though—money is always tight—and she took on a roommate after a while, this chick Andrea from Boston. When they had a falling out it was Cat who packed up and moved, decided she'd had enough of paying rent and joined in with the crew who cracked Cat House. That was stupid. It was her apartment, not Andrea's. She should have kicked Andrea's ass out, kept the place, found a way to make the rent. What she's saved in rent here she's paid a thousand times over in headaches and hassles, splinters and calluses. She's no revolutionary.

"So, Cat," Fletcher's saying, "what do you say?"

"Why do you need me to say anything?"

"I don't know." Fletcher's got his arms crossed over his chest, all petulant.

"Figure this one out on your own, kids, okay? Mama's got a headache." She gets up and heads for the stairs, leaves them to agonize over their petty shit without her.

Places like that one on St. Marks can't be found for less than a grand a month anymore. Maybe Brooklyn, though. That wouldn't be so bad.

Amelia's caught up in a hell of a mess here. Maybe she wants to get out, set off on her own without Gerrit and Steve grabbing after her. She and Cat could find a place in Brooklyn together, make it really nice, with a little room for the baby. There's space out there, cheaper rents. She's getting ahead of herself, maybe, but hey. It's the way things are rolling anyway, their time here running down. Cat and Amelia and that little baby of hers, a big old apartment in Brooklyn. Maybe a garden apartment and Cat can grow her own damn fig tree in a barrel.

How small her dreams have gone.

⊞

Amelia left Cat's and headed for the Thirteen House basement, wanting someplace quiet to be alone. She sank into the comforting musty smell of the old futon mattress in a dark corner by the tools, eyes closed, trying to breathe through the slow-churning panic, trying to sort out what it means to have been truly seen by Cat, to have been laid bare like that. It almost worked, a calm settling over her. But now there are footsteps on the creaking stairs and in walks Steve, pulling the tool cabinet open and starting to paw through it without seeing her there.

"Hey," she whispers, and he jumps back with a shout.

"You scared me." He lowers himself onto the futon and reaches for her. And his hands are nothing like Gerrit's hands. And his mouth is nothing like Gerrit's mouth. He curls his body around hers, his chest against her back, his arm pillowing her head. When he pushes inside of her there isn't the force and hunger she's learned to expect from him, but a gentle easing in. His hips rock against her and his free hand is between her legs, circling her clit, and when she comes he isn't far behind. He moans against her neck, his breath hot on her skin, and she could almost believe he loves her.

When it's over they lie there together, his hand draped over her bared belly. The baby does his swimming thing, rolling and turning and flipping. Sweet boy. Sweet little swimmer. Steve follows the baby's movement, sliding his palm to catch a kick here, an elbow there, a little butt or shoulder or maybe it's his head reaching for the surface, then retreating. Reach and retreat, reach and retreat. It's almost too much for Amelia to bear, to lie there and feel the baby dance with his father like this.

"I saw Cat's scars. On her back," she says.

His hand goes still and the baby gives a quick kick flip to swim down into Amelia's depths. "Yeah," he says. "She disappeared for a while, seventy-two or -three. Came back like that. Never would say what happened. She left Carolyn, came back calling herself Cat. And she was so changed, it wouldn't have felt right calling her by her old name."

"Where'd she go?"

"Sometimes she says South America. Sometimes she says Morocco. Once she said she joined a circus in Wyoming. Hard to know for sure, with Cat. Wherever it was, she came home different. That's around when she started using." He stands, tugs his pants up, arranges his clothes, and hunkers down on his boot heels, facing the futon. At a safe distance, should anyone happen upon them. "How'd you come to see Cat's back?"

Amelia pulls her jeans up but leaves her shirt hiked over her belly, which rolls and bulges as the baby swings into gear. "She brought me to her apartment."

"Really? Brought you home?" He whistles low. "I wonder what she's up to."

"Why's she have to be up to something? Maybe she just likes me. Maybe she wants to help me."

Steve twirls a wood screw from finger to finger, looking at Amelia through that dark tangle of curls. "You be careful of that kind of help. Cat serves Cat." He nods toward her belly. "Is he always that busy?" He sucks his teeth, glances at his watch, and stands, arms high overhead, fingertips grazing the pipes as he stretches that big body. The tenderness is gone from his face. He's shut off from her again, ready to move on. Nothing new. She should be used to it by now, but it still stings. Every time, it stings. *Stomme sloerie.*

"You think he's showing off for your benefit? He's always like this." Amelia pulls her shirt down and struggles to stand.

Outside it's started raining hard. She goes to the back of the basement, through the door and up the steps to the backyard. Salvaged building supplies form silent hills under protective blue tarps. She stands there, letting her shirt get soaked, her hair get soaked. Steve is in the doorway at the foot of the stairs, lit up a sick yellow from the bare hanging bulb behind him. She turns away and when she turns back he's gone. It's just Amelia and the dark and the cold rain, the blue-tarp mounds like sleeping animals all around her.

22

Amelia knocks on Cat's door, a small terror coiling in her throat. She's afraid she's intruding, never mind Cat's open invitation. Afraid she's misunderstood, or Cat changed her mind. No one just walks up and knocks on Cat's door. It isn't done. But here is Amelia, knocking, calling out, "It's me. Amelia," and Cat calls back that she should come in, that the door is open.

Outside it's full noon, a bright clear early March day, but inside the apartment is dark but for a single lamp next to the couch, an orange tabby curled up asleep in the pool of light.

Cat emerges from the gloom. "Hey there, doll," she says. "Glad you came by." She places her small, cool palm over Amelia's eyes. "You look tired. You look worried."

"Can I stay here for a while?" Amelia asks. "I didn't want to stay home, and I didn't want to go to the shop, and I don't know where else to go."

"Sure. You stay as long as you want. Why don't you lie down on the couch and rest a bit?"

Amelia does, and Cat draws a blanket over her. Amelia closes her eyes and listens to Cat moving around the apartment. Washing dishes, making tea, talking quietly to herself or the cats.

When Amelia was a kid, she would sometimes pretend to be sick. Not because she didn't want to go to school, but because it meant that when her grandmother got home from her shift at midmorning and found Amelia home she would tuck her under a blanket on the couch and bring her tea and toast. Amelia would lie there with her eyes closed and listen to her grandmother move around the house.

On those days all the wanting and not having that she carried balled up like a rock in her belly would relax. She would feel happy, exactly where she was and exactly how she was; she would want nothing but what she had—the warmth of the couch, the sound of her grandmother's footsteps on the wide-planked floors. The knowledge that she was not alone, that she had only to call out and her grandmother would be there, at her side. Amelia didn't call out often; it was enough to know that she could.

Cat brings two mugs of tea, hands one to Amelia, and settles her little body on the floor beneath the windows. One of the heavy drapes hangs open and the sunlight filters in, weakened by the dust and the dirty glass, casting Cat in a waxy half-light like some fifties movie siren. Her features are clean-lined, noble, and Amelia sees Cat's lost beauty.

"I was talking to Steve," Amelia says. "He says you went away for a while. In the seventies?"

"I did. Had enough of the city, wanted something new. I was nineteen and I'd never gone farther away than the Bronx." She pauses, takes a big slurping sip of her tea, tugs the drape back into place and her face falls into shadow. "What else did he say, Old Man Steve?"

"Not much. Just that you went away and he doesn't know where to. He said you came back different."

Cat snorts. "Well, you know, travel is so *broadening*." A grimace, and then she lights a cigarette, then a long pause during which Amelia is sorry she brought Steve up at all. "No, it's true. Leaving home will change you—doesn't matter where you go. I'm guessing you know something about that yourself."

Amelia does know about that change. She wishes she didn't. "Where'd you go?"

"You want the story?" Cat says. She casts her voice low, almost a whisper, talking to her hands. Taking slow drags off her cigarette.

"This traveling flamenco troupe came through town the summer of seventy-three. Gypsies, like you hear about in stories. Three men, two women, all of them as young as me but they seemed so much older. Two of the men sang and played guitar, one man danced. The women just danced. Danced like their hair was on fire. Danced like it was the last, best thing they would ever do. And the songs, the voices of the men would rip right through you. *Cante jondo*, they call it. Deep song. That doesn't begin to touch the truth of it, flamenco done right. I'll wake up still, middle of the night, feeling that music in my bones.

"They were just passing through New York, had a few shows booked in supper clubs and then they were heading back home to Spain. To Granada. And then the plan was to travel all around Spain and down into Morocco. I took up with the guy who danced—Jaime was his name—and they invited me to join them. Not to sing or to dance, of course, but they needed some help with the costumes. Those great tiered dresses the women wore, and all that dancing was hell on the seams and the ruffles. I used to be pretty good with a needle and thread and I said what the hell and went along for the ride."

Amelia imagines olive-skinned women, black hair pulled back into severe buns. Imagines lean, dark men with flashing eyes and quick booted feet. Imagines Cat younger even than Amelia is now, riding along in a caravan in Spain, orange trees outside the window and a bold young Gypsy sliding his hand between her thighs.

"And then something went wrong?" Amelia ventures.

"Something went really wrong. In Morocco. Marrakesh. Goddamn city of heat. We reached Marrakesh in full summer. Bad time of year to be in the desert. And no time of year a good time to be a woman in Morocco, especially if you're an American woman; worse still with my light skin, my red hair. Jaime told me to stay close, not to go out without him or one of the other guys, but I didn't believe him. I'd come up on Thirteenth Street back in the day. What couldn't I handle, right?"

She pauses, sucks hard off her cigarette. Goes silent a long time and it seems like she's decided not to say more after all. Some stories being too hard to tell, maybe. Amelia's got stories like that herself.

"So I went out one night on my own. Jaime and I weren't getting along so well and the other women didn't speak any English and I hadn't picked up as much Spanish as I'd hoped I would. I needed to get out on my own and get some air. They came out of nowhere, I swear. This group of men. All ages. Young ones, old ones. Skinny ones, fat ones. I don't even know how many. I lost a bunch of teeth that night—these are dentures, bet you couldn't tell. Got these scars on my back—that was from a belt buckle. When they were done with me they dumped me on the doorstep of the place where we'd been staying for two weeks, like they'd known all along I was there and they were just waiting for me to be stupid enough to come out alone.

"I lay there and Jaime found me. They fixed me up best they could, but there was nowhere to go but home after that. And so I came back. Settled in. Hunkered down."

"Oh, Cat."

"It's okay, you know. Half the women you talk to here, or anywhere, have a story like mine. I just needed to travel all the way to Morocco to get beat down, for some reason. But it's not that special a story."

"Me too," Amelia says. "Before Gerrit took me in. Me too." The rough squats in those first days. Half out of her head with the fear and the dope and always the grabbing hands. The arms, the knees, the heavy hips, holding her back, pinning her down. Street tax. She'd paid up. There was nothing else to do. The dope made it better, until it didn't.

"Yeah. Yeah, I thought so." Cat stubs her cigarette out on the sole of her boot and lets the butt fall to the floor. "You were just a kid when you got here."

"Fifteen."

"Fifteen. Jesus." Cat's big, dark eyes flare up. She swallows hard. "Right, so once my back was healed I got the flames done. Not to cover the scars, you know. But to make them mine. Tattoos are scars, too, but I chose them. And no one sees them, unless I want them to." She sits beside Amelia, shucks her sweater off, her T-shirt. Peels off her tank top, shedding layers down to bare skin. She turns her back, its scars, its tattoos, its knobby spine, toward Amelia. "You can touch them. It's okay."

The scars run in long, stuttering stripes from Cat's neck all the way down her back, disappearing into the waistband of her jeans.

"I want you to." And then in a voice smaller than Amelia would have thought Cat capable, "Please."

Amelia does. She traces the scars slowly with her fingertips. Beginning with just one hesitant finger, but soon growing bolder, using both hands, letting her fingers trail along the gouges and rivets, the raised keloided stripes bubbled up like fat glossy caterpillars. The scar tissue is silky smooth and cool, a landscape in skin and those flames flickering red and orange and yellow across it all.

Amelia recalls a globe that sat on the windowsill of her fourth-grade classroom. It wasn't just flat colors marking borders and nations, continents and oceans. The surface of the globe rose and fell, showing the shape of the land. Amelia would stand at that windowsill every chance she got, spinning the globe and feeling the ridged mountain ranges and the broad flatness of the plains pass beneath her fingers, gazing out the window and imagining she could see all that she felt.

Amelia traces the ridges and plains of Cat's ruined back. She feels the heat of the desert in it, hears the whistle of the belt overhead in the moments before it came down to meet the flesh. She hears the men, feels their hateful hands on this small body. She traces the scars over and over, as beneath her hands Cat quietly weeps.

23

The front wheel of Gerrit's bike meets the Brooklyn Bridge bike path, and with that Gerrit is free. The melee of the Brooklyn streets falls behind him: the horns and radios, the angry cab drivers, the half-crazed dollar-van drivers, the city buses and their dumb bike-hungry wheels. He stands in the pedals and pumps steadily, each stroke a sweet burst of forward motion.

A fool's errand brought him to Brooklyn—he'd seen an ad for a dozen used bikes, in good condition and cheap, in a deserted corner of Gowanus. The guy selling them talked too much and too fast without saying anything, and when he threw open the door to the storage area Gerrit knew the bikes were stolen. The condition was too good on most of them, the price too low for what was there, and some of them still had the severed cables of their locks dangling from the frames. He'd thanked the guy for his time and ridden off. He'd known as soon as he'd heard the guy's voice through the tinny pay-phone receiver that it was too good to be true, which is why he hadn't bothered to borrow a van to bring the bikes back to the shop. It was just an excuse for a long ride. He should have skipped the bikes and ridden Ocean Avenue out to Sheepshead Bay to watch the fishing boats coming in.

A wasted trip, but it's a beautiful day, unseasonably warm for early March, the Manhattan Bridge to his right and beyond it the Williamsburg Bridge, and flowing beneath it all the East River. From up here you can forget how dirty that water is, forget the bikes and bodies and refuse sunk to the riverbed. From this height it's all blue and gold glinting in the afternoon light, flowing fast and steady toward the harbor, where it meets the Hudson and pushes ahead, the waters of Manhattan and Brooklyn, Jersey and Staten Island rushing together, fresh water gone to salt where the ocean swallows the bay.

He pedals, the wind a steady hand at his back, and there, rising up from the river, is Manhattan, the skyline opening up for him like the fanged, glorious mouth of God. He lets the bike coast, surrendering to the gravitational pull of that skyline. The Twin Towers are pure refracted light, the sun blazing up their mirrored skin so completely this time of day that he can't tell where the towers end and the sky begins.

He navigates the ramp on the Manhattan side, riding off the bridge and weaving through traffic, making his way northeast toward Chinatown, pushing through the blocks, plugged into the rhythm of the traffic and feeding onto Bowery, heading uptown. He rides past the crowds of bodies jostling on the packed sidewalks, dodges through the crush of traffic that stutters along the avenue. Past the grocers with their spiky durian fruits and their piles of gingerroot and stinking dried fish. Past the Music Palace with its kung fu double features: five bucks for two movies; faded velvet seats and faded velvet walls; the rise and fall of Cantonese all around him.

Pedaling north, out of Chinatown, past the Bowery Mission, where a handful of homeless sit on chairs in the doorway and ranged out on the sidewalk, groaning and muttering as a double-decker tour bus huffs slowly past in a cloud of excited tourist chatter and flashbulbs. "The zoo is in the Bronx, assholes!" one of the men shouts, flicking a cigarette butt at the departing bus.

Gerrit pulls up outside Irving's building, hoists the bike to his shoulder, and climbs the narrow staircase to the office.

"No news," Irving says as Gerrit walks through the door. He's seated behind his desk, dwarfed by piles of paper and books, an overfull ashtray balanced precariously on the pile nearest to hand.

Gerrit stands in front of the desk, his bike leaning against his hip. "They haven't turned up to make any repairs," he says. "But we didn't think they would."

"But they haven't made any move to appeal, either," Irving says, "which is strange. Very strange. Judge Sykes blocks the eviction and the city goes quiet for almost a month now? Quiet worries me."

"Me too."

Irving fishes a soft pack of Marlboro 100's out of his shirt pocket, taps out a cigarette, then tosses the pack to Gerrit.

"Cheers." Gerrit lights up, drawing the smoke deep into his lungs.

"Keep the pack," Irving says, sneaking glances at Gerrit's right hand.

Gerrit taps his two right fingers on the pile of paper at the front of the desk. Irving wants to see? Let him get an eyeful. "They'll make a move soon. They're waiting for us to drop our guard, get comfortable again."

Irving looks Gerrit carefully in the eye. "You don't strike me as a man who gets comfortable, Gerrit."

"No."

"Well, then we don't have to worry about that. You keep your eyes open, keep your ears open. I'll do the same." Cigarette in the corner of his mouth, eyes squinting from the smoke as he searches through a stack of file folders in front of him. "Damn things like to hide in plain sight," he mutters. "How's Amelia doing? How's that baby of yours coming along?"

"Good. The doctors say everything looks good. She's more than halfway there, now. She's tired a lot."

"Sure, sure. Only natural." He pulls a thick folder from the bottom of the stack and flicks it open. "Anything changes, I hear from the city, I'll be in touch." He's got his reading glasses on now, balanced on the tip of his nose. He salutes Gerrit with his cigarette. They're done here.

Gerrit pauses. "Is that file for our case?"

"Hmmm? This? No. Something else." He closes the folder, laying a palm flat across the blank cover. "Ride safe," Irving says, nodding toward Gerrit's bike.

Gerrit shoulders the bike and makes his way down the staircase, the worn carpet slippery under his feet. It's coming on dusk, the blue sky giving way to encroaching gray. He throws a leg over the bike and pushes on toward home.

24

Three o'clock in the morning and Gerrit is wide awake. He's been lying in bed since midnight, but he can't make his mind stop whirring. Lying in his own bed, small cold cot that it is. There's no more slipping into bed with Amelia—she put a stop to that tonight. Cat had been over for dinner again, and when she finally left around ten and Amelia got into bed, Gerrit had gone to join her like usual. She'd turned to him, put her palm flat against his chest, not so much a touch as a push, and she'd said, "I need to sleep alone from now on. With my belly getting so big and all, and I get so overheated. The bed's too small. Okay? I need my space. Okay?" Then her palm had gone soft and she gave his chest a little pat. "Please," she said.

She needs her space. Maybe so, but Gerrit can't help noticing this need for space in bed coinciding with her sudden attachment to Cat.

Cat. She's all Amelia talks about. What Cat said, what Cat did, what Cat thinks. Half their food goes to feed Cat. Amelia barely turns up at the bike shop at all anymore. She's totally wrapped up in that damn woman. A girlish crush. He'll have to ride it out, like any other of her dalliances. But she's never sent him out of her bed before.

He stands outside the door of her room and hears her breathing slow and even. Asleep. He goes in, creeping to the side of her bed. She's got the covers thrown back and her shirt is hiked up, that gentle globe of her belly tilted down into the mattress. The streetlight through the window plays across her skin and he sees the baby moving, slow languorous rolls just beneath the surface. He lays a hand on her belly, feels the baby flutter and jab against his palm, and Amelia mutters in her sleep, shifting into his hand, deepening the contact. He could slip into bed behind her. He could hold her while she sleeps, one hand cupped around the baby just like this.

There's an explosion of shouts and footsteps outside the window, then someone banging on the front door. Gerrit runs out to the hallway and here comes Steve, who's on night watch, bounding up the stairs, hair wild and eyes wilder and his breathing rushed and shallow, and he shouts, "Fire! Fire at Cat House!" and then he runs past Gerrit, banging on all the apartment doors as he goes, yelling, "Fire! Fire at Cat House!"

Fire! Back into the apartment and jamming his feet into his boots. This time everyone makes it out. He swears it. Swears it to Marrije, to Jurrie. This time he goes back in, as many times as it takes.

Iedereen komt er uit, Marrije. Ik zweer het. Ik beloof het je. Iedereen komt er uit, al wordt het mijn dood. Marrije, voor jou. En voor jou, Jurrie. Ik zweer het.

⊞

Steady banging on the apartment door, the sound of feet running down the staircase, shouts from the hallways and from the street outside the bedroom window. Amelia jolts awake, the clanging din of her nightmare proving true. Gerrit is in the doorway, stomping his feet into his boots and muttering to himself in Dutch.

"Eviction Watch?" she asks.

"Fire," he says. "Cat House is on fire." And then he's running for the door, grabbing a scarf from the table as he goes by. Amelia runs right behind him, stumbling into her boots, forgetting her coat, out the door, down the stairs. Everyone else is headed down, too, or already out. Buckets and fire extinguishers. On the street outside of Cat House, shouts and orders, head counts that come up short. The wail of sirens in the distance.

Lights come on in the windows of the other buildings around them, the commotion startling the block awake. Goddamn all the people in all the cars whirring by, up ahead on First Avenue, oblivious to the burning. Goddamn the streetlights, and the quiet sleeping streets beyond this block. Goddamn everyone who is safely quiet and warm, everyone who isn't here, who doesn't know the street is full of ash and choking black smoke and panic and tears and voices already going raw from calling out the names of the ones still missing.

The smoke curling out from the building is thick and black, coming from the basement door, and from the first-floor windows. It smells nothing at all like any fire Amelia has smelled before. Nothing like burning wood or paper. It is acrid and dark and choking. Burning plaster, old bricks cooking, and who knows what going up and it feels like the ash of Cat House is coating her nostrils, coating her throat. She looks around to see who's already out; she looks around for Cat. The front door is flung open and the hallway is all gone to smoke, flames licking the far wall beyond the staircase down to the basement. She sees Linda; she sees Kim. She does not see Cat. She grabs Kim's arm and Kim leans against her, eyes wide and out of focus.

"Amelia. Jesus, Amelia."

Amelia eases Kim down to sit on the curb. More people spill out of the building. Someone's busted the fire hydrant open and squatters are running back in with buckets, with fire extinguishers. Amelia sees Gerrit running inside, a scarf tied over his mouth and nose. She sees him pass through the front door, get swallowed up by the smoke. "Gerrit!" Jesus Christ, he ran right into the smoke. "Gerrit!"

And here comes Cat, duffel bags slung over both shoulders, the bags alive and wriggling and fighting against her as she stumbles out. Amelia runs to her side, takes one of the bags. "How many cats did you get out?"

"Four," Cat says. "That's as many as I could grab. You take these. I'm going back up for the rest of them. Stow them in your place? Keep them safe?"

More smoke pouring out, and the consuming crack of spreading flames. People come tripping back out with the buckets and the fire extinguishers, faces blackened, coughing, crying. No one's rushing back in again. They're bent over, leaning hands on knees to retch into the street, or falling down, wailing, grabbing on to one another. Gerrit is not among them. Gerrit has not come back out. Amelia grabs Cat's arm, digging in hard to what little flesh is there. Amelia will tackle Cat before she lets her go back in. She'll knock her out cold if she has to.

There's a huge crash and someone shouts, "Back away! Back away!" And where are the fire trucks? Where is the fucking fire department?

Cat lets out a low moan and sinks down, Amelia catching her, holding her in the middle of the street and rocking her as the building sends up bright orange sparks into the cold, and the sirens wail and wail but never seem to get any closer.

⊞

The smoke has a thickness. It has a weight to it. Gerrit feels it settling onto his skin, building up in his lungs, weighing down his eyelids. He had forgotten about that, forgotten how walking through smoke is like slow-motion swimming; forgotten how the edges of the world get erased, leaving nothing but the smoke and the desperate search for more air, more light. He ran into the building before he had time to think about it, because that was the only way he was going to get himself in there, but now he's inside, and he's thinking and his brain is throwing up alarm after alarm to GET THE FUCK OUT OF HERE, YOU FUCK-ING IDIOT. But not this time. Not until he's checked every room. Not until everyone is out. No one is dying in this fire—not if Gerrit survives it.

A shape moves in the smoke next to Gerrit, resolving into Marlowe. The fire is crackling up from the basement, the flames not reaching the first floor yet, but they don't have much time before it spreads. "I'll check this floor and the basement!" Gerrit shouts. "You go upstairs." He turns, and Ben is there, too, coughing, T-shirt pulled up over his mouth and nose. "Okay, Marlowe, check second and third floors. Ben, you have fourth and fifth!" Ben nods and Marlowe nods and they're on their way. Everything else, all the work on the buildings, all the meetings, all the night watches, they were nothing but practice for this moment. Gerrit trusts that they're all doing as much as they can, and working together. That is why no one is going to die tonight.

There are two apartments on the first floor. Gerrit rushes through them, finding no one. The door to the basement is hot to the touch, and smoke pours out from underneath. He runs back into one of the apartments, soaks the scarf in the sink, and wraps it around his mouth and nose again. Then back to the basement door, throws it open, smoke and flames and awful impossible heat blasting out at him. He wonders how much time he has, wonders if this is how he'll die after all, and if he's okay with that. He finds that he is not okay with that. But he runs down the stairs anyway, into the worst of it, waiting to fall through at each step. And then he's in the basement, in a world of smoke and flame, and he drops down to the floor, half-blinded. He makes his way on memory, searching the big community room, the storage area, the workshop, with his hands stretched out in front of him. He works his way around to the front, and just a few feet from the door up to the street his hands find flesh. Gideon is collapsed on the floor. Gerrit can't tell if he's breathing.

The smoke is too thick to see anything and his eyes are burning, his lungs scorched. The fire is roaring now, bits of plaster and lathe falling, cinders. He has to get out. He has to get Gideon out. He hauls Gideon from the floor (dead weight, but he pushes that thought down) and to the door, pulls it open, and drags them both up the steep metal stairs. The metal cellar doors in the sidewalk are mercifully open. He lurches up the last few steps, collapsing in a meaty tangle with Gideon on the sidewalk. Air! Voices calling out from the street. He fights to his feet, drags Gideon by the armpits, and stumbles toward the voices. Between his hands, he feels Gideon's ribs expand, feels him starting to cough.

He sees the streetlights overhead like refracted planets. He feels the cold, clean air scouring his lungs. Hands reach out and take Gideon; hands reach out and catch Gerrit, and he's being lowered to the street, the scarf unwound from his mouth and nose. He turns his head and there's Amelia sitting in the middle of the street, cradling Cat, rocking her like a child.

25

Gerrit stands across the street from the charred wreck of Cat House. Steve walks circles around him, pacing, tugging at his hair. "Are you okay, man?" Gerrit says. All that nervous energy pouring off Steve—he looks manic, unpredictable. Gerrit doesn't like that; he doesn't trust it. Now, more than ever, they need to be clearheaded.

"Am I okay?" Steve says. "That's what you just asked me? For real?"

"Take it easy, man. We need to hold steady, *ja*?"

Steve snorts, blows his hair from his eyes with a twist of his lips. "I'm steady, man. Like a fucking rock over here."

You'd better be, thinks Gerrit. Blue police barricades block access to Cat House. A pair of cops sits in a radio car, and another pair is stationed behind the barricades.

Most of the Cat House squatters have been taken in by Thirteen House, crashing in sleeping bags in the apartments or the community room. The rest have been absorbed by

Utopia. No one will have to go to a shelter. No one will be out on the street—at least as long as Thirteen House can continue to fight off the city lawyers. At least until they come for Utopia, too.

The housing official who arrived last night just behind the fire department, armed with an emergency vacate order before the extent of the damage was even known, said that no one could go back inside but that at nine this morning the fire department would send a few men into the building to collect everyone's belongings. Maybe he expected them each to have a bedroll and a bandana tied to a stick.

There's a lot of talk about how the fire got started. No one believes it was an accident. No one believes it was just bad luck or bad wiring—they did the wiring themselves— and no one cops to having been smoking in the basement, where the fire chief said it seems to have started. No one cops to having been in the basement at all, middle of the night. And why would they lie? That isn't the kind of thing you lie about. You fuck up, you own it. It's always been that way.

Linda said she saw Gideon running down to the basement from his ground-floor apartment holding a fire extinguisher. Whatever he saw down there, he's in no shape to talk yet.

The squatters have been waiting outside the barricades since dawn, even though the fire department wasn't expected until nine. Six firefighters showed up, mercifully on time and not unsympathetic, and have just gone in for everyone's belongings. People shuffle around in small circles or sit on the sidewalk, not really talking. They look tired, beat down. Homeless. Something's shifted in the group, in their voices, in the set of their shoulders.

"If something good doesn't happen soon, I think the city's won," Gerrit says to Steve. "Our army over there looks ready to retreat."

"They've lost their queen bee. That's gonna take its toll, if Cat can't pull her shit together. How is she this morning? Better?"

Gerrit shrugs, spits through his teeth, and the spittle casts a wet arc toward the street. Amelia brought Cat back to their place last night, along with four of her stinking cats—one of which promptly pissed on the couch. Cat couldn't sleep in the wet spot left after they'd cleaned up the cat piss—Amelia wouldn't hear of it—and so Cat slept with Amelia, which was probably Amelia's intention all along. Gerrit paced the floor in the few hours that stood between the fire's end and dawn, back and forth in front of Amelia's open door, watching the two of them wrapped around each other in sleep, Amelia's rounded belly between them. He'd been afraid they'd have to sit up with Cat until morning, she was in such rough shape, but she'd passed out right away, her brain shutting her body down to protect from the overload.

He hadn't expected her to be as soft as that. He'd expected her to be able to weather the fire, weather whatever loss it might bring. No matter what else he thought about Cat, he'd always thought of her as a survivor, but here she

is, crumbling into dust. When he left the apartment at
dawn to see what help there was to offer, to see if maybe
they could sneak into Cat House from the back or from
the roof (they couldn't; cops were posted on the adjoining
rooftops, including their own roof), Cat and Amelia had
both just woken up. All those *godvergeten* animals milling
around and Amelia hovering and offering Cat tea, offering
her toast; throwing her arms around that shrunken little
voodoo body; kissing the cheeks beneath those hollow
eyes. Cat just sat there, not speaking. "She's dead," Gerrit
wanted to say. "Can't you see she's dead? Leave her be."

"Cat's in rough shape," he tells Steve. "Our friends from
Cat House had best find they're more than just the crowd
that walks behind her."

The first load of belongings is hauled out, a tangled
pile of clothes and books, the neck of an acoustic guitar
reaching up from the folds of cloth. They're using rescue
stretchers to carry everything out, which would amuse
Gerrit if it were a different building on a different day.
Where were those stretchers when they were trying to get
everyone out last night?

They did get everyone out, but no thanks to the fire
department for that. Everyone is alive and accounted for,
only five people taken to the hospital, with mostly second-
degree burns, treated and released. Gideon, the worst off,
was admitted, but Kim called Irving's office from Bellevue
to say they'd be releasing him later in the day. The fire department had taken twenty minutes to show up, waiting
just long enough to be sure the damage was done, to be

sure the fire got good and hot. There's no reason it should take twenty minutes to get fire trucks to a burning building in Manhattan.

"Here comes Cat," Steve says. He nods to Irving, who's just stepped out of a cab.

Amelia leads Cat up to the barricades. She looks a thousand years old, creeping along, squinting in the sunlight, clinging to Amelia's arm. She grabs hold of one of the cops and pulls him toward her, hissing in his ear, and it takes four squatters to pull her off before he can reach for his pepper spray or his nightstick. Kim and Marlowe hold Cat back while Amelia talks to the cop, making slow, placating gestures, pointing to Cat, pointing up to Cat's windows.

"I've got a kid coming right behind me with bagels and coffee for everyone," Irving says. "I know, a bagel's not much in the face of a fire, but it certainly never hurt anyone. Eat, keep up your strength." Irving looks to be wearing yesterday's dress shirt and last week's shave. "I talked to the judge, talked to DeMarkis. Cat House is sunk, I'm afraid. I wish I could do more." He waves a hand in front of his face as if to clear away the police barricades, clear away the black soot ringing the mouths of the glassless windows. "Terrible thing, this fire. We'll look into how it got started. We'll ask the questions."

Another stretcher comes through the door, this one heavy with bodies. Cat House was full of animals—not just Cat's strays. Nearly everyone had at least one pet. Gerrit can't recall how many he saw last night, though he does have vague recollections of terrified bundles of fur struggling in arms here and there, fighting against bags and the walls of carriers, so some were saved. Still, the stretcher is full of them. Even from across the street, Gerrit can see the soot and ash thick in the fur. There are twenty bodies, easily. Cats and dogs. A moan ripples through the gathered crowd and Cat falls against the cop with a wail. The cop has the good sense to nod to Amelia and hand Cat off. The firefighters have the good sense to look sympathetic and ease the stretcher down slowly so people can gather their pets up, feel the fur, hold them one last time.

"The firemen are going to have to take those animals with them," Irving says. "Public health issue. I'll go explain that now so it doesn't come as a shock." Irving pats Gerrit's shoulder and crosses the street, going first to Cat. He crouches down where she's bawling on the sidewalk and takes her hand, talking softly to her.

Steve shakes his head. "Aw, Cat."

"I always figured she was tougher than that," Gerrit says.

Steve says, "A person can only take so much. That woman's taken enough. More than her share. She's full up." He lights a fresh smoke off the butt of the old one, his hands shaking slightly. "No. They're not going to have Mama Cat to lean on anymore, are they?"

⊞

Oh God, the cats. Their bodies look so much smaller dead. A pile of abandoned toys, sooty and waterlogged. Griselda, that bony old bitch, she's right on top. Cat's fingers twitch and stroke the air, recalling the feel of the old girl's fur under her hand, the way her sharp spine would arch up into her palm. Old Grizzy dead, Red Tom dead, the kittens X, Y, and Z dead.

The list of Cat's dead grew long way before this fire, the names falling faster each passing year. The cats are just a sick footnote to it all. Aspirin Jack's coat ghosting across the filmy water of the Hudson, caught up in the polluted current, was pointing the way. Float till it pulls you under. No way out but down.

26

Only three days since the fire and already Gerrit wants to put a fist through a wall or a woman through a window. Cat has moved in with them, and she throws a cloud of grief and anxiety around Amelia that he can't penetrate. He's left with peanut butter and jelly dinners and pants covered in cat fur, the *godvergeten* animals tripping him wherever he goes. Cat's mangy strays leaving fur and puddles of piss everywhere, Cat's wasted body filling Gerrit's space in Amelia's bed. It's intolerable.

Meanwhile, on the heels of the fire, the city appealed Judge Sykes's decision and the appellate court overturned it. Thirteen House is unprotected. They need to hunker down and prepare for battle, but everyone is still reeling from the fire and Gerrit can't get anyone to focus on the task at hand.

"This won't do," he tells Amelia, following her into the bathroom and shutting the door, the first chance to catch her alone in days. "You need your rest and this harpy is devouring you."

"Don't tell me what I need." She jabs her toothbrush into her mouth, brushing in sharp, angry strokes.

"Can't you see how this is draining you? Think of the baby."

"You just don't like Cat."

"No," he says. "No, I don't. She's not good for you."

"Everyone's taken in at least one person from Cat House. When did you become too good to help out?" She spits into the sink and slams out of the bathroom.

"You're exhausted. You're running around taking care of Cat when you should be taking care of yourself and the baby."

"You mean when she should be taking care of you," Cat says, her voice only the thinnest sliver of itself. She's a deposed queen draped across their couch, Amelia crouched by her feet. Gerrit could vomit at the sight of it.

"Don't you have somewhere you need to be?" he says. "Don't you have twenty or so comrades—who just lost their home, same as you—looking to you to help them move on, to figure out what comes next? So willing to be the queen of Cat House, but where are you now that they really need you? Cowering on my couch, making a pregnant girl work herself sick taking care of you."

"I'm not making her do anything," Cat says, a hand over her eyes. "And the good people of Cat House don't need me to tell them what's next. There is no next. Or can't you see that yet? Next already happened. It's done."

"Leave her alone." Amelia glares right through him. As if he hadn't been the one to take *her* in, feed *her*, care for *her*. As if they didn't have these years between them. As if this wasn't his home, and he the one who made a place for her in it.

"No. If you don't have enough sense to see what's good for you, I do. Cat, you're leaving. You have other friends to suck dry. You leave my home. You leave my family alone. Now." He tosses one of her duffel bags—stinking of smoke and cat piss and fear—at her. "And don't forget your cats."

He expects her to fight back. He expects it to be harder than that, but Cat isn't the woman she once was. She pats Amelia's cheek. She stands and steps into her boots, pulls on her coat, gathers up the cats.

"You don't have to go," Amelia says. "It's my apartment, too, and I want you to stay." Amelia is crying. *Better this small hurt now*, thinks Gerrit, *than a worse hurt later*. Better to rout out the tumor before it spreads, before Cat really drags Amelia down. It's for the best. For Amelia, for the baby.

"Not like this, honey," Cat whispers, and then she's gone. Out the door. Down the stairs. Thank God.

⊞

"Who the fuck do you think you are?" Amelia says.

"Have you looked in the mirror? Have you stopped worrying about her and waiting on her long enough to feel how she's drained you? She was wearing you down." Gerrit sits on the couch, head in hands. So weary. So put-upon.

"This has nothing to do with what's good for me. At least Cat loves me. Loves me and doesn't want anything from me."

"Cat loves you, does she? Is that what love looks like?" He's back on his feet, moving toward her, face red, gearing up to rage. There'll be some chairs knocked over now. There'll be some stomping, some shouting. But she won't be the one to give this time. She won't be the one to go to him, soothing, conceding. Not this time.

"I've fucking had it," she says. "I'm done. Done pretending we're a couple, done letting you paw me at night."

"Pretending we're a couple?" His face has gone white, mouth closing and opening like a fish's.

"Have you been telling the lie so long you believe it yourself?"

"What lie?"

"The whole"—she waves her hands in front of her face—"all of it. Letting people think we're together."

"We are together. We have been together."

"This is what together looks like to you? Living like roommates and me putting up with you groping me every once in a while?"

"We've been together. All along. We're having the baby together. I don't understand—"

"Calling yourself the father doesn't make the baby yours."

"I don't see anyone else stepping up to claim him." His eyes rake her body. "Or you."

He still sees her like she was in the beginning, she realizes. Still the helpless little junkie, waiting to be saved. "It's Steve's baby."

He shakes his head, gives a condescending cluck of his tongue. "You're being childish. Don't drag him into this just to try to hurt me."

"The baby is Steve's!" she shouts. She's been swallowing it for months and now it bursts out of her, as loud as hell. Gerrit's face is stony, but his eyes go glassy, blinking fast. Good. "I've been fucking Steve!"

Gerrit's face convulses, the muscles fighting against the skin. He tips forward and she thinks he might fall, but he grabs her shoulders, dropping his weight down through his hands. She goes to catch his elbows, but he isn't falling. He's gripping her shoulders hard, shoving her backward, across the kitchen table. He's growling and muttering in Dutch, words she doesn't know, a river of sharp sounds hurled at her.

She struggles against him, kicking out, trying to stand up, but he pins her against the table. He tugs her jeans down. The sound of his zipper, denim on skin, and he pushes inside her. He's hard and he's inside her, his left hand against her chest, holding her down against the cold enamel of the kitchen table. His right half-hand goes snaking through her hair, and terrible keening noises leak from his mouth. His belly slides against her belly, against the baby.

There's a paring knife lying just inches away, and she grabs it. Her fingers close around the handle and she brings it to his throat and says through gritted teeth, "Get off of me." Her voice hard and low and she says, "Get the fuck off of me." She lets the blade dip into his skin, just a nick, just a prick. It blooms up red and he falls away.

She pulls her pants up, pulls her coat on, stumbles out the door, past Anne's dumb stunned face in the hallway, down the stairs, numb to the croaking creaking sound of Gerrit's voice.

Amelia ran out with nothing and now she has nothing. Her clothes, her money, her knitting, her prenatal vitamins, all of it is back in the apartment—in Gerrit's apartment. She wanders hazily from block to block, not quite noticing where she's going, the world around her a vague smear. She'll have to go back for her things. She can't go back. Her prenatal vitamins, her orange scarf, her red sweater. She has to have her red sweater. She focuses on that. Worries around its seams and edges. Plots ways to get it back, thinks of people she can send in after it. The sweater. Focus on the sweater, she tells herself, not on the apartment, on the man inside the apartment. Don't think of his awful, angry face. The bead of sweat that fell from his chin to the hollow of her throat.

Think of the blade against his throat. Think of the blood. He is dead. Gerrit is dead. She wills him dead.

She staggers against a lamppost, leans over into the gutter and retches, vomit spattering the curb, the toes of her boots. This can't be happening.

⊞

Gerrit lies on the kitchen floor taking it all back, wishing it all undone. His unreliable prick picking this day of all days to work. The fear, the surprise on her face. The absolute betrayal. Everything she's ever done to hurt him was erased the moment her back touched that table. Gerrit is now wrong, completely wrong, wrong forever. And the worst of it, how good it felt to see that fear on her face. How right, how just it all felt, in the moment. How she was getting what she deserved, how he was taking what was his.

This is not who he thought he was. Some kind of monster has uncurled in his belly.

And now she's gone, Amelia and the baby are gone.

He rubs at his neck. Already the blood's stopped. A moan, but it's not from him, and he rolls toward the sound, toward the door that Amelia left hanging open, and there's Anne in the hallway. Anne surely heard Amelia yelling, the way sound travels in this building and living right overhead as she does. Anne heard and here she is now, looking in at Gerrit.

Gerrit finds his mind reaching for logic, for explanations, for something to cover the worst of what he's done. But Anne could have heard only Amelia shouting about the baby. She has no way of knowing what came after that. Anne knows only the shock that Gerrit knew before he laid hands on Amelia.

Steve. Amelia and Steve.

⊞

Amelia finds Cat in Tompkins Square, over by the dog run. She's on a bench, duffel bags at her feet, the cats wriggling and clawing against the fabric. Kim's there with her, and Gideon. Gideon with bandages on both hands and a burn across one cheek—an angry red welt weeping yellow beneath a thick layer of ointment. Gideon's beautiful face. Goddammit.

Amelia feels like she's been ripped open, like every bad thing she's ever done, every bad thing that's ever been done to her, is radiating out from her in a toxic haze. There is the baby, who is good, who is pure, and wrapped around him is the rotting, wasted corpse that Amelia hauls around. She is a broken thing; a useless, used thing. But the baby is good; the baby is pure. And so she won't lie down in the park to die; she won't lie down in the street to die.

Kim says, "We've found a couple of spots in a building over on Fourth and D, just opened up a few weeks ago. You can come with us, if you want to."

Amelia nods. Yes, yes, she wants to.

⊞

Steve comes home to find Héctor Lavoe on the stereo and Anne on the couch. Three in the afternoon and she's got a beer in her hand and she's listening to "Periódico de ayer" and crying. "What does this song mean?" she says. "Tell me the words."

And no good could come of it—she never listens to his music, never drinks alone in the afternoon, something is up, something big and bad—but what else can he do but tell her? "Your love is yesterday's newspaper."

"I figured out that much. What else does it say?"

"Anne," he says. "What's wrong?"

"I want to know what the song says."

No, baby. You don't. "A sensation when it came out in the morning, by noon confirmed news, and forgotten by afternoon."

"Yeah," she says, nodding. She swigs her beer like she's aping some coarser, angrier woman. "Yeah, that's what I thought. You play this song a lot."

"It's a good song."

"It's a good song." She stands up, steady on her feet. Not drunk. Something else. "Dance with me."

"What's wrong, Annie?"

"Dance with your fucking wife, Steve." She swipes at her tears with the hand that holds her beer bottle, spilling some onto the floor.

So he takes her in his arms and dances with her. She's warm and there's that good homey smell of hers. He pulls her in close, rocks and sways her through the steps. For once she surrenders to his lead and it's the most natural dance they've ever had. But then her feet stop moving and she's crying harder, shaking.

"I know that's your baby." Her words come out guttural and hoarse, like she's choking on them. "I know . . . oh God." She doesn't push him away; she doesn't scream or beat him or kick him out. She simply leans into his chest and weeps.

A metallic taste, something like blood or maybe it's fear, floods Steve's mouth. "Oh, Annie. I'm so sorry. Oh Jesus."

"You're sorry," she says.

"I love you. Only you. It meant nothing. Annie, listen, I—"

She smacks him hard across the mouth. "It meant nothing."

"Nothing." The one-night stands with girls who'd take him home from the bar, girls he'd meet on the train or on the job, they were never about Anne. Not even the affair with Cat. None of it meant a damn thing. But Anne, she doesn't want to hear that. Let her think this is where it began, because this has got to be where it ends. Hang up your hat, *viejo*. Squeeze those wandering eyes shut. Oh Lord, how he's fucked up. He's fucked it up big time.

"You made a baby, Steve. What the hell are you going to do about it?"

His boy. He's been reaching for the answer for months, but now it comes clear. "I'm going to let him go. He'll have Amelia, he'll have Gerrit. I'm letting him go." And now it's Steve's turn to weep. *Que dios te bendiga, hijo.*

"That's how it feels," she whispers.

She goes to the stereo, puts the song on again. "Dance with me," she says. She looks at him but she doesn't meet his eyes. So he does. He dances with his wife.

27

The squat is so new it doesn't have a name. The people living there don't have names, their faces blurring together. Crusty punks, junkies, mental cases. One arrives, another leaves. No heat, no electricity, no water. Piss buckets instead of toilets and no one ever wants to be the one to empty them, so they don't get emptied nearly enough. A sickening ammonia stench wafts through the rubbled rooms whenever an overfull bucket gets sloshed or tipped over.

A newly opened building is always rough, but as far as Amelia can see no one's working to make this one better. Just a bunch of kids and a couple of truly scary old-timers looking for some walls and a floor, a roof without too many holes. A place to crash while they wait for something to happen to them. It's the kind of place Amelia left behind when she went to live at Thirteen House. She thought she'd left it behind for good. Someone might step up and be a leader here. Kick out the junkies who don't want to

get clean. Lay down some house rules. Form work parties.
Get people moving. But Amelia doesn't see that kind of
leader in the wasted faces she passes in the halls. And she
doesn't see Cat pulling herself together to be that kind of
leader again.

Kim and Gideon lasted all of two days. Amelia is ready
to pack it in, too. But Cat insists on staying, and Amelia
can't leave her. Not here, not like this. They've claimed a
small space in a far corner of the first floor as their room.
No door, so they hung a blanket for privacy, but at least
none of the windows back there are broken, so it doesn't
get too cold. Except at night, when they have to huddle
together for warmth. But it's the end of March already, the
worst of winter behind them and spring coming on soon.
They could make it here, maybe. It might be okay.

It might be okay if Cat can hold on. She hasn't left the
nest of their blankets, except to stagger to the piss bucket,
in days. The remaining four cats ran off, maybe in search
of someplace with more food to offer, or sensing that Cat
had nothing left for them, and she doesn't seem to notice
they're gone.

Amelia still hasn't gone to collect her things from Gerrit's apartment. She may write it all off as lost, start fresh.
Kim and Gideon are settled for now in Utopia, crashing in
the community room with a few others from Cat House,
but that can't last forever and they're talking about leaving New York. Gideon heard things are better out West, in
Portland. Cheaper and cleaner and plenty of squats if you
want to squat, but rents you can actually afford. Amelia

visits them every day, borrows clean clothes, eats some food and tucks some away for Cat, who will refuse to eat it.

The more they talk about getting out, the more sense it makes. To go, to start over—no Gerrit, no Steve. Go and have the baby and raise him someplace quieter than New York. Someplace green. Work a simple job that will pay the rent; have a small, clean place of their own—a place no one can take from them. Just Amelia and the baby. They could have a little garden, maybe. When he gets older she could teach him the things her grandmother taught her: How to train bean plants up a pole. How to tell when tomatoes are ripe enough to eat. They could eat the tomatoes right off the plant, still warm from the sun.

"Cat," Amelia says to the lump beneath the blankets. "I think we should maybe leave the city. Kim and Gideon are talking about Oregon. Portland. I think maybe we should go, too."

A dry laugh from beneath the blanket turns into a hacking cough, the blanket shuddering violently. "I already tried to leave once. Never got west of Ohio. My traveling days are behind me."

"When did you go west?"

"When I left. In seventy-three."

"Before Spain?"

"I've never been to Spain." Cat throws the blanket back from her face. It's grown older in just the past week, deeply lined and shrinking into itself. Her eyes don't quite track as she looks toward Amelia, and for the first time and probably a week too late it occurs to Amelia that there's more going on beneath the blanket than simple depression, and that letting Cat stay in this den of junkies was a grave mistake. "I've never left the country." She waves a skeletal hand toward the dirty windows. "You believed me, didn't you? Morocco and the Gypsies and the gang of men."

Amelia nods, the polka-dot flamenco dresses in her mind crumbling to dust. "You're using again."

"So what if I am?"

"So nothing. Do what you want, I guess."

"That's right. Can you blame me? All those years clean and what damn good did it do me? Just a little bit, just to smooth out the edges. It's not so bad."

"I don't know. Seems like a big step back to me."

"Honey, we already fell so far back we landed in a shit pile. What's another stumble or two, if it makes the shit stink less?"

Amelia shrugs. There's no arguing with her, no talking her clean. Her mother didn't listen, no matter how Amelia cried, no matter how she begged. Cat won't listen, either. Can't tell a junkie what's what any more than you can tell a drunk. They get clean when they're good and ready, or they die. Amelia has to form a steel-cold ball around her love for Cat, or they'll both go down together. She's learned that much.

"Okay, so here's the thing," Cat says. "The truth that you wanted, yeah? There was this guy, Paul. I wanted to leave New York—had to leave New York—and he was headed out of town in an old pickup. So I took up with him.

We were headed for Washington. State, not DC. There was some hippie commune he wanted to find, but what the fuck did I care about a commune? I just wanted to get gone and his truck was pointed in the right direction. We hooked up because that was the price of the ride, you know? We got to Ohio on the third day—Columbus—and didn't get much farther than that. We ran out of gas, ran out of money, and stopped to take on odd jobs so we could keep driving, get to that commune."

Cat bolts upright, squinting toward the window, as if startled by some passing shadow or ghost. Her heavy red dreadlocks have started to uncoil and tangle around her head in a wild orbit. Amelia can see the shape of Cat's skull emerging from beneath the thin, worn surface of her skin. Her mouth twists unnaturally as she talks and Amelia has to push down a small jolt of fear, an unexpected revulsion that makes her want to run from the room.

"He turned out to be an angry drunk, and I should have left the first time he hit me. These are dentures; that much is true. He kicked most of my teeth out one night, but it wasn't till a few nights later that he took a belt to me, buckle side down. And that's what it took to get me to walk away. All these years later, I'm still ashamed to say it took as much as that."

Do the scars matter less if Cat turns out to be just another American woman beaten by another drunk American man? Amelia feels like something has been taken from her, that Cat has somehow been diminished in the light of the true version of the story. If this *is* the true version. Though what could be more expected, more pedestrian than that? You don't make up a story that sounds like the same story any girl on the corner could tell you. So it must be the truth. Hitching a ride out of town, just to get out of town, to get anywhere but where you are now, falling in with a hard-drinking man, getting beaten down. Crawling home. Sure sounds like the truth to Amelia. The dull, ugly truth.

Amelia can't fault Cat for lying. If your lowest point came as part of some bold adventure, doesn't that make it somehow less shameful? You took a wild chance, and you got hurt. Got hurt badly. But look at you, a survivor. You made it through, and what a story you have to tell. But only if you tell it with Gypsies and gaudy dresses and the hot desert sun. Tell it with a faceless pack of foreign men attacking just the once and then leaving you, broken but without having chosen your tormenter, without having the burden of knowing his name, knowing his face. Without the burden of knowing you could have chosen differently.

"So there you have it. Whaddya think of old Cat now, honey?" She collapses back against the mattress, exhausted from the telling. "Now go on, let me get some rest. If you still want to talk about leaving, we can do it tonight. But I'm tired."

⊞

Space, Anne wants space. There's no space here. There's hardly any air.

Steve is going to have a baby. Why should Steve get to have a baby, after everything Anne has lost, after Anne's body turned itself inside out trying to make a baby with him?

She's packing a box to bring to her sister's house. She lied to Cindy, telling her she wanted to get her best things to a safe place in case the eviction went through. She couldn't say, "I want to smuggle myself out of this life piece by piece." She couldn't say, "Tell me to leave him. Tell me I need to get out."

She takes her favorite mixing bowl down from the cabinet, wraps it in newspaper, and nestles it into a box she got from a bodega. Next, the mugs her friend Jessica made for her in college. Jessica was in Alaska last Anne heard—Alaska. Wouldn't that be something?—but that was years ago.

She should leave. She thinks she might leave. But if she does, there's nothing stopping Steve from claiming that baby. He's letting the baby go to keep her. So if she stays it will be to spite him, to ensure his losses match her own.

How small. How terribly, horribly small.

No. She knows she loves him. He has done this awful, unforgivable thing, and yet she wants to find a way to forgive him. She wants a loophole that will allow her to stay without the shame of staying, without the burden of his betrayal.

He said that it was nothing, that this was the only time, and she wants him to mean it. She wants to *trust* that he means it. But there have been so many late drunken nights over the years, so many signs, and always she chose to look the other way. How can she believe it was just this once?

It's unthinkable. How can she stay? She can't stay.

The Chinese candlesticks with the red enamel cicadas, her mother's silver locket, her grandmother's spoon rest: into the box.

Cindy will be there with the car soon. She'll drive Anne to her house, and Anne will stow the box in Cindy's basement and pretend it doesn't mean what it means. She'll smile; she'll tell her sister everything is fine.

So far only Steve, Gerrit, and Amelia know the truth about the baby, and Amelia's gone now, moved out after the fight with Gerrit. There's no telling if she'll be back, or if Gerrit would take her in again. So maybe she's gone. Maybe that part of it is done. And if Amelia keeps quiet about Steve and the baby, and Gerrit and Steve and Anne keep quiet about it, maybe there's a way to walk through the shame, to contain it within these walls and endure.

The shame doesn't come from Steve's faithlessness— that's all on him—but from her choice to stay in spite of it. If she told Cindy, or if others found out, she would have to explain herself, to prove that her reasons for staying with him are not based in weakness, in fear.

Which she first needs to prove to herself.

Her childhood photo album, into the box. Cindy will be there soon. Anne could throw some clothes into a bag, too. She could ride out to Brooklyn with Cindy and just not come back. She wishes that felt like more of an option than it does.

⊞

When Amelia left Cat, it was with the intention of going to find Kim at Utopia Squat. Get some food, bring it back to Cat, figure out their next move. But Kim wasn't at the squat, and she wasn't in the park, and Amelia finds herself now leaving the park, headed north. She finds herself turning right at Thirteenth Street. She finds herself at the bike shop door.

And there is Gerrit inside, working. Still alive, apparently. No obvious signs of suffering. The radio is playing. There's a cup of coffee on the counter, the remains of a bagel. Life is going on, in spite of everything. Gerrit is going on. Damn him. She pushes through the door hard, letting it slam against a folding chair set down too close behind it, half hoping to shatter the glass, but it holds. Gerrit looks up and it's too late to sneak away. She wishes she'd thought of something to say beforehand. Something sharp she could hurl at him, something that would draw blood. She has nothing.

"You're here," he says, half-breathless like he's just taken a punch to the gut, and she thinks, *Well, there's that.* She's gotten to him a little, at least. Just by being there, by showing up like this.

"I didn't mean to come here. I don't know why I did." She'd expected him to look different somehow. She'd expected that when she saw him again her hatred would be strong and pure, as strong as it is when she lies awake at night listening to Cat's ragged breathing, remembering again and again his hands on her shoulders, her back against the table. She'd expected a hatred so strong he would be incinerated by a single look. She had not expected to look at him and have that hate complicated, to feel it mixing with all that came before it—the love, the gratitude, the familiarity. Which makes it so much worse. Pure hate is easy. Pure hate burns with righteous fire. She wants that fire. She wants it to burn him. Not this complication. Not these memories. Not this softness in his face.

"I hate you," she says.

"Yes. Yes, you should. Of course you do." She sees now the deep circles beneath his eyes. Sees the way his throat fights against his words. The tension in his jaw. His hands skittering back and forth along the counter like frightened insects.

"It didn't have to be that way," she says. "I would have let you. I didn't want it, but I would have let you. If you'd asked."

"But why, if you didn't want it? All this time, all these years. If you didn't want me touching you, why did you let me?"

"It didn't seem like so much to ask."

"You felt sorry for me."

"I don't anymore."

"Well, that's something. You never should have. I didn't need your *godvergeten* pity, Amelia. I didn't need your charity. I love you. That's all. I love you and I thought you loved me. Can you really think so little of me, after all this time?"

"No. No, you don't get to turn this around on me. I'm going upstairs for my stuff, and you're going to stay down here. You fucking stay away from me and let me get my stuff and then I'm gone." Screw her stuff. She should leave. She should turn and run.

"Someday you'll understand how I could have done what I did and still love you. Someday maybe you'll see what you were to me. How patient I was, how very little I asked of you. When you're older, maybe." He moves from behind the counter, walking toward her.

She backs up, just outside the shop doorway. Weight shifted back to run. How little he asked. *Jesus.* "I should have driven that knife right into your fucking eyes." And let that be the last thing she ever says to him. Let that be the final word on their time together. She'll go upstairs, she'll take what's hers, and then she'll get gone. Good-bye to Gerrit. Good-bye to Steve. Good-bye to Anne. Good-bye, Thirteen House.

⊞

Young kid, probably half her age. He smells like sardines and shit. He finishes fast, zips up his filthy jeans, cooks up the dope, hands Cat the needle.

Oregon. She always did like the rain.

28

Amelia has to convince Cat to leave.

She peels a twenty off the roll of bills she took from her and Gerrit's savings. She split the money down the middle, though she was tempted to take it all. It would have been reasonable, given the circumstances, but she wanted Gerrit to come back to the apartment and find she'd taken only what was hers. Fair to the last, even if he doesn't deserve it. With that precious twenty she buys groceries for her and Cat. Bread, cheese, oranges. She safes it all away in her messenger bag, not wanting the nameless bodies she's bound to have to step over when she gets back to the building to see the food.

She pushes through the blanket that serves as their door and she knows before she's even inside the room. She pulls back the tangled bedding to reveal Cat's face, still and blue. Eyes closed. Amelia thinks "at peace," but that's bullshit. Dead isn't the same as at peace. It's just muscles gone slack because all the life's drained out.

She wipes the cold sweat from Cat's face with a corner of the blanket. "You just went to sleep," Amelia says. "You were supposed to go out roaring, go out screaming, but you just went to sleep."

Beneath the blankets, Cat is naked, her clothes in a ball by her feet. She is small, shockingly small. Amelia curves her body to Cat's as much as the baby will allow. She puts her arms around her, feels her cooling skin, nestles against her, one last time. "Cat," she croons. "Mama Cat." She holds her and rocks her. And then screams. Amelia screams as loud and as long as she can. But Cat doesn't wake up. And no one in this goddamn wreck of a building comes running. No one at all.

⊞

Amelia goes to Steve for help, because she doesn't know where else to go. She knocks on the apartment door and Anne answers, looking older than ever. Weary. She sees Amelia, shakes her head, and walks into their bedroom, shutting the door quietly. And then there's Steve, filling the doorway, his face an open question.

"It's Cat," she says. "She's dead. She OD'd. She died."

"Where is she now?"

"We've been staying at a new squat over on Fourth and D. I left her there. I didn't know what to do. I don't know what to do. You know . . ."

"With the body. Wait here." He knocks softly on the bedroom door before opening it. He speaks to Anne in hushed words Amelia can't make out. And then he's putting on his coat, he's out in the hallway with her, and they're going down the stairs.

Steve and Amelia and the baby swimming oblivious in her belly, and here they go, out into the harsh clear light of midday, to bring Cat home. Or wherever they're going to bring her. Because they can't bring her home. Cat House is gone.

"What are we going to do with her?" she asks.

"We'll carry her to the park. I'll wait with her on a bench and you'll go flag down a cop. We'll have to say we found her dead on a bench. We can ID her for them so she isn't buried a Jane Doe. We can say she was homeless after the fire."

"It seems so cold."

"I know. But it's the only way. She would have done the same with any of us. We've got to do what we can for her, but we've got to look out for the living, too. You don't want to call the cops to that squat you've been in. They'll clear the building. And you don't want to have to answer too many questions, either. It's better this way."

Steve lets out a low whistle as they walk through the building back to the space she shared with Cat. They have to step over some guy Amelia's never seen before, passed out a few feet from the front door. A piss bucket must have spilled again, because the air is thick with the stench of it. Someone's smeared shit on the walls. Steve says, "You're coming home."

Cat's body is as Amelia left it, blankets pulled up to her chin.

"I can't go back to Gerrit."

"I bet he'd forgive you in time. Anne's on her way to forgiving me, I think. They just need time. It'll be okay."

"No, I mean I *won't* go back to Gerrit." And Anne, she must hate Amelia now. And she'll hate the baby. How could she not? "I'm sorry. For telling. Are you mad at me?"

He shakes his head. "It would have come out one way or another."

"When I told Gerrit you were the father. Gerrit . . . he . . ."

Cat could be asleep. She looks like she's sleeping. Amelia stoops to smooth a hand over Cat's cool forehead, to tuck an errant dread back into place.

"Did he hurt you?"

Cat's back, the deep-ridged scars. The prayer shawl etched in flame over them. Amelia has to be sure Cat is covered before they carry her out. She has to be sure no one sees the scars. Cat would want it that way.

"He did."

Steve kneels, gently lifting Cat's head and shoulders so Amelia can slip a shirt onto her. He traces a flame-covered scar with his finger. They were lovers once, Cat and Steve. Sinking into her own loss, Amelia forgot that. Forgot that it's Steve's loss, too. But you can see it so clearly, the way he cradles Cat's body. He loved her.

"He . . ." She falters and Steve looks up sharply, searching her face. "He held me down. When he found out. He . . ."

"Did he make you . . . did he force you?"

She nods, easing one of Cat's hands through a sleeve.

"I thought you said he couldn't?"

"He did."

"I'll fucking kill him." She is gratified by the angry pulsing muscle in Steve's jaw, by the glassy wet of his eyes. "You come home. Stay with Suzie and Denise. You belong with us. I'll make sure he stays away from you. I'll take care of it."

They finish dressing Cat and wrap her in a blanket as if she were a sick child being brought to the doctor. Steve holds her to his chest, kisses her forehead. "Sweet Carolyn," he murmurs. "We didn't get so far after all, did we?"

Amelia gathers up her and Cat's few belongings and they head to Tompkins. Steve walks slowly, Cat's small, still form barely visible in the blanket. They choose a bench beneath a tree, and Steve eases her down and arranges the blanket around her. He sits down by her head and Amelia takes one last look, then goes to find a cop, to report a dead body found on a bench.

29

It was all over in less than an hour, from the time Amelia flagged down a cop to the time the ambulance drove away with Cat's body and the cops said they were free to go. They watched Cat being carried away, and that feels like permission now to be up on the roof alone together. They returned to the building after a stop at the liquor store for Steve and headed straight to the roof, not stopping to let Anne or anyone else know that they were back.

Amelia leans against the parapet wall, Steve beside her. She nestles in close to him, trying to feel the safety she'd always found in his big warm body. It's gone.

Steve takes quick, frequent pulls off a bottle of whiskey.

"It's my fault Cat ran away all those years ago," he says, his voice whiskey-thick and slow.

"She said she just wanted to get out of New York."

"She got pregnant. I got her pregnant. And we were only nineteen and I wasn't ready to settle down and I told her to get rid of it. She wanted to keep it, but I bullied her, and she did it. Two weeks later, she was gone. And then when she came back . . . " He turns his palms up, empty.

Amelia pictures Cat's body, small and scarred and wasted, in his cupped palms.

"I should have been more careful with you," he says. "I'm sorry."

"Don't say that. Sorry means you're wishing the baby away."

He takes a long swig off the bottle. "I've got to stand by Anne as long as she'll have me, but I'll help you as best I can."

"I think I'm leaving," she says. "I think when Kim and Gideon go to Portland, I'm going with them."

"Your family is here," he says. "In this house. You're going to need us more than ever once the baby comes." He puts an arm around her shoulders, and it feels nothing like it used to.

The sun is starting to set, casting long purple shadows over the rooftops. So much has happened between Amelia's waking up this morning and finding herself here beside Steve. She remembers how hungry she was for him in what now seems a different lifetime. There was the secret of them, what they gave to each other, what they took from each other, quick and hushed. That secret a secret no more, but so much smaller than it once seemed. Such a trivial thing now.

She sees them—all of them—buffeted by change, inevitable change, and she mourns them. She mourns for herself and for her friends. For all this suffering, for all this life.

"I love you," she says.

"I know, baby. I know you do. I'm so sorry."

⊞

Steve feels Amelia's body against his, the new lushness of her. He pictures that soft body pinned to the kitchen table. He thinks of Gerrit's body pressed against the baby.

Against the baby.

"I'm thinking about going downstairs and beating the shit out of Gerrit," he says.

Amelia snorts.

"I mean it."

"No, you don't. You're drunk."

"Would you be angry if I did?" He sees her, awkward and off-balance with that big belly. Sees her held down. Sees Gerrit thrusting into her with frantic animal hips. Staking his claim. Steve feels bile rise in his throat.

"No," she says, looking at her hands. "I want you to."

⊞

Gerrit heard the footsteps coming. He heard Steve's voice, then Amelia's. So when he answers the knock on the door and sees Amelia going down the stairs and sees Steve's face like some mythic god of war shoved into his own, when Steve's hands clamp down around Gerrit's throat and drive him slamming to the floor, Gerrit isn't all that surprised. Steve's fists land in meaty thuds, the pain sharp at first, then duller, radiating throughout Gerrit's body. Steve's fists land, his knees and his elbows land. The blows find their mark.

"Fight back!" Steve shouts, sweat and boozy spit hitting Gerrit's face. "Fucking stand up and fight!" Gerrit has seen Steve rage before, but never from this end of things. His face is terrifying. Wide wild eyes; twisting mouth red and wet; crooked teeth, fierce canines.

Gerrit struggles up onto one knee. His right side is gone to sharp white heat. Broken ribs. "Steve, man, you're drunk. Don't do something you'll regret later."

Steve dives toward him, an elbow hooking around Gerrit's throat, and the two of them crash to the floor. Steve straddles him, palm to Gerrit's forehead pinning his head down. His nostrils flare, sweat dripping from his face onto Gerrit's. And then something gives. He pushes off Gerrit and collapses beside him on the floor. "She trusted you."

Gerrit's right eye is swelling closed, an ice pick of pain pressing down through his vision, scattering shards of light. Beside him Steve's great chest is heaving. Animal stink over both of them; the stink of fear and anger, equal parts. "She trusted you, too."

"I never forced myself on her," Steve says. "I never laid a hand on that girl she didn't want on her."

"Do you love her? Did you let her believe you did? Because I do."

"She says you held her down on the goddamn kitchen table. Six months pregnant and you hold her down and . . . I should kill you. I should fucking kill you."

"What did she tell you when you were fucking her? Did she make me out like some kind of joke? Is that how you made it okay?" Slowly, slowly Gerrit pushes himself up to sit. His head is impossibly heavy, his vision thick and blurring. He closes his eyes against the rising nausea, the stabbing pain in his right side with each breath. Better if he doesn't try to breathe too deeply. Better if he doesn't move. Just sit there, propped against the wall.

"My baby," Steve says. "I should fucking kill you."

"Your baby. We were together. Seven years together, and now she tells me she's having your baby. Telling me everything we had was some kind of act, like she was just doing me a favor, pretending all these years. But it wasn't like that. That's just a lie she tells herself now. Nearly seven years I was in her bed. Just because I couldn't . . . she thought . . . *Godverkutneukenhoeren*." He hears his voice, weak and gasping. The sound comes to him from far off, like he's calling from a great distance, like he's talking underwater.

"All those nights, all those years, lying in her bed, getting her off," Gerrit says. "That's what it was, me giving and her taking, and now she wants to make it out like she was doing me some kind of favor? Like she felt sorry for me? *Krijg de tyfustering allebei.* She was mine. So I'm sorry for what I did. I am. But you have to see it from my side. I love her and she made me into a joke."

"Nothing you say is going to square this," Steve says, his voice hoarse, "and you know that." He heaves himself up onto one elbow, swipes his face against his shirt, leaving a streak of Gerrit's blood on the collar. "I'm sorry for what I did to Anne, but I'm not sorry for you. I was. I felt so low, going behind your back like that. My best friend, right? And there I was with his girl. But that's over. I don't feel bad about you anymore." Steve hauls himself up with a groan. He sniffs, his face gone slack. "You should know, Cat OD'd. She's gone. Amelia's coming home, going to stay with Suzie and Denise. You stay away from her."

Then he's through the door and down the stairs. Cat is dead. Amelia is coming home.

Gerrit crawls to the bathroom and pulls himself up to stand, leaning heavily on the sink. His legs want to give way. His body is a blur of pain. His lungs pinch at each breath—broken ribs for sure. In the mirror, his face is grotesque. A mottled mask, quickly swelling. Not the worst beating he's ever had, not by half. Steve could have done much, much worse. Steve could have killed him easily. The restraint he did show is a sign either of mercy or complicity. Steve is not without guilt. No one, it seems, is entirely without blame here. Not even Amelia, and now she's coming home.

⊞

Steve is filled with fear. The people he loves have gone animal, dying in shitholes, raping each other on kitchen tables. Steve himself beating his best friend until he felt flesh go soft like ripe fruit, until he felt ribs give way under his fists. And Anne—sweet, steady, loyal Anne—caught up in the middle of it, dragged down into the shit of it by

Steve. She got into bed this afternoon with a headache and who could blame her, but it scares him. Anne never takes to her bed.

He goes out, gets her coffee and a doughnut; gets her daisies from the bodega. He finds her still in bed, blanket to her chin and her back to the door. She doesn't turn when he walks in. "Hey, I brought you a coffee, brought you a jelly doughnut." He places the coffee cup on the dresser across from the bed, shakes the doughnut bag. "Ah, shit." The flowers. "I'll be right back." He runs to the kitchen, sticks the daisies in a vase with some water, brings them back with him. "And these. I got you these. Hey. Anne. Annie? Coffee's getting cold."

"I didn't ask for coffee."

"No, I know."

"So let it get cold."

He sets the flowers down on the dresser next to the coffee, where she can see them. She squeezes her eyes closed, rolls away. "Are you going to leave me, Annie?"

Silence.

"I have no right to ask this, I know, but please. Don't leave me."

"Cat's really dead," she says.

"Yes." *She was so small and cold*, he wants to say. *We had them cart her away like garbage.*

"Are you okay?"

"No. I'm not okay. Not about anything."

"Jesus Christ. I'm afraid to ask what's next." She sits up, rubs her face in her hands. "Okay, give me the coffee."

She turns the cup around in her hands but doesn't take a sip. "I should leave you. Every morning I wake up and tell myself, 'Today's the day you walk out on that asshole.' But you know what? I can't do it. I don't *want* to do it. How weak am I?"

"No, not weak. Not weak at all." He sits next to her on the bed, feels for her knee through the blanket and squeezes it. "I'll spend the rest of my life making it up to you. I swear it."

Te lo juro, Annie.

"Don't feed me your bullshit; I'm full up. All I can say for now is I'm not planning to leave you."

He puts an arm around her, pulls her close, but she goes stiff. Okay, so it's going to take some time. He lets her go. "You want that doughnut now?"

"Why not." He hands it to her and she takes a bite, a glob of raspberry jelly oozing out.

"See? You leave me, who's gonna bring you doughnuts in bed?"

"The flowers are nice."

"Yeah? You like them?"

"I do."

"See, any husband—"

"Any asshole lying cheating husband," she says, sucking the jelly off her hand.

"Right. Any asshole lying cheating husband could have blown all the grocery money on roses and fancy chocolates, right? But not this guy. This guy brings you what you actually like, yeah?"

"So you're not a cheap bastard, just extra thoughtful."

"Exactly."

"What a guy."

"This is what I'm telling you."

"I'm lucky, really. A lucky, lucky woman." And her face goes wobbly and she drops the doughnut back into the bag, crying again.

"Oh, babe. I'm the lucky one. I know it."

Jesus, the mess he's made.

30

The community room at Thirteen House is packed, but nobody jostles for space. Nobody complains. Amelia watches as Steve moves to the front of the room and all the faces turn to him, waiting. This was one of the things about Steve that used to thrill her—the way he could make everyone in a room turn toward him without even knowing they were doing it, like plants to the sun.

"Cat wouldn't want a bunch of sappy words about her," he says. "She wouldn't want a lot of tears. But we're the ones left behind, so this isn't about what she'd want. Because maybe we need to say a bunch of words about her. Maybe we need to cry a little bit. Anyone wants to get up here and say a few words about Cat, you can do that. And then we're going to dry the tears and get back down to the business at hand. The fire at Cat House set us all back, but it's time to get that behind us and get moving forward again."

He picks up the sledgehammer that would usually bring a meeting to order, turning it over in his hands. He doesn't square his shoulders the way he does when he's getting ready to make some speech. He doesn't look up. He doesn't pull a piece of paper from his pocket. His voice doesn't boom; he keeps it cast low, talking to his hands, to the sledgehammer, to the walls.

"I knew Cat forever. We came up together as kids, right here on Thirteenth Street. First kiss, first everything with Cat. Carolyn. I'd get her to sneak out of her room at night, down the fire escape. We'd run the streets all night. Sit on the Brooklyn Bridge and watch the sun come up, then race back, trying to get her through her window before her parents woke up. God, they hated me. But that just made Carolyn love me more."

He hunkers down on his haunches, the sledgehammer braced on the floor like a cane. He sinks down into himself. "And I loved her. I loved her and I let her down. Which is, you know, I guess it's how it is with everyone, how we all are for each other. We love each other, and we let each other down. But I'm sorry for it. Sorry for all the hurt I brought her. And I'll miss her." He looks to Anne, tucked into a far corner. Amelia wills him to look at her, wills him to try to catch *her* eyes, but he doesn't. *You hurt me*, she thinks. *You let me down, too. Look at me. Look at me, dammit.*

One after another, people stand to speak about Cat. How she brought Cat House together, how she was their tough-love den mother, their fearless pirate queen. Stories and tears and laughter, and Amelia can't bear it.

"Cat would hate this," she hisses into Kim's ear.

"Steve was right," Kim says. "This isn't for Cat. Funerals are for the living. Just go with it."

All around her, people are laughing, smiling, wiping away tears. *We all hurt each other,* Steve said. *We all let each other down.* But Amelia doesn't want it to be that way. "I'm alone!" she wants to stand up and shout. "Cat died and left me alone!" But she doesn't dare. She knows already what will happen. Someone will say, "Yeah, me too." And then someone else, someone older who thinks they're wiser, will say, "We're all alone." But that's such an easy thing to say, and Amelia isn't convinced it has to be true.

She holds her belly and feels the baby move under her hands. We don't all have to be alone. We don't all have to let each other down in countless, inevitable ways. She won't accept it.

⊞

Gerrit hovers around the edges of the room, maneuvering through the crowd, trying to reach a spot where Amelia can look up and see him, hoping to see something other than hate and fear when she does. He's bound his ribs tightly. The pain's not too bad, as long as he doesn't cough, or move too suddenly.

"Man, are you okay? What hit you?" Gideon winces at Gerrit's black eyes, his swollen cheek and cut lips. Steve must have kept the beating to himself. Steve must have kept everything to himself—and Amelia, too—because no one is looking at Gerrit with anything other than sympathy.

"Looks bad, yeah?" Gerrit says. "I'm okay. I got jumped, picked the wrong block at the wrong time. Bad luck." He motions toward the healing burn on Gideon's cheek. "You should be glad to see someone who looks worse than you."

"Yeah. I mean, they itch, the burns. But I'm good. Alive, you know?" Gideon takes off his cap, rubs at his head with a still-bandaged hand. "Look, thank you, man. For getting me out. If you hadn't . . ."

Gerrit pats Gideon on the shoulder and eases around him. "You would have done the same." He keeps moving, leaving Gideon behind to twist his cap in his hands. He reaches the back of the room and he's just a few feet away from Amelia. There are only two people between them, and he could squeeze right past them to stand next to her. What would she do if he did? Across the room, Steve is watching him. Steve catches his eye and shakes his head. A slow, deliberate shake. A look of *don't you dare.* A look of *I'll rip you to shreds and I don't care who sees it.* Gerrit takes a step back to press himself into the cold cinder-block wall.

There's a knock on the basement door, but no one moves to answer it. The knock comes on the interior door, which means the cellar doors are thrown open on the sidewalk. No one's on the door down here, and probably no one on the door upstairs. All discipline has gone to shit since the fire.

Gerrit makes his way to the interior door and peeks through the small window to see Rick, the cop. What does he know? How much would Steve have told him? Gerrit the rapist opens the door to the cop. He sticks his head out, half expecting to see uniformed officers behind Rick. Waiting for the bracelets. Waiting to be read his rights. "Yeah?"

Rick jolts his head back in surprise, taking in Gerrit's bruised face. "I've got news," he says. "Big news. You'll want to hear it."

No uniforms. No handcuffs. No sign that Rick thinks anything unfriendly about Gerrit. Some cop. Can't he see it in Gerrit's eyes? Can't he smell the guilt rolling off his body? "Come on in." Gerrit pulls back into the basement, where the eulogies drone on, endless. He catches Steve's eye and waves him over. Whatever might have gone to hell between them, Steve still knows when Gerrit means business.

Rick is serious, hands deep in pockets, rocking back on his heels. He nods as Steve approaches.

"You heard about Cat?" Steve says.

Rick says, "I'm sorry for it. Real sorry. My mom cried when I told her. She said what a nice girl she always was."

Gerrit says, "The news?"

Rick cocks his head and squints down at Gerrit as if taking his measure. "Right. Time's up. They're coming tomorrow morning, at dawn. Expect a cast of thousands."

"Thousands?" Gerrit tries to imagine what that would look like.

"Tompkins times ten. Horses. Riot gear. SWAT. You're going to war."

"Jesus," Steve says. "Thanks for the heads-up, man."

"Yeah," Rick says. "You bet." He seems to mean it. "Just so you know, I'll be calling in sick tomorrow. I won't be there. Gotta follow orders, you know. And there are orders gonna come down tomorrow that I don't want a part of. I'm sorry I can't do more for you."

"We've been waiting for this," Gerrit says. He turns to Steve. "Enough with the funeral. We don't have much time."

⊞

Anne breaks away from the work crews putting up the barricades. She goes to the apartment and pulls out the duffel bags she's considered packing so many times in recent months. She's leaving tomorrow. Whether Thirteen House stands or falls, Anne is walking away.

"If you could start over," her mother said when it was just the two of them, finally alone, at the kitchen table back in December, "what would you choose?"

"I don't know," Anne said. "Isn't that awful?"

"No," her mother said. "It's a fine place to start."

31

"It won't be enough to seal the outside doors, or even all the apartment doors," Gerrit told everyone. "We have to do that, and more." He told them how they did it in Amsterdam, how they needed to build layers of defense. "This is how it's done," he said. "This is what we need to do." He drew up plans; he set them in motion. Three levels of defense: the barricades in the street; the protesters outside, arms linked; the windows sealed and the doors welded.

Gerrit thinks of the Vogelstruys eviction. He thinks of Claar and Max and Frits. God, but they were so young then. He wonders what became of his old friends, and what they would say if they saw him now, blowtorch in hand, readying for another siege.

Everyone has been hard at work all night. They've dragged furniture, broken-down appliances, cinder blocks—anything heavy at hand—to build barricades in the street. Marlowe and Fletcher found a burned-out Chevy two blocks down toward the river and pushed it back to Thirteen House. Some of the neighborhood kids helped them flip it over and it landed on its roof with a satisfying rusty groan. "Get past that, pigs!" the kids yelled.

Gerrit and Steve clicked right back into their roles, organizing the anxious, angry, milling crowd into purposeful work crews. Whatever has come between them, it's been left behind for now. "We get through this as friends," Steve said. "Set everything else aside and get through this."

Gerrit raised a blowtorch in salute and got back to work.

At five thirty in the morning, the work is nearly done. The residents of Thirteen House gather in the community room. Outside on the sidewalk, the residents of Cat House and Utopia and dozens more friends and neighbors wait, prepared to link arms and block access when the cops arrive. "Expect a cast of thousands," Rick said. And those thousands will be armed, and armored.

Gerrit stands beneath the open cellar doors and sees their friends gathered and ready to stand up for them. Such a visible, bodily display of love and concern. There are maybe a hundred people out there. It isn't even their building. Many of them aren't even squatters.

Irving says he'll wake up every judge in town if he has to, but Gerrit doesn't see any point. They've gone too far for judges and lawyers now.

Gerrit turns back to the group in the community room and fires up the blowtorch. "Last chance to leave," he shouts. "Get moving now or you're here for the long haul."

José is looking toward the door. Gerrit saw him with his family in the vestibule last night, just before Nena and Carla left to stay with a cousin. They held fast to each other, whispering in tender Spanish. The girl was crying as her mother led her out the door. Gerrit catches José's eye, sees the man falter a moment, but then he nods. He's in. No one else moves to leave, and Gerrit pulls the metal cellar doors closed flush with the sidewalk. Together he and Ben weld them shut and then seal the interior door, too, as they already welded the ground-level door closed, and the back door. The first- and second-floor windows are nailed shut and boarded up as if in anticipation of a hurricane.

"And now," Steve says, "we wait."

⊞

Dawn comes and goes. It's almost 8:00 AM and still no cops. Gideon radioed in on the walkie-talkie more than two hours ago to say the cops were mustering at Tompkins, but they haven't budged at all since then. Amelia and Suzie wander the halls, restless. Amelia is exhausted already and no telling when this day will end. No sleep last night and now going on two hours of being on guard, listening for the attack that was bound to come at any moment. Any moment now for two hours, and she's circling like a dog, desperate to lie down, to come to rest.

Suzie carries a sledgehammer balanced over one shoulder, patrolling as they walk, stopping to listen at the sealed doors and windows each time they pass them. Never any sound but their friends outside. Even from inside the building, Amelia can hear that the excited predawn chatter has given way to a weary, determined silence. Everything is on hold. The world has stopped spinning, the city gone still. Everything, everything is holding its breath, waiting for the siege.

The crackle of the walkie-talkie from somewhere upstairs cuts through the nervous silence. Gideon's out on the streets on bike watch, and his voice comes across the radio, sharp and broken, and then Steve's voice in response. Amelia can't make out the words. And now Steve bellows down the stairwell. "Okay, folks!" he shouts. "Here we go! Gideon says they're on the move. They're headed our way!"

Gerrit runs down the stairs, banging on the wall as he goes. "Get to your posts! To your posts! Here we go!" His face is flushed, his eyes all broken blood vessels, and dark bruises around them like a mask. When she first saw Steve's handiwork last night, Amelia gasped, wondering how Gerrit could walk around after a beating like that. How could he have absorbed that much pain? She thinks of Steve's massive fists, Gerrit's slight body.

She recalls the stories Gerrit told her about the fights with the cops in Amsterdam. The building clearings, when he stood on rooftops with his comrades and threw down rocks and bricks. How he fought as they dragged him away, billy club against his throat. How as soon as he was released he'd be back out, opening another building.

For the first time she lets herself imagine how it could go down today, beyond the point of the cops reaching the doors. There could be nightsticks. There could be tear gas.

There could be guns. For the first time she lets herself understand how very badly this could all end. Gerrit stops as he passes her in the hall. He looks at her, and beneath the bruises his face is utterly calm. This is what he's made for. This is all he's ever expected. All these years of playing house, the cops turning their backs, the city turning its back. This was always coming, and he knew it. He tried to tell her. He tried to prepare her.

"I'm scared," she says, forgetting for now that he has become the last person she ever intended to say such a thing to.

"We'll look out for you. You'll be fine." He reaches out to touch her arm, then stops himself and his hand falls heavily to his side. "If the cops make it through the door, you go toward them, slowly, hands up. You let them see your belly, and you tell them you're pregnant. Got it? No room for assumptions, no taking chances. You yell, 'I'm not resisting.' You yell, 'I'm pregnant.' They'll take you out first that way, and they'll probably go easy on you. Okay? No heroics. If they get through the door, you go to them and you get out safely."

"Yeah. Okay."

"They might want to search you to make sure that's all baby there and not an explosive belt or anything. You let them search you. You don't put up any struggle. Got it?"

"Yeah. Yeah, okay." Explosive belt. Jesus. Who do they think lives here?

"I'm looking out for you. Steve is looking out for you." He lifts his hand again, brings it to rest, hesitant, on her arm. The awful calm slips from his face, and there is the fear, there is the uncertainty. It's comforting to see it, the soft animal underbelly he keeps secreted away. *I still know you*, she thinks. *There you are.* He says, "If we make it through today I will do anything you want me to. I'll leave Thirteen House. I'll leave New York. Anything you want. *Ik zweer het je. Maakt niet uit wat.*"

I swear it to you. Anything. *I want you to take it all back*, she thinks. *I want you to erase everything that makes my guts knot up when I see you. I want you to make me forget that look on your face, that look that said you hated me, that said I was getting everything I deserved. I want you to say I didn't deserve it.*

"I can't do this now." She pushes past him, into Suzie and Denise's apartment. Suzie is in position at the window and Amelia joins her. Outside the door, she hears Gerrit take up the call again.

"Posts! To your posts!"

"Here we go," Suzie says.

And there the police are. Where Avenue A meets Thirteenth Street, just beyond the barricades the squatters built last night, the cops are gathering. Cops in dark blue riot gear, bulletproof vests, heavy helmets, and boots. Cops with rifles, with machine guns. Mounted police, their horses the only calm bodies to be seen.

"The fucking SWAT team is here!" someone yells. The squatters of Thirteen House are all crowded around the upper-floor windows, trying to catch sight of the gathering forces. The warnings were true. They're late, but they're here. More police than anyone can count, innumerable because their helmeted, armored bodies blend together. They are a teeming blue wave poised to crash.

"Jesus fuck," Amelia says, pushing away from the window, feeling panic rise and swell around her, panic closing off her ears, closing off her eyes so the room is a muffled swirl. The air is too thick to breathe. She finds the wall, leans into it, counts to ten. She wills her heart to slow, wills her lungs to take in the air. *Hold it together, hold it together. Look out the window again. Look down, look at everyone gathered there. You aren't alone, not by a long shot.*

Outside, the crowd of supporters has swelled to rival the crowd of cops. The street in front of the building and the sidewalks on both sides are full, people surrounding the overturned car and all the way up to the dumpster, the bed frames, the garbage cans and plywood they dragged out into the mouth of the intersection—the final barricade that separates the people from the cops. The street is full of familiar faces and unfamiliar faces. They're shouting encouragement up to the windows of Thirteen House. They're shouting at the cops. They're holding signs.

NO HOUSING, NO PEACE!

GENTRIFICATION IS CLASS WARFARE!

HOUSING IS A HUMAN RIGHT!

"This is unreal," Ben says. "Where did all these people come from?"

Two men Amelia knows only by sight climb up onto the belly of the overturned car. With a roar they hoist a big hand-painted sign overhead, turning it first to show the squatters in the windows, then turning it to the cops.

LONG LIVE THE REVOLUTION OF EVERYDAY LIFE!

"Oh, fuck yeah!" a voice Amelia recognizes as Kim's shouts from the group that's linked arms in front of the building.

Fuck yeah!

Suzie tugs on Amelia's sleeve and it's up to the roof, running up the stairs, the sheet they painted last night tucked under Suzie's arm. They burst out into the morning sun and Amelia gives the finger to the police helicopters buzzing overhead. Fuck yeah! Over to the parapet wall. They unfurl their sign, anchoring it in place with bricks.

Simple, in the biggest letters the sheet could take.

HOME

⊞

But the cops don't move. They mill around, they shift their weapons from hand to hand, but they don't move past that first barricade. An hour passes. Anne goes through the building, keeping everyone posted as the reports come in from outside, but soon there's nothing new to report. No sign of Irving, or word from him by way of his assistant. On the other end of the walkie-talkie, Gideon says that the cops have shut down access to the block and he can't get back to the building. Steve paces up and down the stairs, rooftop to basement, then back up. Gerrit wanders the halls, blowtorch in hand, muttering in Dutch. Overhead, the helicopters drone. Amelia wonders if it would be perverse to take out her knitting.

"What are they waiting for?" she says. "I'm gonna lose it if they just stand around much longer."

"Beats the hell out of the alternative, though," Marlowe says. "A lot of guns out there."

Amelia squints to try to make out the faces of the individual cops, to try to pick some kind of identifying features out of the unified swarm of blue. These cops, each of them is somebody's son or daughter. Maybe somebody's father, somebody's wife. How do all those sons and fathers and husbands, those daughters and mothers and wives, disappear into a single terrifying wall like that? How do they get so swallowed up? Do they feel swallowed up? Do they even feel like themselves, once the visors on their riot helmets drop down over their eyes? Behind those visors, are they thinking about what their kid said at the breakfast table? Are they thinking about their father's last heart attack? The game on TV tonight? A few beers after shift, God willing we all get through this and go home? Or are they just thinking about the weight of the gun in their hands? Thirteen House just a target to be moved through?

"They don't seem real to me, the cops," Amelia says. "Do you think we're real for them?"

Engines whir and a horn blasts and the sea of blue parts to let three vehicles through: a tow truck, a bulldozer, and something that looks like a souped-up school bus painted NYPD blue and white.

"Here comes the short bus!" somebody jokes, but the laughter dies down pretty fast when burly men in hard hats spill out of the bus and start breaking the first barricade down.

⊞

Steve insists that Irving can still save them. He keeps checking in with Gideon on the walkie-talkie, but there's never any sign of Irving's runner.

"Steve, man," Gerrit says. "Put down that walkie-talkie. That's done. You want to know what's happening, look out the window. They're coming. That walkie-talkie's only good now as something to throw."

"No one's throwing anything. We've still got a shot in court. You go throwing shit at the cops, that's only going to hurt us." Steve is nervous, faltering. Gerrit sees that now, the way he keeps thumbing the TALK button on the radio, the way he keeps glancing toward the windows but doesn't get close enough to look out. This wasn't part of his plan. He's sunk down against a wall, those big shoulders hunched, those big hands unsure.

"You didn't think it would get this far," Gerrit says.

Steve bangs his head back against the wall, the drywall giving up a dull thud. "What do we do? Just let them come in and march us out?"

"The first barricade is down!" Ben shouts, setting runners off through the halls, passing the word along. "First barricade down! First barricade down!" echoes through the building.

"Irving might come through yet," Steve says.

"A lawyer isn't worth a damn once it gets to the point of riot helmets."

It could be said—Gerrit himself has said it—that you don't really know what someone is made of until the cops are coming through the door. He wouldn't have expected this of Steve. Nothing in the past twelve years would have led him to expect Steve to crumble like this. Gerrit would have predicted hellfire. He would have thought he'd have to hold Steve back to keep him from charging out and dying in a hail of bullets. He always thought Steve was the cowboy among them. Then again, Steve probably thought as much himself.

"It's happening. This is what is happening." Gerrit shoves Steve's chest. "It's time. Fight or flight." He wishes Marrije was there. She would be up on the roof with him, shouting at the cops to bring it on. She'd be the one to throw the first brick.

"Second barricade is down!"

One barricade left—the overturned car—and then their friends outside, waiting to link arms. Then nothing stands between them and the cops but the dumb strength of the battering rams against the welded doors. This is bigger—much bigger—than anything he and Marrije faced down. There is an army out there; there are helicopters hovering overhead. This is the fist of the city of New York, clenched and ready to smash them.

⊞

Amelia doesn't know what to do with herself. The barricades are coming down. The cops are on the move. With the kind of force they've gathered today, a line of people with linked arms won't hold them back. They'll slow the cops long enough to get themselves arrested, and then the cops are coming in. It's not if, anymore. It's when. *I'm not resisting. I'm pregnant.* And maybe they're not so rough as they lead her out, but what comes after that? The building is most likely lost. Or maybe Irving will come through. Maybe they'll be out for a few days and then Irving can get them back in.

But she knows it's never happened that way before. Either they don't manage to get you out, or once you're out the squat is done. Better prepare to move on. Better count yourself as on the street. So why are they all roaming the halls? Why is Gerrit pacing around with a blowtorch over his shoulder like an assault rifle? Why aren't they just packing their things? When the police come through the door, they can file out quietly with their bags, like they're getting off a bus.

They claimed this building with crowbars and bolt cutters. They held it with hammers and nails. Giuliani is taking it back with battering rams and guns. Possession, apparently, comes down less to law than to force.

Home. The defiance that moved Amelia to paint that sign with Suzie last night has given way to something else. Beneath the anger and determination, there's fear. And a longing for it all to be over, one way or another. If they lose the building, at least there will be the relief of an ending. No more waiting. No more wondering how it's all going to end, because the worst that could happen already did. Is that how Cat felt, after the fire? All that fight in her, all that anger, and then the fire took the fight for Cat House away and she lay down and died. How long had Cat been waiting for permission to stop fighting?

Where would she have gone, anyway? Forty-one years old and back to the beginning in a fetid den of junkie-thieves and trust-fund punks.

Where will Amelia go? It wasn't too long ago that the answer would have been wherever Gerrit goes. Because Gerrit would know what to do. Gerrit would take care of her, and it would be fine. And isn't that how this mess between them got started in the first place? Amelia drifting along, letting Gerrit take care of everything, letting Gerrit take care of her. She doesn't forgive him what he's done. How could she? But she sees it now, the innocent beginnings of it, how she let those seeds of possession get planted, and how they grew and vined around her, tying her to Gerrit. And he came to believe that she was his, that she would always be tied to him like that.

When she leaves Thirteen House, she wants to leave with everything she needs to move on. She's going out that door with eyes open. No pretending someone will swoop down and save the day. No pretending they'll be allowed even to go back in for their things once they've been forced out.

Most of the things that really matter she's already gathered up. It isn't much—it all fits pretty well into her big messenger bag. When she went back to the apartment to get her stuff the first time, she was surprised by how much of what she'd once thought essential had become incidental. She left her books, most of her clothes, her music. She left her stash of recycled yarn. She took only her two pairs of maternity jeans—she'll worry about getting regular jeans after the baby is born—and a few shirts big enough to stretch over the belly. Two sweaters that don't fit now but will again. Her prenatal vitamins. She took her grandmother's knitting needles, and the handful of photos she's been carrying around since leaving home going on eight years ago now. And her half of the money. That was it. That day it seemed like there would always be another chance to go back and get everything. But it's done. So one more time through, to be sure she isn't leaving anything behind that she'll regret later.

Anne is sitting on the floor outside the apartment, leaning against the wall. "Were you waiting for me?" Amelia asks.

"You? No." Anne's nails are dirty, her shirt stained with coffee and paint, remnants of last night's preparations. "I wanted a moment's peace. I thought they had you squared away with Suzie."

Amelia taps the messenger bag slung across her chest. "Gonna pack my bag. Looks like they're coming in." She pauses, taking in Anne's weary face. "You hate me."

"Hate's strong. I pity you. Go on, now. Pack your bag, Amelia." Anne looks past her, down the long empty hall. Her fingers scissor around a phantom cigarette.

"You do hate me." Amelia sits down opposite Anne. Her belly rises up between them. "How could you not hate me? I would hate me."

"Did you think he would leave me for you? Did you think he would save you? How does it feel now? You're all on your own. How does it feel?"

From outside comes the groan and whine of metal giving way, a clattering crash and a mechanical moan. The barricades falling, piece by piece.

You can give yourself away without knowing what you're giving. But you can take it all back, too. You can take yourself back. "Good. It feels good."

"Hunh." Anne's gaze falls to Amelia's belly as the baby does one of his big swooping rolls. She screws up her eyes, peers at Amelia, searching her face for something. A sign of something, though Amelia doesn't know what. "Steve says Gerrit hurt you when he found out about you and him. He says he raped you, and that's why you ran off with Cat."

It's the first time anyone has used that word. When she told Steve what happened, she didn't say *rape*. And when Steve talked about it, he talked around the word, too. But there it is, bald and true. "Yeah. He did. He raped me."

"You didn't deserve that. Whatever else I think of you, I was sorry to hear that."

Amelia's guard dissolves, and she can't remember what it was she was trying to ward off in the first place. She wraps her arms around the baby in her belly, drops her head against the wall, and cries in quiet hiccupping sobs. With everything Amelia has taken from Anne, Anne still offers up this small kindness. The kindness of seeing a wound and acknowledging it. The kindness of not looking the other way.

"Third barricade down! Last barricade down! Get ready!"

"Go on inside," Anne says. "Get your things together. We've got to get you and that baby out the door first anyway."

⊞

Steve sits on the couch in his apartment, probably for the last time. Why didn't they pack anything? Photo albums, records, the stereo? Anne's bread bowl? His *books*? Now, when it's too late, he thinks of all the things they've accumulated over the years, all the things he'd like to save. They're going to be marched out of there—it's only a matter of minutes now—with nothing. He goes to the closet to grab the duffel bags, to save what he can, and finds they're already packed. Anne. The first one is full of clothes, hers and his. The second one holds a plastic bag full of their photos, the heavy albums left behind; their bankbook; a roll of cash; Steve's notebooks; Steve's records: Dylan, Nieves, Springsteen, that *maldito* Héctor Lavoe album.

He searches the kitchen cabinets and finds her bread bowl is gone, as is the soup pot and the good tea mugs. Even her favorite wooden spoon is gone. She must have been squirreling things away at her sister's, afraid to mention it to him, worried he would accuse her of faithlessness, of fatal pessimism. She would have been right, but only because he never let himself imagine this moment would actually come. Here they are. It's done. And Steve is so grateful to Anne, yet again, for recognizing what they will need, for knowing that they are too old now to have nothing but the clothes on their backs, that they will need to carry some things with them from this life into whatever comes next.

But what does come next? He goes to the bedroom window, looks out at Thirteenth Street. All these years he thought he was moving ahead, but he's never gotten anywhere at all. He's just been closing in on himself, pulling time around him in choking concentric circles.

There's nothing in these rooms he wants that Anne hasn't already packed. He hefts the duffel bags, carries them out the door.

⊞

The tow truck hauls the junked car away, and with that the third barricade is gone. Watching from the roof, Gerrit expects to see the cops swarm forward on foot, grabbing up the bodies of their supporters, throwing them into the paddy wagons waiting down the block, behind the blue wooden police lines they've set up along Avenue B, but the cops don't move forward on foot. The blue sea parts again and a tank rolls through. An armored tank, and behind it a crane with a wrecking ball, big and impossible as the moon hung from a rusty chain. It creaks and rattles as it advances steadily forward.

Below him, he hears his friends outside the open windows. "A tank? What are they going to do with a fucking *tank*?"

There's no gun on the tank, and it's painted NYPD blue and white rather than military drab, but it's the real deal. It's something you'd expect to see rolling across a foreign desert on the news. It's ridiculously out of place here, in the middle of Thirteenth Street. A nuclear bomb to take out an anthill.

This is it. They'll be at the door soon. That wrecking ball makes Gerrit's decision easy. If they get everyone out of the building, there will be no going back. The building is coming down. So it is important, vitally important, that they do not get everyone out of the building. Gerrit is staying.

⊞

The first time she came back to the apartment, Amelia rushed straight to her bedroom, not wanting to look around, not wanting to feel the fear or revulsion or panic that would rise up. But the apartment is as she left it. The couch is just the couch, the floor just the floor. Even the kitchen table fails to stir much in her but a vague sense of loss. She lived here and now it's time to leave. Simple. So much simpler than she would have thought it would be.

She rifles through the drawers and milk crates in her room but finds nothing she needs or wants. Let the city haul it away. Let some sanitation worker's wife wear her jeans. Let his kids listen to her CDs. Screw it. Let the police knock the door down and just get on with it already. She peeks out her bedroom window and sees the human barricade is starting to break down. The protesters make their bodies go limp but keep their arms linked with each other, and it's slow going for the cops to pry them apart. Here and there, though, already she sees friends being dragged away from the building.

Footsteps in the living room. Gerrit.

She leaves her bedroom and he's standing there, swaying, rooted by his heavy boots. Making small, sharp noises, like he could split open from the pressure of whatever he contains.

"Amelia," he says. "*Vergeef me.*"

Forgive me.

"*O God, alsjeblieft, vergeef het me.*"

She looks at him, and his face is supplicant, grief-stricken. *Vergeef me.* His face is as kind and open as the night he first brought her home. So many claims and assumptions built up between them like silt in the intervening years, making it impossible to trace a clear path from then to now. She has no idea who this man standing before her is. She knows only what her idea of him was, and how it changed.

She takes a step toward him, and then another. Another step, and she's by his shoulder, almost past him. He is a bright body of pain and hope. He is not her idea of Gerrit; he is not even his idea of himself, but something else entirely. She leans in and kisses his mouth. His lips reach toward hers, wanting another kiss, but she touches his chest, steps past him, toward the open door.

"I'm leaving," she says.

"Amelia."

A heavy metallic clang rings through the building, the walls and floors vibrating with the force.

"Battering ram," he says. "I . . ." He shakes his head, waves her out the door. "Go stand on the landing of the first floor, hands up. Not right in front of the door, because they'll be coming in with a lot of force. You let them see you! You tell them you aren't resisting! Go." He follows her out the door, urges her toward the stairs. Steve is in the hallway, Anne at his side.

"She's going now," Gerrit tells Steve. "Make sure she gets out safely."

"What about you?" Amelia says.

"They can't swing that wrecking ball with someone inside." He raises the blowtorch. "Go on now. All of you." And with that, he slams the apartment door shut. Bits of flame and spark fly out around the edges of the metal door as he welds himself in.

"Come on," Steve says. "They'll be through that door in no time."

⊞

Anne stands beside Steve in the hallway outside Gerrit's place and watches him send Amelia forward with a gentle hand at the small of her back. Then he reaches out to Anne. He's got both their bags slung over his shoulder. Amelia descends the stairs silently, head bowed. Anne takes a bag from Steve's shoulder and slides it over her own. She is tied to this man; she does not want to be without him.

"You ready?" he says.

⊞

Steve sends Amelia out the front door, a cop on either arm and the sun lighting her up like the Virgin Mary and he wants to call out to her, call her back to him, take it all back. But he lets her go; he lets the baby go.

And here's Anne now, sliding her hand into his, and they walk out together, duffel bags slung over their shoulders. It's done.

⊞

Gerrit has sealed the door enough to do the job. There will be no coming in without a real fight. They could always come in through the window via the fire escape, but they never seem to go that route, for some reason. Cops. They'd rather break down a door than slip through a window.

He hears shouts and scuffling in the halls as some of the squatters do the passive-resistance thing. "You're going to have to carry me out of here, man," he hears Ben's voice say, and then there's the muffled thud of fists or maybe feet on flesh and booted feet past the door and Gerrit guesses Ben is going out the hard way.

A look out the window shows Amelia walking through the front door, a cop on either side of her. They're taking it easy with her, walking slowly. They lead her across the street and position her behind a wooden police barricade. She's holding her head up. She looks calm, steady. *Good girl*, he thinks.

He hopes Amelia can forgive him one day. He hopes she knows he loves her. He hopes she remembers him to her son, and with kindness. Gerrit hopes she tells her son that he was mostly a good man.

⊞

The building looks so small, so unprotected from across the street. Amelia stands behind the police line, Suzie and Denise beside her. Steve is there. Anne is there. Marlowe. Just about everyone from inside was brought out and deposited behind the line, except for Ben, who got led out with handcuffs and a bloodied face. It was the people defending them on the outside who got the worst of it. Got clubbed. Got carried off, tossed into the paddy wagons.

Two cops come out through the front door. "All clear!" one of them calls. There's a whistle, and the guys in the hard hats move forward, the wrecking ball rolled into place.

"Jesus, it's not all clear!" Amelia turns to find Steve in the crowd. "It's not fucking all clear!"

Murmurs through their group now, turning to shouts. "Wait! Someone's still inside! It's not empty!"

"Gerrit!" Amelia shouts. "Gerrit, show your face!"

"Gerrit!" they're all yelling. "Show your face!"

Irving is running down the block, escorted by two cops, waving a piece of paper and running toward the wrecking ball. He's shouting, "Stop! Stop! By order of the court!"

The cop in charge gives a nod to the foreman and the crane swings its arm back in preparation to strike.

Gerrit appears in the window, face calm.

"Someone's still inside!" they all shout. "Stop!"

The crane's arm swings forward, the wrecking ball hitting the building one floor above Gerrit's window, and there's an awful crash, a groan, shattering glass and splintering wood and a puff of dust. The front of the building is gone, three stories collapsed, caved all the way down to the second floor.

No sound but the sliding and settling of the wreckage. Plaster dust and pulverized brick hang in the air. Amelia holds her breath, searches for a sign of Gerrit, waiting for him to emerge from the front door, having managed some kind of Houdini trick, but the building is a silent wreck, utterly, terribly still.

32

It took four hours for the fire department to reach Gerrit in the rubble. Amelia couldn't bring herself to look, so Steve identified the body, and they carried it away in an ambulance.

"There will be hell to pay," Irving says. "They've got to answer for this. It's murder." Steve nods, teeth clenched so hard the muscles in his jaw twitch. Gideon glares down at his boots with big wet eyes, his energy already spent kicking lampposts and overturning trash cans and howling at the wreck.

The great faceless hordes of cops have gone, just a couple dozen uniforms left to keep people behind the police lines. Some suits have arrived, along with a city attorney. Not DeMarkis. Some white-haired guy in a slick suit. They've traded up.

Steve flicks a spent cigarette into the street and sits down next to Amelia on the curb, his thigh pressing into hers. Anne left hours ago, barely a good-bye to anyone, barely a glance back. "Me and Anne, we're going to be staying with her sister for a while," he says, his voice cast low. "Get back on our feet, figure out what's next. You can find me there. Even after we move on, she'll always know where I am. Okay?" He slips a piece of paper into her hand. Cindy's address and phone number in Brooklyn. "Are you really going?"

"I am. Kim and Gideon found a ride west in some guy's van, leaving first thing tomorrow. I'll crash with them in Utopia's community room tonight."

"You let me know when you get where you're going. You stay in touch." He presses more paper into her hand. Money, a sueded old twenty wrapped around more bills. A lot of them. More than he can afford to give. He stands, jamming his hands into his pockets. "Don't lose that address." His voice catches and he looks away, eyes squinting small in the sharp, insistent light of afternoon, last rays stabbing through before sunset. He tells himself that he isn't crying. It's just the sun in his eyes. He crouches down to kiss Amelia, soft on the lips, for anyone to see, and a hand trailing across her belly, then heads west to catch the train out to Brooklyn, to Anne and her sister and whatever comes next.

Steve doesn't know if his tears are for the baby or Amelia, for Anne or himself, for Gerrit. The sun is setting on the rubble of Thirteen House. Tonight the rats will move in and tomorrow the pigeons, and they'll make it their home until the bulldozers come, until concrete is poured and pipes laid, until a new building rises, a building never meant for the likes of Steve.

He wants to scream at the people walking past him; he wants to grab them by the shoulders and shake them until they understand. *Look at everything you're losing! Look at everything you've lost!* A man died here today, in an avalanche of wood and brick, in a building he helped bring back from ruin. From ruin to home to ruin again. A man died here today.

⊞

Amelia sits on the curb, feet in the gutter, looking out across the landslide that had been their home; the empty air where her bedroom window had been, Gerrit's face in it in those last moments.

When he's old enough, she'll tell her son about Steve and about Gerrit. She'll tell him that she had been young once, in a faraway place called the Lower East Side. She'll send pictures to Steve. She'll send letters and copies of report cards. And maybe one day Steve will meet his son, and he can be in his life in some small way.

If she brings her son back here, there won't be anything left of this old life to show him. She'll stand with him in this spot, and point across the street to some slick condo building, and say, "That's where it was." How will he picture Thirteen House? How will she make him understand where he came from? "Used to be, there was room for everyone here," she'll say. "Used to be you could be whoever you were, however you wanted to be. I knew artists and activists. I knew junkies and thieves. We were pioneers," she'll tell him. "We were pirates."

But her son won't be of this time or place. This is the past now. Her son is of the future, and she needs to carry him toward it even as she carries Marlowe and Ben, Suzie and Denise, Steve and Anne with her. Even as she carries Cat. Even as she carries Gerrit.

Amelia will have to love this baby enough for all of them.

You've turned on us, New York. We who see your jagged-tooth skyline rise up and want to weep because we are so full of you. We who know that the tumbledown tenements are beautiful, that the cracked sidewalks are beautiful, that the iron and cobblestones, the soot and the stink are beautiful. That the musty old bookstores are beautiful, that the tired old shoemakers are beautiful. That the bodega cats, the gutter rats, the endless clouds of pigeons are beautiful . . . We mourn for you, New York, because you are forgetting us, your brash and ragged children.

ACKNOWLEDGMENTS

Thank you to everyone at Tin House Books, especially my amazing editor, Meg Storey, for her insight and guidance, and Nanci McCloskey for her infectious enthusiasm and drive. Thanks also to Masie Cochran and Jack Mahaffy for their close readings, which helped to guide my revisions.

Tremendous gratitude and respect to my teachers Michael Cunningham, Ernesto Mestre-Reed, Robert Kelly, Carey Harrison, Jenny Offill, Jonathan Baumbach, and Rosemary McLaughlin.

Thank you to Jim Handlin, who ran around the classroom in his socks and shouted "WRITE! WRITE!" to our crew of hopeful, terrified young writers as we groped our way through freewriting exercises at the New Jersey Summer Arts Institute in the summers of 1989 and 1990, and who gave me permission to be a writer.

Thank you to Susan Choi for her generosity and sound advice, and for taking me on as an honorary student.

Thanks to Caroline Leavitt for her encouragement and support.

Thank you to Rachael Herron, who reads my first, second, third, and twentieth drafts and helps me to see them so much more clearly.

Thank you to Lon Koontz, whose sharp critical eye has improved everything I've written for the past ten years.

Thank you to my draft readers for their essential feedback: Emily Mitchell, Sara Shepard, Anina Moore, Adam Pollock, Reyna Clancy, Michelle Scheraga, Mindy Weisberger, Jessica Brown, Regina Joskow, Katherine Lynn, Heather Lee, Alicia Marie Howard, Joe Meyer, and DC Donohue.

Thank you to Marrije Schaake, who taught me how to curse in Dutch and kept me in line in regard to Dutch culture. All correct Dutch in this book is thanks to her, and any errors are entirely my own.

My gratitude to the Ragdale Foundation, for granting me the time and space to begin this novel.

Thank you to my family for your love and encouragement, and for not trying to talk me into going to dental school when I announced I wanted to be a writer.

And most of all, thank you to Billy and the kids for absolutely everything.